Code O

The Journal of
Edwin Underhill

By the same author:

KILLER

The Journal of Edwin Underhill

Peter Tonkin

HODDER AND STOUGHTON
LONDON SYDNEY AUCKLAND TORONTO

What profit is there in my blood;
When I must go down to the Pit?

British Library Cataloguing in Publication Data
Tonkin, Peter
The Journal of Edwin Underhill

I. Title
823'.914 [F]   PR6070.0498
ISBN 0 340 26242 7

JOURNAL

January to July

THE STAKE

It is midnight and I cannot sleep. Therefore I have taken up this book and started to write in it. First I borrowed the pencil old Mr. Agee in the bed next to mine keeps by him, then I sat on the window-sill here with my legs drawn up as supports and my left arm in its sling against the panes. I am sure there must be a full moon tonight — it has flooded all the ward, and I can see as if it were day. My left hand hurts where it is pierced, but endurably.

I have loved Rebecca for more than a year. This journal is a present from her. She is the daughter of the Reverend Hugh Gore, vicar of my home parish, Dunmow Cross. "Is this the new English teacher, Miss Featherstone? My God, he is a plain little man!" This aside, painfully audible, was said on our first meeting at the school staff Christmas ball a year ago.

But by July she was calling me Underhill, by September sometimes Edwin. Often she spoke to me kindly, and I hoped. Then came the invitation to her New Year's Eve party and, even though everyone who was anyone in the village was going to be there, my hopes grew.

I presented myself at the vicarage door on the dot of nine last night, with a small but expensive box of chocolates in my overcoat pocket. I rang, and after some considerable time Rebecca herself answered, holding a glass of champagne. She was dressed in a gown of green velvet cut tight to the hips and low on the breast. She waved me in and I entered, suddenly terribly aware of the shabbiness of my appearance. I hung my coat in the hall and followed her hesitantly into the loud brightness of the party. I was so overcome by the heat and the din that it was a moment before I realised my mistake: the room I had entered in my blue lounge suit was

7

full of people in formal evening dress. Overcome with embarrassment, I turned to escape when I heard her call me.

She came through the crowd towards me, playing the perfect hostess: but when she saw how I was dressed she stopped abruptly. "Oh, Eddie!"

"I didn't know," I said, far too loudly in the sudden silence.

The moment passed as these moments will. My colleagues from school did their best to hide their smiles while certain other guests didn't even try — the local Rugby Club and Young Farmers' Association sniggered openly.

I took the offered glass and retreated to a corner where I spent a dreary evening watching Rebecca dancing in the distance. Even the champagne tasted strange . . . it was some time before I discovered it was in fact champagne cocktail. I had eaten nothing before coming out and by the time food was announced — some time after half-past ten — I was ravenous and rather drunk. I tried to reach the buffet table but was elbowed aside by Rugby Club members and Young Farmers, all in a hurry to get their escorts fed and watered in preparation for the inevitable subsequent bedding.

All they left me was some badly undercooked beef, some pungent rice salad, and a piece of ham which was mostly fat. I ate little, but continued to drink. One by one the groups I tried to join ostracised me. As in all country villages, our society is strongly stratified, and as a schoolmaster — and with a degree from Exeter rather than one of the senior universities — I did not fit. Thus I was left with no one to talk to. It was not yet midnight. I could not leave. And there was worse to come.

At about eleven thirty I decided to give Rebecca her box of chocolates, and fetched them from my coat in the hall. However, she was nowhere to be found. I wandered through the vicarage until finally there was only the conservatory left where she might be. It was in darkness, but through the icy glass I could just see her seated on an ornamental bench. The skirt of her green dress was high above her knees. The bodice was partly undone. There was a man kissing her. As I blundered in, her eyes flicked up at me over his shoulder.

Completely lost for words, I stood there, dazed, swaying

drunkenly as she put one casual hand against her lover's breast and pushed him away. "Yes, Eddie?" she said to me quite calmly.

The man turned. It was Andrew Royle, the heir to Bishops End Farm whose lands march with the A130 most of the way to Chelmsford. She put a restraining hand on his arm so that he could not rise. "Yes, Eddie?" she said again, mocking me.

"I've brought you a present," I blurted. She held out her hand in an imperious gesture, and I placed the chocolates carefully in it. She looked at me but I could not read her eyes. "Your present is under the tree," she said. "It is the one in the blue paper." My heart leaped. A present: a sign that she had thought about me after all.

As I rummaged confusedly throught the pile of presents beneath the bright Christmas tree the room seemed to empty behind me. Although it would soon be midnight, I thought nothing of this: my mind was on the search. The blue package was at the bottom. It was weighty and solid, slightly concave on three narrow sides — a book, obviously: this journal, in fact. I removed the wrapping paper, admired the rich red binding. Of course, I went back to thank her.

This time she was alone. I held up the present. "I found it," I said.

She patted the bench and I went over and sat beside her. Then suddenly my hopes and my passion overflowed and I found myself on my knees before her, the book forgotten, fallen to the floor. I searched desperately in her velvet lap for her hands as I gabbled drunkenly, "Rebecca, I have loved you since I first saw you. Oh Rebecca, I love you so much. Please say you'll be mine . . ."

There would have been more but I paused for breath. And then, deep in the shadows, someone tittered. The titter spread, was joined by giggles. The shadows moved, attained substance, became people. It was then, as their laughter bellowed round me, that I realised where all the dancers had gone, and the cruel trap they had set.

Rebecca suddenly rose to her feet and shouted, "Shut up and get out!"

I thought she was talking to me and I was glad enough to go. I rose to my feet and ran. Behind me she called, "Wait, Edwin, wait!"

Perhaps the joke had gone further than she had intended. Perhaps she wished to apologise. I turned, part-way across the vicarage lawn, and waited. But out of the darkness came no apology — simply my Christmas present to smash into my chest. I caught it and for some reason then I understood: the plain wrapping amongst the bright paper; the lack of a label — it had not been specifically for me at all. It was a general purpose gratuity, kept in reserve to be given in return for an unexpected gift.

I took to my heels once more and pounded across the back garden, through the gate and into the churchyard, weaving drunkenly down the path between the ancient graves.

Beyond the covered lich-gate leading out of the graveyard is a path and beyond that the village green and the cross-roads. The green has always been there — perhaps an acre of rough grass, even allowing for the roads and pavements. I ran across it heading for the crossroads themselves and the sanctuary of my one rented room in the ugly Victorian terrace beyond. I was drunk and full of black, bitter self-recrimination. My glasses were misted. My mind, like my vision, was anything but clear. I do not remember crossing the green itself, but suddenly I was at the crossroads. Behind, the church clock began to chime the quarters of the midnight hour. Then the ground seemed to give way under me and I fell.

I landed flat on my face, legs splayed out, my right hand clutching the frosted grass verge. My chin crashed down with stunning force, and my glasses spun away. Beneath my left shoulder the clay at the edge of the tarmac had crumbled. My left hand, fingers forced back by the soil, reached incredibly the full arm's length straight down into the earth and, as the hand went down into the black ground, the palm was pierced by something long and sharp. The pain was more than I can describe. The point entered the middle of my hand and, forced further through by my full weight, ripped out at the other side. I could feel the bones being forced apart and I screamed.

I found my arm was caught fast. I could not move it. In an instant I was covered with the icy, sweat of shock. I vomited, choking on the sweet iron taste of blood in my throat, and began to call out wordlessly for help.

It was thus that they found me, Rebecca and Andrew Royle. Amongst the midnight chimes of the church clock came his bored, supercilious voice. "My God, look at him: too drunk to walk. Heavens, what a noise . . ."

But then Rebecca, approaching, quieter and more gentle: "No, Andrew, look at his arm. I think there's something wrong."

A moment later they were beside me. A small crowd was gathering, but I could see Rebecca's feet before my face. "Miss Gore," I said, "I think my arm is broken."

"Careful now, old chap," said another voice, deep and warmly sympathetic. "The ground seems to have caved in . . . What on earth has happened?"

I felt fingers at my shoulder, pulling. The agony in my hand intensified. Everything was very clear for a couple of seconds. Distantly, in the vicarage, they were singing 'Auld lang Syne'. The stranger released me and said to Rebecca, "His hand seems to be trapped. We may have to dig him out."

"No," I said, feeling strangely calm. "No, hang on, it's all right . . ." I tensed myself, held my shaking body still, breathed deeply once and jerked my left shoulder up. Deep in the earth something tore, and blood suddenly began pumping out of me.

"Mr. Underhill! Edwin! Wait!" cried Rebecca. I paid no attention. I jerked my shoulder up again. Agony. Blood turning the soil around my hand to warm ooze.

And then I seemed to feel something move. Slowly, almost voluptuously, it writhed against my spread palm as though awakening from a long sleep. I made a guttural sound, jerked my shoulder up again, and a few inches of my arm was resurrected. Then my strength failed.

"Help me," I cried. "Miss Gore, please . . . please put your hands under my shoulder." She did so: taking firm hold. A pair of man's patent leather dancing pumps shifted anxiously before my face as the stranger watched over us. My hand felt more movements in the ground below and, "Now!" I yelled, my voice breaking, "pull!" We tore my shoulder upwards in unison, and the arm came free.

I rolled over completely on my back, my arm high in the air. I could see it silhouetted by the beams of a street-lamp

11

and I held it there for a moment, gazing at it. The sleeves of both jacket and shirt were pushed up past the elbow. The light hair on my forearm and wrist was matted with mud and blood. My hand was clawed against the yellow light, the fingers twisted. And through the centre of the palm there was a thin stake of black wood more than a yard long. Almost a foot of the point had been pushed out of the back of my hand. With the black bolt of wood through it, my hand had ceased to look like a human hand at all.

Sunday 7 January:

THE FIRST VISIT

Today she came to see me, her visit sandwiched between tea and early Evensong. I had passed the day, like many of the last seven, in an uneasy doze born of my inability to sleep much at night. I awoke from a cat-nap and she was there, thoughtlessly smoothing a lock of her dark red hair.

"Hello, Edwin," she said quietly. "How's your hand?" I got it out from under the blankets. It is covered by a light bandage now, and is healing fast. I pulled the gauze away from its back to show her the pink mass of the scar where the stake had come through. Long ridged legs reach out to the edges of my hand where the skin tore open, all held together by stitches and smeared with yellow ointment. It looks evil, somehow, like a spider crouching on the back of my hand. Rebecca drew back, pale.

I covered it up. "I'll be out soon," I said. There was an uneasy silence. "Who was the man who helped me?" I asked.

"Oh, haven't you met him?" She welcomed the change of subject. "That's Richard Burke. He's just taken Whitethorn Cottage for a few months. Until the end of the summer, I

12

think. He's a psychiatrist. He moved down here from London to do consulting work at Morden Hall, the asylum."

Morden Hall was the psychiatric hospital where Mrs. Gore, Rebecca's mother, had been receiving treatment for several years. I looked away, embarrassed. "How did the party go?" I asked, more for something to say than out of any real desire to know.

"It broke up almost immediately."

"No one left to laugh at," I said, suddenly bitter.

She looked as though I had slapped her. "I can hardly be responsible, Mr. Underhill, it you become too drunk to control yourself! Still, now that you've brought the subject up, there *are* one or two things I'd like to say . . . ."

It was clearly a prepared speech: the reason, in fact, for her visit. I had done enough to merit it, I know, but it hurt nevertheless. I ought to look at myself, she said: what sort of a person was I — how fit was I to offer myself to any woman? Perhaps, before I started making protestations of love, it would be better if I pulled myself together and tried to make something of what few qualities I did possess . . .

She was soon finished. The doors slammed shut-open-shut behind her, leaving me to contemplate wretchedly the sad truth of her words.

What sort of a person am I? Well, to be frank, I am a slob. My hair, what there is of it around a large bald patch, is too long and always looks a mess. My clothes are baggy and usually grubby. I'm five foot six inches tall, my shoulders stoop, and I have no chest to speak of and a pot belly. All this might be acceptable were I an absent-minded professor-type, unworldly but creative. But instead I'm simply a down-at-heel schoolmaster in a fairly down-at-heel private school . . . In short, Rebecca was quite right: I've precious little to offer any woman, let alone one as beautiful and intelligent as she.

It wasn't a happy realisation. But at least, once I had faced the truth about myself, I felt better for it, knowing once and for all where I stood.

And now, tonight, I have been visited by something else: a nightmare at the very least, a horror so terrible that I can hardly write of it. It began as I seemed to waken out of a fitful doze into the quietness of the midnight ward. Outside, a

13

faint wind moaned against the windows, making them rattle. The beds stretched away in ranks, curiously indistinct to me, even in the achingly bright moonlight. I found myself sitting up, looking round anxiously as if I expected something to happen. The air was so cold my breath clouded upon it. An inexplicable shiver of fear shook my whole body.

Old Mr. Agee in the bed next to mine grunted, coughed, and turned over. Then the moment was gone. Silence flowed in. Even the wind died. I lay down again. The whole hospital seemed then to be held in a vibrant stillness, as thought the night's dark cloak had fallen over the sprawling building and deadened every sound. Then out of the silence there grew the tiniest of whispers. I turned my head like a dog towards the door, the better to hear the sound. One faint voice infinitely far away, seeming to sing a song without words. Was it in the hospital? Some child in a distant corridor humming dreamily, perhaps. The whisper in the silence sang a little louder. My skin rose to gooseflesh. My scalp too tight from neck to eyebrows. The strange voice quavered, gaining strength. I thought, *I must move*! but the voice chained me down, nearer now, louder. Surely someone else must hear it?

Was that a movement? the night-light immediately outside the ward flickered, dimmed and died. The glass door-panes seemed black as though painted. The air in the ward freezing, and thick enough to drown you. I shuddered as the absolute knowledge came to me that it was there, whatever it was, just outside the doors in the corridor.

The doors began to rattle. The voice, a woman's now, lingered hauntingly on the air above the abrupt sound of the shaking wood, utterly strange and beautiful, terrifyingly sinister. Then, all at once, silence, more terrible than a scream.

CRASH! The doors slammed open. I jerked back, smashing my head on the iron bedstead. Blackness flowed in through the door, a shadow of impenetrable dark, perhaps five feet high, twisted, almost human in shape, and yet totally unhuman. It soaked up all the light around its twisted, stump-limbed body into two points of eye-brightness. How could a monstrous thing like this, I thought, have a woman's voice?

I leaned across to the vague mound of Mr. Agee in the next

14

bed and shook him wildly. No reaction. The dark was coming towards me, its feeling of absolute evil washing over me. I froze once more, as the thing lurched to the end of my bed and rose erect there, shadowy stumps waving from hunched, uneven shoulders. For a moment of utter terror I felt it watching me, the light soaking up from around it focused in two bright eyes, red, like almonds of blood — eyes without iris or pupil. My left hand came up off the bed, reaching towards it, thrusting it away, still like a claw from the wound.

It seemed to laugh: for a moment the ice-heavy air bore the foulest stench imaginable, and then the presence was gone.

Light flowed back into the ward. Heat. Breathable air. I slumped down on to the pillows and gradually my horror passed and the pounding of my heart slowed. The glass door-panes cast a warm, reassuring glow on to the ceiling of the ward. I looked across at Mr. Agee — he was lying flat on his back, peacefully asleep, quite undisturbed . . . so my dark visitation had been a private fantasy, a nightmare, no more than that. And I'm writing of it now, in the moonlit ward, while its frightfulness is still fresh in my mind, with the simple intention of exorcising its evil memory.

I do not, indeed, ever mean to dwell on it again, and I pray that it may never be repeated for I fear for my sanity should I be forced once more to suffer such mindless, all-encompassing terror.

Sunday 4 February:

CANDLEMAS

My strange experience in the ward was not repeated. I was released from hospital within the week and returned at once to work. The other teachers from my school who had attended Rebecca's party had circulated the story of my embarrassment, so that I found myself even more ostracised than usual. By everyone, that is, except Jane Martin, a colleague of mine in the English department.

A warm-hearted young woman with wide brown eyes and a ready smile; the friendship she offered me was sorely needed. It even included cheerful advice upon the diet which Rebecca's cruel words had prompted me to begin, and the suggestion that my general fitness might be improved if I took up jogging. And two days ago, last Friday, it came to a climax with an invitation to dinner at her house that night, an invitation that I was delighted to accept, little thinking what horrors it would bring.

Jane's family have resided in Dunmow Cross for many generations. It was not surprising, therefore, that, after attending teachers'-training college in Bristol she should have returned here to teach. Her parents, like mine, are both dead, and she now lives in a rambling old house on the southern outskirts of the village, tucked discreetly behind a neat garden and a tiny, but impenetrable, coppice of ancient elm trees.

At half-past six precisely I pushed the white gate open and crunched up the ice-brittle pebble path. A light wind made the branches above me click and whisper together. I pressed the bell and the door opened almost immediately.

Jane smiled at me. "Oh, Edwin," she said, "how cold you look — you should have worn a coat." Hot air washed over me, making me dizzy for a moment. "You'll get pneumonia," she told me.

"No, it's all right," I said. "I don't feel the cold."

"Well, you'd be better in the warm anyway." She stepped aside to let me in, but just for a moment something seemed to hold me back. I stood there on the doorstep, unable to move, until she said, with a hint of impatience, "Come *in*, Edwin, I'm letting all the heat out."

It took me a second to get used to the warm brightness of the hall. It was my first visit and I was very nervous. "What a beautiful old house," I said.

The walls were oak-panelled. A gracious staircase led up to a shadowed gallery landing. "It's Elizabethan," she said as she led the way through to the living room.

The living room was cluttered: too many chairs were

16

gathered round too large a fireplace with far too hot a fire. Too many tables carried too many photographs. A great black sideboard with an open cupboard above it bustled with decorative plates. Adding to the busy clutter was a stiff-backed old lady. The ramrod in her back extended up through her neck, throwing back her head so that her vivid blue eyes glared disdainfully down a great beak of a nose. Her mouth was a tight line pulled down at the corners towards a white-powdered turkey's neck. She was perched on the edge of a hard chair by the fire. Her twisted, arthritic hands lay crossed on an ebony cane. She offered me the right one as Jane performed the introduction before vanishing towards the kitchen. She was dressed in black bombazine. Her name was Miss Royston, and she was Jane's aunt, there on a winter visit.

"So," she said, "you are Jane's young man, are you? Come over here, young man: let me get a good look at you. Sit here opposite me." She peered at me sharply as I hesitated. "Don't like the heat, eh? Well, you must have thicker blood than I — that's all there is to that."

I sat opposite her beside the roaring fire as ordered, and she surveyed me for a while in silence. "You've quite a strong aura," she said at last, "I have seen many very much stronger of course, but I would say you have *some* force of character."

"Thank you very much," I said.

"I can tell, you know; tell at a glance." She clicked her false teeth knowingly.

"Oh yes?"

"Oh *yes*. It is a great gift. I can see right inside most people. Into their very souls. See that in them which is eternal and will abide."

Such things as abiding eternally anywhere have always been a source of absolute indifference to me. Out of common politeness, however, I held up my end of the occult small-talk until she suddenly said,

"You know the village has something of a history in that line? Oh yes: they say the old crossroads up by the church are haunted. Why, when I was a girl no one in the village would go near them after dark on a night like this. Or to the Broken Woods, of course."

17

She lapsed into silence. Something of what she said had got under my skin, though: after all, the crossroads had featured largely in my own recent experience. My left hand clenched painfully at the thought. "On a night like this?" I queried.

"Oh yes. Didn't you know?" She leaned closer. "Tonight is the second of February: the Feast of the Purification of the Blessed Virgin. Candlemas. For some reason the chains are light on all things evil tonight: It is a Sabbat."

"You mean a Witches' Sabbat?"

"Yes indeed. Not far from here I know of at least one coven which will be at their dark deeds . . ." She paused melodramatically, looked up, suddenly very still, as if listening. A tall old clock in the corner struck the hour of seven. I jumped . . . which was, I suppose, what she wanted. She gave a sort of leer. "In five hours' time . . . preparation will have begun long ago of course, but in five hours' time the witches will be calling on . . . *evil*."

Such mumbo-jumbo didn't interest me, and I came near to saying so. But at that moment the door opened and Jane announced "There, almost ready. Time for a drink, I think."

As soon as we were grouped around the fire again after dinner, Miss Royston made a suggestion which, from another source, might have been surprising. But not from her. "Jane," she said, drawing herself up on her long, straight back and staring down at us, "you may fetch the table. I feel a Presence."

Her eyes closed in apparent ecstasy. Jane glanced at me with apology and embarrassment. "But, Aunt," she whispered, "surely Mr. Underhill . . ."

"Mr. Underhill may not know it, my dear, but he is a part-believer. We must guide his feet, Jane; guide his feet." Her voice sank to a vibrant whisper on the repetition.

Jane returned with a small round table, a wine-glass and, of all things, an old Scrabble set. The old lady rummaged around the plastic chips and with the speed of practice set out a circle of letters spelling out the alphabet, a clock-face broken at nine and three by the words YES and NO. In the centre of this circle she put the glass, base upwards.

"Now," she said, leaning forward, body tense and eyes compelling, "we will communicate with the Other Side by

18

placing our index fingers on the glass. Do not press. Do not try and control the movement of the glass, you will find it moves of its own volition when the Presence wishes to communicate with us.''

She placed the top of a bony finger on the glass. Jane followed suit. They both looked at me expectantly so I leaned forward, suddenly reluctant to be dabbling in this, and did as I was told. The base of the glass was icy cold, pleasant to feel in the oven-like room.

"Concentrate," whispered Miss Royston. "Empty your minds of all thought. Leave yourself open to be influenced!" This is childish, I thought, swept back suddenly to a rainy Saturday of childhood when, with some friends, breathless with delicious terror, I had experimented with the letters of the alphabet scrawled on pieces of paper and a plastic mug on the linoleum. Scrabble chips and a cheap wine-glass seemed hardly more conducive to success. "There are negative thoughts!' rapped Miss Royston, her voice suddenly brisk and authoritative. Her eyes on me. "You must empty your mind." Obligingly I tried to do so, bored already with the stupidity of it.

The glass under my finger was giving off a blessed coolness, so I concentrated on that. "Is there anybody there?" said Miss Royston. Again: "Is there anybody there?"

And the glass moved.

My eyes, which had been closed, jumped wide. The hairs on the back of my neck prickled uncomfortably.

YES: said the glass. As simple as that. By moving across the table, making a slight scraping noise, seemingly suddenly imbued with a life of its own, the glass said YES.

I tried to jerk my hand back, but it would not move. "Don't," Miss Royston hissed at me. "You'll disturb it!"

"Who is there?" she continued, full voice. I looked at Jane. She was white as wax, seemingly in a trance. "Who is there?" repeated Miss Royston.

The glass said: US.

"Who are *you*?"

ME AND ANOTHER, laboriously.

"What is your name?"

The glass lurched into motion once more: ANNE.

"Ah!" said Miss Royston, "I thought so. Anne is my spirit

19

guide . . . Hello Anne. Do not be afraid. There are only friends here."

NO. The glass slid across the table urgently.

Miss Royston frowned. "There are only friends . . ."

NO. NO: said the glass.

"I am a friend," said the old lady.

YES: said the glass.

"Jane is a friend."

YES.

"Mr. Underhill is a friend."

The glass did not move. I could feel my mind shutting again. It was obviously a fake. The old woman was guiding the glass. "Mr. Underhill!" she snapped. "Your negative thoughts are a serious handicap."

Unaccountably, the glass said NO then.

Miss Royston took a deep breath. The clock ticked. A sudden wind made the windows rattle and the room seemed less stifling for a moment, as though there were a cool draught. "Mr. Underhill is a friend," she repeated.

NO. YES: said the glass.

"What do you mean?"

NO. YES.

Suddenly my arm was unbearably heavy. There was sweat on my face. My left hand in my lap twisted and throbbed. "Explain what you mean!" snapped Miss Royston.

ANOTHER: said the glass.

"Please be clear."

BAD.

"Who is bad? Mr. Underhill?"

WICKED.

"Mr. Underhill?"

EVIL.

And everything went out. The lights went dim. Even the fire died. The burningly cold glass screeched across the table with a new and savage force, dragging us after it like puppets.

"Who is evil?" Miss Royston demanded, still undaunted.

I: it said.

"Who are you?"

I.

20

"What is your name?" patiently.

COUNTESS.

I wanted to call out a warning, to cry out, to scream . . . but I was dumb.

"Who are you, Countess?"

I AM I ALWAYS. Terribly fast, almost tearing our fingers free of our hands. I could feel the shadows dancing. The sense of mortal evil around us was utter and complete.

"Will you tell us your name, Countess?"

NO.

And still the old woman persisted. "You will not?"

NO NAME.

How could she be so totally unaware of the danger? I felt I knew the creature the nameless force in the room, and I knew it would feed on fear. Feed and gain strength on Jane's fear and mine. But old Miss Royston was questioning still. "If you have no name, at least tell us how you are known."

KNOWN I AM KNOWN.

"What do you do here?"

I AM FREE.

"What do you do?"

I AM FREE

I AM FREE

I AM FREE

Perhaps Miss Royston at last felt something. Her voice wavered, "What do you want?"

FREE

She straightened, and held up her other hand. "By all the powers of Light . . ."

FREE

Miss Royston broke then. "Tell me what you are," she whispered. And the thing seemed to laugh. D spelt the glass, and E. It scraped more slowly across the table, suddenly webbed by a network of white cracks, as if crushed under some terrible strain and held together only by the will of the malevolent force around us. The glass spelt out A and, moving back, gouged the wood into trenches. Back and back and back it scraped, towards the first letter — D.

D—E—A—D.

Suddenly Jane screamed, a howl of animal terror which splintered the moment and the room slammed back to reality. Light blazed. Heat swirled like boiling water. The glass wrenched itself away across the room and shattered by the far door. The table came up into my face, scattering Scrabble chips. Jane lurched sideways and crashed down on to the floor. I watched, paralysed, as Miss Royston was hurled backwards out of her chair and seemed to fly across the room, heels dragging on the carpet, until she crashed against the wall to hang there as if held by the throat, crushed against the plaster six feet from the floor. Her heels drummed against the black wainscot now, well clear of the carpet, and her hands fought to shake off the invisible thing that seemed to hold her there.

Then the drumming of the heels slowed and her bulging eyes rolled up. The appalling reality of it penetrated my daze: Miss Royston was hanging there. Really. This was not imagination . . . this was not a dream — there was something in the real world which was actually choking the life out of this poor, crazy old woman. I hurled the table aside sprang out of my seat, and ran full-tilt towards the wall. "Let her go!" I screamed. "Let her go!"

My hands waved uselessly through the empty air until with stunning suddenness I was struck in the centre of my forehead. Something was in front of the wall exactly level with the old woman's throat. I could not see it, but I could feel it. Its end was the stub of hardness on which I had hit my head. It was surrounded by a slight, slimy softness, cold as a slug. My shaking hands explored the length of the thing. I found a shape I recognised — an elbow-joint. Then a forearm, a wrist and hand.

Miss Royston was being held against the wall by an invisible, rigid, unbelievably powerful severed arm.

"Let her go!" I screamed again. My open palms slapped against icy, invisible flesh, bunched muscles, steely tendons. "In God's name, let her go!" And abruptly it did so.

She fell in a heap to the ground, slumped on to her side, and moaned faintly. Jane sat up, the terror still in her eyes. "Get your aunt some brandy," I said firmly.

It was something for her to do, something to distract her mind from the full horror of what we had just witnessed. She was gone for several minutes while I crouched beside the motionless old woman, and when she returned with the brandy she was pale but composed.

I moistened Miss Royston's lips with the brandy and she sighed deeply and stirred. "Are you all right?" I asked.

She nodded gingerly. I gave her some more. She coughed and sat up.

"Phone for a doctor," I said to Jane, but Miss Royston whispered, "No. Help me to my bedroom. I shall be quite all right in a minute."

I protested that she really ought to see a doctor, but Jane's aunt was not someone with whom one argued for long. And besides, she was clearly making an amazingly quick recovery. So I helped her up to her room, and then waited uneasily downstairs. To pass the time I tidied away the Scrabble tiles and swept up the broken glass. The room, in fact, was distressingly normal — it was almost impossible to believe in what I had seen in it with my own eyes, and felt with my own hands, only such a short time before.

When Jane had put her aunt to bed, the old lady sent word for me to stick my head round the door. I did as she asked.

"I have to go home to Scotland in a day or two," Miss Royston told me, "so I won't be able to do much more. It'll be up to you, now."

"What will be?" I asked, surprised.

"Why, to find out what that thing was, Mr. Underhill, and how it got loose. *Free*, it said it was . . ." She smiled at me wanly. "Well, you're just going to have to chain it down again, you know . . ."

Her voice wandered away and her head dropped sideways on her pillow. On her throat, already darkening into bruises, I saw the unmistakable marks of four fingers and a thumb. At the tip of each mark was a curved wound, as though fingernails lengthened into claws had cut into her flesh. The wounds were not deep but blood welled in them softly, bright and strangely beautiful against her wrinkled, powdered skin.

THE CROSSROADS

Miss Royston returned to her home in the north on the fourth, two days after the seance, and last week Jane was called away to nurse her. We both hope her illness will prove to be nothing serious. In Jane's absence my life has seemed to centre around my increasing interest in jogging. I have also pursued a rather dilatory search for information about the ghostly Countess. This has proved difficult. Dunmow Cross, it seems, has seen nearly two millenia of countesses, and following up every single one of them has been a task quite beyond my limited enthusiasm. Until this very evening, in fact, when a chance encounter — for I would not believe it otherwise — has at the same time sharpened my interest and eased my difficulty.

I have made a habit of jogging most evenings and today, after church, lunch and a long boring afternoon, I suddenly felt wildly restless. I changed into my new tracksuit and set out into the gloom. As usual I felt full of running almost instantly. The east wind caressed me, tugging my hair, making my flesh rise in goosebumps. Even the pavement seemed to spring up beneath my feet, thrusting me forward in the darkness. I decided to run out of the village into the surrounding fields.

I do not know how far I ran or for how long, my course dictated only by the windings of the paths I followed: past Jane's house, out of the village, across the A120 main road and up the western edge of the Great South Field to the Broken Woods. The naked branches of the high hedgerows glistened against the black sky. Even in this dead season I seemed to be sailing through a sea of life. Birds soared above me, calling as they settled for the night. The hedgerows and frost-white grasses were alive with scratchings and scurryings. I closed my eyes and ran.

On the coppiced hillock of the Broken Woods I overlooked the distant diamond lights of Great Dunmow. The evening seemed so full of life that I actually sang out loud. Utterly at one with nature I ran from tree to tree, exploring their rough bark with newly sensitive fingers. I felt their quiet life pulsing beneath my hands.

Then I turned and sped down the hill until I came to the great straight Roman road, where I turned for home. In the distance, a mile or two before me, the church bells began to ring: Evensong, I supposed. I ran on, then slowed to a walk as the bells quietened. What I was thinking about I cannot clearly remember. The bells had punctured my euphoria but I was not tired. If anything in particular, I was thinking of food.

I have been very pleased with the way my diet has been going: I have lost more than a stone now and need to wear belts with all my old trousers. It is a simple diet, consisting mainly of meat, fresh fruit and green vegetables. Recently, however, I find I have grown sick of plant pap. And the only drawback to eating meat on its own is its effect on my digestion. I seem to awake occasionally in the night with a terrible burning thirst.

Such mundane thoughts, I believe, occupied my mind as I jogged down towards the village. The church tower reared dizzily on my left, the vacant threatening stare of old empty houses on my right. I speeded up a little. Henry Francis Lyte's immortal 'Abide with Me' lingered like incense on the air behind me and it was that, if anything, which raised the short hairs on the back of my neck. A few hundred yards ahead of me lay the crossroads themselves. The street-lamp which normally illuminates them was not working, but the road seemed to contain its own dim brightness amid the heavy shadows, and the grass positively shone. The signpost stood like a complicated gallows, its four wooden arms pointing urgently away from the place. In the far distance, thunder rumbled again. New clouds moved across the dark heavens, lean and grey, slightly luminous, like a pack of ghostly wolves hunting. The east wind pulled my hair gently, an invisible lover, and I thought suddenly of those other fingers that I had not seen, clamped around Miss Royston's throat. I shivered. For a moment everything was absolutely still. Even time itself seemed to pause.

And at the birth of that moment there was suddenly a figure beside the signpost. It was crouching or kneeling by

25

the thin wooden post. Naturally I went towards it. As I came nearer it began to pull itself up, almost as if out of the ground. "Is everything all right?" I called.

By the time I was within five yards of it I could see that it was a woman, even though her back was towards me. She was fully erect now, leaning against the signpost, looking up at the church. Her head was held at a strange angle, almost resting on her left shoulder. I knew now that here was something wrong. Her hair fell in rats' tails of colourless darkness down her back. Her left hand came away from the post and fell to her side. It was the absolute silence of her movement which triggered the most vivid alarm in my mind. She had on a full skirt which reached the ground and bulked out strangely on either side of her slim waist. Her arm should have made some sound as it fell against the shadowed cloth, but it did not. I froze, every nerve in my body suddenly aflame with an agony of cold. She began to turn. A high lace ruff flashed a pinpoint or two of light. I noticed then that there was no cloud of breath above her on the icy air. Something inside me recognised what this was, and who.

I turned and ran. Ran from the Countess; ran from her who was dead. And free . . . Head down and elbows pumping, bruising the balls of my feet on the black, icy road, I sped out of the haunted shadows down into the bright heart of the village. As I ran I thought of Miss Royston's words: there is something evil loose — and you must chain it.

And soon now, I will have her, my Countess. Already I have begun to tie her down. For I have seen the style of dress she wore in countless illustrations: she was an Elizabethan, my Countess. And it should be easy now to learn her history, to discover why she walks, and armed with that knowledge — to chain her as the old woman said.

26

THE RECORDS

Every evening after school for the last ten days or so I have gone straight into the Central Library in Great Dunmow to consult all the histories of Essex I could find, but there was no reference to any Elizabethan countess.

By last Wednesday I had looked in all the books immediately available to me and had found nothing. My next step was obvious: the parish records. It was time to go and visit the Reverend Gore. And, of course, I thought that if I was lucky I would see Rebecca also, and could show her how fully I have followed the advice so mercilessly given at our last meeting in the hospital. My jogging continues, I am running faster and longer, and I swear I stand taller these days. And it is all, at least to some degree, thanks to her.

This evening, accordingly, after a high tea of rare steak, I went up the hill to the vicarage. It was a misty spring evening and the declining sun seemed unbearably bright. Dunmow Cross was quite busy and yet I found myself walking alone. Only slowly did I realise that whereas everyone else was crowded on the sunny side of the street in the brightness and warmth, I had elected without conscious thought to walk amongst the shadows.

The vicarage is a huge house for one old man and his daughter to live in. There must be eight or ten bedrooms. It is, as Rebecca had told me, early Elizabethan, built in the distant days when Dunmow Cross was a thriving community and its vicarage one short step only below the bishop's palace. Nowadays, of course, the income from this wasted parish cannot begin to support it, and it is terribly seedy and dilapidated.

I walked up the drive and knocked on the door. Rebecca opened it almost at once. Not long ago my heart would have been in my throat at the prospect of seeing her, but today I was expectant rather than nervous. She was wearing a big, red, floppy, woollen, polo-necked pullover and faded blue jeans. She squinted at me for a moment, slightly puzzled, until I said, "Hello, Rebecca."

"Oh. It's you, Edwin. I didn't recognise you." Her face was pinched. Her eyes were dull and dark-ringed. She did not look well. "What is it you want?"

"Can I see your father for a moment?" I asked.

"My father? Yes, of course. Come in." She held the door open wide. I stepped into the cool, dark hall. It was neat, tidy and sparkingly clean. Even the wainscot glowed dully. They had a woman in, of course — old Mrs. Hope. She had been coming ever since Mrs. Gore had gone into hospital. When was that? Five years ago now?

"He's in his study. This way . . ." She shut the door behind me and led me into the big airy sitting room.

"How are you?" I asked.

"Fine. You?"

"O.K." I held up my left hand, the scar white now, as though I had drawn a starfish with chalk on the palm and the back of the hand alike. On the far side of the sitting room, down two steps, was a dark little corridor. We went along it.

"What do you want to see father about?" she asked.

"Ghosts, actually," I answered.

She stopped and I collided with her.

"Please, Mr. Underhill — under no circumstances mention ghosts to him!"

The tone of her voice was strange, almost frightening. Then she swung away and rapped smartly on a big dark door. A distant voice called, "Come!" She pushed it open, ushered me in, and left me.

It was a tall room, packed with books of all kinds and ages. Mr. Gore sat at a huge desk littered with paper. There were crumpled balls of it on the floor round the desk and in the wastepaper-basket. His white mane of hair was dishevelled as though he has been running his fingers through it. "Ah, Mr. Underhill!" he said, swinging his chair towards me and half rising. "How are you? I haven't seen you much in church lately. What can I do for you? Sit down, do."

I sank into an overstuffed armchair and put on my lap the pile of file paper purloined from school. I cleared my throat a little nervously. The Reverend Hugh Gore is a large, powerful man. They say he was a rugby blue at Oxford. Physically,

28

emotionally and spiritually he is overpowering. Rebecca's warning lingered in my mind: there would be no mention of ghosts. But I had come well prepared.

"I would like to consult some parish records," I said. "I shall need a little guidance as to which ones would be best. I've never done anything quite like this before. It's for a project with one of my classes about the history of Dunmow Cross in Elizabethan times."

"Why the Elizabethan period particularly?"

"Well, I teach English rather than history, and the Elizabethan was the Golden Age of English Literature, after all."

"I see." His tone made it clear that he wished he didn't. "Well, the best place I can recommend to you is the *Victoria County History of Essex* . . ."

"Yes. I've looked there. I was hoping for something of more local note. I thought, perhaps, if there are any parish records . . ."

"Oh, I think you'll find very little of use in there. Baptisms, marriages, funerals . . . Dry old stuff . . ."

"An exploration of local history. Old family names, forgotten relationships. The very fabric of our past," I insisted.

"But I'm sure you will be disappointed. Really. There's nothing of note at all!"

"Does it mention where people were buried?"

"Some family plots, yes. But you can see more by looking at the gravestones in the churchyard . . ."

I was not to be put off. "Some of them are defaced . . ."

"Oh, very few . . ."

"And I have heard that some graves actually lie outside the churchyard wall."

Silence. An icy silence. "Well, Mr. Underhill, I see you have a scholar's tenacity and that weakness of youth which refuses to learn by any experience other than its own. I suppose you wish to see the marriage register."

"No. The records of burials, please."

"Really, Mr. Underhill, you must let me guide you some of the way. There are hardly likely to be any family relationships recorded in a register of interments." His voice had taken on the strange iron edge which had made Rebecca's tone so sinister when she talked of ghosts. He was clearly not

29

going to give an inch.

"Of course, you're quite right. I didn't think of that. The marriage register is exactly what I want." It was on a shelf far back in the room. I paid careful attention as he got it.

For the next hour I ploughed through the several hundred pages of a fat dusty tome dated in faded but beautiful writing: MARRIAGES IN THE PARISH OF DUNMOW CROSS 1560–1575. I sat bemused as the youngsters of a large and bustling provincial town married and inter-married. Dunmow Cross must have been by far the largest town in Essex when Elizabeth was still a young woman. What had happened to it? I was tempted away from my search for any reference to a Countess by that question. "Could I see the next one?" I asked.

"What?" Mr. Gore glanced up from his work.

"The next volume. What is it, 1575-1590?"

"No, no. The next one is locked up. Not available. It would really be most inconvenient."

"Oh, I'm sorry," I said. "I'll just put this one back."

"No. Leave it there. I'll put it back."

"Please don't bother," I said, rising and walking across towards the shelf. "I really don't want to disturb you."

He was on his feet immediately, thrusting his great square body between the shelves and myself. "It's no trouble at all," he said, holding his hand out for the book. But my eyes were busy over his shoulder. Beside the space left by the removal of this fat volume of marriages 1560–1575 was a curiously thin companion labelled MARRIAGES IN THE PARISH OF DUNMOW CROSS 1575–1620. Apparently it had needed several hundred pages to record fifteen years of weddings in the earlier volume and less than half that number in the next to record the following forty-five. Stunned, I pushed the fat volume into his outstretched hand. It was extremely heavy. One hand was really not enough to hold it in. He dropped it, half caught it, fumbled with it, stepped back to give himself more room, and collided with the shelves. As I helped him regain his balance my gaze wandered once more along the dusty rows of books. Three shelves up the words REGISTER OF BURIALS caught my attention, and I ran my eye along the line. 1540–1550 . . . 1550–1560 . . . 1560–1570 . . . 1570 — and then suddenly, on its own, an entire weighty volume, labelled 1579. In that one year, then, there must have been a thousand burials — no, many, many more! A plague, perhaps? The Black Death? or . . .

One of the vicar's great hands closed on my shoulder. I turned to him. He had followed the direction of my gaze, and now in his smile there was a terrible, menacing coldness.

"Is there anything else you'll be wanting, Mr. Underhill?" he asked, challenging me.

"N . . . no, thank you." I'd had enough already. More than enough.

"In that case, Mr. Underhill, I suggest that you leave me to get on with my work. I have a sermon to prepare." He gestured indifferently at the crumpled balls of paper that littered the floor. "And if you *really* wish to interest your pupils in literary history, might I suggest another period? Milton's perhaps? I'm sure they'd find it far more rewarding."

He pointed to the door. "You can find your own way out, I imagine."

I could. And I did. Rebecca was nowhere to be seen, but that did not particularly concern me. What *did* concern me were the reasons of the vicar of this ancient parish for wishing to keep its doings in the 1570s so deeply shrouded in mystery. They would hardly, I thought, have been on account simply of the plague. If there had been a visitation, then there would be more than just the Black Death involved.

Friday 16 March:

THE CHASE

Last Monday brought a letter from Jane. Miss Royston was fading fast, poor old soul, and had been asking to see me. She said she had something of enormous importance to tell me, and I was preparing to travel up to her sick-bed this weeekend when a telegram this morning forestalled me. Miss Royston died last night. And her secret, whatever it may have been, died with her. I do not know what Jane will do, but there is sadly no help I can offer her.

This week, since my confrontation with the Reverend Gore, has been very strange. I have been searching down all the old records once again, my mind full, not only of the Countess, but also of the visitation that Death itself seems to have made to the village four hundred years ago. But all available documents seem to be wilfully silent on the matter.

My concentration on these questions is such that they seem on occasion actually to intrude upon reality. Even at school, once or twice this air of unreality has proved unsettlingly powerful: shadows glimpsed out of the corners of my eye, movements where nothing moved. I am sleeping badly again also, and such rest as I do get is disturbed by visions and dreams. One especially has been repeated: I seem to awaken in my room in utter silence, a silence which is broken, as it was in the ward, by the approach of some terrifyingly evil entity. I can feel it, hear it, on the landing outside my bedroom door. The handle turns. The door is locked. The handle turns further and rattles impatiently. And then the door itself begins to shake as though something enormously powerful and dangerous is about to burst into my bedroom.

In spite of the strong temptation, I have not seen the vicar again until this evening — and even then it was not a social call, but simply an accident. I had gone jogging over my familiar route down through the village, up to the Broken Woods through the fields, and down again towards the crossroads. As I came past the vicarage in the dark, I was startled to see the Reverend Gore astride an ancient bicycle. On the back of the old machine there was a square parcel bound with string. I was about to turn away when in my mind's eye I suddenly saw that bundle once more. It was made up of books . . . All at once I knew they were the parish records! I almost panicked. Where was he going with them? What was he going to do? By the time I had brought my thoughts under control, my legs had taken over and thrust me forward in pursuit.

And so the chase began. The vicar turned off the main road

32

into one of the little hedge-bound lanes and veered south, squeaking away in the dark. I bounded after him along the silent byways, mouth agape and gums stinging. My glasses — a positive hindrance nowadays — kept slipping down my nose. I took them off and thrust them into my tracksuit pocket.

Low clouds filled the sky. City dwellers are not acquainted with the dark as we are out here. Beyond the realm of street lamps the darkness can be absolute. The dark wraps itself around your head like a black sack, even seeming to impede your breathing.

But this evening there was light from a rising moon, filtering through the clouds and I could see the hedgerows glinting with dampness. I ran in the middle of the road between the busy rustlings of the night creatures in the hedges and the fields, and always, ahead of me, drawing me on, the squeaking of the bicycle.

Abruptly there was mist. It lay in flat sheets on the dead air. Mr. Gore pedalled through it unconcernedly but as I met the first pale swathe I brought my hands up to my head as though there were cobwebs entangled in my hair. I began to shiver. Where was he going? Each step forward made me colder and more tired. The squeaking of the bicycle began to draw away. I gritted my teeth — how my gums throbbed — and ran on at full-tilt. Then, over the sound of the bicycle I heard the first sinister whisper. The hissing, gurgling, bubbling song of running water. The vicar was heading for the River Chelmer and I knew what he was going to do. He was going to throw the books into the water.

I put all my power into the running now, leaping forward in great bounds, grasping the ground with spread toes as though I were barefoot, thrusting onward with every sinew. Suddenly the squeaking stopped. The sibilance of the water filled my ears as though I were surrounded by snakes. By the time the stream came in sight I was drenched in an icy sweat of terror. Why was I so afraid?

The road went down to a tiny ford. The banks gathered up, mist-shrouded, and meandered into the dark on either side. The water was inky. It seemed to give off an aura of night. And the nearer I came, the more strongly it reached for me. I faltered, my fear of it incomprehensible yet sickeningly powerful.

Mr. Gore stood with the square parcel in his hands and his chin sunk on his chest, at prayer no doubt. For all his unhelpfulness I wished him no ill — it was the books I wanted. So I gathered my courage and worked my way left, nearer to the water.

Finally the vicar stopped praying and raised the bundle high above his head. He hesitated. I crouched. Then he turned towards me and the heavy package crashed into the reeds a little to my left. Silent as a cat I dived after it, but the rushes rustled and cracked around me.

"Who's there?" cried the vicar. I scrabbled in the icy ooze at the edge of the water. "Come out, whoever you are," he shouted, his voice ringing on the watery air.

The stream closed on my left hand like jaws. My bones ached. I moaned in terror, wriggling forward, my ears closed to what Mr. Gore was yelling. Elbow-deep, shoulder-deep I pushed my arm, seeking the bundle. Agony. I could scarcely breathe. Past the shoulder. Half of the chest, my hand among the riverbed weeds and slime, numb yet afire. I gulped one agonised breath, mouth stretched, nostrils flaring, and plunged into the water. My finger brushed the package, nails scraping recklessly over the sodden paper, cutting through the wet cord as if they were steel claws, so that the bundle, destroyed by my clumsiness, burst apart.

A book brushed my face. I opened my eyes beneath the water, saw its pages wafting in slow motion on the stream, saw the lines on them blur, run, and fade away as the book itself disintergrated. Then my feet touched bottom and I thrust up.

I exploded out of the river with manic force. Mr. Gore had taken several steps forward and was staring into the dark, obviously perplexed by the noises I was making, and blinded by the darkness. Now his pale face twisted into a mask of horror. He cried out, and something silver sailed lazily over my head to sink into the black water safely behind me — a crucifix and chain. Then there were only his hurried footsteps and the dying squeal of his bicycle.

It was not until then that I realised I was screaming. Screaming with terror and rage and frustration. Screaming like an animal. Screaming so that all the farm dogs for miles around were answering my cries.

ALL FOOLS

After the episode in the river things have quietened. My sleep is uninterrupted, the corners of my eyes are untenanted. All avenues towards a discovery of the Countess's identity seem closed off to me. And I have been glad enough to let it lie, to concentrate instead on the inevitable mountain of school-work which seems to collect at the end of term — added to this term by the portion of Jane Martin's work that I also have to do in her absence. As the holidays were approaching she has decided to stay up in Scotland and try to come to terms with the shock of Miss Royston's death.

Yesterday night, however, by the merest coincidence, interest in my ghostly lady stirred again. It was a gusty, uneasy night. The windows rattled, and strange little draughts disturbed curtains and papers like unseen fingers. The whole of my tiny rented room seemed suddenly packed with ghosts. My unease was so drawn out that when a strange, slithering scratching sound began against my window I jumped from my chair and cowered back against the room's far wall.

The sound persisted, like the whisper of long nails against the curtained glass. It took all of my strength and courage to drive me across the room to it. My hand trembled on the curtain. And when I jerked it back I cried out as if in a nightmare, for a wizened yellow claw was pressed against the dark glass, tapping and tapping, its skin lemon-coloured and scaled . . . It took me anguished moments to recognise it as simply a chicken's foot on a pole. When I pressed my face to the glass it vanished, and I saw half a dozen dark shapes scrambling away across the garden. They were children, and they were playing the ancient Fools' Game.

In Little Dunmow they have their famous Flitch Trial in which, for a side of bacon, husbands and wives are tested. All over Britain we have the bonfires of November 5th. In America, trick or treat on October 31st. Here in Dunmow Cross we have the Fools' Game.

35

The idea is simple: on this night each year one child — a girl always — begins to creep through the village at sunset. She taps on the windows, summoning the other children out to her. They in turn tap on other windows for other children, until all the children in the village and the neighbouring farms have been called out into the night. Then they all flit from shadow to shadow up to the Broken Woods, where they dance around a bonfire.

The game has not been played for years however, and as I put on my coat to go downstairs I wondered who had started it up again. Of course it had to be the newcomer, the new tenant of Whitethorn Cottage, Dr. Richard Burke the psychiatrist, working extra hard to become an accepted member of the village community. I found him alone in the now-silent street, and joined him.

"Hello, Mr. Underhill," he said affably. "How's the hand? No ill-effects, I hope?"

I showed him the scar, which was fading now, and we chatted amiably about village life while the children flitted between the dark buildings, individuals becoming couples, groups and gangs. Their giggling increased, only just short of hysteria.

"It's one of the most fascinating historic games I've ever seen," said Burke. "What do you think it means?"

"I don't know. It's extremely sinister, though."

"I quite agree. Does it ever start spontaneously?" He tugged at his beard. "I mean, I set this game up myself, arranging permission with parents and suchlike, but does it ever just *happen*?"

I told him it hadn't, not that I'd heard of since coming to the village. We began to walk up towards the Broken Woods where the Fools' Game would end. We talked about children's games and how they made play out of fear.

Here comes the candle to light you to bed,
Here comes the chopper to chop off your head . . .

And the horrific 'Ring-a-ring-a-roses', which is a catalogue of the symptons of bubonic plague, a memory of the Black Death. Like these, the Fools' Game, we decided, seemed to tap some forgotten terror.

36

Dr. Burke went on up the hill to watch the bonfire. I left him on the edge of the woods and returned to my room. There was something about the prospect of seeing the children dance around that fire that made my hackles rise. The children and my ghostly Countess seemed suddenly to be inextricably connected . . .

I met Dr. Burke this afternoon as well, when I called round to Jane's house after school to see if everything was all right there.

He was in the garden. "Look at this," he cried as I went in through the gate. "It's those damn children!"

A small rose garden at the corner of her lawn had been trampled underfoot so that the bushes lay about with their roots starting out of the soil like black bones. "I was keeping an eye on this one in particular," he said, pointing to a tall standard lying on its side. "It's Miss Martin's favourite — it needs tying up, and I've nothing . . ."

"I have," I said, and went quickly back to my room. A few minutes later I returned with the stake which had stabbed my hand four months ago. We thumped it into the ground and tied the rose to it. "There," I said when we had finished. "That should hold it."

This evening, after correcting a set of exam papers, I changed into my tracksuit and padded out into the night. I had been running for perhaps twenty minutes when in the darkness something squealed. I knew the sound. Looking neither right nor left, the Reverend Hugh Gore cycled determinedly past me.

Without pausing to think I followed him. Down the road we went, through the village heading south. After half an hour or so, Mr. Gore turned into the driveway through a great pair of gates. Interest quickening, I moved forward. By the time I reached the gates he was gone and the gates locked again behind him, but I could hear his bicycle squeaking away up the drive.

There was a notice on a dark brick column: MID ESSEX HOSPITAL PSYCHIATRIC UNIT: MORDEN HALL.

I loped into the darkness. There had been an urgency in Mr. Gore's manner that told me something was afoot. The wall of the asylum grounds was perhaps ten feet high, but a few yards back from the road a small coppice reached up to the cloudy sky. It was the work of only a moment to shin up the tree nearest to the wall, swing out on a limb and drop down on to the other side.

Some two hundred yards away stood the irredeemably ugly building, squat, and square, five storeys high, like a huge Victorian workhouse. It had an air of brooding hopelessness. Windows blazed, yet there was absolute silence. I moved forward. The grass was shaggy — it would soon need its first summer cutting and it pulled my feet. Along this wing of the asylum there was a stair-well with steps leading down to basement doors, and around it a wrought-iron railing painted black: uprights about nine inches apart, rising to ornate points above a single, flat, horizontal bar at shoulder height. I followed the railings along to the end of the building but there was nothing of interest.

I turned and began to walk back across the lawn. The silence of the place depressed me, I found it dangerously at odds with the tension that seemed to crackle everywhere in the night air around me. I had taken perhaps a dozen steps when the sound of breaking glass made me stop and turn.

High on the wall a window burst outwards, the glass falling in bright arcs like crystal snowflakes. A figure dressed in black dived through the broken frame to pause on all fours like a huge cat balanced impossibly on the sill. It was shrieking the high-pitched cry of a woman. Outlined against the brightness I saw long wild hair, great breadth of shoulders, legs as thin as bones.

Its shrieking ceased as the moon broke through fat clouds, and the creature raised its arms in a frantic gesture of oneness. Then it hunched forward. Its hands sought purchase on the rough brickwork, the hips and buttocks were outlined for a moment and then it began incredibly to crawl head-first down the wall like a gigantic black spider.

Another figure appeared in the vacant square of the window-frame. "Rowena!" cried the Reverend Gore.

He hurled himself out over the sill, reaching down to grasp the foot hooked on to a drain-pipe. "Hang on, Rowena!" he cried, inching forward.

Other figures joined him, held his legs as he pushed clear of the sill, leaning down to grasp the hooked foot with both hands. As he did so a great silver crucifix swung free of his breast and dangled glinting in the moonlight. The creature on the wall saw it and one hand lifted free of a projecting overflow pipe to make a wild gesture. "Hang on, Rowena!" he cried again "Don't let go!"

But the creature howled and kicked against him. A heel slammed into his face. His grip on the other foot slipped. Suddenly the creature looked down and its eyes met mine. It gave a low, thrilling howl, and lifted its hands once more, as it had to the moon.

Lazily, turning in the air like a coin flipped for a bet, it fell clear of the wall. Over and over it went, its scream growing like the whistle of a train approaching out of a long tunnel. It seemed to fall forever.

She was on her back, face up, legs in towards the wall, when she hit the railings. Warm, heavy drops rained on me. One moment she was falling, the next: still. No transition. Suddenly, absolutely, as though she had always been there, she was hanging on the rails. Heels against the iron uprights, hands at the end of arms swinging behind her back to clap quietly in the silence. Upside down and silent — though still wide-eyed — dangled the white face of Rowena, mother to Rebecca and wife to Hugh Gore.

Five years insane, and at peace at last.

Friday 13 April:

THE INQUEST

The Coroner's Court was a small, dusty room, rather like a lecture theatre in a university. There were public seats at the back, seats for a jury at the front, a couple of tables, a witness box and an august bench for the coroner. The coroner today was Miss Hortense Simcox J.P., a formidable lady with hair like steel-wool and the face of a pink frog. But she had sharp, intelligent eyes. I sat at the back, enjoying one of the first days of my Easter holiday. The court was crowded.

The preliminaries were surprisingly swift. A jury was sworn in. The coroner gave a brief talk about the circumstances of Mrs. Gore's illness, about the Gore family and its feelings.

The pathologist was a fat, bald man with a black moustache and artist's hands. He spoke briefly, and forcefully. There was no doubt of his meaning, although many of his technicalities were foreign to me.

The psychiatric expert was Richard Burke. Mrs. Gore, he said, had been under his care for the last few months of his consultancy at Morden Hall. She suffered basically from paranoia, a specialised persecution complex. She slipped into and out of reality quite unpredictably, and was capable of the greatest extremes of violence, both to herself and to others.

Put at its most simple, he said, trying to sound matter-of-fact, Rowena Gore believed that she was a vampire. She feared sunlight and water. She fed only on raw meat, and on her own blood licked out of bites on her forearms. The clearest pattern of her behaviour — if the court would indulge an unmedical reference — would be that of the lunatic Renfield in Bram Stoker's novel, *Dracula*.

My God! I thought, no wonder the Reverend Gore and his daughter sometimes seemed to be carrying a heavy burden! And, even as I thought this, the vicar himself got up to give evidence.

His face was haggard, and he seemed to have aged a dozen years since I'd seen him last. But he spoke out strongly, and with impressive dignity.

"For many years," he began, "my wife believed that there was a curse on the female members of my family and blood. There is a legend in our village about a beautiful foreign lady of noble birth who brought a terrible plague to what had been, up to then, a prosperous town. An ancestor of mine was apparently instrumental in whatever revenge the townspeople took on this noblewoman, and she is said to have cursed his line through its female descendants.

"There is a doggerel which run thus:

Women of blood, look to blood,
Make of blood your bread.
Feed on blood until your blood
Feeds the Dead.

"I myself have never placed any credence in this tale, although it is a matter of record that the women of my family have not led long or happy lives."

Mr. Gore paused, took a drink of water, then calmly continued.

"When she consented to become my wife, Rowena knew nothing of this, but Dunmow Cross has been the cradle of my family through many generations, and soon after the birth of our daughter Rebecca I decided to live there. Somehow, not long after we moved in, Rowena discovered a reference to this curse. She brought it to my notice of course, but I explained that is was nothing but a folk tale. My wife and I met at Oxford University where we were both involved in academic study — myself in theology and Rowena in history — and she used her training in methods of research to the very worst ends. In such places as the Bodleian Library and the library of the British Museum she began to check back on the history of the folk tale. In doing so, she became insanely convinced that some powerful supernatural agency was involved, and that the curse would in fact work out its full power upon her, and eventually upon our daughter Rebecca."

Here he paused again. The feeling of concentration in the room was absolute. Every eye was directed towards his tragic, black-clad figure. This was not a ghost story. This was real. He was talking about a woman who had actually lived and believed in such things, and who had died in that belief, because of that belief.

Mr. Gore sighed deeply. "The ideas took root. I offered to give up living in Dunmow Cross and move away, but her fixation was absolute and she refused. She believed that the curse would find her out no matter where she was, and that research in and around the village presented her best chance of fighting back.

"Ten years ago I first took her to see a psychiatrist. Five years ago I was forced to have her committed." He stopped,

41

his head drooping at last.

The coroner cleared her throat, "Can we turn now to the night in question?"

"Certainly, madam." He drew himself up again. "Since the beginning of this year, my wife's illness had become even more pronounced. She seemed convinced that the curse was coming to some sort of climax. That its author, the Countess, was in fact returning to complete her revenge."

"Let me get this quite clear, please," said the coroner. "Your wife believed that someone was returning — returning from where?"

I sat forward, waiting for his answer, fascinated.

"From beyond the grave. From the dead," said Mr. Gore and a stir went through the silent room like a night wind through trees.

"I see," said the coroner. She made a note. "Please continue, Mr. Gore."

"I went to see her as often as possible, of course, to try and bring her some spiritual comfort. But it was no use. She was convinced that she was beyond divine aid. That it was only a matter of time, of very little time, before this creature returned to claim her for ever."

"And in the meantime, she was sure she was a vampire?" You could hear the conflict between sympathy and utter incredulity in the coroner's voice.

"That was just it, you see," cried Gore, his voice growing hoarse now with the strain. "That was the cure: that she should become like that. She believed the curse was that she should become a vampire, completely and absolutely, one of the un-dead, feeding on blood alone."

Miss Simcox waited for the commotion to subside in the courtroom. When she spoke again her voice trembled, but she kept her tone brisk. "I see. Thank you, Mr. Gore. Now to the night in question, if you please."

With a visible effort Mr. Gore took up his story again. "I went to see her as usual, around eight o'clock. It was after dark. She was seated in her room surrounded by her books. At first, she seemed very glad to see me and asked how I was. We talked of the family and the village, just chit-chat really. Then she began to grow restless. She said she could feel something evil coming close. I tried to change the subject by

42

referring to some parish records which she had spent many years studying. I told her, quite abruptly, hoping to shock her back to her senses, that I had thrown them away."

"Just a moment, please," said the coroner, "you mean to say that you have thrown parish records away?"

"Yes," Mr. Gore admitted. "But only records of the late 1570s, now unfortunately so badly aged and damaged as to be utterly indecipherable."

"I see. So you told your wife you had disposed of these. What was her reaction?"

"She asked me why I had done this. She seemed shocked, as I had hoped — and suddenly quite rational."

"So your shock tactic worked."

"So I believed."

"And then?"

"I explained to her that someone else had been going through the records in her absence."

"Who had?"

"A local schoolteacher. He was checking for a lesson. He mentioned something to my daughter about tracking down a ghost also."

"I see. Is this relevant?"

"Not at all except that Rowena also asked who had been looking at the books and why. And when I told her she became most agitated again. She asked me, what ghost? I realised I had committed a serious error in mentioning it and immediately rang for aid. My wife started to scream. 'It is she. It is she!' I tried to calm her but she suddenly went completely berserk and threw herself at me screaming that I had summoned back the Dead."

"What did you do?"

"I have for some time been using the delustions of her illness to control the malady itself — under the advice of course of Dr. Burke. I showed her my crucifix."

"Did it work?"

"She drew back from me, yes. But at that moment two attendants came in and she threw herself between them, and out through the door. I ran after her but I was too slow. She hurled herself through a window at the end of the corridor and tried to climb down the wall. I leaned out of the window and reached her. I caught her foot but she kicked free —"

Mr. Gore choked, and turned his head away. The coroner waited until he was in control of himself again, and then she said, very gently, "Your wife fell?"

"Yes. No. Yes."

"You're not sure?"

Mr. Gore hunched his shoulders. "Not entirely. You see, it was more complex than that. I . . . I think she saw the Countess down there waiting for her."

"*What?*"

"There was something, someone, down there." He stretched out one hand as if pointing. "Rowena saw it. I too — I am certain there was a figure on the lawn. It was tall and gaunt. It gave the impression of being terribly crippled in some way . . . I am sure Rowena saw it and tried to fly down and join it."

Far too quickly the coroner said: "It was obviously someone from the hospital."

"No," Mr. Gore whispered. He was almost sobbing now. "They were all accounted for. It was no one from the hospital. And there were footprints of a sort across the long grass of the lawn. It was gone, of course, before anyone else saw it. And yet *I saw* it. I know Rowena saw it . . . Why was it there? Where did it go? And so quickly?"

He collapsed then. His testimony was at an end. So was the inquest to all intents and purposes. He was led sympathetically away, and the coroner summed up as best she could. A verdict of Accidental Death was returned almost immediately.

On the way out the Reverend Gore was cornered by well-wishers and newspapermen. I caught up with Rebecca who had gone on alone. My part in her mother's death was troubling me. "Hello," I said, as lightly as I could.

"Edwin," She jumped. "I thought you'd be back in the village. Where did you spring from?"

"I just happened to be in town," I gestured apologetically. "I do hope you don't mind, but I was in there for the whole thing. Is there anything I can do?"

She just looked at me.

"I feel so responsible." I wondered how much I dared admit to. "It was I, after all, who started it all, digging around

44

in those old books."

"Oh, Edwin, don't be so silly! Poor mother was quite mad — we've known it for ages. Come on. Let's have a cup of coffee."

Over coffee — which I did not drink because my lips and gums have grown very sensitive to heat these days — I suggested that her mother might not have been as mad as everyone thought. There might in fact have been a curse after all, I said. And my own researches, taken up since I had seen an (I glanced uneasily over my shoulder, certain that someone was standing there) . . . an apparently genuine apparition, had more or less proved the existence of the Countess.

She went marble-white. "What?"

"Wouldn't it be of help to you and your father's peace of mind if I could prove that there was a solid historical foundation to this? That your mother's fixation was not *all* madness?"

"That there really was a curse?" she cried. "On all the Gore women? Are you saying that I will become like that, too?"

"No! No, of course not. I'm just suggesting that if we can discover the historical basis of the story, then perhaps you will understand your poor mother a bit better. I really don't think she was half as mad as people like Dr. Burke care to make out."

Rebecca drifted off into thought, as though she were simply too bone weary to bother with the strain of reality any more. As I watched her I wondered what it must be like to suspect that, like your mother, grandmother, like ten generations, all you have to look forward to is madness and violent death.

Finally she sighed. She picked up her spoon and slowly stirred the coffee in her cup. She had come to a decision. "Yes, it's a good idea," she said. "We'll try it. Come to the house sometime next week. We'll go up to Mother's old library in the attic and look through what's left of her papers."

THE PAPERS

It was a long, low room with dormer-windows and sloping ceiling, immediately under the vicarage eaves. It was lit by three naked light-bulbs. The wind whispered all around it. Things scurried behind its rough plaster walls. Somewhere nearby a tree-branch tapped on the tiles with mindless insistence, as though something were out there, like Catherine's ghost in *Wuthering Heights,* begging to come in.

"I hate this place," said Rebecca with unaccustomed violence. "It's full of death and ghosts."

Now I rather liked it. For all the strange business associated with it, it had an atmosphere I personally found restful, but I agreed with her out of politeness and pretended to shiver. The constraint between us following her New Year's Eve party has mostly been forgotten these days. We meet seldom, but never unfriendlily.

On the right of the attic the ceiling sloped down to the floor, but on the left the room was ten or so feet high. All along that wall were book-shelves loaded with books. In front of the shelves was a desk. I went over and opened it. It was full of stationery.

Behind me Rebecca shifted her feet. "Well," she said, "I'll leave you to it."

"Thanks," I said, hardly bothering to look at her. On the desk was a plastic box full of file-cards. An index. I pulled up the chair which stood by the desk and sat.

"You know your way down," she said. "I'll be somewhere around."

But I was already leafing through the index at random. POLIDORI John: *The Vampire*; POE Edgar A: *Berenice*; STOKER Bram: *Dracula's Guest*; STOKER Bram: *Dracula.* In fiction and in fact, in old editions and in new, in English and a whole spectrum of other languages she had amassed a library on the occult which centred, as her obsession had dictated, on vampires.

Piled on the floor beneath the lowest shelf were older,

darker tomes whose names were not on the cards. *The Clavicle of Solomon; The Grimoire of Pope Honorius, The Arbatel of Magic.* Lists of devils and demons of all sorts — box upon box of them — but always the same basic theme: vampires. Their formation, their habits, defences against their strength, methods of exploiting their weaknesses, their place in the patterns of Earth, their position in the hierarchies of Hell.

All of it interesting enough to anyone obsessed by vampires, I suppose, but all of it useless to me. I was very near to despair when I found, right at the back of the room, a plain brown cardboard box. The top was folded shut and sealed with tape. I peeled this off and tore the flaps back.

I cannot fully describe what happened then. It was as though I had opened a jack-in-the-box, some sort of booby-trap. Something formless seemed to leap out of the box and hit me with considerable force full in the face. A stench as though of putrefying flesh, a white light hurled me back in a strange explosion of power right across the width of the room. Inevitably my head hit the slope of the ceiling and I rolled, helpless, into the narrow dark corner where the roof met the floor.

I was knocked partly insensible, I think, because it seemed only seconds before Rebecca was at my side. She later said that it was some minutes for she was downstairs when she heard the distant crash of my fall. She helped me up and supported me over the chair. "What happened?" she asked.

"I don't know. I was opening that box when . . ."

"This box?"

"Yes."

She leaned over it. "There seems to be something —" She broke off "What a terrible smell! There's something here. *How disgusting!*" She dipped cautiously into the box and brought something out. "No wonder you were startled," She said. "Look at this."

She held up the decomposing corpse of a bat. On its breast there was a tiny silver crucifix tied in place with white strings of garlic. Nausea burned agonisingly in the back of my throat. "Take it away," I croaked. "Please!"

She took it away. My head began to clear. After a few moments she returned. "Are you all right?"

"Yes," I said "I'm fine now."

She stood above me, lingered for a few moments, and then left me again. I waited till she was gone, then turned to look in the box. Inside there were three green files. Rebecca's mother had placed them there, and then the corpse of the bat on top of them. I wondered why. Was the bat intended to discourage innocent intruders? Or had not the crucifix perhaps been placed there to protect the files from evil? I lifted them carefully out and carried them over to the desk.

In many ways those three files have absolutely dominated my days and nights ever since. From mid-morning to mid-afternoon I pore over them in that strange long room which whispers and rustles all around me with such quiet mystery that at times I imagine, if I were only to turn quickly enough, that I would see the spirit of old Mrs. Gore scribbling away in the corner. And even when I walk or jog abroad on the busy streets or in the open fields in the evenings, that whispering still seems to teem about my ears.

The first file looked initially to be innocent enough. It was a history of our village of Dunmow Cross from its beginnings right back in the Bronze Age. A stone circle was built on the hill, its ruins cloaked today by the Broken Woods. In later years the circle was fortified to stand with Boadicea and the Icenii. When Governor Suetonius Paulinus brought his legions over in A.D. 61, the Romans moved the fortress down the hill, and settled the site of the present village where two of their roads crossed: the rule-straight *via* up the Roddings and Stane Street which ran at that time due west from Camulodunum.

The Romans fell in their turn, to be followed by the East Saxons, who gave the whole region their name — Essex — and the town the name it holds to this day: Dun Mow — the Field on the Hill. Then, after them came the Danes, up the River Chelmer one night in the mid-ninth century to slaughter the townsfolk and put everything to the torch.

And yet by the time the Domesday Book was compiled two hundred years later, here was a thriving town again. It grew during the Wars of the Roses to be the premier wool-market of East Anglia. By the reign of Elizabeth I it was set fair to become a force to be reckoned with in the South of England: at least five thousand people dwelt there in the 1570s.

But then it all ended. Not temporarily, as the slaughter by

the Danes had ended it, but permanently. Inexorably the records in the file revealed that something had happened there so evil, so powerful, that the whole town had died. It had ceased, never to live again.

Rowena Gore had photocopied the pages from the Register of Burials which I had not been allowed to see. There were thirty-seven pages for January 1579 alone. Fifteen entries per page. More than five hundred deaths in that one month. As many as 150 dead in a week, for week after week.

'Ann Spooner 18 yrs Spinster this P'sh. Dead of the White Plague. St'd.'

Page after page like this. All dead of the White Plague, all young, each with that cryptic 'st'd.' at the end of the entry. January, February and March of 1579 went past. The graveyard became too full. They put the bodies in the crypt of the church. When that too became full, they found somewhere else.

By All Fools' Day 1579, the busy town of Dunmow Cross was dead. It fell out of history. Even the roads moved. Stane Street, nowadays the A120, bent north, while the B184 up the Roddings bent east. They circled away from the accursed, derelict spot where the Roman roads had originally crossed. A new crossroads was made, and a new town: Great Dunmow. So it remains on the maps today — two perfectly straight roads, which look as though they will cross at right angles, turn aside instead and cross at Great Dunmow, only to turn back afterwards to their original straight ways . . . Dunmow Cross is the place they avoid, a tiny shabby village now, unremarked upon even by the makers of maps . . .

After this brooding, sinister history, the second green file came initially as something of a surprise, for it began with methodical examination of the probable locations for an old house, now long vanished. The place had been called Coul Hall. When Dunmow Cross had been an important town, Coul Hall had apparently been one of its most famous buildings — amongst the greatest architectural wonders of East Anglia. And the conclusion of the first part of the folder surveyed the geographical evidence and suggested that the hall had stood close by the Broken Woods, on the top of the hill.

Turning to the second part, however, I saw at once why Coul Hall had clearly been so important to Rowena Gore.

In 1578 the hall had suddenly acquired a new tenant. A beautiful lady, a member of some foreign aristocracy, took up residence there. As the year aged, she became the hub of Dunmow Cross society; as it died she threw party after party in the bright rooms. In the icy mid-winter her guests thronged the place. They danced, they ate, they drank . . . Then they began to die. According to the records, almost every person in the town aged between ten and twenty-five sickened, infected others, died. Their disease came to be known as 'The White Death'. They were buried in the graveyard, in the crypt, finally even in the cellars of Coul Hall itself. And in the spring the few remaining townspeople took the house, stone by stone, and tore it down with their bare hands, so that only the faintest memory of the place remained.

And what of the curse that so weighed on Rebecca's mind? And what of the beautiful tenant of Coul Hall herself? The third folder told of both, the curse and its originator: Stana Etain, Countess Issyk-Koul, bringer of the White Plague, witch, monster, the Dead.

Certainly that was what the townspeople had believed her to be. Rebecca's mother had documented their sufferings with obsessive thoroughness. And if she herself shared in their belief, did that make her crazy? When I finally went downstairs carrying the folders, late on that first afternoon, I had little enough to tell Rebecca, and nothing for her comfort. The curse was historical fact. She could believe in its effectiveness or not, I had to say, as her own convictions persuaded her . . .

And now dear Jane Martin has returned, seeming to bring the spring with her. All through her long absense we have corresponded, letters full of increasing affection. She had told me more or less how long she would be staying in Scotland, of course, but not the exact date of her return. Indeed, I did not even know she was back in Dunmow Cross until yesterday afternoon, when a note from her was pushed through my landlord's door.

She's looking well. As soon as I received her note yesterday I put aside the folders and went to take tea with her. The sky was cloudless, radiant, and there was a south wind full of the scent of young blossoms. The elm trees round her house were delicately green as their new leaves unfurled in the balmy air. So warm was it, in fact, that we took tea on the lawn.

She seems slimmer, a little quieter than I remember, but full of a new strength that I find both appealing and impressive. She embraced me in the doorway and kissed me warmly on my check. "Oh, Edwin!" she said, "it's so lovely to see you again."

"Welcome home!" I said, returning her hug enthusiastically. "You've been away too long. I've missed you."

With our arms still around each others' waists we walked through the house. "You *do* look well," she told me. "You've lost so much weight! It makes you look much taller, you know."

In the garden, Richard Burke was sitting with a bone-china teacup expertly balanced on his knee. He rose as we came out.

"Edwin! How are you?" he asked.

We shook hands. "Very well, thank you. And yourself?"

"Fine . I was just telling Jane how we've been keeping the garden in line."

"Oh, come now! You've been much busier than I have. I haven't been round in a week or more. I've been . . ."

"Well, it was you who saved the standard rose . . ." he gestured across towards the rose tree we had bound to my stake.

There was indeed a tall bush, rich in branches and buds. We went across and examined it with increasing interest. The rose, in fact, was stunted and dying. It was my stake which was branching into life. "That's amazing!" said Jane. "What sort of bush is that?"

We didn't know, but such was our fascination that we decided to check there and then. Jane kept much of her gardening equipment and several books in the cellar. This was a large dark room at the foot of a flight of stairs, tucked behind a narrow door beside the entrance to the kitchen, in the hall. As Richard and Jane pored over assorted gardening books, I explored the cluttered dusty room and discovered,

51

beyond it, a tiny room behind another door. Here Jane's grandfather had kept his woodworking tools on an old trestle-table. The windowless little room was very snug — there was even an old gas fire there. I would have lingered for some time, had not Jane called, "Well, that's it: it's not here. We'd better give up. Come on, Edwin, The tea will be getting cold. And I want to hear what else has been happening while I've been away . . ."

The most lurid news current, of course, was that of Rowena Gore's death. "Yes," said Richard, nodding sadly over a new cup of scalding tea, "I was involved. Mrs. Gore was the main reason I came down, you know. I'm spending the second half of this year doing a series of lectures both here and on the continent about certain types of criminal lunacy. Several of the lectures will centre on so-called 'Vampirism', and Rowena's case was the most vivid example of it in years. Well, since Haigh, actually . . ."

Richard Burke is a charming, friendly person and he was so naively excited by the prospect of the lecture tour, it was a delight to listen to him. The tour was the goal he had striven for during many heart-breaking years of obscure work. He was determined to take the establishment by storm. Over-night — well, within six months — he was going to become famous. Rich.

But Jane, my quiet, fair-minded Jane, did not let him have all the limelight. "And what have you been up to, Edwin?" she asked at last.

"Well, it brushes against Richard's concerns really . . ."

"Is that so?" Richard leaned forward eagerly, interested at once.

"Yes. It arose out of Mrs. Gore's inquest. I was there, you see, and heard your evidence, and it occurred to me that there might be some basis in fact for her obsession."

"That's fascinating!" Richard tugged excitedly at his beard. "And is there?"

"Well, I've been going through her folders —"

"Folders? I never knew . . ."

" — and it seems that there *is* a certain basis. You see, in 1579 there was a woman living in a place called Coul Hall just outside the village, up in the Broken Woods somewhere. This woman, whose name was Stana Etain, Countess

Issyk-Koul, brought some sort of a plague to the village, and —"

"What sort of plague?" Richard demanded. "Black Death? Bubonic?"

"I don't think so." I shrugged. "They called it the White Death, whatever that might have been. Anyway, so many people died of this plague that the villagers who were left took revenge upon the Countess. They accused her of witchcraft. They said she was a creature they spoke of as the Dead. They tried her, hanged her, and buried her at the crossroads."

"That's fascinating. *Stana Etain* . . ." He thought for a moment. "That wouldn't have been her real name, of course. It's obviously a cypher for Satan Innate . . . so it's no wonder that they buried her at the crossroads. And I tell you what — it must have been *her* grave you pushed your arm into on the night of the party!"

"Obviously." I had already worked that much out for myself. "Perhaps that's also why . . ." I went on to tell him something of my experiences with the ghost, the apparition at the roadside.

"And you think your disturbing her grave has been enough to bring her back?" he asked when I had finished.

"Well, I can't think of anything else I've done," I said.

Richard swung round dramatically, and pointed at the black bush growing strongly beside the dying rose. "You've done that!" he cried.

At first I did not understand his meaning.

"The stake," he explained. "The stake through her heart — you've removed it. If — just for argument's sake — you admit that vampire lore has any basis in fact, then the removal of the stake is bound to bring her back. Isn't it?"

I hesitated, sensing from his manner that he was trying to trick me "I'm not sure," I muttered.

"Wise man." He smiled at me approvingly. "You see, the snag is that if she were truly a vampire then her *body* would have risen. She wouldn't appear to you as a ghost — she'd seem to be an apparently normal person."

I was about to agree with him when suddenly Jane spoke up "Unless," she said, looking from me to Richard and back again, "unless the people who buried her found some other way of destroying her — something more than just the stake through her heart."

Richard frowned, momentarily nonplussed. For me, however, her words came as a blinding revelation, for I remembered all too vividly my terrible experience at her aunt's seance — the powerful presence of evil, and the severed arm that had tried to choke the poor old woman. There had also, before that, been the shapeless, semi-dismembered apparition in the hospital ward.

"Of course!" I cried. "The townspeople must have cut her up. Chopped her limbs from her body . . . perhaps her head also . . . That's why, even though the removal of the stake has released her from her grave, she *still* cannot take on human flesh again. She needs another body. *And I think she's looking for one.*"

Silence fell across the garden like a sudden shadow. Richard shifted uneasily in his seat. "It's an interesting theory," he said.

His words were calm enough, scientific, carefully objective. But behind them lurked a fear, a primeval dread, that would not be hidden. Even a man of science such as he would not be arrogant enough to deny the existence of the Unknown. Nor, deep in his bones, would he be too arrogant to fear it.

Monday 7 May:

THE HALL

Now a new urgency has entered my researches into the life and times of Stana, Countess Issyk-Koul. Jane helps me with them, and together we have come to the conclusion that there is little more to be wrung from the general history of the village, while Mrs. Gore's maunderings about the Dead itself bear far too much the stamp of lunacy to be worth our

54

serious attention.

Not so her work on the location of Coul Hall, however, and here we have concentrated our main endeavours. Although all reference to the place has been expunged from records after 1579, Mrs. Gore discovered some hints in earlier documents, and, so finally with the aid of her notes, a large-scale map and a good deal of guess-work, we set out this afternoon to find the site.

We started near the road and, with the hulk of the Broken Woods towering on our right, began our slow exploration of the ground, pausing every now and then to consult our maps and diagrams. The day wore on: we found nothing. At sunset, with the road far behind and out of sight, we sat down side by side like lovers to watch the red disc of the sun settle behind the smoke-grey horizon. Jane rested her head on my shoulder, rubbed her cheek there thoughtlessly like a child, and fell asleep.

The view was beautiful. The slight roll of the countryside, the chequered fields, the hedgerows already plump and green. The first twinkling lights in the vales on the shady sides of hillocks. A distant spire stark against the sky.

As the last of the sun vanished, threads of mist appeared among the hedgerows. Even as I watched, the threads became webs and the webs tiny white clouds. A coldness crept out of the woods behind us. I shivered and glanced back, careful not to move my shoulders for fear I should awaken Jane. The woods seemed more threatening now, the black tree trunks breeding shadows. Everything was expectant, silent and still.

"What's that?" cried Jane suddenly.

I jumped, looked where she was pointing. There was a glimmer of movement. We froze. It was repeated. Someone was wandering silently in the twilight at the farthest edge of the coppice, a mile from the quiet road, five hundred yards from us.

"Hello?" I called, and the faintest of echoes came: "Hello?"

The figure did not pause or turn. I did not call again. My skin prickling, I caught Jane by the hand, rose and plunged forward up the slope. It was the Countess Stana, I was sure, pacing the vanished ruins of her home. The figure became

55

clearer as we ran, and yet somehow it remained indistinct. I could make out only paleness, silently moving among the great black columns unhindered by undergrowth, unencumbered by brambles.

We drew level with the edge of the trees and, turning right without letting go of each other, entered the wood. Our progress slowed and when we reached the place where she had walked there was nothing. She had vanished. We began to cast about for some sign of her, but it was useless. Darkness began to gather. I had matches in my pocket and lit one. Even with the maps shading it, the match blew out immediately.

And then the ground opened beneath me.

One moment I was standing on firm ground, the next, incredibly, there was a sharp crack as the earth tilted and tore itself into ragged jaws. I fell between them precipitated down into a musty, echoing dark. My ghostly Countess had led me well.

Immediately I was knee deep in soft soil. I panicked and floundered about, fearing I would sink as though into quicksand, until Jane's head thrust into the rough square of light above my head. "Are you all right?" she asked anxiously.

The need to reassure her calmed me. "I'm fine," I said. And I was. My feet had found firm ground now, paving stones or levelled rock.

"It looks as though you trod on some kind of trapdoor. Are those steps under that earth?"

I felt about. "I think so.'

"Good, I'm coming down."

In a moment we were both standing in what seemed to be a shadowy little room, perhaps one-quarter filled with earth. Straight ahead of us a doorway gaped absolutely black, the soil flowing through it like a stream in suspended animation.

"Someone went to a lot of trouble to fill this room with earth," Jane whispered, "but then the door there must have given way."

I did not answer. She clutched my arm and we both moved forward, blundering through the strange clinging soil. At the doorway we were stopped by the stench. We stood there for a moment. There was just light enough to see that the floor fell away again into another set of steps.

Beyond that there was only darkness.

But the atmosphere of the room told me what we would see if there were more light. It was the distillation of all the terrors felt at midnight in a thousand graveyards. Some timeless memory in me knew well enough the peculiar odour of ancient putrefaction.

And yet I was utterly unprepared for what I saw when I lit a match and held it high in the still air. It was a sight I carried with me as I fled with Jane up the soil-slick stairs and out of the gathering shadows of the woods. It was a sight that burned a vision of horror indelibly upon my mind.

They had not rotted to skeletons. The atmosphere must have been kept dry by the thick, stone, cellar walls and the location high on the hill. Nor had it mummified them — not properly. And of course worms and insects had been busy for four hundred years.

Like grey-green leather the skin clung to their bones, holding thigh to hip and arm to shoulder, holding wild-haired skull to neck. Nearly a thousand children, the records had said. They were piled like wood — one row atop another. Once, no doubt, neatly and reverently. Now the weight of those on the top had crushed those beneath. The highest rows were toppled outwards as though, even in death, trying to escape. They had fallen in attitudes of crawling, and the match flame's guttering flicker made them seem to move. But it was not the corpses which so deeply shocked me — not their number nor their condition. It was the final understanding they gave me of the White Death, the cryptic 'st'd.' after each name in the register of burials: for through the breast of each tiny corpse there was a sharpened piece of wood.

In that nightmare winter four centuries ago the towns-people had staked their dead children for fear they would rise again, with stakes like the one I had removed from the breast of the Dead itself.

Tomorrow, I think, we must go and see Mr. Gore. At last we have something to tell him.

57

THE GRAVE

That Saturday, the twelfth, we went to see Rebecca's father. She was out, and the old man answered the door himself. He was not pleased to see us, and let us through into the library only after I insisted that we had discovered something of great importance.

"Look, sir," I said as soon as we had sat down, "I know you don't believe any of this, but let me put it to you the way I think I see it. Your late wife's records show that four hundred years ago a witch lived at Coul Hall. She called herself Stana, Countess Issyk-Koul. The villagers called her the Dead, believe her to be a vampire. Early in 1579 they summoned a 'Cunning Man', as they were called, a sort of folk-wizard, from the village of Theydon Mount to help them destroy her. This man, Gore, was the progenitor of your family, and he advised the people of Dunmow Cross how best to lay the witch to rest. Eventually this was done, but as she died she cursed Gore and his family. You repeated the doggerel yourself in court:

> Women of blood, look to blood,
> Make of blood your bread.
> Feed on blood until your blood
> Feeds the Dead."

He nodded, an expression of extreme distaste on his rugged face. I continued, undeterred. "By that time, however, nearly a thousand young people in the town had died and the townspeople, believing this to be the work of the vampire, drove a wooden stake through the hearts of each person before they buried them."

"But this is preposterous!" he exploded, "a childish legend."

"They did the same to the Countess."

"Nonsense! She was hanged for witchcraft. There were records. I have seen them. *Hanged!* This vampire stuff, the

58

curse, the Dead, it is all make-believe, childishness and lunacy."

"No," said Jane quietly, "it is not!"

"Hah! I'm sorry, Miss Martin, but if you believe that then you are as mad as my wife, poor soul!"

"No," I said. There was madness, but not ours. Nor, at the beginning certainly, your wife's." I leaned forward, intensity burning in me. "And not your daughter's either . . . yet!"

"What do you mean?"

"The stories, they are true," whispered Jane. "What those people did is true. As for what they believed . . . well, of course, that is another matter, but they did stake the children. We've seen it. We can prove it."

He sat back in his chair, stunned, as though she had hit him *"Prove it?* How can you prove it?"

"We found where they buried the children."

"In the crypt . . ."

"No," I said, "in Coul Hall."

Again he lurched. "The Hall? But it is gone. People have spent years searching . . ."

"We found it. There are cellars. We have been down. The children are there."

"Sacrilege! *Blasphemy!*" He rose, arms raised, white hair wild and floating.

"Neither!" I snapped. "Accident. Good luck. Perhaps I was guided. Have you thought of that? Guided? What does it say? 'To give light to those that sit in darkness and in the shadow of the Dead, and to guide our feet into the paths of peace . . . ' "

He swung towards me. For some reason my throat burned as though I had drunk acid. "I have not heard that translation before," he said, more calmly.

I said nothing. Jane reached across and touched my hand.

Mr. Gore considered the two of us. "You must show me what you have found," he said.

He brought a briefcase, I took a torch. Jane begged to be excused: she said that once was enough for her, and went home.

The sun was bright as Mr. Gore and I set off at a brisk pace. He began to perspire almost immediately, mopping his face

59

with a great white handkerchief. We talked hardly at all until the Broken Woods closed over us like a black wave breaking.

My companion shivered as soon as the shadows of the trees clutched at him. We walked more slowly, both of us suddenly reluctant to reach our destination. It must have been after six when I found the hole. It gaped silent and sinister like a dark wound in the earth. I lit the torch. The blackness gulped at the puny beam.

"The steps are covered with earth," I said "You'd better watch it."

I put one wary foot in, and explored until I found the faintest edge of stone. Then I went down, backwards, until I was in the antechamber, up to my knees in soft black earth once more. I shone my torch around, briefly illuminating walls, floors, the squat lintel on the inner door.

Mr. Gore came down as I had done. "It smells horrible," he said. The darkness seemed to consume his words, as it did the light. We paused for a moment.

"There's nothing here," I said. "We have to go through there." I pointed with my torch beam into the shadows of the second room.

He took another torch from his briefcase. We waded over to the doorway and stumbled down the slope into the vaulted chamber beyond. It was not until we stood together on a sure footing that either of us looked up. Mr. Gore retched drily. His torch beam wavered up the walls of the dead to those few still packed up high against the ceiling, and fell again to the floor. "I would not have believed it!" he cried. "It's incredible. They must have been mad. Oh, the stupid, criminal, *blasphemy* of it all!"

His voice rang out and dust filtered down among dead bones, disturbed by his echoing words. He fell to his knees, opened his case, and began to set up a little altar.

"There is no need for that, surely," I said harshly, turning away, "I'm sure they were all blessed and shriven by good Christian men just after the stakes were driven home."

"Don't, don't," he whispered. "A sacrilege. A perversion. How terrible."

He began to mumble prayers. The stench upon the air grew richer. It was then that I noticed that all the bodies seemed to be directing the gaze of their cavernous eye sockets at one spot in the centre of the room. The impression was so strong that I stepped forward, past the man and his prayers, to the long tongue of earth which thrust down from the antechamber above. At the place at which the skulls were staring so fixedly, I kicked desultorily at the earth and my foot struck hollow wood. "There's something here," I said, and knelt.

Mr. Gore did not hear me. I began to scrape away at the earth with my hands. Several prayers later I had uncovered the head of a stone tomb. There was a thick lid of rotting boards. I scrabbled the earth away down its length and hooked my fingers under the edge. "Help me!" I cried to Gore. "Help me here."

The prayers faltered into silence. I tugged again. There came a quiet grating. *"Help me!"* I tugged once more as I spoke, and the lid burst free, tumbling earth into my lap. The torch cartwheeled away, slicing the darkness with its beam.

As I picked myself up the old man came over, his torch aimed strangely high, like a knife in my eyes. He hesitated, staring oddly at me. "What is it?" I asked. He mumbled something about shadows. I laid my hand over his, guiding the torch beam down into the stone box. He resisted momentarily, shuddering, then acquiesced.

There was no body in the coffin — only a piece of parchment marked with dark writing. I picked it up and looked closely in the torch-light. The writing glistened slightly as though there were scales on it. I rubbed a dot with a thumbnail. It flaked away. I wet my finger and it stained my flesh dull red. It was blood.

In blood upon the parchment someone had written: THE DEAD WHERE SHE RESTED.

And through the parchment they had driven a sharpened wooden cross. Disgusted, I tore it out and threw it away. As I did so, the shadows seemed to leap around us. I looked over my shoulder and thought I saw a crippled shape lurch away into invisibility. I swung back towards Gore. He was dead white. Had he seen it too? His eyes went down to the parchment. "Blasphemy," he whispered. Then he turned back to his makeshift altar.

"There's nothing more we can do here," I said. "I've shown you as I said I would. Now we must look to Rebecca.

Here is the origin of the curse — we must find a way to lift it."

Then he did a strange thing. He turned towards me, still on his knees, the light of his torch lending fire to a silver crucifix. I stepped back easily and turned away to recover my torch. "What's the matter, Vicar?" I asked as I straightened again.

Leaning forward, as though against a strong wind, I walked towards him. Something — proximity to so much putrefaction, perhaps, brought bitter vomit to the back of my throat. I lifted my right hand as if to protect myself, although against what I did not know. "Mr. Gore?" I queried.

He seemed confused for a moment, then he lowered the cross, took my hand and allowed me to help him up. "You're right," he said. "We should seal this place and bless it. Perhaps erect a cross, an epitaph."

"Your wife has an epitaph in a book in her library," I said. I was not serious but he did not realise it. "The vampire's epitaph: 'What profit is there in my blood: when I must go down to the Pit?' "

"Yes," he said, his eyes strangely bright. "Yes. Let us do that immediately."

"Not yet," I answered. There was an idea suddenly forming in my mind. On the way up out of there, and on the way home, I explained it to him — how we should take the Countess from her grave at the crossroads and return her to this place where she had rested, so that she perhaps might find eternal rest again.

He heard me out. "Well, I don't know," he said uncertainly, "I suspect we would need a special dispensation from the bishop, not to mention the civil authorities . . ."

"For Rebecca," I said. "If she believes in the curse then this will surely lift it."

I needed to say no more.

The arrangements took him a fortnight. While we waited, Jane and I left off our ghost-hunting. It was a quiet, gentle time. We saw each other every evening for tea or dinner and I could feel a mutual regard blossoming almost minute by minute. Once I had loved Rebecca and perhaps I loved her still. Is it possible for a man to love two different women in two different ways? Jane and Rebecca. Calm and passion.

And now, this evening, the exhumation has taken place.

Jane and I reached the crossroads at seven. Five minutes later a police car drew up quietly, and then a blue van. Three constables in shirts-sleeves began to unload a set of green canvas screens which they erected in a rough square on the grassy corner of the green where I had fallen on the night of the party. Then they produced a small generator, a battery of lights, spades and a pickaxe and some black plastic bags, all of which were taken behind the screens.

At a quarter-past seven more people arrived in official cars. There was quite a crowd of villagers now outside the first terraced houses of the Cross on the far side of the road to the village green. A representative of the Department of Health and Social Security talked briefly with a uniformed police inspector. The coroner, Miss Simcox, arrived. At half-past seven precisely Mr. Gore came down through the churchyard with the sexton, Rebecca, and a tall stranger dressed in black clerical robes. Jane and I moved forward at last.

I had not seen Rebecca for some time, and her simple proximity set my heart racing. Jane fell into conversation with the stranger while I drifted across to Rebecca. "How do you feel?" I asked her solicitously as we moved into the floodlit square.

She was pale and her face was marked with strain. She smiled wryly.

"Frightened," she said.

I had no time to react to this, for Jane was at my side again: "Edwin, this is Brother John Warlock. Brother Warlock, Edwin Underhill."

He was tall, his hair thick and wavy. His eyes were bright blue and piercing, and his hand was almost as cold as mine. I grunted some reply and turned away.

The grass was floodlit, flat and green. The sexton and two constables had spades. We witnesses gathered round. The place where my arm had gone through the earth by the road was still visible. The coroner nodded and the men began to dig there. It was as simple as that.

They cut the turf into rough squares and laid them to one side. Then the medical officer turned to Mr. Gore and said, "Are you sure this is what you want?"

The vicar's arm tightened round his daughter's shoulders

63

and, loudly and clearly, he said, "Yes. I am."

The spades bit into the earth, wrenched it free, dumped it with a dead sound on a mound by the graveside. They were no more than two feet down when the first spade struck something solid. They dug the hole wide enough to leave a walkway of a couple of feet on one side of the coffin, and stood on this as they carefully uncovered its plain wooden boards.

These were completely featureless except that in the centre, above the heart, there was a ragged hole, presumably caused by my hand. The sexton reached for the pickaxe. One blow wedged it under the boards. He tugged, but they would not yield. The nearest constable joined him and they leaned on the haft together, rocking with all their strength, trying to prise the stubborn lid up. The rest of us gathered round the head end, the floodlights blazing above us. Every crack in the board stood out clearly.

There was a groan, as of someone in great pain. The constable and sexton strained at the lever and abruptly there was a sharp crack as the ancient wood split apart. About four square feet of the head sprang free and fell back thunderously against the hollow length of the coffin.

On the other side of the lid, uppermost now, there was a severed head, fixed to it by an iron staple driven into the gaping eye sockets. Incredibly, greenish skin still stretched to obscene fullness over rotten flesh. Long hair, matted, writhed with worms and insects. The flaccid mouth fell open as the lower jaw swung down. Teeth projected over swollen black lips, the canines two shining scimitars of white bone.

Rebecca fainted, was caught by the medical officer as she teetered on the edge of the hole. Jane staggered back, dragging me with her, and Mr. Gore fell scrabbling to his knees. The three men in the hole leaped out, vomiting as the first putrid stench on the thing tainted the still air. Brother Warlock, however, moved forward unafraid. He prayed in silence, tranquilly, over the shattered coffin until order was restored around him.

Eventually the head was placed in a plastic bag and the exhumation continued. There was little more of note: the rest of the skeleton, mere dry bones, was put into further plastic bags for later examination. Then the hole was filled in. I left then, taking Jane home and then returning to my

64

rented room. I dined here alone, on rare steak and warm milk.

Afterwards, for some reason, I found myself terribly restless. I crept downstairs in my tracksuit and ran out into the dark. I was running with no object other than for the exercise, and along my usual course, out of the village and on to the pathways between the fields, then across the main road towards Great Dunmow. As I neared the westernmost corner of the Broken Woods I saw a flicker of light in the blackness.

I froze. Then I realised that it was not the ghostly glow of some spectre but the flashing of an ordinary electric torch: nothing supernatural about it at all. I crept forward, both curious and silent. As I drew near I heard voices.

"*I must!*" Rebecca's voice.

"But you don't know what is down there, Rebecca." They were by the entrance to the vault. "Brother Warlock and I will do it."

"I don't care. I'm not frightened of dead children. I must come down. I want to be there when you read the service over her remains."

A pause. Then the deep, infinitely calm voice of Warlock himself. "Let Rebecca come, Hugh. If we do ill, we will protect her. If we do good, she must share in it."

The light went out. I reached the trap-door and paused. After a few moments I followed them down.

They knelt by the side of the stone tomb and their heads were bowed in prayer. In the coffin lay the bones and, still stapled to its piece of wood, the head of Stana, Countess Issyk-Koul, mistress of Coul Hall. In the coffin lay what was left of the Dead, and all around her lay her children.

They had placed a candle on each corner of the great stone box and these illuminated the cellar with a clean holy light which seemed obscenely out of place. It drove the shadows back, revealing each separate horror of the thousand tiny mouldering corpses. And yet even as I looked, a shadow seemed to creep in front of my eyes. I took a step forward; the shadow lingered; I took another step. Then my foot slipped and I crashed sideways against the door opening. All three of them leaped to their feet. Rebecca's arm hit a candle and it tumbled, miraculously still alight, to roll away across the floor. Before any of us had time to react the bodies burst into flame, first their brittle hair and then their paper skin. In an instant the whole wall was a sheet of crackling spitting fire.

"Run!" I yelled and grabbed the vicar by the shoulders, hurling him towards the steps. Warlock needed no second bidding. Rebecca stood still, riveted by the speed and ferocity of the inferno. I swept her bodily into my arms and ran with her up the stairs, behind Brother Warlock and her father.

Outside, we paused for a moment, and only for a moment. There was a roar from within the earth's heart. The ground quaked. A column of fire swirled out of the vault's dark entrance as if from a gigantic flame-thrower, shrivelling the grass and blackening the rich summer green of the trees overhead. Then we staggered gasping away, Rebecca still close against my breast, and seeming to me so hot there that she might have been a live coal herself.

The service of commital, I gathered, had not been completed. I saw this as in some measure my fault, and I apologised. But my words were waved away, for none of us then — not even the wary Brother Warlock — doubted that the destruction of those foul remains would have led inevitably to the laying of Stana's evil ghost and the lifting of her four-hundred-year curse.

Now, however, as I write this in the quiet of my room, I begin to have my suspicions. The dark calls to me, and somewhere, somehow, the Countess is waiting.

THE STAKING

In the week since we opened her grave I have slept only fleetingly. Listless and sick by day, I am restless and burning with energy at night. This is not sudden, I know: looking back I see the process starting at the beginning of the year — sleeping through the alarm in the morning: too overtired to do more than catnap at night. And of course there have been the dreams. Even now as I write this in the empty hours before dawn, I could swear that I hear my bedroom door begin to shake as though there were something terrible out there battering the flimsy wood to come in to me.

And this is what happened last night. I seemed to awake from a fitful doze at the first whisper of sound — like the lightest brushing of long talons against the wood. I sat up, mesmerised, as the round porcelain handle began to move. Three-quarters of a turn one way it went, screaming softly, then three-quarters of a turn the other way. The door stayed closed. I could see the key that I had turned before getting into bed, locking it. The talons scratched the paint again. Then the door began to rattle back and forth as whatever stood outside it tried to break it down.

And at last, goaded beyond endurance, I cried, "If you must come, come then. Come in! *Come in!*" And the rattling stopped abruptly. Silence clotted my ears. The door did not open but shadows obscured it for a moment. I lay back, half propped up by my pillows, and suddenly she stood there, inside the room. How can a sane man describe a nightmare? She was tall, her body clothed in a plain white robe which fell from shoulder to ankle. Her hair was a dark mass tumbling. Her face was pale, on her full lips glinted the points of sharp white teeth, and her eyes were blood-red almonds. I have never experienced such absolute terror in all my life. My breath clouded on the icy air. She walked towards me, and as she did so her left hand reached out. I shrank back into the corner between bedhead and wall.

When the white cloth of her gown touched my counter-

67

pane she stopped. Very faintly through the fullness of her body I could see the door. She was not a thing of muscle and bone, then, I thought. Those sharp white teeth would break no skin.

Her hand reached out to touch my forehead in its centre. She did no more than stand there for a moment, then turn and vanish into shadow. But it was as though a splinter of ice had been driven into my brain which lingered even when she had gone. Exhausted by the excess of my terror, finally in my dream I slept.

But in my sleep of dreams I had a dream. And in this dream I stood at the foot of a gallows high on a hill. From one arm of this gallows hung a body bound by strange ropes woven with dead white flowers. There was an odour of garlic on the air. The body was that of a woman, dressed in a long white nightgown. Its hair was long and Titian red. A great blade of tongue lolled out of the side of the mouth. Its neck was broken and yet, beneath the ropes, the body writhed, fighting against the knots and the garlic which bound it. If she could release herself, the neck would heal in time. And she had time, Stana Etain, Countess Issyk-Koul, she had all eternity. Unless . . .

Unless down in the town of Dunmow Cross hard at the bottom of the hill, Master Rawley looked to his daughters. Or Napier, or Potter, or any of the rest to their children. Unless Cunning Man Gore returned, for he had dangerous knowledge.

In the distance, suddenly, a great scream mixed of heartbreak, revulsion and terror. The scream was echoed throughout the Cross. They cried as they must have cried in Egypt when Moses also had loosed the Angel of Death to the firstborn of the land. Time would be short now. Swaying even in the calm, the Countess writhed against the ropes — but long before an inch of freedom could be gained they came. Lights like a river of fire surged through the town.

They were led by the Cunning Man of Theydon Mount and their cry was all *revenge*! Great carrot-topped Rawley and his friend Tom Piper followed, then Napier the blacksmith and the rest. Napier cut the rope which had hanged her and she fell, broken-boned, in a heap to the ground. The Cunning Man made a sign. They moved forward, silently and with terrible purpose. They lifted her and threw her on to the bare boards of an open cart as though she were a sack of offal, the depth of their hatred far beyond words or tears. The cart creaked into motion, down towards the crossroads at the heart of the town.

The long watches of the winter's night were drawing to a close when they came to rest on the green outside their tall old church. Some had already started digging the grave at the foot of the four-armed signpost. A coffin of plain, white wood stood ready, its lid leaning erect against the upright of the post. Cunning Man Gore pointed to this. The only sounds still were the roaring of the wind in torch flames, and the crunch of frozen earth yielding to their spades. They dragged the white body off the cart and held the lolling, inert length upright against the coffin lid while the Cunning Man lashed her with more garlic ropes to the rough wood, then stood back silently.

Then Piper, overcome with a lust for personal revenge, reached forward. "This strumpet," he roared grasping the bodice of her shift, "this Countess whore shall not go to her grave in virgin white while I yet live!" He tore downwards with all his force. The white material yielded, revealing white flesh. The shreds of fine silk writhed about her as the man, his eyes fixed upon her cold nakedness, pulled them free. The last jerk dislodged the rope from her arms.

With the speed of a striking serpent her left hand reached for his throat, the strength of the dead sinews choking his scream before it was born. Like a puppet he was jerked towards her. Her head, lolling on the ruined column of her neck, was suddenly alive. Eyes like pools of blood sprang wide. There was a grating of broken bones loud on the air as her head moved, then the great blades of her teeth were like daggers in his breast. Blood gushed steaming down her naked body.

Her gruntings, like those of a feeding hog, seemed to fill the air and the spell was broken. "Her eyes! Look away from her eyes!" cried the Cunning Man, and they were all quick to obey.

Already she had cast Piper aside, dead and drained, and was plucking at the ropes which bound her — she could not break them, but if she could unloose the knots she would be free. But once again they outwitted her. With loops of their garlic rope they caught her wrists and lashed them once more safely to her sides.

She tried all her tricks upon them then, writhing and howling in such a manner that every movement drew their eyes and every sound was a promise. But there were a thousand dying children in a wall between these men and her wiles. They did not look at the flawless beauty of her body. They did not look at the limitless power of her eyes. They finished the grave yawning silently at her feet, put the open coffin in it and stood back.

Then Cunning Man Gore threw a sack on the ground and drew from it a jumble of iron and wood. There were staples, a mallet, an axe, a stake. They pushed the points of the first staple into her left leg, just above the knee. There was no blood. Her screams held no pain, for she felt none: they were those of a beast defeated. "Look to your daughters, Gore," she screamed. "Look to your daughters to the end of time. I am the Dead and I will abide."

Gore pushed the staple home until the points grated the bone and then, with a stroke of his heavy mallet, drove them through and into the wood. He did the same with her right leg. The metal was like two grey scars over her dimpled knees. The flesh seemed to smoke. In a few moments more, he had done the same over her elbows.

And she cried out again in a high sing-song — "Women of blood," she cried, "look to blood. Make of blood your bread. Feed on blood till your blood feeds the Dead."

The last staple was more than a hand's length long, but half a finger's length wide. A length of rope hauled tight in her grasping mouth stopped its motion and its screams. Gore rested the points of the staple on the blood-balls of her eyes and pushed home. For the first time blood flowed as they burst, and cascaded down her face. The man from Theydon held the cold, slippery metal with a shaking hand and then drove it home, home, home. Even then she screamed. But there was one more wound: one more lesson that Cunning Man Gore had learned.

He rested the point of the plain wooden stake on her breast above her heart. Napier took up the great mallet and swung with all the might of his great blacksmith's shoulders. The point went through her torso, through ribs and heart,

70

through the thin wing of her shoulderblade, through the white cold flesh of her back, through the soft wood to stand there, more than a foot of its bloody point clear of the back of the coffin lid.

A great torrent burst from her. It did not pulse as though driven by a heart, it simply roared out of her, pushing the flesh back from shattered stubs of bone, to thunder into the coffin at her feet. Gallon after gallon, as though her sagging body were just a shell filled to bursting with it. As the coffin filled, so she seemed to shrink. On to the skin sprang a web of wrinkles, the flesh beneath it wasting away, until finally the flow faltered, slowed and died.

But the man were otherwise occupied, making assurance doubly sure. Cunning Man Gore caught up the axe at his feet, then, reaching forward with careful aim he struck with all his strength at the top of her thigh. The flesh parted at the first stroke, the white stick of bone at the second, and at the third the leg fell free. When each limb was held only by a staple, and the head by its staple, and the torso, anchored only by the stake through the breast, was beginning to slide to the right, Gore gave the back of the lid a mighty kick and it fell into the grave with a great dead crash.

Rawley said, "Now it is over."

But the voice of the Cunning Man echoed in my ears as I awoke, saying, "No. It has just begun."

Sunday 17 June:

THE CHANGES

For some reason, when I woke on that morning after my dream, I was struck at once by the paltriness of the room in which I had lived for so long. It measured a mere twelve feet by ten. One mean window, for ever rattling in its warped and twisted frame, overlooked the back yard of the

71

George public house next door, and to it the stench of putrid rubbish rose with clouds of fat iridescent flies whenever the sun came out.

One thin-mattressed bed pushed its foot at the crooked door. One narrow wardrobe stood in a corner where two outside walls converged, its interior always cold and damp, breeding pinmould on my clothes. A low cupboard was topped with a single electric ring, upon which I did what little cooking I now care for. There was a bookcase beside this, infested with some nameless life form which ticked in the night like a hesitant clock.

On one wall there hung a cracked washbasin whose ancient taps gushed rust-red water, and above it a mirror so marked and flyblown as to be utterly useless . . .

It was, I think, the sudden recognition of all this tawdriness that Sunday morning that told me how far I had outgrown the place. For months past I had been striving to bring myself up to the standards of fitness and self-assurance demanded of me so long ago by Rebecca. I believed I had been successful. And could the new man, the new Edwin Underhill, remain in the den of the old?

In less than an hour I had packed my bags, run down the rickety stairs, slammed the front door, and posted through it a letter of explanation enclosed with my last week's rent and the keys. It was almost noon, so I went into the George, dumping my cases beside the bar. There was a sign of the wall which said ACCOMMODATION: BED AND BREAKFAST, £10 A NIGHT. A week's rent every night! But I was feeling reckless enough not to care — especially when the landlord's daughter came bustling in.

Theresa Potter had just turned eighteen and was in the sixth form of my school. She gave me a beer, chattering gaily with that self-conscious mixture of familiarity and formality that pupils use to teachers out of school. A pity I didn't teach her any longer, she said, making eyes at me across the bar. I was taken aback. She had always seemed to dislike me. Yet here I was, unshaven and undeniably scruffy, and she was quite blatantly propositioning me. I asked her about the room to rent and, with more teenage ogling, she said she must talk to her father.

At last she drifted away to serve another customer and I

was left staring, still somewhat amazed, into my beer. Then the bar door opened behind me and Jane came in. "Hello, Edwin," she exclaimed. "I've never though of you as much of a pub-goer — what are you doing here?"

I told her my story, and when I had finished there was a little silence. Then she smiled as if she had thought of the most wonderful thing. "You must come to me," she said. "I have spare rooms, spare bathrooms, spare everything. It's such a big house really — you can have the whole east wing for twelve pounds a week."

I stared at her. "The east wing?"

"Well, it's not a wing really, of course — I just call the two halves of the house 'wings' to sound grand."

"But — "

"But what? The gossip?" She tossed her head. "Who cares?"

I thought again of the dingy little chamber of horrors upstairs next door and smiled gratefully. I said I didn't want to be any trouble and she replied eagerly that she would be glad of the company.

The east wing of Jane's house is fairly well self-contained. When you come in through the front door you find stairs leading straight up opposite you out of the spacious hall to a gallery landing. This leads off right and left — each side to a small bedroom, bathroom, large bedroom with smaller withdrawing room *en suite*. We share the kitchen, dining room and lounge downstairs.

That first afternoon I unpacked, while Jane fussed happily about with towels and suchlike. She was obviously delighted to have me there. Later on, while she made tea, I lay full-length on the bed and felt my being fill the room. It took only a few moments, but in that time the whole east wing seemed to become mine more comfortably, inevitably and absolutely, than the vision-haunted kennel above the George's dustbins had ever been.

During the following week Jane and I settled down well together. We were fond, loving even, but we did not become lovers. Something held us back — I thought at the time it was propriety.

At the end of the week, when I went shopping in Great Dunmow, a couple of strange things happened. I had decided to buy a new suit, and therefore went into one of the larger gentlemen's oufitters. But the size I asked for, the size I had worn for fifteen years and more, came nowhere near to fitting me. Clearly the constant exercise over the last six months had shrunk my waist and deepened my chest more than I would have believed possible.

I was undeniably taller also, and I ended up buying a black three-piece suit that fitted me excellently but that only a few short months ago I would have said was made for another man altogether.

The second episode was even more bizarre. I went to get my hair cut. Jane had recommended Richard Burke's hairdresser so I chose this establishment, thinking more about my elegant new image than about my growing aversion to water. As soon as I was seated in the chair, however, things started to go wrong. The huge mirror in front of me was so disgustingly marked that I could not bring myself to look in it. The barber gently pushed my shoulders forward, over the white porcelain bowl immediately below the spotted glass. I leaned forward but when he turned on a hand-shower attachment and water was suddenly swirling within inches of my face I could not stop myself from jerking back. The terrible hissing filled my head. Clouds of steam threatened to choke me. The very droplets seemed to scald my skin. "Is anything the matter, sir?" asked the hairdresser, surprised.

I controlled myself as best I could. "No. It's just a bit hot."

"Sorry." He adjusted the heat and leaned me forward again. I managed to stay calm until the stuff actually touched my head then I jerked away once more. "Still too hot?" He adjusted it further. "There you are: dead cold."

For ten minutes I had to control every jumping muscle in my body as the stuff ran like scalding slime over my skin. Lather. Rinse. Lather. Rinse. I watched it pour away as one watches something utterly disgusting, nauseated but unable to close my eyes.

Finally, to my profound relief, it was over and he began to cut. We fell into a strange conversation: was I an actor? he wanted to know. No, I was not, I was a school teacher. Ah. Had I just been in the school play, then? No, I had not. Had I just been to a fancy-dress party? Dressed as a monk,

74

perhaps?

At that I lost my temper. "No!" I snapped. "Why do you ask?"

"Well," he said huffily, "I could have sworn you've recently had your head shaved in some sort of tonsure, and now it's growing back." His fingers were on my bald patch. "You feel it?" he asked. "Stubble. Hair growing here."

All I could feel were his fingers, hot and distasteful. I brought my own hand up — it was true, there was stubble there. My hair was returning, and thicker than it had ever been!

I had used my left hand, and now I heard his quick indrawn breath as he saw the scar on it. His reaction gave me just the clue I needed to come up with a reasonable explanation.

Of course!" I exclaimed. "The doctor *told* me there might be side-effects. I used to be going bald, you see, but when I injured my hand I was given a massive blood transfusion and the doctor said it might effect my metabolism . . ."

Now, at last, over the last few days, I have been forced to admit and to come to terms with my steadily changing appearance. I do not consult a mirror — I do not need to for I can sense the changes within me, coursing powerfully through my blood. Inevitably Jane has noticed them also, and earlier tonight she came to me.

I had awoken from yet another strange but unremembered vision with a burning thirst, my teeth and gums aflame. I found myself half in and half out of bed, and at first I did not recognise the figure that stood over me.

"Edwin?" she whispered. "Edwin — what's the matter?"

Relief flowed through my body. I eased myself back into the bed and sat up. "What do you mean?"

"Edwin — oh, I've been so frightened. What's happening?"

When I didn't answer, she collapsed on to the edge of my bed and reached out her hand like a child seeking reasssurance. "But you must have felt it! There's something *evil* here in the house. It must be the Countess. Oh Edwin, I'm so frightened . . ."

Spontaneously I threw one arm round her quaking shoulders and hugged her to my breast. She came willingly

75

enough, pressing her fiery cheek to my cool flesh.

"But now that I'm with you, it will be all right," she murmured. "Six months ago I wouldn't have dreamed this could ever be possible. But you've changed so much."

"Me? Changed? How?" I was wary.

"Oh Edwin — you know very well you have."

I snapped on the light by the bed. "I haven't changed *that* much," I protested, still unsure of her reaction.

She sat up, and cradled my face in her long hot hands. She looked at me, frowning with concentration. "Yes," she said, "even your face. It's different somehow."

"It can't be."

"It is," she insisted. "I suppose it's partly what you said Richard's barber has done to bring your hair back, but your forehead looks definitely broader. Your eyebrows are shaggier, too. And now you don't wear you glasses any more, your eyes look bigger . . ."

Her hands moved down from my face, down my neck to caress my shoulders and the new, hard muscles of my chest. Her cheeks were flushed and she was smiling. There could be no doubt now that, whatever the changes in me might be, she found them to her liking.

She leaned forward, looked up into my eyes. "And you're different in *yourself*, Edwin. One's body is so important, my dear . . . yours is so strong now, so powerful — it's made *you* strong and powerful too. You're . . . you're the most exciting man I've ever known, Edwin —"

She pressed herself against me, passionately, tenderly. The need for words between us ceased . . .

I write this now in the grey light of dawn. Jane has left me. I have slept fitfully, and now I am awake again. And in my sleeping I have dreamed, for once a dream of exaltation, and it is with me still:

It seems in my dream that even as I close my eyes I open them again and find myself in the charred undergrowth of the Broken Woods. The smells of ripeness and ash are bitter on the air and burn at my tongue and throat. I lift my nose, sniffing shallow breaths, trying to sort out the different scents around me. The high moon makes my blood reel. I move, and so discover that I am on all fours, although there is none of the uneasiness of movement associated with crawling. I slip through the shadows gracefully and without sound until the trees part before me and I am on the edge of the meadow watching its rolling bosom in the moonlight.

I run forward, my presence upsetting the calm of the summer's night. Panic movement spreads out in ripples from my dive into this pool of life. An owl drops noiselessly on to the back of some creature I have disturbed. Silently I trot onward, breaking into a gentle lope, bouncing off my broad grey pads as though I had springs in wrist and ankle. The rich air smells good. The waxing moon calls with her timeless call, and I begin to run in earnest, bursting with the eternal joy of it, forelegs close together grasping the ground, shoulders hunching, back arching. The wind tears at my face and body and howls in my ears . . .

The Great South Field speeds past beneath me. A hedge with a gate which I clear in one bound. Sheep scatter in panic. Another hedge. Along deserted roads and pathways. Then into a farmyard, setting all the dogs tugging at their chains to join me — to join the spirit of the wild and free.

Saturday 23 June:

THE PSYCHIATRIST

When we arrived home from work on Wednesday evening there was a letter awaiting us. Would we like to go to the vicarage on Friday evening? Miss Rebecca Gore would be celebrating her birthday.

When Friday came — yesterday, in fact — Jane was dressed in a brown evening gown which left bare her arms, shoulders, and the upper slopes of her breasts. I had shaved carefully with a new electric razor and I wore my new black suit. We wandered arm in arm up to the vicarage, past the crossroads with its sinister square of dead grass where Stana's grave had been. We talked quietly of intimate things, already like lovers of long-standing. The night wrapped itself around us gently and delicately, free for once of the shades which frighten us. I felt buoyant, excited. I was with a woman I possessed, going to see a woman I desired. I was massively self-confident — the feeling dizzily stealing over me that I, and I alone, was ordering events.

Rebecca answered the door, immediately, as though she had been waiting for my knock. "Edwin, you look magnificent! Positively Byronic. Come in. You will break a few hearts tonight."

We went in and handed over cards and presents. I had brought her also one of the blood-red blossoms which have sprouted on the strange tree in Jane's garden that grows out of Stana's stake. She fixed it to her fine silk corsage. Against its fullness her flesh looked utterly white so that it revealed the fine blue traceries of the veins just beneath her skin. Then we went through to the room of my humiliation of six months ago.

It was full of the same people: the headmistress, her deputy, half the staff from school. Andrew Royle, of course. The Rugby Club, the Cricket Club, the Young Farmers.

As with my last entrance, many eyes turned towards me, but this time it was very different. I had Jane on one arm and Rebecca on the other: the two most attractive women there. I was dressed with a great deal of elegance, newly shaved and with my hair (so much more of it) well cut. I felt as though I were master of all I surveyed.

Jane and I danced every now and then but both of us were content to circulate. Most often I saw her beside the bearded Richard Burke. Once or twice they appeared to be deep in heated conversation, but I saw no cause to interfere. Theresa Potter openly offered me drinks and, almost as openly, herself.

A little later Rebecca appeared at my side. She pressed my hand fondly, and kissed my cheek. Then she moved reluctantly away. "Father would like to speak to you," she said. "He's in the study."

I went through and knocked quietly. A voice called, "Come in." I went on through. He was sitting in the great wing-backed chair. John Warlock perched on the edge of the desk, his keen blue eyes hooded but watchful. "Edwin," cried the old man, half rising. "We were just talking about you."

"That's very flattering, sir. Good evening, Brother Warlock."

He half smiled and nodded at my greeting. There was a feeling of power about him which made me feel uneasy. "You seem to have become something of an expert in occult matters," he said.

I pretended modesty. "Not really," I said. "I just found a few old books in Mrs. Gore's library and hoped to help Rebecca by using them."

"Yes. Your strategy seems to have been quite faultless."

"I'm glad to hear it. She certainly looks much happier tonight."

"Yes." The Reverend Gore laughed — it was the first time I had ever heard him laugh. "She's calling tonight her first birthday. She says it's a completely new start."

"Oh, that *is* good news."

"It was very selfless of you to risk both your sanity and your salvation in the way, just to help another," Brother Warlock persisted, probing like a dentist at a suspect tooth.

"Not really." I dared play with him. "I don't actually believe in it."

"In what?"

"In any of it — black magic, ghosts, vampires."

"I see. And you found this a source of strength when dealing with the Dark Powers?"

"There are no Dark Powers," I explained patiently. "It's all in the mind."

"There are few people who really believe that," observed Mr. Gore.

"Oh, I don't know. There's a great deal of the Doubting Thomas in us all, I think. We have a scale of incredulity, our own thresholds of belief. For myself, I simply do not believe in ghosts. Nor in exorcism."

Brother Warlock smiled tolerantly. "Exorcism is only as powerful as a man's belief in it. It isn't all like that sensation-mongering film. Most of it is quiet and mundane. People get worried — they think they see things. So a place gets a reputation and the local priest or someone like myself requests permission to hold a special service there. The

79

bishop or Synod eventually agree. Then the service is read and . . . well, things quieten."

I folded my arms, "It *is* all in the mind, then?"

"No, no, — by no means. But actual physical manifestations are rare. It makes good sense if you look at it logically from the Devil's point of view. If he manifests his powers too clearly — as in the case of demonic possession, overt diabolic influence and so forth — then he will only prove his own existence and therefore, in so doing, prove equally the existence of his eternal antagonist, God."

"And you believe in all of this, do you? That in and around us there are hierarchies of Good and Evil involved in our every action?"

"Except that I include the element of free will, yes. The Powers of Light and those of Darkness."

"And life after death?"

"Certainly."

"If you can really believe in that, then why don't you believe in all the rest of it?"

"All the rest of what?"

"All the other occult mumbo-jumbo. The un-dead. Werewolves. Vampires. All that sort of thing."

He paused for moment. "There is no need," he said, "to step outside the formal structure of my religion to explain these things. Ghost, vampires, even Satan himself — if these are not all a part of my spiritual framework, why do they fear my holy symbols?"

"But they fear other symbols too. How does your theory fit with their aversion to garlic, mirrors, silver, iron, running water?"

"You have answered your own question of course. These are all chosen as symbols of goodness, concentrating their power more fully against things of evil."

I shrugged easily. "It's all magic really," I said. "And who believes in that these days?"

"So in your world," Brother Warlock observed, "the exorcists you need are psychiatrists, not priests."

It was a good point — and the psychiatrist was what I got later on. Warlock, Gore and I chatted amiably through one or two of the more ridiculous conundrums of occult theology, and then I excused myself. Almost immediately Jane came

80

up to me with Richard Burke in tow.

"Richard wants you to fill him in on the final chapter of the Stana saga," she said, but her troubled eyes suggested there might be more.

I was reluctant to say much, but under her gentle prompting I lowered my guard and told him the tale. Jane, who knew most of it, drifted away.

"I see," Burke said when I had finished. "And how has this affected you in yourself?"

"Me?" I laughed. "Hardly at all."

"You find your sleep undisturbed by nightmares? It's given poor Jane a few. It would give me nightmares too, I can tell you."

"No." I met his gaze squarely. "I don't dream much. Quite honestly, I don't sleep much anyway. I'm a bit of an insomniac."

"Have you always been like that?"

"Not really." Burke too, like Brother Warlock, could be played with. "Only this year or so."

"That's very interesting. And the ghost — why did you see her, I wonder. You had experiences like this in your childhood?"

"Not that I remember. No."

He paused, looked down at his drink, spinning it in his glass. I thought back to our last meeting over tea at Jane's. How could I have actually *liked* this man? He glanced up, as though divining my hostility. "One or two people say you've changed a good bit, you know. I was just thinking as you came in tonight that if I hadn't seen you on and off since the New Year I would hardly have recognised you at all."

"Is that so?"

"Yes." He watched me keenly. "Strange, isn't it? You even seem to be taller."

He was boring me now. "Look," I demanded, "where is all this leading? What is it you want to know?"

"Do you ever dream of being an animal, Edwin?"

"Certainly not. No."

"Do you dream about death? Blood?"

"I told you — I don't dream."

"Do you still see the Countess Stana? The Dead?"

"What are you talking about? Look, what *is* this all

81

about?"

"Listen to me, Edwin. Here's my card — feel free to call me, any time, day or night. I'll still be at Whitethorn Cottage for the next few weeks. It's just across the road from Jane's."

"How dare you! What exactly are you getting at?"

"It's Jane. She's worried about you and I think she may have good grounds. I know what I'm talking about, Edwin. Remember Mrs. Gore."

"Don't be ridiculous . . ."

"When did you last look at yourself in a mirror?"

Months ago. "That's none of your —"

"You eat your meat raw and bleeding, Jane tells me. And you only drink milk."

"I'm on a diet."

"Come and see me when you need to, Edwin. I can help."

"This conversation is serving no purpose. Good evening, Mr. Burke!" I turned and stalked away across the floor.

After the party, when we got home last night, Jane and I quarrelled bitterly. I did not think she should have told Burke so much about me, and I said so. Inevitably she defended herself. We fought again this morning and she took a train to London in a huff. I went out for a walk instead, up past the vicarage, my mind a strange mixture of regret, of exultation and terror. In every distant propect I saw the promise of Rebecca, while in every nearby shadow I saw the terrible spectre of Stana Etain, Countess Issyk-Koul, mocking my paltry assumptions of power.

I needed Jane, but my pride and my harsh words had sent her away.

THE LORD OF FLIES

I am worried about Jane. Our quarrel that Saturday two weeks ago was soon made up. But she is looking most unwell. Her colour has gone and her hair is dull and lank. Although we are still lovers we sleep apart for I cannot stand the burning heat of her body in the night. I keep telling her to go and see a doctor but she won't. I think she sometimes visits Richard Burke instead.

For myself, after a restless week, dream-infested, I went for a walk this afternoon. I wanted to think things through. The ghost-woman Stana keeps me company continually, filling every shadow with her obscene presence. It is only a madness in me, of course, I have no doubt of that. Only I am not sure what to do about it. Perhaps I should go and see Richard, like Jane. Or Brother Warlock. There is a rumour in the village that he wants to exorcise the Dunmow Round, the small circle of Bronze Age stones up in the woods close by where Coul Hall once stood. Perhaps he should exorcise me while he is at it. It would be as much use as anything else, as far as I can see. But something must be done.

On my walk the weather was overcast and threatening. Great fat clouds rolled in, their black bellies slick as though drawn tight with the strain of containing the deluge. The wind was hot, clammy on the skin, and the whole afternoon slowly took on the aspect of a huge dank cave full of hot fetid air.

I walked through Dunmow Cross in my shirt sleeves. The suffocating weight of a jacket was too much even to consider. I was lost in thought, and shouldered my brooding way through the mass of early weekend shoppers. A woman half turned towards me: she had Stana's face.

I walked up past the crossroads and towards the Broken Woods. There was no beauty in the wretched fields. No growth, no movement, no life. Only columns of flies and mosquitoes humming and dancing in the sullen grey air. And she was there again, filling the shadows with her pale form. I found a stick but my wild slashes and thrusts passed through her as if through a mist. At last, striking at her dull red eyes, I broke my stick on a tree and hurled the stump away.

The afternoon gathered stiflingly around me as I stumped on. A headache throbbed behind my eyes. The phantom woman, the exorcist, the psychiatrist, Jane, my life, the weather — all sickened me. I carried a weight of agonised frustration which eventually bore me down. With the hog's back of the hill humped up on my left, the woods like a strange, spiny cloud at its top and a quiet little valley cloaked with clover at my feet, finally I flung myself on my back to look at the low grey sky.

In a moment I was asleep.

And awake, in a dream, once again in the great wolf's body. I raised my long head. Odours rose to my nostrils in stunning array, but in the breathless heat of the afternoon they brought no pleasure to my keen animal senses. Silently I padded forward into the rough undergrowth. Each touch from a fetid leaf brought a rumble of anger to my throat. Every whiff of the damp fullness of life just on the edge of rottenness caused my black lips to rise in a snarl.

Only slowly as I crept forward, moving my body with relentless deliberation, did I realise that I was hunting. Abruptly, the lust to destroy suffused me with an excitement that was almost sexual. My heart thundered in my throat. My grey flanks rose and fell . . . Then, suddenly, a scent of the hated prey swirled along the delicately nerved corridors of my muzzle. Cleanness, soap, a hint of perfume, they were all on the air and I was tracking them.

The sound of voices came. Whispers at first, then words half heard. I crept forward, my belly sweeping the lank grasses. The smell of flesh; young and sweet. Saliva pumped so fast I drooled great threads of it. A growl rumbled in my throat. Careless in my ravening, I put one pad on a dead twig and it broke like thunder.

"What was that?" She.

"Nothing, darling. It's all right. No one comes here." He.

They were lying on a rug in the middle of the circle of the Dunmow Round. On the ground beside them articles of clothing — a green blazer, a pullover, his shirt, her blouse.

He lay half on top of her, his gray-flannelled thigh cunningly pushing up her skirt. Their hands, mouths and minds were busy. I crept forward, three long steps, and my grey tail was free of the bushes. Pause. Crouch. And then the charge.

I leapt on to his back. His head turned, looking up over his shoulder, too stunned even to react. My jaws closed on his fat, freckled face and I dragged him back, worrying at him, ripping his flesh away from forehead to chin. He struggled, his hands beating at me, trying to fight back, choking on screams. I jerked my head from side to side until his writhings weakened.

But a distraction disturbed my feeding. The girl. Coming out of her shock, she leaped to her feet and ran. Instantly I bounded across the body of her lover, and was after her. Wild with panic, screaming uselessly in the empty woods, she tore through the undergrowth between the sullen trees. Bushes laid traps for her. Branches clubbed her. Crab-grass tripped her and I caught her.

She was pulling herself to her feet as my forelegs landed on her. And then there was only the blood.

I awoke screaming. My body arched, writhed with the dream sensation of blood on my skin. I lay for a moment, waiting for my head to clear. Then I looked down. My shirt ballooned out from my chest. The wind might have moved it but there was no wind. I brought up my shaking hand to open the buttons. My shirt sagged apart and beneath it my breast was black and shiny.

At first I thought it was blood from the dream, but then my vision cleared. The blackness was flies. Like a shirt of mail they clothed me, several layers deep. Those on top were crawling down, trying to reach my skin. Even as I watched, the ghastly sensation, as though I were being touched by millions of cold pins, spread to my arms. The back of my hand was abruptly thick with them.

I lurched to a sitting position. My face was immediately in a hovering screaming cloud of them. They settled like cobwebs closing on my skin, and clung buzzing. My nose clogged. My ears. I could feel on my lips each individual foot with its scratching hairs and sucker, each individual tongue kissing. I squeezed my eyes shut and felt them clotting on my

85

eyelids. They infested my hair. All over me, on every inch of my skin, they crawled.

My mind said: This is not happening; you are imagining this. Do not believe what your senses are telling you. Be calm and it will end. Be calm.

I was calm. I did not open my mouth or my eyes. Blind, I rose and took a step. Blind and dumb, I began to run. If I beat my arms across my chest, I thought, I will kill some and the rest will fly away: but I did not beat my arms. If I find a stream or lake, I thought, I can jump in and they will drown: but I found no stream or lake. If I fall down and roll on the ground I will crush many and the rest will fly away: I did not fall. If I open my eyes I will at least see where I am going: I did not open my eyes. If I open my mouth I can call out and someone will come to my aid: I did not open my mouth.

Running full-tilt, I tripped. Blind and deaf and dumb I fell, rolling over and over, until mercifully I lost consciousness . . .

When I recovered I looked frantically in all my clothes and ran my fingers through my hair: there will be many dead flies, I thought. But there was none.

Wednesday 25 July:

THE LAST DAY

It was the last day of summer term today. Jane went to work alone this morning. Her sickness is worsening: she has about her now a constantly haunted look, as though she sees in every shadow something too horrible to express. I wonder whether I too look like that. Even as I write this, waiting for the end, if I glance up I can see the phantom Countess where the shades are thickest, her eyes like blood, the red rose of her mouth beckoning.

86

This morning I stayed at home, nursing my madness. But she drove me out relentlessly into the streets, and wherever I went she was before me still. Finally, desperate just to talk to someone, I knocked on Richard Burke's front door. Once — how long ago now was it? — he had offered me his help.

He welcomed me in, strangely unsurprised to see me, and we sat in his chintzy front room. I came to the point at once, asked him if he believed in malignant spirits.

He shook his head gently. "They're all in the mind, Edwin."

"They have no will, intelligence, or power of their own?" I insisted.

"How could they have, when they don't exist? They're pure imagination."

His words gave me little comfort. "And vampires?" I asked. "Does the same apply to them?"

"Of course." He smiled. "I could hardly write off ghosts and then grant genuine powers to other occult creatures. No — vampires, werewolves, they're both simply the products of our own fears: hysterical attempts on our part to explain phenomena that are really not at all supernatural."

"I can't believe that."

"You *must*, Edwin. Look at vampires, for instance. All the great centres of vampire folklore are in mountainous areas — the Carpathians, the Hartz Mountains, the middle of Greece. Now, in areas like those the soil is thin and graves are therefore shallow."

"Obviously. But—"

"Listen to me, Edwin. Vampires are linked with bubonic plague in the Germanic tradition, right?" I nodded eagerly, thinking of Stana and the White Plague. He went on: "The scenario is easy to imagine. Great numbers of plague deaths, bad medical facilities growing worse under the strain, increasing numbers of cataleptic trances being mistaken for death . . . and therefore premature burials, victims awakening out of their catalepsy, being able to dig their way easily out through a couple of feet of light soil and returning to their families for help." He spread his hands. "Hey presto, the myth of the un-dead — vampires!"

He became suddenly serious. "And so, Edwin, from vampires to wolves. In those same mountainous areas the woods must have been full of wolves. As one lay in bed at night listening to them howling, how easy it must have been to imagine them possessed by evil spirits."

"But all that was hundreds of years ago — if there's really nothing in such ideas, why should they have lasted so long?"

"Because they answer some of our darkest fears, Edwin." He looked at me narrowly. "Tell me, what are *you* most frightened of?"

I thought of the Countess. "The dark," I said. Then, "And dying."

"Exactly — darkness and death, the two things most men fear worst of all. And the vampire, in its own mad way, is lord over both. Hence the lunatic-based fixations; lycanthropy and vampirism. There are well-authenticated cases of both, you know."

I looked up at him, surprised.

He nodded. "Oh yes — there was a Countess Elizabeth Barthory in the Middle Ages, and a Marshal of France called Gilles de Rais a little later — both drank blood and bathed in it. They really did. Haigh, of course, is the classic case in this century, but there are many others. In one particular strain of chronic anaemia the sufferer will actually try to suck blood in a vain attempt to replace his own missing red corpuscles . . ."

"But such people are quite mad," I cried.

He frowned. "I prefer to think they're sick. And I find it perfectly understandable that a certain sort of mind — one with a morbid fear of death and darkness, for example — once presented with the complex of legends surrounding vampires and werewolves, should become interested . . . and then pathologically fixated. After all, a vampire is a creature of geat sexual power also, and how many of us have not wished at one time or another that we had only to say a girl's name and look into her eyes for her to be ours?"

I left him soon afterwards. His calm rationality irritated me — *he* might find such things understandable, but I did not. And sick or mad, the difference seemed to me to be one of words, nothing more. And how understandable would he have thought it if I had told him of the Countess, standing all the time in the shadows by his fireplace while we talked, standing and silently laughing?

88

Jane returned in the afternoon. School had closed early.

"They've found them," she said, as if I would know what she meant, And when I asked for an explanation she gave it coldly, almost dispassionately.

Children playing in their lunch hour at the edge of the Broken Woods had discovered two corpses, inexpertly covered with broken branches. The face and throat of the male corpse had been torn away, and the female's head had been crushed. The sixth-former, Theresa Potter, had been missing from her home the previous night, and evidence pointed to the female corpse being hers. The dead man had not yet been identified.

When Jane had finished she just sat and looked at me. It seemed that she could not know the terrible visions she had conjured up in my memory.

"It . . . it must have been a dog," I said at last.

She nodded. "Something like a dog."

"What do you mean by that?"

She hesitated. "Sometimes when I wake up in the middle of the night, you are not there," she said slowly. "But if I listen carefully, I can often hear a wolf, howling in the woods."

"NO!" I cried, lurching to my feet.

She shrank back. I cannot describe what went through my mind then, as all the careful layers of self-deception which had bolstered up my sanity crumbled away. For weeks I had supposed poor Jane to be frightened of the horrors I thought I saw in shadows: now I looked into her eyes and realised that all that time she has been terrified of *me*.

She ran from me, out of the house and I followed her. Bright burning sunlight splattered like acid on my skin. Defeated, I covered my face with my hands and felt the flesh blister as the sunlight touched them. Blinded and agonised I staggered back into her house. She had fled, to fetch the police no doubt.

I slammed the door. Locked and bolted it. "I am not mad!" I cried.

In the bathroom was a mirror. I put my hands on either side of it and stared full into the glass. At first I could not hold my head still. It would jerk away to either side like the pole of a magnet approaching the like pole of another. But eventually I held it unmoving and looked into it. There was no reflection. Nothing. Like a square black pit it reached back into infinity beckoning so strongly that I almost tumbled down it to who knows what damnation.

But I did not: somehow I forced my gaze away — and I sit there now writing these words so that everyone may know. Richard Burke was right, it is a sickness after all. The figure in the shadows leers and shows me the face of poor Mrs. Gore. Looking into her mind I have caught her madness.

I am in the little room in the cellar. There are no windows at all. I have blocked the flue and the bottom of the door. Jane had an old gas fire in here and I have turned it on full. It is not lit.

Had it not been for Theresa and her dead, nameless lover, I might have tried to face my madness and even seek a cure. But the thought of myself, wolflike, creeping through the woods to leap upon them and kill them in such a way is more than I am willing to accept. To be such a thing is more than I can bear.

This not a large room. The gas from the fire roars like a storm of wind. It should not take long. It is very cold.

NOCTURNAL

August to December

AWAKE

My first thought was: I am not dead. But there crept through me, with that realisation the first stirring of unease. I felt the weight of my face. I catalogued its vague outline traced by tension in the muscles of the brow, a movement of eyes behind closed lids, the flaring of nostrils, the turning down of the lips. The mass of the flesh pressed upon the bones at the front of my skull and cheekbones jutted prominently. My tongue lay along the roof of my dry mouth, its tip caged by teeth. My chin pressed a shirt-collar and the knot of a tie into the hollow of my throat.

These things on the one hand: my mind was alive, sensation existed. But on the other hand, I felt no pressure of the weight of my body on shoulders, back and buttocks, nor from the weight of my head on the back of my skull. I felt no weight of arms on my breast although my fingers felt, as though through thin gloves, the material of a jacket. There was no all-pervading throb of heartbeat sensible to innumerable delicate nerve-ends. There was no rustle in nostrils and throat from the tidal surge of breath. There was no automatic pumping of ribs and diaphragm. And there had been, before awareness came, no dreams.

Now I lay in silence, feeling nothing in my body, two trains of thought in my mind debating one simple question: am I alive or dead? How long I would have lain thus I do not know had it not come: terror, unreasoned but overwhelming. My eyes jerked open, dry lids sliding back, and saw nothing. My ribs rose fractionally. So the first sounds I heard were the hiss of breath in my throat, the catch of it jerking across the back of my tongue. I screamed, and my body exploded into action. But each part of me that moved came into contact almost immediately with an unyielding

93

surface. Head, foot, sides, floor, lid, all inches away.

Thus I discovered the coffin.

No other explanation for the presence of these strange restrictive walls even occurred to me. What else could they have been? The terror stilled in me. I lay quiet. My movement had brought about several results.

Wads of cotton wool and gauze had been knocked loose in my mouth. I turned my head to one side and spat it all out. Bemused, I ran my tongue around the inside of my mouth, finding rudimentary molars at the back, and at each side a complex of canines building up to the thrust of fangs. They crowded my gums so that the whole shape of my mouth was different. It was squarer and a good deal longer. The whole shape of my face was different: I jerked my right hand up to feel the shape of the new face. My knuckles crashed against the coffin lid.

It was then that the unreasoned feeling of restriction began to squeeze in on me again. Breath hissed through my throat again as I prepared to make animal sounds of distress. My hands slammed palm-up against the quilted lid of my coffin and pushed up until the wood screamed in protest. It was in my mind to break open the fragile wooden roof and dig my way up through the thick earth to the surface. But there was something in me which knew better than that. *Do not destroy your home.* It was as though there was a voice which whispered in my ear. *Do not tear down the wall when all you need do is open the door.*

Slowly my arms relaxed. The lid settled back above me. I lay absolutely still. At the very centre of my mind a lake of utter blackness beckoned. I relaxed my grip on the reality which surrounded me and slipped into the dark. There was a moment of absolute terror as the totality of it swept over me, then the earth around me trembled and heaved, thrusting me upwards and out into the light. The rich stench of the living world washed into my nose and I knew, at last, that I was no longer of its number.

I stood at the head of a new grave in the silent graveyard amid the crystal purity of a summer's night. It was precisely that time of evening when the trees lose colour and form to become intricate silhouettes against the stained-glass sky. The west was pale gold, edged with rose and crimson, the east

94

smoke blue and shadowed. The first star gleamed like diamond. My joints creaked as I turned. Like a cat I stretched, clawing my hands and pushing them up towards the sky. I rocked my head back, mouth agape, experiencing an overwhelming desire to howl. It would be a first-quarter moon tonight.

There was no surprise in me. A moment before this body had been entombed. It had just passed through six feet of earth. And yet it was real enough. I struck my chest with my hand. My chest was hard. I looked down. My hand stood out against the shadowed soil. I moved my fingers, watching the play of the muscles as they stretched and tensed. And it seemed to be wearing a white glove. Above the glove, the arm of my black suit. I lifted my hand closer to my face. There was something strange about the glove: it had features — wrinkles, finger-prints. It looked like white wax. Like an animal I brought it to my mouth. I tasted it: sniffed it. It had no particular taste. It smelt of me. I fastened my new needle-sharp teeth in it and tugged. It would not come free. It seemed to be attached to my wrist. I tugged again. It remained stubborn. I released it and folded my cuffs back expecting to find the top of the glove neatly tucked away. There was nothing. The white of the glove ran into the pale skin without a flaw. It was then that I realised. As in the coffin, the dark animal in me took over, knowing what to do. The new razor fangs traced lower wrists with gentleness and care until I felt the skin part beneath my lips. I did the same with my left hand, and peeled off my old hands like gloves. My new hands were long and thin. Thick, horn-yellow nails curved wickedly at my finger-ends. When I closed my fists the points of the nails lay on my wrists and in the centre of the palms there was a pattern of dark silky fur.

I wadded up the waxy skin from my hands and eased the cold ball past the incredible array of my new teeth. I could not chew. My lower jaw, used to moving from side to side as the molars worked, could only move up and down now. As the tasteless thickness of skin was slowly shredded in the dry cavity I studied my wrists and forearms more closely. The edge of skin cut away by my fangs was like an obscene lace cuff below my shirt cuff. The skin of my forearm seemed to be covered in tiny white blisters. There was no pulse in my wrist.

I stood in the middle of the graveyard as the night gathered about me. I could not at first get used to the absolute stillness of my chest. No breathing. No heartbeat. A part of me wailed with utter horror. I choked down the lumps of half-chewed skin and went questing into the night.

It was the beauty which held me first and holds me still. I found on every side *light* — as though a rainbow had been shattered at my feet and lay now glittering on the earth. Everything living seemed to have an aura of energy flowing about it: from the tall majestic shimmering of a tree to the bright bolt of the sparrow nesting in its bosom. I walked upon a lambent carpet of grass broken only by pools and rivers of non-life: gravestones, slabs, paths, eventually the roadway. But even here there was magic: the faintest glow of a lichen, the sudden irridescent scurry of a beetle. On the pavements, bright filaments of grass and moss at the square edges of the flags. The lingering glow of a leaf dying in the gutter. I began to run silently north towards the Broken Woods.

A little bolt of lightning hurled above my head: a house martin hunting. A ball of fire before me on the ground: a cat, turning and gone even as I reached out towards it.

Then the meadow gathered itself before me in a great lucent wave, breaking at its crest into the brightness of the Broken Woods. The splendour of it made me reel as I went in among the trees: would have robbed me of breath had I been breathing, would have made my pulses race had my heart been beating.

I paused and brushed a bright leaf with my finger. There was a thrill like a tiny electric shock. The skeleton of life upon it flickered and died. Something massive in me stirred at the sensation. By tomorrow, it told me, the little spade of green would be sere and crisp. I had killed it with a touch. The dark thing in me stirred again, rejoicing in the destruction, leaving the slightest memory of laughter on the air. I examined its power. The thing was evil. Unhuman. It is the thing which keeps me un-dead, of course: it is the Dead. I half expected it to have character and personality — to be Stana herself; but it had neither and was far more elemental even than she.

They say that vampires go home first. Richard Burke had

told me this was natural — the victim, confused, starving, terrified, would go home, looking for aid. I was not looking for aid. I was not even fully in control. It was the Dead itself which directed my feet home to Jane's house.

I approached it from the back, scaling the garden fence with supple ease and dropping silently on the phosporescent lawn beside the strange tree which had grown out of my cursed stake. Only that plant, alone among all the others, had no glow of life-force. It has a shadowed aura like that which surrounds me, and its crimson blossoms are like black holes in the very fabric of my new reality.

The house was in silence and shadow. It was midway through the night. I thought she would be asleep. I pushed the French windows and they opened to me. As I crossed the threshold I felt a tug as though there was some force warning me that I should not enter lightly, but it had been my home in life, therefore I went in.

The house itself glowed with electricities, life-forces, the dying memory of life. The doorway had a faint sheen: it was wood. I could distinguish the wooden parquet flooring in the hall, the wooden banisters, and the wooden stairway, which I now ascended. Anticipating her body asleep between the sheets, I felt the stir of animal excitement, but by the strange alchemy of the Dead, it set my sharp new fangs to throbbing — and not my loins. My long claws clicked against the faint ghost of her door and it opened. The Dead led me in, prowling across the carpet to her bed, filling me within, massively burning. How can I describe what I, Edwin Underhill, felt at the presence of this commanding cancer of the spirit within? At the casual ease with which it had started my body awake and sent it hunting through the night.

But she was not in her room. She was nowhere in the house. I searched it from attic to cellar, and laughed to see the brute within me frustrated. My clothes were all there untouched, but many of her clothes and two of her suitcases were gone. She had clearly gone away, presumably on holiday. So that the beast, which had waited so long, must wait a little longer.

For the rest of the night I have been busy. Close by the graveyard, in the sexton's garden, I found a spade and rope. By the light of the fattening moon I parted the earth above my coffin. The rope slid around it and tore it effortlessly out of the grave. By moon-set the hole was filled again. I cleared the coffin's silken interior of the wads of gauze packed into my cadaver by the undertaker, and half filled it with soft earth from the grave. There was nothing on which to transport it, so finally it was rested on my shoulders and my new-clawed hands grasped the handles.

I have put it in Jane's cellar, in the small windowless room where Underhill succumbed to the gas. Among the books in my old bedroom I discovered this journal, and the thought has come that I may continue to record my experiences. While just beyond the curve of the earth the gaudy sun approaches, and the Dead within me awaits Jane's return.

Friday Night 17/18 August:

COMPANY

She returned on Wednesday afternoon. My eyes sprang open. I knew it was not yet sunset, and I lay still for a moment, every nerve at full stretch. I heard footsteps on the path and the grinding of a key in the lock. Against my will my face twisted in anticipation and a growl rumbled in my throat. My long hands were suddenly pressed on the white silk above my face, but I saw in my mind's eye the great gold disc of the sun and I could not lift the lid. The front door swung open. She put heavy things on to the hall floor. Iron rivets on wood: suitcases. I hissed, helpless. Leather on wood, click-click as she walked. The door swung closed: she was alone. The footsteps moved from thick parquet on to planks masked with rugs. A stair creaked. Then she was on the gallery landing, and then in the west wing. I had ears in the floors but my body was bound down here.

I listened to her unpacking. I needed no chronometer to tell me the length of the chain which held me.

Wood on wood, screaming: drawers. Wood on wood, with a faint whisper of hinges: doors. Light doors brushing wood, heavy doors sweeeping over carpeting. Feet on the carpets.

Feet on the stairs. Feet in the hall. She would make supper now. And the sun yet twice its diameter above the black blade of the horizon.

As I listened to her, my lips stretched back on the bone-blade teeth. The weight of the lid above my hands became intolerable. Blackness seemed to exude from every dry pore of my body and fill the coffin like smoke. Her mind opened to the questing of the Dead. A vision — Burke the bearded psychiatrist; then an emotion — tenderness. Then fear: *What was that noise?*

I realised I was screaming. I closed my mouth, the points of my fangs meeting and sliding down upon each other. I fell silent. Too late. Her footsteps approached on the parquet of the hall, on the cellar stairs, hesitantly on concrete floor. Click of light switch in the next room. My hands slammed down flat on either side of me, grasped the black earth filling the black box beneath me. The sun was still high in the sky. If she came in here she would see the coffin on the trestle-table among her grandfather's tools. There was nothing I could do.

I saw through her eyes the outer cellar room. The cob-webbed and shadowed walls. Red-brick and cankered whitewash. The canes, spades, forks, rakes, the gardening books. Emotion came to her — again a poignant stirring of fear. She looked round the room until her gaze fell on the closed door leading in here. A sudden vividness of memory: the trestle-table, the swinging light, the choking stench of gas, the hunched body, my own, the hands which clasped the open journal . . .

Terror flooded her body and she turned and fled. Doors slammed. Cellar door. Front door. Two things lingering: her scream and the face of the psychiatrist in her mind. She would go and seek his help.

Like the first kiss of the returned beloved, the rim of the sun touched the horizon. Moments now, mere moments. I writhed slowly, arching, falling, my fists like thunder on the cushioned wood, as the Dead sifted information, trying to find her and predict the moment of her return.

The sun vanished. The night lay upon me. The coffin lid slammed open of its own accord and I was out, a vortex of sensation still swirling in my head. The woman was returning, and now he was with her. Feet running on wet gravel. Front door . . . "I don't know, Richard — somehow there was a feeling of such *evil* . . ."

Two pairs of shoes descended the cellar steps. Outside the cellar door they faltered. I crossed my dark sanctuary and positioned myself, towering beside the doorway. They stumbled into the main cellar. In her mind there was still terror. His mind assessed: admittedly the air was icy cold, but that was not uncommon in cellars; and the sensation of evil could well be more than an association of ideas.

His voice came then, professional, soothing. "It was only to be expected. I should never have let you come home alone. Look. There's nothing here . . ." He looked at the shut door to my sanctuary. Our minds met. *You will not come in here,* I thought.

Time stopped. Then: "Let's just go upstairs for a cup of tea and a chat . . ." They turned and walked away. The light snapped off. I swirled through the door, silently into the cellar where their scent, their very heat, still lingered on the chill air.

I stood in the shadowed hall outside the kitchen door and heard the man say, "Look, Jane, perhaps it would be better if you came and stayed with me for a while."

"No," she said, with iron in her voice. "This is my house. I will stay here."

"Then let me move in for a couple of nights, until you've settled down again." Silence, then, "Shall I get my overnight things? I've put off my lecture tour for a month so I can look after you for a while — I might as well do the thing properly." He was Daniel, and he did not know it, coming to the lion's den.

"Yes," she said at last. "That would be very kind."

I would have to find some way of keeping them out of my cellar, I thought. But no: "What about the cellar?" she asked.

"Take out the gardening stuff, then lock it up and throw away the key," he answered.

I turned away across the hall, out through the front door and into the night.

When I returned in the grey time before dawn, I stole like a shadow into her room to stand at the foot of her bed. Such was the beauty of her simple humanity that I felt tainted. She

100

writhed and moaned in her sleep, and a vision came to me of her dreams: a hideous terror, bestial, without mercy. The psychiatrist rose in the next room, coming to her. I fled carrying with me that loathsome vision of myself.

It has not occurred to me before to see myself like that. But I realise now that the beast that keeps me company within knows well enough what sort of thing it is. And rejoices.

The cellar door is locked now, bolted and barred against all save myself, a safe stronghold, yet despair has opened like a pit. And at its bottom lurks the black strength of the Dead — the desire for destruction, for revenge against the beauty of the world.

Dawn is like the breath of dragons on the roof-top: the upper windows catching fire, the dawn chorus and a cock-crow. I must lie down upon my stinking earth. Gently I must close the lid.

Saturday Night 25/26 August:

JANE

The shadow-stalker, the skulker in shade, the thing inside me grew impatient as night after night Burke lingered. Each sunset it took me far away creeping from darkness to darkness, haunting the fields, learning the fleetness to feed on animals. First it caught a stupid rabbit in a field. How horribly it lingered on its feast, feeling the little body convulsed in terror between long hands, rubbing it over my face and mouth before forcing its head between the bone blades of my fangs. As the Dead was at its feast I thought, *This then is what I have become: a creature without glory, a horror.* And hatred burned in me for everything that was greater than the thing I have become. For everything that has life, that has hope, that has the slightest tincture of divinity about it. For everything which *is*, and which is not the Dead. That hatred burns

101

in me still.

Sometime yesterday the psychiatrist left, with protestations of affection and mutual promises to write: he has gone at last on his lecture tour and will not return until Christmas. The house once more belongs only to Jane and myself, and the tension of awaiting the dark racked me more than I can tell.

As soon as it was evening I arose and prowled the house. It was empty, but I knew she would return. I went out into the fields to feed but my mind remained clear. I wandered amongst the Broken Woods lost in thought. I had no mirrors: I did not know what I looked like any more, and I feared the knowledge, yet burned for it. Reflectively I ran my fingertips over my face. They discovered smooth cheeks, thick hair. My body was almost invisible to my eyes for it gave off only a tiny part of the energy I saw in other creatures and, like the strange stake-tree in Jane's garden, it has no life-flame. Were there bloodstains on the dark suit? Was there mud caked all about me? Was there a stench of death like a miasma on the air I inhabited?

With these thoughts darkly in my mind I sat beneath the moon. The reason for them all was the same: Jane. I thought — feared — that the Dead would take this opportunity to kill her. But if my hatred of it were strong enough, then there was hope. In the small hours of the morning, therefore, I rose, my senses tingling and began to walk towards the village and the little white gate to Jane's house. As I reached it the trees broke in a wave of brightness up and over its roof. Ivy clung to its walls like a seaweed made of fire. There was a rush and roar of air: leaves flew in a blazing spray. I glanced up. Thunderheads closed across the face of the moon and a wind whipped through the village, armed with lashes of dust. The trees roared again. Thunder snarled. Shutters rattled. The houses trembled.

I pushed the gate open. A sharp twinge of pain in my arm warned me that I had touched something toxic to me. I glanced down: the iron latch. I walked up the gravel path, the wind wild about me. The door opened itself to me, then closed against the storm. I paused. The hall glowed dully. A bolt of lightning flashed like the flicker of an enormous arc lamp and thunder boomed. The stairs were drenched in a waterfall of light. I crossed towards them and stood at their foot. Rain and hail combined like pebbles on the window-panes above. Step after step, I slowly mounted to the gallery junction. The easternmost window went livid blue. A fiery wave of static electricity rolled down the hall. Dazzled, I was forced to turn my back on it. Thunder crashed like the feet of giants running over the sky.

I stood before her tall bright door for some time, my mind seized in a paralysis of conflicting fear and expectation. Then I reached out towards it and it swung open.

Instantaneouly the cavern of the room was lit, surfaces blue, angles black. Each vertical tuft of carpet stood out. The chairs were littered with clothes, nylon glowing with electricity, silk and wool with filaments of life-brightness. Swiftly then I moved until my back was to the windows and I looked down upon her from the foot of the bed. Lightning visited the black sky behind me. The bed lit up stark with the dazzling blue. She lay revealed by the light, restless on her back, caught in mid-movement, tossing her head. Then the light was gone and I saw her with my vampire's eyes. The first woman the Dead within me had looked upon.

The clothes had fallen back a little from her breast. Filaments of electricity flickered on her nightdress as it rose and fell. She herself was a creature of flame and darkness, of light contained in layers and planes as in the heart of an opal. The dark ruby thrust of her life constricted in the channels of her throat. The electric impulses of motor-nerves relaying bright messages to restless muscles. The golden filigree of sensation all about her. The plain, untarnished depth of the silver life-flame which clothed her, shining even through the heavy blankets. I could do nothing but stand there and look at her, robed as she was in beauty. I could not move or utter sound. Until another lightning flash lit the bed with absolute clarity and I realised with aching bitterness that, in the face of so much radiance, so much vitality, I the vampire lacked even a shadow.

I do not know what prompted me to wake her in the way that I did. I might have aroused her in many ways, but I chose to wait for a silence in the storm and, with tongue and strange jaws unused to words after more than a month of rest, the consonants fitting ill against my teeth, I quietly called her name. "Jane," I whispered to her. "Jane."

She stirred. My face slipped into her dreams. My old face. Emotion: love. Emotion: horror. The dream released her then and her eyes flickered. "Edwin?" she murmured.

And I again, her name like bones in my long mouth: "Jane!"

Her forearm moved across her bright brow. Her mind filled with things of the Dead, a grave, wreaths . . . Terror. She sat bolt upright, the flame of her bright against the wall behind her. A creature reared vividly in her mind, a thing of immense horror. Tall, wild, utterly evil. Blood-red eyes ablaze. Hands armed with yellow talons, great fangs in a cavernous mouth. A sense of evil beyond the bearing of sanity.

"Jane," I cried. "That is not I. That is the Dead. *It is the Dead.*"

But there was madness in her face, madness in her head. I stepped forward, seeking to help. The vision in her mind loomed. Her last faint hold on reality began to weaken. And it was I, I the Dead, I the vampire, who was doing this. Another moment of horror and she would be insane.

It was then I found within me a new sort of strength, a power of command. It closed on her mind and all thought stilled there. And even as I concentrated so completely on the matter in hand, I remembered Richard Burke's words and reeled with exultation at my power. *You have only to say a girl's name and look into her eyes for her to be yours . . .*

Eventually it was done and to the utmost limit of her mind she belonged to me. "What is it that you want?" She whispered. "This?"

She threw herself back upon the pillows arms wide. Her movement jerked me forward, my attention focused to the curve of her jaw, and the soft round flow of her neck down to the hollow of her throat. She turned her head to the right a little, the long muscle pulling from the inner point of her collar-bone up and back beneath the tumble of her hair. In the shadow of the ridge it made, the powerful thrust of life flowed on her skin like a river of ruby. I felt the tug of her invitation in my fangs and on my lips.

But she leapt up then and stood beside me, shrugging off the shoulders of her nightdress to let it tumble crackling down her life-bright length. "Is this what you returned for?"

she cried.

I reeled with Burke's sense of power. The woman was mine to command. Her mind was in my control. I caught her by her blue-veined shoulders, and felt my finger sink into the pliant flesh. "Tell me," I whispered. "Tell me what you *see!*"

I felt the wildness and some of the strength draining out of her body. I could have torn into her at that moment, fastened wolf-like on to her throat, drinking her essence. Temptation answered only with hunger. And my hunger the hunger of the Dead. Unchecked, it would bring destruction.

I released her and she swayed. Only the iron rivets of my gaze held her erect, like the staples hammered home in Stana's eyes. Her will rose like a candle in a storm, only to gutter out. Her terror crumbled. "Tell me what you see," I said again.

She described me to myself then. She was my mirror of words. We perched, knees almost touching, at the edge of the bed and she told me of myself.

A tall man, she described, long of arm and leg, whose hands, though claw-nailed, could fly into sudden courtly gestures. The fur on their palms somehow divided the broad spades of flesh into the plump bulges of a dog's foot. "Or a wolf's," I said.

"Yes," she answered her voice blank, "yes, I suppose so."

There is about his long body a feeling of suppressed power and savagery — revealed in its stillness and rapid, precise movements. The clothes are marked with mud and spotted, especially on the lapels, with points of green mildew. A white shirt, unstained. A dark tie. Shoes crusted and scuffed.

My head, she said, is long and lean. My hair thick, my ears high-tipped without lobes. The long brindled hair all but covers them. My forehead has become broad. It slopes back sharply above the shaggy thrust of brows. Beneath these brows, in deep caves, dwell huge almond-shaped eyes. These would be of surpassing beauty were it not for the fact that the eyeballs themselves are a blazing blood-red. My cheekbones are high, my cheeks hollow. My nose, although long, is flattened and spread at the nostrils by the forward thrust of my upper lip and strong, square chin. Although my full, red lips almost conceal my teeth, when I move my mouth to talk, an array of bone-white, finely honed points comes instantly

105

on view.

Then I stood as she undressed me. Suit to one side, shirt to another, underwear. And all at once, her stomach was heaving and my mind was forced to close around her once more, and bend her will to mine again. I saw in a flash what she saw — the tall, lean, well-muscled body marred by strange blotches: from shoulder to thigh, front and back, my torso was covered by huge blisters of dead skin, beneath which matted tufts of black hair curled like sleeping worms.

I stood for an hour or so while I made her remove the dead skin from me as though I were somehow terribly sunburned and peeling. And I made her find pleasure in this simple service.

At last the cold tide of dawn washed inexorably across the roof-tops. My hands reached out towards her. "Come," I said, "it is time I was at rest." Her hands came up, fluttered and settled in mine. She looked entirely lovely. "What can I give you?" I asked.

"Please," she said — filigree golden sparks among her hair as she began to think a little — "please, I would like to sleep . . ." Her head raised, her eyes sought mine. They were dark-ringed, red-rimmed. Her face was lined with fatigue. "I would like to sleep without *dreaming*."

I threw back my head like a wolf and laughed — my first laughter in many months. My right arm slid across her back and beneath her arms. I scooped my left arm across the backs of her thighs, sweeping her up against my chest. I felt the vital heat of her in my hands and on my face. "Come down with me and you will sleep without dreams," I promised.

And so I lay down in the coffin and she lay by my side, thigh curled over my loins, left arm on my breast, face burning in the crook of my neck. We slept thus, I at first aware of her few movements as she pressed more of her body on to my chest. But her weight on my ribs, and her heat, no longer disturbed me as it had done once. Why should it, when my ribs no longer rose and fell, when my coldness was impregnable, that of the Dead, and when the sleep I granted my Jane for that first day was that of the Dead also — the dreamless sleep that only the Dead know?

106

ENEMY ACTION

I am still in two minds as to what to do about what has happened this evening. An incursion of the enemy into my lair, you might say, though probably no more than the result of simple curiosity. Alternatively, of course, the visit might have been an excuse for poking around. They might, after all, suspect something.

I heard men's footsteps on the doorstep just before sunset. My eyes opened wide. The bands of day still tight about me, I writhed in the coffin but could not open its lid. Deep in the house the doorbell jangled. Jane's soft footsteps came downstairs and across the hall. She sleeps up in her own room again now but still, whenever her routine allows it, in the daytime.

The door opened. "Good evening, Miss Martin." It was the voice of Mr Gore.

'Good evening." Jane's quiet voice in return. "What can I do for you, Vicar?"

"May we come in?" Warlock's voice now. What was he doing, still here? Had he not exorcised the Broken Woods and gone about his business? I writhed the more on hearing him, for I feel he is deadly dangerous to me. "May we?" he repeated.

"Well. . . " she hesitated. With Burke away, I had not expected many visitors, and so I had not told her how she should react to them.

"Please?" Warlock, pressing.

"Of course." Inevitably she yielded. Footsteps moved above my head, turning away into the lounge. I tried to reach her with my mind. I caught glimpses of the room, cavernously dark behind curtains kept constantly closed. The two men stood courteously till she had seated herself. Then they too sat down. She did not open the curtains or switch on the light. I have trained her to love darkness like myself. Neither did she offer them food or drink: to offer sustenance is to give of your strength — that too I have taught her. "What can I do for you?" she asked.

"We were asked to call by a mutual friend," said Gore.

"Oh, who?" Interested, but distant.

"Richard Burke," said Warlock. "He hasn't heard from you for some time. Your telephone seems to be out of order. He's on his lecture tour now, but he's asked us to call and see how you are."

"I am fine, thank you."

"We haven't seen you in church lately, Jane," Hugh Gore probed gently. At that moment, as the last curve of the sun slipped out of the sky, my coffin lid slammed open. I sat up slowly, still listening to the conversation above.

"No," said Jane.

"Is there any reason for that?" Dear, gentle old Gore. Look to your own child, man, I thought, and to Stana's curse . . . Immediately I noticed that the thought of Rebecca stirred within me something I had thought to be dead — lust. With Jane I have so succeeded in subduing the emotions of the Dead within me that only domination remains.

But Gore had asked Jane if she had a reason for avoiding church. "Not really," she answered calmy.

"Richard is really most concerned. Will you write to him?" Warlock, his voice now impatient.

"Perhaps." Still that quiet, dead intonation.

"Is someting troubling you, my child?" Even the vicar had noticed that something was not quite right.

"Nothing," she said as indifferently as ever. I frowned: she should be getting angry. If the two men were to be convinced by her behaviour then there should be hostility in her at their inquisitiveness — but of course there was not: there was nothing I had not formed and put there. I could feel Warlock's mind seething with uneasy questions. I stepped out of my narrow bed, crossed the cellar and caused the door to open to me. Silently I mounted the cellar stairs and crept into the hall.

"Excuse me," said Warlock quickly, "but might I use your bathroom, please?"

"If you wish."

I faded back into the shadows as the door swung open and he came out across the hall. He did not see me. At the foot of the stairs he stopped and looked around. Supposing the coast to be clear, he passed the cloakroom door, climbed the steps two at a time, and vanished on to the landing. I had to follow him, or course, even though I was acutely aware of how much I was risking, for I still do not know the full extent of his power. Or of my own, for that matter.

Had he the knowledge to unmask me and the power and means to destroy me? Quite possibly. But I had to know what he was doing.

I took the stairs as he had — two at a time, and in silence. A movement in Jane's bedroom. I crept to the door. He had left it slightly ajar; the pressure of my will swung it silently wider. He was searching the place quickly but thoroughly, and what he was finding elicited the occasional click of his tongue against his teeth. One muddy footprint: a man's. A man's shoes, with a little earth on one. Supposition in his mind: a lover.

I realised for the first time how noticeable the change must be that had come over Jane's behaviour. From a cheerful extrovert she had become a virtual recluse. Clearly Warlock and Gore had supposed — prompted no doubt by Burke — that it was the shock of Underhill's death; now Warlock thought again. He swiftly searched the other rooms, found nothing more and returned to the head of the stairs. I withdrew into the shadows at the far end of the landing. He glanced my way, paused, frowned as though he thought he could see something, and then went down.

I watched him as he crossed the hall. At first I thought he would return to the lounge, but he did not. He went instead towards the doors which lead to the kitchen and to the cellar steps. I took the stairs in a rush. He was just turning to go down into the cellars as I arrived outside the lounge. Desperately I sought Jane's consciousness. Savagely, more savagely than I needed to have done, I sent pain into her. The response was a keening scream of agony and the slump of a falling body. Warlock left the cellar steps and rushed back into the darkly-curtained room. As he did so, he came very close to me.

He paused, feeling something of my presence in the thick shadows. I stepped back and back, burning under the hostile awareness of his mind, then Gore called his name and he went in throught the door. Jane lay curled on the ground. They picked her up and sat her in a chair. She quickly regained consciousness.

"I'm all right," she said. "Please go." I was totally in control of her every word now. She became righteously angry. "Really, there is nothing the matter with me. If I was upset then it is you who are upsetting me. Just go away and leave me alone!"

Suspicion sparked between them then. But they left the house as she had demanded and quiet returned.

By now Jane remembers nothing about their visit. I wish I could clean Warlock's mind as easily, as completely. He remembers too much and I'm sure he will come back a second time. Perhaps during the day when I am powerless to stop him.

School opens on Monday. I will allow Jane to go back to work. If there is gossip, then perhaps that will still it. And she will write coldly to Burke, telling him to stay away from her. If he comes, I cannot let him escape again.

After they had gone, I recalled the previous spark of lust I had felt, that Jane cannot arouse in me. Soon I must see Rebecca, therefore: the tiny flame of passion was for her. And perhaps I will also see the interfering priests.

Monday Night 24/25 September:

FIRST BLOOD

It has been a period of savage frustration. It is becoming impossible to follow any train of thought or action for any length of time because some tiny stimulus will always bring out the Dead lusting for blood and then I must go ravaging about the countryside on orgies of destruction.

Only two nights remain in my mind with any consciousness of my own will — two visits to the vicarage. The first

110

was some ten nights ago. The church clock struck seven as I passed it like a shadow on that bright evening. I swung in an arc round the churchyard to where the trees around the old house almost reached the road, offering me shelter and easy access. Between the trees all was quiet. I slowed my steps and crept through the shadows like a panther, alert with dark purpose: Rebecca. The bright specks of animals and insects were few tonight — they had been thinning out for some time, learning to avoid the black figure which fed on them in the night. I spat and hissed at their fleeing forms. I would have howled but I fought for control, choking into silence as I crouched behind the vicarage garden wall.

I heard voices: "What was that?" Brother Warlock.

"What? I didn't hear anything." Old Mr Gore.

"It sounded like some sort of animal."

"Perhaps it was a cat. The woods are full of them, you know."

"Yes. That must be it," said the first voice. Brother Warlock's words were clear, his intonation revealing that he did not believe for a moment that the noise I had made was the cry of a cat.

"We are fortunate to have such an evening to sit out in this late in the summer," observed Mr. Gore tranquilly.

"Indeed," agreed Warlock. But his mind was elsewhere.

I pressed my cheek against the cold brick and sent my thoughts hunting his. At first his mind was tense, concentrating, alert to the slightest sound or movement.

Then he began to relax. He lowered his defences, and I crept into his memory and looked around. I saw surprisingly little at first: a childhood obscured, a restless youth, a young-manhood like many — like my own. And then the finger of belief touching him. And from that belief coming a tireless quest for knowledge never to be quite slaked in seminaries and universities. The paths and patterns of his knowledge twisting into distances beyond my ken. But then, suddenly, one path which riveted me, leading through the years of his experience: the memory of his first exorcism.

My hackles rose. More terrible memories, exorcism after exorcism. Here was a man who fought devils, witches, ghosts, all on their own terms. My panic made me clumsy, and suddenly he knew I was there, something was there, in his

111

mind. I felt him jump into awareness and begin to identify the essence which had invaded him. My panic increased. Then abruptly, I saw two women stand in his thoughts. Rebecca, beloved daughter of his oldest friend — he was worried about her. He suspected that she was involved far more deeply than she realised in something which even he feared. But the other woman in his thoughts was Stana Etain, Countess Issyk-Koul. I froze, stunned.

And yet, I told myself, he did not, he could not, know her true, dark, evil power as the Dead. He only knew her as the priestess, the wanderer, the plague-carrier, the witch . . . an entity he must fight and finally control. Which would explain why he had remained in the village — he would not want to leave until he had laid her to rest.

But even as I considered this strange new situation, Brother Warlock's mind closed in upon me. As I was seeing into his own depths so he would see into mine in an instant. There was no time for coherent thought — the Dead, timelessly practise in deception and survival, took over and disguised me. I blundered forward, batlike, into the light of his awareness, fingers spread, body squat, broad, and dark-furred. I fell forward and flitted, screaming, towards freedom.

His mind started back in instinctive revulsion. I saw myself in the mirror of his thoughts, twisted by the instant of his fear, hardly recognisable. But as I broke free, the talons of his recognition raked along my back. My essence, and not my shape, stirred someting in him and word VAMPIRE filled his mind. There came a crash as he jumped up, overturning his chair, then reeled and nearly collapsed.

"John!" cried Hugh Gore. "What is it? Are you all right?

Footsteps stumbled on a path. Then Gore's approaching, firmer. "Here, John — lean on me."

"I'll be fine in a moment. A . . . a passing faintness, no more . . ."

I saw then in his mind another word: EXORCISM. He had applied for the bishop's permission, and so far it had been withheld, and now he feared that his strength was failing. I smiled,

"Come inside." Gore was solicitous.

"No . . ." Receding, too weak to enforce his wishes. "No,

112

really" — his friend leading him away towards the house.

The French windows screamed shut behind them. I was back in my body now, crouched against the garden wall. I rose and faded into the shadows, trembling yet from the narrowness of my escape. And then the Dead in me broke loose again.

Nights passed: the more it hunted, the leaner became the pickings. It was as though the cold of winter came each sunset to the countryside around Dunmow Cross. Small animals died, even a few dumb sheep. But there was no fulfilment, and the beast was never satisfied.

Last night, however, it seemed to remain asleep inside me when I stirred. Underhill's mind — *my* mind — drove me out into the night as soon as possible, seeking Rebecca still, and I prowled restlessly round the vicarage until all the lights were out. Then I crept up to the door and silently it yielded.

The hall was a bright cavern around me. I paused. Faintly from above came the sound of someone snoring peacefully: the old man. But other sounds were not as I had expected. As I crept up the stairway, my head moving from side to side, ears alert for the least noise, tiny gasps and murmurs of ecstacy came to me on the still air. The gallery stretched to either side like the arms of the letter 'T'. I turned left. The vicar's peaceful grunting came from behind, the sounds of lust from before me, on the right. And not from Rebecca's room but from Brother Warlock's!

His door was closed against me. I willed it to open and it swung inwards. But when I stepped forward my foot came to the threshold and would go no further. Yet the door was fully open. Confused, I put out my hand. It went as far as the edge of the door-frame and there, as if the door had been replaced by a sheet of glass, some invisible force prevented it from entering.

Brother Warlock might not know *whom* he fought against, but the power of his spell and the faint hated whiff of garlic showed me that he had all too clearly learnt *what* he confronted: he confronted the vampire . . .

Like a child outside a sweetshop window I pressed my hands against his defences and peered through. And the Dead, which I thought had left me to myself tonight, was there before me.

Within the room Brother Warlock writhed on his jumbled bed. And astride the sleeping man's loins crouched Stana Etain, Countess Issyk-Koul, ghost, pure spirit, *succubus* . . . His spells were powerless against her. As in a rodeo she rode his bucking body, her head lashing forward and back as he jerked. I hissed her name but she did not hear. She was in a kind of ecstacy, her face and senses closed to me, her long hands grasping his shoulders.

At last their movements reached a climax, and then quietened. "Now!" I thought, and stepped forward, but still my entry was prevented. Stana sat, slumped forward, her whole pale body jumping. There was no brightness about her, no life-flame. "Stana!" I cried, beyond control, but still she would not hear. She drew back the tumbled, red curtains of her hair with shaking hands and began to move again. Warlock groaned, and started to writhe in helpless response.

I whirled away from the doorway, hot with rage and passion. I stood erect, rigid in every fibre of my being. A great scream for Rebecca built in me. I fought to control it. Suddenly I sensed a movement, downstairs in the hall. I moved to the landing, but remained cloaked in shadows, staring down.

The door of the lounge opened and Andrew Royle came out. He turned and I heard this whisper, "Goodnight, darling." She, on the couch no doubt, make some noise in reply. He began to creep on tiptoe across the hall, slipping on his jacket as he did so. As he opened the front door I stood halfway down the stairs and watched him, the air about me suddenly cold as ice. The door closed behind him.

For a moment I hesitated, torn between my hate for him and my desire for Rebecca. Then I moved forward once more, passing across the parquet of the hall like the first north wind of winter. The door opened to me and I glided out. I was not aware of walking. I seemed to float over the ground, a column of darkness like smoke. My eyes burned. My wolf's tongue lay along my lower jaw, waiting. I was aware of every tooth in my long hot mouth.

He hurried down the side of the house and then along the path towards the graveyard. He vaulted easily over the low wooden gate and threaded his way amongst the tombstones.

I followed, drawing closer to his unsuspecting back with silent speed. Was Stana with me then? I do not know.

For some reason, in the very centre of that dead place he chose to pause. I saw my left arm reach out towards the shoulder of his jacket: a long hand, impossibly thin, absolutely bloodless. It closed on the cloth, sucking his warmth already through the bright strands. He did not jump. It was far too late for shock. As though deeply hypnotised he turned towards me. He had a young, open, innocent face, not unlike the little I remember of Underhill's face. His hair was tousled. He needed a shave. And behind his eyes a picture of Rebecca, naked and welcoming on the couch.

My left hand rested like thistledown on his left shoulder now. I pulled him towards me gently, like a lover. His chest brushed against mine. Our lips could have met. Gently, I took his soft-stubbled chin in my right hand, resting on my curled index finger, thumb closing on the girlish roundness beneath his lower lip, thumbnail brushing his white teeth, inches away. I turned his face into the crook of my arm lifting the lower jaw a little until his head tilted fully backwards and the column of his throat was mine for the taking . . .

There was an open grave close by the churchyard wall. I cut an extra niche in it two feet deep and laid what was left of him there. I smoothed the bottom of the grave flat over him. He will not rise. It was to have been like a lover's first kiss, hesitating, gentle. But the hunger overcame me and I lost all control. Now his body is completely destroyed and his spirit utterly vanquished . . .

Saturday Night 20/21 October:

PLAGUE RETURNING

They are still looking for innocent young Andrew, but they will never find him unless they exhume Mr. Berry and look under the old man's box.

Now, today, Jane tells me that they are bringing in a crack medical team to be centred at the hospital. All the children at school have been inoculated. "Against what?" I ask.

"Some sort of flu epidemic, they think."

"Why is that?"

"Some of the children have been kept at home, complaining of sore throats and fever." Some fourth-years are ill, she tells me, many fifth-years, almost all the sixth-form girls. They complain of sore throats, restlessness at night, listlessness in the day, terrible nightmares, raging thirst, fever. Hospital tests reveal anaemia. There is talk of some strange infestation. Many parents want the school shut down entirely and fumigated from top to botton.

"What makes them suspect infestation?" I ask.

"Well, nothing concrete really. Just that in one or two cases pinpricks have been noticed on the children's skins as though some sort of insect had bitten them."

"Has any of these insects been found?" I enquire.

"On close inspection a flea or two. At least one case of nits and some ringworm. Pretty much what you would expect. Nothing unusual at all. It is so strange. Nobody can understand it."

I agreed. Oh, I agreed.

The sensation of lips pressed to hot hollowed flesh is among the most exquisite. Yet it is only the prelude to subtleties and complexities beyond belief. From the pulsing richness which bursts from the smallest incision in the throat to the cooler, lighter draughts coaxed gently from a vein below the ankle.

Ah, you will doubt me. This is a monster, you will say, without sense or sensibility, a night-walker capable only of the torn joys of the wolf. But, as is evidenced by what Jane says, my feeding since then might be confused not with the savaging of a hound, but with the sipping of a flea.

Like fine needles, my fangs break the skin. My tongue moves like a butterfly's wing to lap and savour. Is this then the feeding of a beast?

Take Margaret Allen, for instance, captain of the school. She is among the infected. She lives near the crossroads in Dunmow Cross. She is an only child. Her father, a farm labourer, caught mumps from her when she was three and is now impotent. He is a great simple giant of a man, quiet and gentle. He loves her more than life itself. He and his highly-strung little wife are distraught. They do not know what to do. There is nothing to be done, of course. She will not live for long.

Each night when they are all asleep I come tap-tap-tapping at her bedroom window. She rises like a ghost from her bed, lets me in and returns to her deep, troubled slumbers. I steal to the end of her bed.

Margaret sleeps, curled like a child, on her left side. I draw the blankets back gently. She may stir then, but she will not wake. She wears childs' pyjamas, decorated with pink kittens. I stand before her, lost in wonder at her simple beauty. Then I lean forward, dipping my face into the cool flame of her flawless silver life-force. My lips just brush the peach-down at her waist, then move of their own volition, exploring the curve of vital flesh cataloguing each miniscule change in temperature until a fat vein wanders like a hot wire from point to point across my tongue. The slightest pressure, the least movement of my head and the hot blood comes. And more, much more; the wonderful complexities of her life, her hopes and dreams, loves and hates — everything that makes the succession of the days worthwhile for her.

What animal could appreciate such things? What monster employ such artistry? More deeply than the most impassioned lover ever could, I have partaken of the essence of this girl. She is mine, but, in a strange and haunting way, I also am hers.

Thursday Night 1/2 November:

ALL HALLOWS

In Rome it was a saturnalian orgy in honour of Pomona, Goddess of Fruits. They call it Cake Night, Nutcrack Night,

Holy Eve, Hallowmass, Hallowe'en, All Hallows. To the ancient Celts, worshipping in their strange stone circles, it was Samhain, the first night of winter and of their New Year. Even in these enlightened times, the fires of the Druids, lit millenia ago to placate Arawn, lord of Annwn, the Abyss, have not moved away into folklore but just along a few days to Bonfire Night.

Whatever its name, for more than a week beforehand I felt All Hallows building in the atmosphere. In the corner of my eyes I glimpsed strange movements. There was the scent of the charnel-house on every breeze, and the taste of something rotten in the air. Such heart as I have was stirred at the promise of it. My restlessness dwelt in my long mouth; I fed often and widely. They expect to close the school soon for more children are ill, and one or two parents also. But no one will die as long as I can hold the Dead in check, for deaths such as this would breed my disease — Stana's Plague, the White Death — and reprisals. I cannot have that. My greatest strength, the most massive bastion protecting me, is the fact that so few people believe the Dead exists.

A year or two ago, in the Midlands, a man choked to death on a clove of garlic which he had placed on the back of his tongue to protect him from vampires as he slept. In his room were talismans. You smiled, I'm sure, if you read of it, more shocked than amused of course, but thinking : poor fellow, he must have been a *little* mad.

If you thought that, then you are mine. You could not even begin to protect yourself if we met one dark night, because you do not believe.

But if children began to die, then people might begin to wonder. If children began to rise again, hungry for blood, then even you would believe.

My nets, therefore, cast wide and shallow. I am the locust disguised as a butterfly — what I might devour, I sip instead.

On 28 October we returned from British Summer time to Greenwich Mean Time, and from that day, of course, my potential prey was multiplied and my hunting became less hit-and-miss. When the sun sets it is no longer nearly six o'clock, it is a little after half-past four, and there is still some bustle and vigour in the day. For a quarter of the year I have been chained to the night, but now it seems I have a toe-hold in the afternoon. Now I can follow the schoolchildren home, the office-workers, shopgirls and city secretaries returning from work. And when selection is make, addresses noted, company and possible protection sounded, then I simply wait until they are alone or asleep in bed.

But I was not the only one finding such easy satisfaction. Other things moved upon the air, thickening it like wood-smoke. What ever these ghostly essences were, their dark dancing grew wilder during those strange days until All Hallows Eve, and the evil of their power grew.

The sun set that night at five-and -twenty minutes to five. Even with the lid closed down upon my narrow bed I could feel the boiling of the air. I rose, caught by it, bubbling with excitement. Great things should be afoot tonight. Because it was a special occasion Jane exercised herself to the utmost, trimming my hair and shaving me, and by five I was abroad. The night wound around me, unnaturally warm and vital.

There was a wind and a thick toil of clouds overhead, as if the sky were an inverted cauldron full of sooty water at the boil. A new moon, thickening towards fullness, would slice the sky later like an ancient Druid's golden sickle, cropping mistletoe among the stars. The laughter of children, barely contained, whispered in the shadows. I thrust my taloned hands deep into my pockets. Had they been free, I think I would have leaped into the air as though I could take wing with sheer excitement. It was a night to ride the skittish winds like a leaf in autumn.

Already the graveyard was astir. Mist clotted among the gravestones, concealing the first thrusting fingers and arms as the smoke-thin essences of awakened spirits clawed into the air. I paused, looking over the black, dead, wrought-iron fence. The wind sending icy coils of mist to writhe around me. A quiet came as the ghosts strangely sensed my presence and paused in their unearthly movement, fearing me.

A lone hunched figure from the material world hurried down the side of the church — Hugh Gore, going about his futile business. The tall, pointed door creaked open, light flared within, the door screeched shut behind him. I turned restlessly away. Rooks rode the wind above the skeletal trees like untidy black kites, screaming. Rebecca . . . I turned into the long arm of the wood behind the vicarage. Only the plants glowed, already growing winter-dull. There were no animals out at all.

The tops of the high trees shook in the wind but I strode in still air as though I were just below the surface of some strange ocean. The garden wall loomed. I crouched behind it. Silence from the garden. I rose and looked across the long lawn. The back of the vicarage seemed to huddle in upon itself, the thickly-curtained windows glowing dimly. Smoke rose from a tall gaunt chimney only to be torn to rags by the wind, now sucked in a long thin column to the stars, now rolling in slow billows down the ancient tiles. I vaulted the wall and stole across the shaggy lawn. Splinters of quiet conversation were thrust into my straining ears. It was not until I stood right against the glass of the French windows that I realised the television was on. Round the edge of the heavy curtains I saw Rebecca. She was sprawled on the long sofa, tensely watching the screen. What she was watching I cannot tell, for the box to my eyes was a dazzling maze of electric circuitry, all so vividly ablaze that the lines which formed the picture were lost in the pervading fire.

I was content to wait there and observe her. Simply having her under my eye seemed to calm my restlessness. I ceased all movement and stood like a shadow hour after hour. She watched the screen intently, as if it were a shield against the night's unease. Her father returned. Warlock came and went. At last she rose reluctantly and snapped the bright machine off. As the church clock chimed out eleven o'clock, she went slowly upstairs. I did not enter yet. My ears sending threads like spiders' webs to catch the sounds of her movement, I listened as she climbed the stairs and went to her room.

Wanting to be sure the household was all asleep, I lingered another hour in the roaring dark. The church clock was tolling midnight as the front door yielded to me. There was silence as I crossed the hall, silence, and a potent whisper of evil. Something powerful in the house waited in ambush. My whole body prickled. My nerve-ends tingled. As I mounted the stairs I remembered my first blood, Andrew Royle. I smiled: Rebecca had not been too upset by his disappearance — there'd been no hysterics, no decline. I'd known she did not love him, but it amused me that not even the slightest gesture of remorse had been offered.

At the top of the stairs I became aware of a faint whisper of sound, the merest movement of lips. I paused. There was sanctity in the air: someone was at prayer. My interest roused, I moved forward.

Warlock's door was wide. I stood in the shadows outside the white-edged door-frame. My hand pushed round the wood and immediately met invisible resistance. Wise man — he was taking no chances. He sat at a darkwood desk, fully clothed, reading his prayers by the light of two votive candles. Around the yellow cones of light, the darkness danced like the waves of the sea. He sat on a hardwood chair, hunched forward, his elbows on the slope of the desk's lid, a book before him. His head was supported on his broad hands. His eyes followed the lines, his lips the words. I pushed the faintest trace of my awareness into his mind. It blazed with holy fervour. I staggered back from the doorway one arm up.

Such was the brightness of his prayers that the reason for them was almost hidden. But, narrowing my mind, I soon sniffed it out. It was the memory of his dreams that tormented him. With Stana, once sleep had stripped his defences away, he had plumbed the depths of sexual depravity. Underhill was bemused and sickened by what lurked there, but the Dead in me laughed savagely at the cesspit Stana had created within him. I choked on its laughter.

The shadows at his back were thicker now. He dozed, and his head slipped off his hands. He jerked awake. Too late. The moment his grip of prayer had faltered she was standing behind him, the candlelight glowing in the red pools of her eyes and on the terrible white blades of her teeth. I look like that, I thought.

She stood immediately behind him. She was naked. Her hands, long and almost transparent, reached forward to stroke his hair. The flight of prayer began again, faltered. Forgetting everything but the weariness she placed in him, he yawned. She leaned forward, her arms sliding around his neck. He shook his head, trying vaguely to clear it. She soothed his brow until his tired head was cradled on her breasts. Every shadow tempted, and Stana was already

121

behind him. Her hands moved on him, her breasts cushioned his neck. He breathed deeply, stretching his ribs with the fullness of his lungs as he arched his back, thrusting his head down into Stana's pale embrace.

He groaned in his passion and the sound broke into his sleep that was no sleep at all. He opened his eyes, saw her looking down at him. And into his mind there flooded the memory of the greatest of his strengths, his bishop, in full regalia, arms raised as he spoke the simple, dreadful prayer commanding a blessing on Brother Warlock in the Office of Exorcist . . .

He lurched to his feet and cast himself on to his knees by the bed. As I reeled from the renewed force of his prayers I saw Stana herself turn and take flight, all her shadows following in her wake. His prayer was like a cathedral towering in his mind, all its windows blazing with light. And its radiance tore at my senses as I staggered away, across the corridor and into the icy sanctuary of Rebecca's room.

I leaned by her bed. The power of Brother Warlock's prayers was left behind. I looked down, and was transfixed.

She lay in a cave of wonder, aglitter with life, resting on a double bed beneath a quilt ablaze with silk. She had slept so peacefully, the ghostly tensions of the night forgotten. Now she moaned in her sleep and the Dead awoke.

"No!" screamed poor, weak Underhill, "I must not . . ." But it was too late. One long hand, brindle-haired on the back and palm, yellow-clawed, knotted with tendons, had grasped at the edge of the quilt and thrown it back.

She lay on one side. The cold hand took her burning shoulder and laid her on her back. She unfolded like a rose, the long flame of her life-force lambent on the pale net of the sheet. How long we stood, the Dead and I, hypnotised by the rhythmic pulses of life beneath her silken skin, I do not know. The beast within me drew dark and savage strength from the sight. The lust she had once roused in my loins was nothing beside its power.

At last I moved. Left hand beside her right shoulder, right arm taking my weight, I lay on her gently, like a lover. She stirred voluptuously beneath me but did not wake. I rose on my elbows and turned her head on one side. The wind shrieked and beat upon the windows with invisible fists as though it would break in. Beneath her right ear the life pulsed, and my long mouth throbbed in answer. I lowered my lips until they brushed the warm curve of her throat. The wind screamed in the stone throat of a bricked-up fireplace deep behind the wall. The power of the beast hunched over me, its one love, destruction, its one joy, death.

I would have torn her throat out then. I was but the slightest gesture away from doing so. Then there was a noise behind me: tiny but significant enough to cut through my delirium. Like a lover caught *in flagrante*, I looked over my shoulder, and Stana stood in the doorway watching me. She held out one hand towards me. In it was a sheet of paper. I rolled off the bed, rose to my feet, and took the paper. As I did so she stretched her arms out like wings and crossed them over her breast. She was clothed now in a gown of the lightest of faery green. I unfolded the sheet of paper and read it.

Dear John,
I apologise for the unpardonable length of time for which the Synod has considered your urgent request. The last six months cannot have been easy for you under the circum-stances. I am pleased to inform you, however, that agree-ment has now been reached and with all our blessings you may proceed with the full *Rituale* to exorcise those abodes of the noonday devil as you ask.
                    Your brother in Christ
             ·   Ralph
                    Archbishop

When I looked up into the doorway she was gone, but I followed her out into the night, for I knew well enough that she expected us to stand together against the terrible threat of exorcism. And I think I hear her now as I write these words. *Together*, she whispers, *we will never be defeated.*

THE ROMAN RITUAL

Last Saturday afternoon Burke the psychiatrist returned. His footsteps on the gravel path roused me and I sprang awake in my narrow bed. There were hours yet to sunset and I was all but helpless where I lay. The doorbell rang. Jane was marking books from the school and did not immediately answer, but eventually the insistent ringing penetrated her apathy and she climbed wearily to her feet.

"Who is it?" she called from behind the closed door.

"It's Richard Burke, Jane. Hurry up and let me in — I'm freezing out here!"

"What is it that you want?"

"I want to talk, Jane. I must talk to you. Please open the door!" He banged upon it impatiently with his fist. She paused, uncertain what to do. "Jane!" he yelled, "open the bloody door."

At last, inevitably, the strength of his demands was answered by the obedience I had engendered in her. With arm at full stretch she unloosed the latch and jumped back like a startled rabbit as the door swung inwards.

Burke strode in, sweeping her into his arms at once and hugging her tightly as he kicked the door shut. Confused by his affection — for I had locked off that area of her experience amongst many others — she answered his embrace in the only way she now knew. Her body moved against his licentiously.

Shocked, he sprang back and his distaste washed through the place until I could smell it like smoke. "Jane!" he cried. "Jane, what has happened to you?"

Through his eyes I saw a thin pale characterless woman, washed-out and old. Her hair was lank. Her forehead was deeply hollowed at the temples. Her dull eyes were purple-ringed. Her cheeks were as hollow as her temples. Her neck was lined and scraggy. Her shoulders were hunched, her hands restless. Her clothes hung off her at breast and hip, and she was dressed in a slovenly, careless manner.

124

With a deep sense of shock I realised that I had seen none of these things. I, or perhaps the Dead, had seen her simply as Jane the body-slave, and noticed nothing else.

Burke led her, unresisting, into the lounge. He sat her in a chair and perched on the edge of another opposite her. "Jane, what is it? What is happening to you?"

"Tired?" It was a question. I had made her senses so dull. Yes. Yes, indeed she must be tired: working all day, being used each night by my unrelenting unfulfilled lust. She was not an individual to me, of course — no one was any more. Little by little over the weeks, the whole human race, with the possible exception of Rebecca, have been reduced to one function in my eyes, which is to be used for my sport.

"Look Jane, you must come with me! I'll take care of you, my darling. Dear goodness, why did I ever go away. I should never have left you." He ran his fingers distractedly through his hair. ". . . Look, I'll cancel my next few lectures. Take you to London. See you're all right."

A thin enough gesture, I thought, for the man who had left her in the first place to go on this lecture tour, content with the formal letters I made her write in reply to his own, happy to speak with her once in a while over the telephone, relying otherwise, on old man Gore and a strange priest to look after her.

And yet how well the Underhill in me remembered the bright dreams of fame poor Burke had had. How they had filled his life, given him a goal worth striving for in the dark days after his failure to cure Mrs. Gore. His love for Jane had been real enough, was still real. But first there had been Underhill between them, then Underhill's memory. How easy, therefore, to convince himself that the lecture tour, which would bring fame, position, enough clients for an exclusive private practice, was the surest way to win her in the end.

"You should have told me — you should have told me about all this in your letters!" he cried. "I would have come sooner. Made arrangements to stay." He sprang to his feet and began to pace. "What am I to do? I have to deliver a talk to the Royal Society on Monday. It is the one thing I cannot cancel. Jane! I must go back tonight. Come with me for pity's sake. I will take care of you. Come with me — *please*."

125

Jane can have understood none of this. She sat quietly in the armchair, twining her fingers in her lap. Finally he took her by the hands, sinking on one knee before her. "Jane, you must come with me . . ."

And at last I opened her dull mind and, as though she were a puppet taken up suddenly by the puppeteer, she sprang to her feet. "Now you look here, Richard," she said, "you have no right to come charging in here. There's nothing the matter — nothing at all. I may be a little tired, but that's all. And it's not as if you *really* cared!" She tossed her head scornfully. "How many weeks is it now since you left me here alone? And sending the vicar down to see if I'm all right: hardly the act of an impassioned lover. You're a hypocrite! You profess undying love, but do you actually bother to come and see me? *No* . . .!" She collapsed in tears on to the armchair.

He was thunderstruck. "Jane! I . . ." he came towards her, arms reaching out to comfort her.

She jerked erect, eyes blazing, suddenly almost vital again. "Oh no you don't! You can just leave me alone, Richard! Get out of my house and leave me alone! Do you hear me? Just get out — and don't come back!"

Oh, how avidly did the Dead feed upon this delicious irony. That in striving so hard to win her he had finally, irredeemably lost her. And he was beginning to see that bitter truth for himself.

And so he went, sadly, back to London, and out of her life.

But there were other enemies to hold the centre of my interest at this time. Brother Warlock, having at last received permission from the Archbishop to perform his exorcism, was deep into his preparations. These were deceptively simple. He took communion morning, noon and night. The wafers and the wine were all that he consumed except water. Like a monk he rose every few hours through the night or paused in his labours during the day and said the service due to the hours. After the wild, dangerous, murderous strength of the Dead which so nearly consumed her, I did not dare to visit Rebecca again, but even had I desired to do so the way would have been barred against me by the priest's ceaseless rituals.

It was barred also against Stana Etain, Countess Issyk-

Koul. As if by mutual — though unexpressed — consent we sought each other out during at least part of those long restless nights and talked. She told me of herself, her lives. She told me of the night, of its wonders and beauties. She showed me places, holy and unholy, which might be important in our fight against Brother Warlock. For there was no doubt that we would stand together. In that we were of one mind. *We* were, after all, the Dead.

On Thursday evening as I swung open the lid of my coffin she was there, an emerald flame in the most shadowed corner of the cellar. "It will be tonight," she said. "His preparations are complete. It only remains for us to complete our own and then await him at the Round in the Broken Woods. He will come at midnight." She sneered: "With bell, book and candle no doubt!"

"What must we do?"

"To each his own. An evil deed, to give us strength."

"Is that all? An evil deed?" I was disappointed by the mean-mindedness of it. Where was the grandeur in a mere evil deed?

"To give us strength," she said again. "The more suffering it brings, the greater the power it leaves." Her blood eyes blazed, and I began to understand something of the enormity of the act required. And, as it chanced, I had a deed ripe for the doing.

Margaret Allen's protracted illness had caused devasting results in her family. Her mother had suffered a nervous breakdown and was on the edge of suicide. That quiet giant of a man, her father, had aged ten years and more, taken to drink and become dangerously violent. The destruction this simple sipping of the child's life was causing, gave the act an almost transcendental significance. There were moments when I felt like Macbeth, spreading wretchedness around me like a plague.

An evil deed.

They had removed her to a private room in the hospital for tests. The window yielded easily enough to me, and she lay fortunately sound asleep, on a white-painted, iron-framed bed. Careful not to touch this, I folded the bedcothes back. She did not stir. She rested on her side, one arm pushed under her pillow. She wore a pink-checked cotton hospital-smock tied with three laces down the back. I turned her until she lay face-down. The smock rode up around her, revealing her upper left thigh and both of her calves. In the warm hollow behind her left knee I let my lips alight. She smelt like a puppy, and whimpered in her sleep. My fangs probed like a lover's fingers.

Where is the great evil in this? you will ask. Where is the grandeur in this painless leeching on the leg of a child? Tear her throat out if you would be wicked! Rip out her heart if you would lend strength to your damnation! Ah but wait, my hot-blooded friend. I look to the future. Her simple death will be the undoing of the mother. If I am gentle, my mark invisible, she will die apparently of pernicious anaemia. She will be buried in a week or so; but she will not *rest*. She will rise, return home to her father who must either destroy her or be destroyed. So they all will be undone — damned, perhaps eternally. All from a moment's sipping at the back of her leg . . .

Slivers of needle-sharp bone, too keen to waken her dull nerves with pain, probe her. Sliding past fine-stranded tendon, careful of swelling muscles above and below, avoiding the electric white worm of the nerve, nudging aside the slack-walled vein to stab down into the twitching tube of the artery. The long fine points opening the convulsing wall with more precision than any scalpel, and holding it wide while the blood gushes out, two tiny geysers fountaining on to my avid tongue. For moment after moment as the light thickens, there is only the sound of quiet sucking.

Then her breathing becomes hoarse and ragged. Her body writhes on the bed, shivers convulsively once, and lies still. The deed is done; the well is dry. And when the points of the fangs withdraw, why, you would need a magnifying glass to find the wounds. They are so fine at the tip, so razor-sharp and delicate, these fangs of mine. You will laugh, I know: but I must take care when licking the blood from my lips or I will lop off half my tongue.

I withdrew outside the window and towered in darkness, awaiting visiting time. Duly at half-past seven the door opened, the light went on, and, by the best of luck, both parents followed the nurse immediately into the room. As soon as she saw her daughter's abandoned position,

Mrs. Allen knew. Even as the nurse reached Margaret's side and grabbed for her wrist, the thin, grey-faced little woman turned away and soundlessly collapsed. Her slovenly husband caught her under arms, and looked stupidly into the glazed surfaces of her suddenly doll-like eyes. Then he gave one great bellow of animal agony, cast his dead wife down beside his dead daughter and stumbled out into the busy corridor, weeping like a demented soul.

Evil enough? I laughed, believing so.

At midnight we waited, cloaked in black, among the trees of the Broken Wood beside the Dunmow Round. The church clock in the distance laboriously chimed the hour. The wind performed a devil's dance among the tree-tops, tearing away the last of the autumn leaves. Black clouds closed off the stars and moon. There was no light, except, to my eyes and to those of the phantom Countess, the lambency of life, dull green and winter-low, in the tree-trunks, branches, mosses, lichens, fat toadstools and stunted grasses all round. This was light enough for us to see by: the exorcists required a torch.

"It should have been done in daylight, surely, "quavered Hugh Gore as they came. At the first hint of doubt in this voice, Stana moved away from me, and when the two men entered the glade she walked beside the vicar, her serpent arms entwined around his neck.

"John, this is just plain stupid. We're playing the Devil at his own game here." At the mention of His name, she burned more brightly. Warlock silently erected a small portable altar. Sanctity dwelt on the air until a gust of wind tore through the trees at Stana's command to tip the table over.

"We should be home in bed," continued Gore. She pressed the icy length of her body against him. His mind filled with sensual thoughts and suddenly his defences began to stir — she had almost alerted him. Now she fell back and he quietened.

"No," John Warlock said. "It must be here. It must be here, and now"

They had to weight down their altar-cloth for fear the wind would claw it off and carry it away. It took them some time to fight their way into their flapping, recalcitrant robes. Stana's wind danced and howled more wildly around them.

Twigs began to fall like a rain of ice-green fire. Savagely the branches whipped each other. The whole glade began to tremble as though the earth would quake. Then Warlock, before his makeshift altar with its paraphernalia, religious junk, water, wafers and unlit candles, raised his arms and cried, "*Our Father . . .*" And the wind stopped.

The service got under way then, the young man saying the versicles, the old man the responses:

"*Save thy servant,*"

"*Oh my God, that putteth his trust in thee.*"

"*Be unto him, oh Lord, a strong tower,*"

"*From the face of his enemy.*"

And so forth.

And so on.

And there were prayers. An infinity of prayers, each word like fire in my ears: "Deliver this place from ruin and from the noonday devil send thy fear, oh Lord, upon the wild beast . . ." And worse: "I command thee, whosoever thou art, thou unclean spirit . . . that thou *tell me thy name*, the day and the hour of thy going out . . ."

While Warlock and Gore had been conducting their ritual, a wind had sprung up again, but this time it blew against us, Stana and me, where we stood shoulder to shoulder a little outside the circle, to the north, in the direction dedicated to the name of Uriel. Uriel, Raphael, Michael, Gabriel . . . As the prayers multiplied, so the wind seemed to grow, threatening to hurl us away, through Scotland and even over the end of the earth.

But as Warlock spoke these words, ". . . *tell me thy name* . . ." it seemed that a great bolt of lightning danced between the two of us. The darkness around us fell away so that our enemies could see us where we stood, bathed in vivid electricity. And it seemed that the lightning between us had, not only thunder, but a voice. From the deepest part of the sky it roared.

"I AM THE SHADOW IN DARKNESS, THE SILENCE WHICH SEEMS TO WHISPER. I AM NOT THE WALL BUT THE CRACKS IN THE WALL. NOT THE BONE BUT THE DUST OF THE BONE."

Warlock and Gore were blasted back by the force of it. Stana and I reeled alike and only the icy strength of it held us up.

130

Warlock held up his Book of Exorcisms. "I exorcise thee, most foul spirit, every coming in of the enemy, every apparition, every legion . . ." but his words were drowned by the thundering of the Dead.

"I AM NOT THE AIR BUT THE POISON IN THE AIR. NOT THE FIRE BUT THE ASH. I AM NOT THE EARTH BUT THE POISON IN THE EARTH. NOT THE WATER BUT THE DUST. I AM WHAT LIES BETWEEN THE STARS. NOT THE SPACE BUT THE ANGLE."

Gore was broken now, but still the man Warlock was granted strength. He crawled towards us awkwardly in his robes, on two knees and his left hand. Still with that black book held up before his face he cried, "I adjure thee, thou old serpent, by the Judge of the quick and the dead, by thy Maker and the Maker of the world. I adjure thee . . ."

"I AM THE VIRUS. I AM THE WORM. I AM THE FLEA. I AM THE SPIDER. I AM THE BAT. AND I AM THE WOLF."

The man was beaten now and he knew it. If he had other powers, they were not to be invoked this night. He caught up the fainting Gore and together they backed away. Still the black Book of Exorcisms was held up between us so that even we, victorious, were powerless against them. Staggering backwards down the path together they cried, "We pray thee oh Almighty God, that the spirit of wickedness have no more power over us but that he may flee away . . ."

But this last prayer also was drowned out by the thunder:

"I AM THE RELENTLESS HUNTER. I AM THE STEALER OF SOULS. I AM THE BRINGER OF TERROR IN THE NIGHT. YOU WILL KNOW ME WHEN I COME FOR YOU—

I AM THE DEAD AND I WILL ABIDE."

TO REST IN PEACE

Last night, more than a week after the Dead overcame Gore's and Warlock's canting, I found myself full of a burning restless energy. As soon as I was free of the shackles of the day I strode abroad. Only the greatest control kept me from finding my favourite victims and letting the Dead in me drink its fill and drain them until they died. But what I had done to Margaret Allen and her family seemed jest enough for the time-being, and I was still — though more faintly — concerned about the dangers to myself inherent in a return of Stana's Plague.

Soon, therefore, I found myself in the Broken Woods at the site of our victory. The air smelt strange. There was a heavy odour of burning and, indeed, the bushes around the point where the Countess and I had stood were badly scorched. But it was more than this. There was a distinct aroma of burned soil, a strange overlay of charred wood, leaf-mould, of the ash of dust and stone and this was mingled with the stench of long-dead air.

I started at north of the circle, where the smell was strongest, and began to explore the crisp black undergrowth in the mystic house of Uriel. All the bright life had been drained from the place and I searched almost blindly. I was used to seeing a green lambency about every plant around me, but here there were only shadows multiplying.

I believe now that Stana guided me. But at the time I thought I had found the pit by chance. A lifeless crater nearly six feet deep, I could not tell whether it was under the exact point where we had stood or if it was a little behind. In either case it took me utterly by surprise. The ground just tilted suddenly and fell away sharply, and I slid down into it until at its bottom my feet struck a strangely flat stone slab. I knelt down and let my fingertips investigate it. A little more than a square yard was laid bare — a granite slab cleft, as though by a thunderbolt, so that there was a crack in it just large enough for a man to squeeze through. From this cleft came the strange smell of stale air long entombed. Not unnaturally such an odour called to something deep inside me. Blinded still by the lack of life-flames, I crawled forward and sat on the edge of the hole so that my feet dangled below. Then, with the utmost care I eased myself over the edge and dropped into the black tunnel below. At first I did no more than stand there, then my eyes cleared a little. There was life down here: sparks of tiny animals, filaments of root, faint clouds of lichen — life enough to see by.

I was in a long tunnel, perhaps seven feet in height, which sloped steeply downwards on my right. After a moment more of exploration I faced downhill and began to follow the slope. After several yards I came to a flight of steps leading down to a high narrow door. Without thinking I ran down them and reached one hand out towards the handle. What made me hesitate I do not know — some ancient wisdom of the Dead. My fingers merely brushed the handle, yet even so a great flame seemed to erupt there, almost consuming my hand. I staggered back. For a second more, blue flames danced around my strange flesh. Then they died.

Cunningly wrapped around the iron handle I had touched there were wolf's-bane and garlic flowers, dead for so long that they contained no warning life-force — only their eternal magic, deadly to me. I went closer again. Carved on the door itself there was a feared and hated symbol. This place had been closed against such as I. Therefore I longed to see inside.

An hour later I once again stood beneath the cleft stone slab. I called up to the woman whom I had brought back with me and she lowered first the bag and then herself into my waiting arms. "It's dark," Jane said.

I remembered about the light she would need in order to see. "You have the torch?" I asked.

"In the bag."

"Get it out. You will need it."

Abruptly the beam sliced the shadows. "All right?" she asked.

A strange relationship, ours. To me she is a creature, totally bound by my will. To her, in the shadowy world I allow her to see, I am her mysterious lover, creator of and sharer in the adventures of the night. She does not talk of me:

133

our love is secret. My name in the daytime? Ah, a shifting thing like sunlight in water, glimpsed but not easily caught. My identity? A black cat amongst dark shadows. Sometimes far above her, sometimes at her side.

"All right," I said. She, bearing the light, went first down the slope. She moved slowly: careful but unafraid, lighting the place with her clear life's flame more vividly than did the torch. Over the fire-edged silhouette of her head, the bolts of thought flashed. Down her lithe back ran the electric river of her spinal cord.

It was the work of a thoughtless moment for her to break the spells on the old nail-studded blackwood door. She turned the iron ring of the handle and pushed her shoulder against the graven symbol. The door swung a little open, the hinge protesting bitterly, then stopped. There was a scent which in life I would have said to be the scent of roses. "What do you smell?" I asked her.

She took a deep breath and began to retch drily, leaning against the door-frame. Beyond the smell there was nothing to guide me. I felt a power in the place even more ancient than that around the door. I went in front of her and rested the fingers of my left hand on the edge of the door. Behind me, Jane straightened. The torch beam brightened the wood. There should have been the shadow of my head. Of course, there was no shadow. I pushed. The door swung away from me. The smell of roses intensified. She sank to her knees, choking.

I went forward but even to my eyes there was only the faintest light. A candle-power of old magic. Enough to make shadows loom. I called the woman. After a moment, still fighting for breath, she brought the torch to me.

It was not a large chamber — perhaps twelve feet across, made up of at least ten short-sided walls each mounting in a curve to a pointed vault. It was as though we stood inside a huge bullet looking upwards towards the point. On each of the walls there were painted scenes of sadism and sexual perversion. The torch light wavered, lighting more obscenities. I caught the woman and held her cradled in my right arm. The faintest of sensation as it brushed her clothing told me that feeling was returning to the blackened fist of my right hand. I willed it to move, but muscles beneath the

134

blistered skin remained recalcitrant. I took the torch in my left hand and guided the beam myself. There was an altar in the centre of the room, its sides like the walls, lovingly decorated. A forest of stakes were painted there, each bearing strange fruit. White bodies, impaled, transfixed in a grim mixture of agony and ecstacy. Amid the laden stakes danced naked, blood-speckled children. So vivid was the artistry that the impaled ones seemed to writhe as you watched, and as you glanced away the children seemed to move. Lingering on the utter silence of the place there came the faintest echo of childish laughter.

There was about the room an air of brooding agony which I could not bear. If Stana had wanted me to find this place then it was here, no doubt, four centuries ago, that she herself had been discovered at her blasphemies and dragged away by the townsfolk to face the rope, the axe, the stake. Abruptly I wanted to get away, even from the leering, licentious gaze of the children dancing on the altar's side. "Come," I said to the woman. She led the way out of the tiny chapel, waited like a porter as I passed, and closed the door behind me.

I left Jane to walk home alone, content myself for the moment to dawdle. The restlessness which had filled me earlier was stilled. I wandered darkly through the deserted, silent village. Winter was well upon us now, and what had been a clear, starlit night adorned with a crescent moon was rapidly becoming palled over with a massive winding sheet of clouds. A wind blew from the north-east, bitter and still with a faint breath of the great black-pined steppes which had given it birth. That at least suited the new mood building up in me.

As I strode towards the crossroads, however, I detected a distant flicker of movement: someone, in the dark heart of the night, was creeping throught the back gardens of the little terraced houses away on my left. I suddenly caught the stirring of a familiar old excitement. I knew it but did not recognise it. Something deep within me was aroused. Hunched forward, cloaked in thicknesses of shadow, I crept down the tiny path between two houses.

There! Again! In the distance, a pale flicker. The air seemed to contain laughter — as had the air in the under-

135

ground chapel — and the hair down my long back stirred. Eagerly I ran through the neat-clipped, winter-bedded gardens, vaulting easily over hedges, fences, walls, slowly drawing closer to the pale thing which scurried noiselessly down the length of the village. Every now and then it would pause, disappear into the shadows behind a house, and reappear a few minutes later. As I came closer I could hear, each time this happened, a gentle tap-tap-tapping on glass.

Down one side of the village we sped, then across the road and into the gardens to creep up the other side. This time the figure did not simply tap on the windows, but lingered longer as though expecting answers. At last an answer was received. A window opened. Another figure climbed out. I caught right up and watched them: two children in night-clothes whispering to each other and giggling in the shadows.

I realised then: it was the Fools' Game again, but strangely out of season. I drew closer still. And then I understood. The child who had just climbed through the window was bright and blazingly vital. The child I had been following was not: it was Margaret Allen, three days buried, now playing the Fools' Game in earnest.

And even as I thought this, the darker figure engulfed the bright one. The silver life-frame quivered and began to die.

I strode forward, but at my first movement Margaret, or the thing she had become, let go of the child she had been feeding upon and flitted away into the darkness. Her victim stood for a moment, dazed, then fell to the ground. I picked her up, put her in through the open window to the stifling warmth of her own lounge and left her there where she would come to no further harm. The longer the villagers remained unalerted to what was abroad, the better.

In the moments it took me to perform this act, Margaret had disappeared. I cast about in the gardens further down, but she was gone. But then, as I turned to go home, the wind carried a snatch of drunken song to my keen ears and, down past the shops from the direction of Braintree, came Margaret's father. Where he had been I have no idea, nor how he had contrived to arrive home at this time. But he was as drunk as any man can be who is still able to move.

I followed him as he wove down the dark, dead road. I

stood under the four-fingered signpost at the corner of the green as he fumbled at the front door of his house on the corner opposite. Eventually the door opened and he staggered in. I had no difficulty in slipping in after him a few moments later. He was crashing around downstairs. He had switched on the kitchen lights and was searching for something. Eventually he raised his voice and bellowed hoarsely to his dead wife, "Enid, where are my slippers? Enid . . .?" Then, even in his drunken stupor, he remembered.

He stumbled past me at the bottom of the stairs, blinded with hot, boozy tears. I followed him up, into his bedroom. He switched the light on at his third attempt. The room was tidy — strangely so, considering the mess in the rest of the house — and the bed was neatly made. Arthur stared around, as if trying to make some sense out of things. Then he dumped himself down on the edge of the bed and set about pulling off his boots. That done, he hurled them across the room, lurched upright, threw the bed-clothes back and froze.

She was lying where her mother used to lie, dressed in a long white nightgown. As the light struck her she opened her blood-red eyes and smiled, the needle-points of her fangs glinting. "Hello, Daddy," she whispered.

I cannot properly describe the sound he made. He staggered back. She rolled across the bed and rose before him, her arms wide in mute invitation.

"No!" he screamed and, turning, he blundered into me, where I stood on the landing. At the time I didn't think he even noticed the brief contact as he swept past on to the stairway. He took two steps and his knees gave out, precipitating him bodily down the stairs. The hunter in the child followed. With a snarl which rid her face of its last vestige of humanity, she bounded after him and threw herself bodily from the top of the stairs on to his back as he staggered erect. The weight of her pitched him forward again and she rolled over his shoulder. He was on his knees as she cast herself at him a third time, but now he was better prepared. A great ham-fist swung across her face, hurling her, snarling, into a corner as he rose finally to his feet.

I watched from the top of the stairs. Even the Dead was given pause, fascinated by the boundless, evil ferocity it had let into the girl's body. For the fourth time she charged, all white-bone fangs, red eyes and yellow claws. The man caught her by the throat as she leapt at him. They swayed together for a moment as her talons tore at his shoulders and chest before he hurled her away once more. As soon as he was free of her he turned and stumbled towards the back door. He left it swinging and ran into the yard. I thought he was making an escape, as did the thing his daughter had become, for she hurled herself across the room to pause in the open doorway, hands on the door-post level with her head.

For a second this tableau froze, the girl outlined against the dark rectangle as her eyes probed the shadows beyond. Then there was a great cry and a glittering arc of light swung past her head to crash into the upright of wood. The vampire staggered back and something fell to the ground. At first I did not realise that it was her right hand. Then, with a great scream, as mad and animal as her own, Arthur Allen erupted back in through the doorway, wielding a great woodman's axe. Like any creature wounded and cornered, she hurled herself into the attack but the man had her measure. The axe-head buried itself in her side, flinging her back against the wall. She attacked again, spitting blood, reaching out even with the stump of her right arm, only to be hurled back once more, gushing the blood of village children over the floor and walls.

I turned away long before it was over and vanished out of the front door into the shadows. My mind ablaze, I ran home to Jane. There was an hour or two before dawn yet and the sight of blood had aroused my lust.

Half an hour later he came. The great thundering of his fists upon the door jerked Jane out of my arms. She threw on her dressing-gown and went downstairs. I stood at the head of the stairs as she crept towards the bolted door. "Who is it?" she asked.

"Where is he?" cried the man outside.

"Who? Who do you want?"

"Underhill!"

"Oh, but Mr. Underhill is dead . . ."

The head of the axe burst between two planks of the door tearing the bolt cleanly from the wood. The door slammed back and Arthur Allen stood there, fired with a terrible lunacy, in one hand his logger's axe and in the other the head of his daughter, swinging by its hair.

"Where is he?" he screamed. Jane staggered back, her mind, thankfully, blank. After a step or two she fell, stuck her temple and lost consciousness.

Arthur swung his axe across his great chest, catching the haft just beneath the steel head, and strode in on stiff legs. I stood at the top of the stairs and watched him as he prowled, muttering, about the hall. Every now and then he would whirl and send the bloody blade of the axe howling through the thick shadows at his back. It was not until he reached the foot of the stairway that I heard what he was saying: "Here, boy; here, boy; come along, there's a good boy. Come here, boy: I won't hurt you." As though I were some kind of animal to be fooled by his kind words.

He would say this four or five times, then whirl around to hack at the shadows.

Satisfied that I was not lurking in the hall, he stumped off to explore the kitchen and the dining room. I flew silently down the stairs, scooped up Jane's inert body and carried her up to the landing, out of harm's way. Then I returned to the hall, and went to hunt the hunter.

He never really stood a chance. Even if his constant muttering had not given away his location, the bright flame of his life-force would have guided me. But finding him and finishing him were two different problems. Half a dozen blows from that axe had reduced the lithe, powerful body of his vampire daughter to something fit only for a butcher's shop. I did not want to share her fate. My right hand was still charred though beginning to heal. I crept into the kitchen which he had just vacated, looking for a weapon myself. There was a great crash from the dining room as he attacked the grandfather clock. His muted drone never varied. There was nothing in the kitchen which I could use as a weapon. My own talons would be more effective even than Jane's sharpest carving knife.

With stunning suddenness his mad blaze erupted through the door behind me. "HA!" he cried, swinging his axe up. I whirled and rushed forward in one movement, catching the kitchen table and pushing it before me. The narrow end of it crashed into his lower belly, hurling him backwards so that the axe blade cleft, not my head, but the table-top a foot before my face. The massive blow destroyed the table completely, and Arthur hurled himself forward once again through the mess of kindling he had made. I met him in the doorway.

For a moment we stood there, swaying, our arms raised and interlocked while blood from his daughter's ragged neck ran down them. Then, almost of their own volition, my lips spread wide and I struck at him like a snake. He staggered back. I turned and vanished once again into the darkness. This time there was a weapon in the kitchen — a heavy mahogany leg in the ruins of the table.

Arthur was on the prowl again, whispering, "Here, boy, here, boy," in his crazed undertone. Somewhere far beyond the edge of the world the first light of dawn was threatening. An early bird swooped across the black sky heralding the hated chorus. I crept into the hall. Repeating his lunatic phrase for the fifth time, Arthur swung round on the third step of the staircase and destroyed the banister behind. He paused, then hunched his shoulders and began to climb once more. He was on the fifth step when I rose up behind him and brought my makeshift club in a great blow on to his left ear. The power of it hurled him to his right, through the banisters, and flat on his face on to the parquet flooring below. The axe slid away across the hall. Not so his gory trophy, its hair wound tightly round his fingers. Incredibly, he heaved himself on to all fours and began to go after the axe.

I threw my club to one side, for it had splintered as I struck, and thrust myself after him. As luck would have it, I did not land well and sprawled half on to his heaving back. He shrugged me off with almost contemptuous ease, leaving his daughter's head now for me to catch up in my turn, and crawled on. His fingers closed upon the axe just as I skittered round in front of him. He reared up, trying to control the shining blade sufficiently to strike a final murderous blow.

I had no time for thought — only for action. I swung the weight now in my burned right hand, swung it back and downwards, then powered it up again in the most powerful blow I could muster. It took him under the chin, lifted him

140

upright, drove his lower jaw up out of its socket, and hurled him back amid the wreckage of the stairs.

At that climactic moment there came a terrible, soul-destroyed scream from the landing. Jane stood up there. My concentration on the battle had been so total that I had not felt her stir and waken. Neither had I closed off her mind. Too late, I tried to do so now, only to find it already possessed with a thousand variations on one frozen, hideous image.

She had seen me clearly at last — she had seen what I had become, and she had seen what I was doing, and the vision of it filled her mind with revulsion. The creature at the foot of her stairs seemed more vile than any product of mankind's darkest fantasies. Yet she knew that it was real, that she had loved it . . . *and that she had made love to it.* And it stood now, astride the bleeding body of a man, frozen in the act of clubbing him to death with the severed head of a golden-haired girl.

This picture was the last thing that Jane saw. As I watched, the silver flame around her faded. The golden filigree of living thought about head and body disappeared. The pulse beneath her skin faltered and stilled.

"Jane!" I shrieked.

She toppled forward and pitched down the staircase. I flung the head away and went forward to where she was lying. If the shock of what she had seen had not killed her, then her fall had, for she was quite, quite dead. Gently I lifted her and, cradling her pale blind face to my breast, I carried her upstairs and put her to bed. The carrion down in the hall I buried. This house is isolated and its garden large: the chances, even if Arthur were traced here, of anyone finding him are remote.

The task completed, I returned to Jane and sat at her side and held her hand until dawn began to burn my eyes. Poor Jane: I would have cried for her once, but the Dead has no tears.

ALONE

I had not thought I could have felt grief, but for nights on end I have just wandered disconsolately through the old house like some mindless spectre condemned to repeat a pointless eternal round. Only her bedroom contains anything of her now: everywhere else is full of her absence. Her school-books unmarked, clothes to be washed, dishes piled on the draining-board. There are telephone calls in the light hours which interrupt my rest with their urgency, and letters piled each evening at the foot of the door. Letters from old pupils, people I have never heard of. Letters from Richard Burke begging forgiveness and understanding. Then there are letters from school demanding an explanation for her absence. People come knocking on the door, but of course I never open it. But I read the letters aloud to her each evening, in the lingering twilight.

One night I decided to return to the mysterious chapel we had discovered together beneath the witches's circle of stones in the heart of the Broken Woods. A sentimental journey or an answer to a summons? At the time I did not think to wonder. The wind was up, and gusting black clouds low across a moonless sky. The weight of the winter night pressed down on my shoulders like a coat of lead. I walked slowly along almost deserted streets, between seasonably festive shop windows. Nobody saw me. Never before had the sense of my otherness been so poignant within me, the totality of my loneliness so terrible.

Beyond the last street-lamp, the dark gathered round me like a congregation of old friends. All around, even in midwinter, life was bright. Only the dead road and I were dark. The Broken Woods enfolded me like a shimmering cloud columned with green. I shivered with the intensity of my hatred for all this mindless burgeoning.

At the bottom of the black pit the cleft stone slab still gaped. I stood for a moment looking down at it, remembering how I had stood here once before with Jane at my

142

shoulder. The wind died. Silence crouched over me, and I swung round, fully expecting someone to be there. But only mocking shadows met my eyes. I slid alone into the hole, paused on the edge of the broken slab, then dropped into the dark, musty passage. I waited until the roots in the roof gave some of their light to my eyes, then I moved silently down the dust-carpeted slope. The door stood a little open, faintly aglimmer. This gave me pause, for I remembered that Jane had closed it behind me as we left. I crept up to the smooth lambent wood, therefore, and ran my fingers warily down its cool surface. Its magic against me was still strong. I braced myself, and pushed it further open.

Stana sat upon the altar as though upon a table-edge, one foot swinging in the air, her upper body leaning back on the rigid prop of her right arm. With her left hand she drew the red tresses of her hair across the bone-white dome of her brow. A delicately curved eyebrow was raised interrogatively above the expressionless blood-almond of her eye. "What is it that you search for?" she asked quietly. Did she mock me? I could not tell.

"Nothing," I told her. She looked down, smoothing the folds of her faery-green dress, her claws whispering.

"What is this place?" I asked.

"Surely that is obvious." She gestured to the painted walls, the point of the roof towards which the eyes were directed by the painter's artistry and which I now saw to be adorned with a picture of a beast, half-man/half-goat. "It is a place of worship."

"Your place of worship?"

"It is mine but I did not worship here. I came here. Others worshipped here."

"Because you know that what they worshipped was . . . is . . . a plaster painting only?"

"I know many things."

"But not that. What they worshipped, what you worshipped, you do not know its nature."

"Perhaps. Perhaps not."

"To know that," I said suddenly, "to know that for certain would almost be worth becoming this." I gestured towards my body. Immediately I knew I had enraged her, although there was no change in her expression.

"And what do you truly know of *that* or *this*?" she demanded. "You know nothing. Nothing at all. Come with me!" Abruptly she stood erect, her hand held out imperiously towards me. "Come — there is a thing I wish to show you."

Obediently I took her hand. The walls of her strange temple began to waver. Slowly she led me forward towards the door, but by the time we reached it, it had vanished. Like Dante led by Virgil down to the Pit I went, or seemed to go.

After some time we paused and she turned to me — we were at the very top of a precipitous cliff. She gestured down. It was black basalt rock and sheer as a wall. An ocean beat against the foot of this cliff, but it threw no spume or spindrift up into the whirling wind. It was an ocean of bodies stretching far beyond the shadowed horizon. How deep it was I had no way of knowing, but there were bodies enough to make it heave like a restless sea. Great waves swept in relentlessly. Greased by blood and sweat, those in the depths tried to claw their way to the surface. Those on the surface dared not rest or sleep, for fear that those below, made wakeful by agony, might supplant them.

Those on the surface who were strong enough crawled forward, hoping to reach the cliffs. If they could reach the cliff-foot, perhaps they might scale the massive basalt wall and escape altogether. And there were some that made it. The rock was glass-smooth and lined only with the tiniest cracks. Some who were thrown upwards by the heaving below caught hand-holds here. If they could avoid the clutching hands beneath which sought also to be pulled up, and could wedge fingers and toes into hair-thin seams, they could begin to climb. But the higher they climbed, the greater became the danger. If they fell more than a few feet, the human ocean below would open and they would sink to the bottom once more. And as they climbed higher, the cracks, blunted at first by the fingers of those unnumbered ones who had made it some way up, became sharper, glass-edged.

Even so, as we stood and watched at the outermost edge of the cliff, a pair of gaunt hands appeared. Bleeding fingers tipped with filthy, broken nails, pulled thin, torn arms into view. A bearded head rose with aching slowness over the

144

black rock. The man saw our feet and looked up, eyes ablaze with hope of salvation.

Then his gaze fell on my companion. His motion froze. His face twisted in a mixture of terror and hatred. "You!" he cried.

She stepped forward towards him, hand stretched out to help, but he jerked away from her in an uncontrollable gesture of revulsion. "Do not touch me," he hissed. His hand-hold failed. His chin crashed on to the cliff edge. Screaming, he fell away.

She turned to me. "He loved me once," she said.

I went to the outermost edge of the cliff and looked down upon the ocean of writhing bodies which stretched as far as my eyes could see on all sides. How many millions were entrapped down there? Their cries gave life to a great rushing wind.

"But how strange it is," I said, "that, out of so many, the one who climbed the wall should know you . . ."

She looked at me then and I thought I detected sorrow in her still face and the surfaces of her crimson eyes.

"They all know me," she said. "These are those dead at my hand who died in sin. Some rose again, their corpses filled with vampire-spirits, some did not rise. No matter whether their bodies moved or remained at peace, this is where their souls abide."

Behind her, the hurricane of their cries almost drowned the surf of their agony as they lapped against the rock. "I knew them all, loved them all, destroyed them all. This is what *you* have to look forward to. This is what being the Dead means. You tear, you sip, you infect and pollute others. We are the White Plague you and I. We are the tall figures in black robes who take the scythe to such as these. Behold! a pale horse, and he that sitteth upon him is the Dead."

I stood, stunned, scarcely understanding her bitter words. Then, abruptly she smiled and held out her hand again. "Come," she said, "enough of this. Let us return to reality: it is almost dawn."

I swung towards her, stung by that word 'reality', for I had thought myself to be in a circle of Hell, in a mansion of the Pit. And my mind had already raced towards that glowing conclusion: if Hell exists, then so does its opposite. So that all the evil and good in all places and times had fallen into a beautiful pattern.

And now she had destroyed the symmetry with that one sharp word. I swung towards her, therefore. "Reality?" I said. "Returned to reality? Is this place then not *real?*"

She laughed, a joyless sound. "Real?" she whispered. *"This is a dream!* You did not think any of this really exists, did you?" She threw her head back and howled with triumphant laughter. And before the echoes had died we were back in the underground chapel.

I have not visited that cavern again. In time I will find out for myself what is real and what is not. Certainly I cannot rely upon Stana for guidance. But why should I do so, in any case? I do not begin to understand her. I think my most fundamental error has been the assumption that because she takes the outward shape of a human she is in fact touched by some humanity. She is not. And on those rare occasions when I can see myself clearly nowadays, I am appalled by the extent to which even my own humanity has withered quite away. And yet I crave sensation. I am sexually insatiable, which is no more than a metaphor for the most delicate sensations of the soul. I am sexually insatiable because my organs, although functioning perfectly, are without feeling. And because consummation is forbidden, it is the more avidly sought.

Only the grossest excesses seem able to move me now: rage, lust, agony, terror. Because I cannot feel the gentle delicacy of love, I crave it. I crave conscience also, but that too has gone. Ah, how early that began! With the fear of water, with the failure of mirrors, I cloaked a growing ruthlessness under the urgency of my pretended mission to save Rebecca, not seeing for a moment where this would lead. How could I have been so self-deluding? Only self-pity remains, and is exquisite. Let me wallow a little longer. After all, no matter how wise I might have been what could I have *done?* Once Stana's stake had pierced my palm, my path was fixed. And now . . . and now I feel, ah, *I feel*, so sad . . .

Burke came back last night. There were letters at the door's foot when I rose and I collected them together to read in the evening to my quiet Jane. A little after seven o'clock, the doorbell rang below. We sat in silence, Jane and I. The

146

ringing was repeated at length and with great urgency. The door-handle rattled and fists beat upon the still scarred wood. I have buried Allen's body, but I cannot make the door perfect again.

"Jane!" Richard cried.

I put the letters down and rose to my feet. The bell began to ring once more. I moved along the landing and down the stairs. The hall was full of his noise. His finger on the bell, his fist on the locked door, his voice on the evening air like the howl of a hunting-dog. "Jane! I know you're in there! Answer the door. Jane! It's Richard! I've come to take you away."

I stood beside the door scant inches from him. My left hand reached out until its fingernails stroked the black wood where his face must be. Feeling came: hatred, ice-cold and welcome. I stood with my mouth stretched in a smile and felt wonderful, beautiful hatred for this importunate man.

Then the sound stopped. He stood silently, lost in thought, then turned away. His footsteps receded down the path. I knew very well what would happen next. There was no need for haste. I went along beside the stairs and down into my cellar to await events.

They began with the smashing of a pane of glass upstairs in the study. A window slid up coming into position with a bang! There was a scuffling sound as he climbed carefully across the sill. Feet placed individually and almost silently on the carpet. Would he open the curtains or creep forward in the dark? A footstep, a stumble, a crash!: he had become entangled in the curtains and upset the small table beside the window. He had chosen the dark, and it was not his element. Silence. He stood frozen. He had been in communication no doubt with Warlock and Gore, so he knew that something was terribly wrong. Yet he had come here alone, to face he knew not what. What brought him? Mere professional curiosity? The need to challenge his disbelief? Even love? I could not tell.

Footsteps moved across the room. I smiled to myself. Childe Roland to the Dark Tower had come, in search of a fair damsel to rescue. He would find her soon enough. Hinges squealed as he opened the lounge door. His leather soles clicked on parquet flooring. I seemed to grow: I had the momentary impression that if I moved at all my head would strike the ceiling. I towered there in the cellar's blackness. He came past the locked door at the top of the cellar steps, his heavy footfall growing louder and them softer again. He went into the kitchen. My eyes burned. My teeth throbbed as though a tuning fork had been struck against them. My hands, the right one fully healed now, were hooked at my sides.

"Jane?" he called.

My whole body shook with tension. His footsteps drew near once more. As they receded towards the front door again I sped up the cellar steps and into the thickest shadows of the hall. He stood looking at the wreckage of the banister. He wore jeans, a black shirt open at the neck and a ski jacket. As I arrived, he glanced up as though startled, but he could not distinguish me from the sea of blackness all around. He had a flashlight which he turned once more upon the stairs and crossed towards them. He paused, swung round suddenly. The torch beam cut through me where I stood in shadow behind him. His breathing filled the hall like a gale of wind. His cheeks were white, his hair and beard were wild. He had the face of a man who has been terribly torn on the rack between duty and desire. Abandoning Jane, albeit at her angry command, had cost his conscience dear. How I envied him. And how I hated him — that such a creature should have feelings so much more subtle than my own.

He turned back to the shadowed staircase and began to climb. I crossed the hall in three long strides and crept up close behind him. I could hear his heart thundering in his chest. A web of light flickered all along his back and down his legs as the muscles jumped with tension. A stairboard creaked. He cried out in sudden terror, his scalp a vivid crown of gold as all the tiny muscles jumped to raise his hair erect. Then he moved on, his breath clouding above his head as he panted on the freezing air. He reached the landing, hesitated.

Once more he called, softly, "Jane?" Then he crept away from her bedroom as if he already suspected what he might find there.

Together we checked the rooms in which Underhill had once lived. He searched the bathroom — I preferred to stay outside its maze of iron water pipes. But at last there was nowhere else for him to go. He crept up to her bedroom door and stopped. Terror flickered over his skin like sparks. It was as if he knew there was something terrible in there. Did he have second sight? Or . . . I sniffed the air: ah yes — he could smell her. And yet he still went in.

The door squealed open for him. The torch beam wandered around the room and found her as I had kept her, in a warm nightdress, propped up in bed. The yellow light made her face livid. The look of horror with which she had died was faded now, for the flesh had bloated and sagged. The eyes were dry and filmed with grey. A small track of something green wound over her slack, purple lip, down her chin, and on to the neck of her nightgown. The smell of her was overpowering. He choked, staggered, and yet moved on forward.

I moved backwards then, sweeping towards the head of the stairs. "Jane!" he cried again, this time in the unbelievable certainty of what he had discovered. I heard his fingertips against the cloth of her nightgown. Then he gave a sobbing scream and came back through the door at a stumbling run, his mind a whirl of images overlaid most strongly by the idea of the police — to whom someone should have gone long ago. He tripped on something. The torch fell from his hands to land on the floor, pointing uselessly at the wall. He did not see me at first. He was still looking back over his shoulder as he staggered to regain his balance. Then he stooped, groped for the torch, and there I was, towering above him. As I could see him amid his silver life-flame, so he saw me, darkness of darkness, shadow of shadows, red-eyed, white-fanged. He cowered away, his face convulsing in horror. "No!" he choked. "Oh God, no!"

"Yes," I whispered, moving slowly forward.

Disbelief, like a cloud, around him. But it could not save him. Gently I leaned down and gathered his face in my left hand, thumb down the left side of his jaw, the spider-scar crouching on my white skin. His eyes bulged over the edge of my hand. His breath and the beginnings of a scream trembled against the sensitive fur on my palm. I tightened my fingers until I felt his cheekbones begin to crack. Agony cleared his mind. And in it I saw, in this his dying moment, his reason for having returned to the house. Love. Love for Jane. In his own way, no matter how imperfectly, he had loved her.

I closed my hand to a fist. His face crushed like a sheet of paper. I twisted his jerking head back until the neck snapped, and sank my fangs into the offered column of his throat. I hurled him away and down the stairs. As he crashed from step to step the bright flame of him began to fade. Finally it guttered and died on the dim parquet. I descended, kicked his remains away from the foot of the stairs, depression suddenly weighing me down.

As midnight stirred, my mind cleared and I seemed to be sickened by what I had done. By what the Dead had done. A confusion of feelings lingered briefly: sadness for the dead man rapidly became sadness for myself. Sadness and bitter loneliness.

Even Jane, my creature through many months; Jane, consigned by chance to oblivion and silence; even Jane had had someone to love her, to search for her and try to save her.

Who could ever love me now?

Sunday Night 9/10 December:

STANA'S PLAN (i)

As soon as I shrugged off Underhill's vapid melancholia I began to look for the Countess Stana, and pursued my search to the exclusion of all other things except feeding in the night. She was not in the strange chapel beneath the buried circle of stones in the Broken Woods. She was not in the graveyard or the crypt or the tombs of the church, though I waited for several nights hoping she would come. She had no lair in the village that I could find. She did not rest beneath the finger-post at the crossroads on the green in the grave where once she had lain.

150

I did not see her as I followed the shopgirls and the secretaries to their snug homes in the evenings. I did not feel her near me as I sipped willing bodies. How full this winter will be of laryngitis, pharyngitis, bronchitis and the mild blood diseases — iron deficiency, anaemia: if only the local doctors knew. Stana was not there in the night as I moved about silent streets, sated and searching for her. Nor in the cold grey dawns like this when Edwin brings me home to keep my journal, no, my *nocturnal*: my journal of the night, in the house with Jane in her yellow-stained bed, and the remains of the psychiatrist at the foot of the stairs. Sooner or later someone, the police no doubt, will come and find them and take them away. But until that happens they are at least company for me, of a sort. Tiring of the search and growing impatient with my helplessness, I decided to console myself with a sight of Rebecca. I had not visited her for some time, fearing my weak control over the Dead, and what the beast might do to her. At midnight, therefore, I went to the vicarage and stood before its blackwood door. There was no wind or movement in the earth during those moments, and as the chimes struck the door swung slowly inwards at my command. The house was quiet. The old man and his daughter were in bed. I mounted the stairs. The landing lay open and dark on either hand. The door to the spare room where Brother Warlock had slept was open. Idly I entered. Much of the man remained — clothes, shoes, cases — but of the exorcist himself no sign.

I was lingering there, trying to ascertain the reason for his absence and the date of his return, when I heard the faintest breath of laughter. At first I did not see her for she was lying cloaked by shade, but then, as I stood bemused, Stana rose in a parody of Venus from the sheets. She was clothed from throat to ankle in her gown of faery green. As she swung free of the bed she smiled at me, teeth agleam, eyes lighting the room like the embers of a fire. "He is not here," she said. "But he is not so far away that I cannot reach him when he sleeps."

We talked then. It was her time, sated as she was with her torture of Brother Warlock's sleeping mind, for confidences. She told me of her suffering after the staking and dismemberment, when she had existed, blind, deaf, dumb, bound to the grave by the crossroads. This was as near to Hell as she could imagine, fighting through countless days and nights to remain as an entity, to hold together a character, a mind, an identity as all her strength was sapped away by the nothingness around her. She told me how memory faltered and faded. Madness beckoned. What lay beyond the final plunge when all knowledge of self would be gone she did not know, but it was the only thing which truly terrified her. So she had used it, for four hundred years, used her terror and her hatred to remain individual, to remain strong, to remain the Countess. Until by chance I had at last released her into personality and the spectral semblance of a body, so that she could wander freely.

It was a sombre night, this night, and we talked of sombre things. One subject of discourse especially held my interest. In all the centuries of her existence as the Dead, before she came to Dunmow Cross that one last time, she said, her sole abiding grief had been that she was always alone. In all that time there had been no single companion immortal like herself. Solitude was a state of being I should try to avoid above all others, she said. Even the burden of immortality grew light if shared. And here she was willing to help me. She would have offered herself, of course, but she had form only, and no flesh, while I was young and great in power. Now was the time, therefore, for me to choose one and fit her to be my eternal companion.

How would I do this? I asked.

There were rituals, she said: if I would allow her, she would aid me in their performance. My part, after choosing my companion, would be to ensure that her spirit was educated swiftly in the ways of the Dead — swiftly but gently, for some spirits were weak and might break beneath the strain. Further, the carrion flesh must be stripped away skilfully and in a certain manner. And I must not only take the essence of my chosen mate, but give to her also of my own essence, in so far as I am able. I must wrap her gently in toils so thick and strong she could never escape, even should her wishes be contrary to my own. Had not even I tried to escape my fate? — my victim might also try to seek oblivion rather than eternity.

"Choose your partner carefully," she told me, "and then we will begin."

But she knew as well as I did that the choice was already made.

(ii)

When all the vicarage lights were out on Monday night I commanded the front door to yield to me. Impatience barely held in check, I crossed the glimmering hall and mounted the stairway to the landing. The old man was deep in sleep, his dreams stinking of purity. Stana was not in Brother Warlock's room but I knew well enough what to do, even without her.

Rebecca's gown was of white cotton buttoned demurely to her throat. I sat upon the edge of her bed and slipped quietly into her dreams. We dreamed together through the long dark night.

At the first most distant stirring of dawn in the restless air I unfastened the buttons of her nightdress and pulled the bodice wide. The column of her throat beckoned me from its shadowed hollow to the full curve of her chin. Yet fearing the ravening of that monster, the Dead, even though it grows sluggish within me at the ending of the night, I pressed her wrist, only, to my mouth, content to ease my needle teeth amongst the tendons there. In a moment I had searched out the strong beat of her pulse and filled my mouth at its perfect fountain.

Tuesday night passed in the same way — as did each night for the rest of the week. Remembering Stana's instructions, I interfered more in her dreams, until she came to regard my intrusion there as something natural and desirable. Our dreams were always chaste. It was not until later that I wished to feature as lover and master — for the moment I was content to be her friend.

153

And I talked. I talked about everything under the sky, promising her such experiences, such wild visions. Her body jumped with anticipation; her heart pulsed with excitement — and yet I was careful to sip at her wrist only.

Tonight, however, I felt it was time to move one step further. As her dreams stilled in the dullest hours of the night I decided to awaken her.

How many times I actually placed my hand upon her shoulder only to pull it back again before she stirred, I cannot tell; but eventually something in me was sickened by this timorous hesitation, causing my long fingers to close on her burning flesh and shake her with unnecessary force. She sprang awake immediately and I felt ripples on the air as her senses expanded around her. "Father?" she whispered — why she whispered I do not know. "Father, is that you?"

Already my will was closing around her, not absolutely, as it had closed around Jane, but strongly enough to hold her. She smelt me first, and that alerted her. Visions of graveyards came into her mind because of the stench of my body. Then she saw some dull light on my face from the uncurtained window. Curve of eye-socket, thrust of cheekbone, resolute line of jaw. A wing of brindled hair above an ear. I turned a little towards the light — it was as though I could see my reflection red-eyed in her mind. At last recognition came. "Edwin," she breathed.

An avalanche of conflicting emotions came. Love, respect, trust engendered in her dreams. Terror, revulsion, disbelief born of her waking mind. I raised my left hand and rested it on her broad brow, gathering her throbbing temples into finger-roots and thumb-joint. Her mind lost force and power. "Edwin," she said again. Then, "How can it be you?"

But before I could answer she had thrown herself forward, arms about my neck. With my chin pillowed on the muscle at the back of her shoulder I strove to hold back the beast within me while the flame of her body pressed against mine. Such breath as I chose to take fanned her hair as her sighs stirred mine. Warmth drained out of her full flesh and into my chill bones. I felt only that, only that and the burning needles of lust, the joys of coming destruction, a heady sense of victory over a formless good. The first step was taken and there had been no stumbling. She loved me. I took her to the window and let her gaze upon the night. "All this is mine alone," I told her, as though the darkness were some precious jewel, "but I have awoken you so that you may share it with me. I am King here. I want you as my Queen."

For the rest of the night I told her, while awake, what I had promised her in dreams. This time her face shone, her dark eyes glowed with the thought of it. Then I led her back to her tumbled bed. "Tomorrow night," I told her as I raised her wrist for the last time to my mouth, "we will begin a little Odyssey upon the ocean of the night."

My lips moved upon her burning flesh. A moan whimpered almost silently far in the back of her throat. At that passionate sound my gums burst aflame. I fought the monster down. Shaking as though with fever I placed her arm beside her body on the bed. She slept immediately. I was crouched over her when the door burst open. In the twinkling of an eye the Dead had whirled me away into the safety of the shadows.

Mr. Gore's head came round the door. "Rebecca?" he whispered. "Rebecca, are you all right? I thought I heard . . ."

His voice trailed away as he saw by the light from the open door that she was asleep. He stood in silence for some moments, his eyes probing the darkness beyond her. Perhaps he sensed my presence. Certainly the stench of his fear was strong about him. His hand brushed the light-switch, faltered, and dropped to his side. He turned and walked away down the bright corridor as if all the weight of the world was resting on his shoulders.

Friday Night 21/22 December:

(iii)

On Monday night the vicarage door was bolted and barred. Faintly but potently on the blackwood was marked a cross in holy water. The old man thought he could keep me away . . . My laughter was lost amid the chimes of midnight as I went round to the side of the house where the ivy glowed, winter-dull, but strong against the brick. In a moment I was outside Rebecca's bedroom window. She paced restlessly in the room, not yet undressed for bed. She wore a black polo-necked pullover against which the silver crucifix upon her breast caught the light mockingly. There was a stench of sanctity, as though prayers had been said in the room. The window also was barred against me with more holy water. "Rebecca!" I called to her with my mind.

Her pacing stopped. She looked fearfully at the window but saw only the night. I called her again. Her will rose. Something in her forbade her to listen to me, but when I called her the third time it died.

Without further thought, she crossed her arms upon her stomach, fingers to the waistband of the pullover, and with one sensuous movement she lifted it over her head. The silver cross and chain became entangled in the woollen folds and were cast aside. Then, bare-breasted, she crossed to the window. She used a hand-towel to mop up the water from the sill and threw the window wide. Immediately I was in, forming out of a tall column of darkness behind her.

She turned back towards me, shivering suddenly in the icy night air. The church clock intoned the half-hour. I held out my hand and the last of her resistance crumbled as she accepted it. I said, "Dress quickly. We have much to see."

Our path took us past the churchyard. We stood outside the wrought-iron fence and I passed my hand before her eyes so that she would see as Stana and I saw. The mist billowed up above the frosted ground. The graves lay in neat rows, trim, well-tended, full. A rat crept from the splintered corner of a tomb. A breath of wind set the mist to rolling like a strange sea. From the grave nearest to us there suddenly thrust a dead white hand, clawed and clawing. Another. Arms like sticks. A face like a skull half covered with grey clotted clay and ill-tanned leather. Rebecca turned away, revolted. Another and another rose, mindless horrors capable only of echoing the wind and stumbling a few yards from their resting-places. Neither cursed nor damned, I told her, too insignificant to warrant anyone's attention. Pity warred with her revulsion, a lingering vein of humanity. I recognised it, but it was a stranger to me. What sort of a sickly power would care for these? I thought. "This is what you may expect from life after death, my dear, in spite of all *their* cant!" I gestured up at the quiet church. "They are things of no account. Come," I said, and led her onwards.

I took her then to my house. I showed her this place, my lair, the chair and desk I have moved down here so that I can keep my journal of the night. I showed her this book itself and read her some passages from its crowded pages. I showed her my narrow bed, saying, "It does not look much, I know. And yet what else is there to look forward to?"

I took her through the hall, past the stinking wreck of Burke at the stair's foot, and up to see my Jane, bloated now almost beyond recognition. "That is the best you can hope for," I told her, leading her out into the night.

Tuesday night found me picking my way easily through Gore's ineffective maze of charms. I took her to the Broken Woods, to the circle made of stones. There was an oddly confused reaction to these things in her mind. Writing it down now, it strikes me more forcefully than it did then. She knew the place well enough and the half-buried, mossy stones of the Dunmow Round, scarcely more than ankle-high but all aglow with occult power. Folk memories danced vividly and erotically as she recalled rituals once held here. Behind these memories, strongly associated with them, was her fear of madness and the curse of the Dead which she had for so long sought to escape. But underlying all, so deep and devious as to be almost invisible, there lurked another drive, the strongest by far. A drive not wholly Rebecca's own. At the time, when the Dead was strong in me, I hardly paid it any attention. Now in the dawn when the Dead is weak I am more disturbed.

157

But it was not the stones alone which were my object. I took her to the pit which had been hollowed by the power of the Dead as it fought the Roman Ritual through Stana and myself. I lowered her through the cleft stone down into the passage, slipped down behind her and we walked to the chapel. A sort of revelation overcame her when she opened the door and saw inside. Breathless with wonder and growing passion she studied the walls, craning her head back to follow the paintings to the pointed roof. Abruptly, she took me by the hand and led me to the altar. She climbed upon it and lay back, extending her neck and throat. Then, like the couples on the walls, she writhed as I drank at the bright thrusting fountain of her life.

The next night, Wednesday, presented even more spells to forbid my entrance to her room, but still, for all Gore's senile cunning, they proved ineffective. His defences were half-hearted and without pattern or force. He had meant to await my arrival himself armed with some paltry protection, but he had gone to sleep kneeling at his bedside.

Rebecca wore a nightgown woven of pure white silk completely apt to my purpose, for I had come to baptise her. She lay still as death but when my fingers brushed her forehead her eyes sprang wide and her lips parted in invitation. Deep, rhythmic breathing surged in her throat and she writhed slowly in an excess of desire.

"Sit up," I ordered. She obeyed immediately, thrusting herself erect, her back straight, hands folded and pressed into her lap. I sat half turned towards her on the edge of the bed. In some distant part her mind suddenly exploded into absolute terror. As I controlled it, my fingers brushing the hair away from her face, her cheek rubbing sensuously against my hand, I was moved for a minute to self-recrimination. The power of the Dead hid it well from whatever vestiges of humanity still remained in us, but the woman and I both knew, somewhere deep in our hearts, the true horror of what I was doing to her. I was taking a creature of light and life, of joy and mortality, and making from it a monster like myself. And, for all the deluding passions of power, a monster is what I knew myself to be. A thing that rational creatures, whether of no account like Gore, or capable of wielding power like Warlock, must loathe and condemn. I was the leper infecting his most dearly beloved so that I might not be lonely in my obscene damnation.

And this was the moment for such thoughts, while there was still time. The blame was not mine that I was what I was: and from that a whole dreadful sequence of events must follow. Yet now, now the step I was taking was new, and newly vile . . . But the power of the Dead, like a thunder-cloud over the moon, effortlessly rode down my stunted conscience. I smiled, feeling my lips stretch over my fangs. Her chin rose fractionally, her eyes opened, heavy-lidded, and her throat was offered. "Not yet," I told her, "later. First it is your turn."

Slowly I pulled my tie off and began to unbutton my shirt. A second or two was sufficient time to open it fully, revealing my lean chest, ridged with ribs and forested with rough black hair. Only down the very centre of my breastbone did the flesh gleam dully. Rebecca's eyes rested here, entranced. I rested the long curved yellow claw of my left index finger at the hollow of my throat. For a moment it remained there, then it began to move downwards, the edge of the talon parting the dead skin and flesh as efficiently as any razor. Cold blood came, pale and thin. I took her by the back of the neck and pressed her mouth to it. As she sipped like a kitten from a bowl of milk, my fingers unloosed buttons at the back of her nightgown. By the time I had them all undone her mouth was at my throat. The wound was healed beneath her lips. Her eyes glowed with a new light. Her breathing was raucous — she had become a thing compounded entirely of lust, and this was the time to answer her desire with my own.

The final stages of Stana's ritual were simple. I must show her the beauties of my state so, for the next two nights, as the old man snored obediently in his room, I led her out again. She no longer needed to change out of her long nightgown. She no longer felt the cold. My power over her was so strong that she might already have been dead. Looking through her eyes I saw it all anew, and the dizzy joy of it washed over me once more. It was all too beautiful — how I longed to destroy it.

Street-lamps soared around us, elegant curves of bright blue power exploding into their dazzling brightnesses like

159

sky-rockets frozen. All around us, fine indigo nets of cables sparkled. People and animals made her catch her breath with the beauty of their living as they hurried past.

When the village was quiet I led her up the still, dead ribbon of the road to the Broken Woods. The faint phosphorescence of winter-dead fields called to her with soothing beauty. The tall trees clothed in green fire made her laugh with joy. Even in this season there was some life here. I caught her a dull-burning rabbit. Together we tore its flesh and drained it.

Now there is only the final part of the ritual to be performed. The time is not quite right. I will kill her on a night of power; when, I do not yet know. She lies there now upon her distant bed. If I wish it she will open her eyes and I will see through them. She is mine now utterly. I sit here, sated — for I have drunk her blood and used her to the full — keeping my dark nocturnal at my desk in Jane's cellar while the sky begins to lighten. My body does not need to be with hers any more. Even should oceans part us I can touch her with my mind. Wherever she is, or will be, ever, I can feel her, hold her, see what she sees, know what she knows. She will do what I tell her instantly and without question. While still she is a creature of flesh, until I grant her the final power, I am the puppet-master and she the puppet. We are utterly and completely one.

Saturday Night 22/23 December:

FINAN'S EVE

Finan's Eve is the Winter Solstice, Lucy's Day, Midwinter. The day has seven hours and the night seventeen. No sooner had the sun set behind flat, slate clouds than I was up and about. Long before the street-lamps could surge into life, when even the old man Gore would still be awake, I stood before the blackwood vicarage door. It was bolted, blessed, and would not yield to me. I tried to form with my mind the cavernous hall so that I might enter there as I had exited my grave so long ago. All I saw was a bowl of holy water and a prayer. Laughing at this dogged repetition of his aged folly I proceeded to look in at the windows. All were sealed against me. There were more prayers. White wafers. Water. In Rebecca's room there were strings of garlic and a terrible excess of worship.

She lay still and sleeping on the bed, her night has become the day, and her day the night. But she was bound down and protected. A new hand here: someone who knew the Dead for what it is. Even before I saw him I had guessed who it would be. Rebecca's bedroom door opened. Brother Warlock came in and sat on the edge of her bed. Gore entered also, dark-eyed and bowed with fatigue. Warlock said, "Sunset." They both looked fearfully at the window.

I could not see Rebecca clearly for the rituals forbade the entry of even my mind into the room, but I knew well enough how she would look — pale and languorous upon the sheets. To the men's eyes sick unto death; to my eyes more beautiful than ever.

"Thank God you're back, John," whispered Gore. "This thing has grown terribly since the Roman Ritual. I had given up all hope for her."

"No," commanded Warlock. "You must never give up hope, Hugh. With God's help she will come through."

"But you have not seen the new power of this Hellish obscenity, John. I warn you, have a care. Each night for the last week I have laid out the charms exactly as you suggested and waited up myself, but each night it has come regardless and taken her. My flesh is too weak, John. My flesh and my faith . . ."

"No, Hugh. Do not doubt your faith. I have been trained to this for many years and practised the rituals all over the world, but even I have never come across an evil such as this. How such a power has been allowed to escape from the Pit, I can hardly imagine, but we can only pray faithfully for sufficient strength to chain the beast again."

"I am frightened, John. Not only for my daughter. I am terrified for my very soul."

"So am I, Hugh. I am fearful for all of us. God send us grace. And power."

"Amen."

Rage came, that they should stand in my way. Thunder rumbled in the clouds. *Rebecca!* I called silently, battering with all the power of my mind against all the walls of prayer and magic. Faintly and at a great distance I felt her stir.

"John! I think she is waking up."

"Yes. The night is upon us." There was the sweetest sound of terror in his voice.

Rebecca! I called again, summoning all my monstrous strength. She sat up, but her eyes remained fast closed. "Dear God," whispered Gore. "It is summoning her. Even through your prayers and spells, John. It can reach out its foulness and she will answer it!"

Come to me! I ordered, and she began to move, swinging her legs off the bed, placing her feet on the floor. *"John!"* choked the old man, such agony in him that I nearly howled with joy. But then Warlock took her, whispering some foul prayer. I felt my grasp upon her slipping. "Here," whispered the white wizard, "drink this". Something was pressed to her lips. I heard her teeth chime against silver and I lost her.

"God!" she screamed, her shrill voice filling the room like the most sickening stench, "God help me! Father! Brother John! Give me strength! I don't want to die! Daddy, Daddy, I don't want to die."

"Hush, my child!" The old man enfolded her in her arms and half carried her back to bed. "With the Lord's help we will come through. Hush now, go to sleep."

"Oh Daddy, it is so horrible. Oh dear God!"

"Hush now, Rebecca. Save your strength."

"Let us pray," said Brother Warlock. He came towards the window, his suspicion like a hot wind upon my face, but he did not see me there. He turned his back, broad shoulders blocking the room from my sight, and the three of them filled the night-time with the terrifying volume of their worship.

Anger bitter in my throat, I climbed down and began my search again. No door would open to me. At first it seemed that all the windows also had been sealed with spells, but then I found that the window of a cellar, its sill at ground-level behind a rosebush, had been forgotten. At my insis-

162

tence it began to open, my will upon the rusty hinges like oil. In a moment or two I slid through it and dropped like a shadow to the floor.

Sensing nothing untoward, guided by hate and thwarted desire, I crossed the little basement room and mounted the steps. Silently, again at my will, the door swung open and with the merest whisper of sound I walked into the hall. Facing the stairs, I closed the door by leaning back against it with my shoulders. The place was heavy with holy magic. I felt as though I had suddenly walked into a stifling tropical storm. Bowls of water gave off their steamy power. Wafers filled the air with clammy warmth. Everywhere the fetid, overpowering stench of garlic. Crosses everywhere fashioned of wood, silver and iron, filled the place with a thunder of their potency. There was even a sort of fence made of black briars at the foot of the stairs. As soon as I moved the powerful lightning of the spells cracked about me. My hair stirred with fear and yet I *would* go on. Some way or other I would reach Rebecca now. Therefore I strode forward across the hall in spite of everything they had placed there to protect themselves against me. Therefore I fell into their trap.

Suddenly the old man came out of the bedroom along the passage at the head of the stairs. Before I could do anything, his eyes met mine. "Sweet Christ!" he whispered.

I pounced towards him, but my steps faltered even before I reached their briar wall because light caught the great silver cross he was wearing round his scrawny neck. "It is here!" he cried. "Warlock, the thing is here!"

His right hand took the silver and thrust it out before him as he stumbled down the stairs. I staggered back a step or two as it flamed in his hand with dreadful power. Then Warlock too was at the head of the stairs above the old man. He held in his hand a bottle of water and as soon as he saw me he hurled it. I threw myself sideways instinctively, but I was not the target — it shattered against the cellar door, painting across my only escape-route a pattern of brightness whose strength I would not easily overcome.

"I was right," he called to Gore. "It *is* Underhill."

Prayers stumbled into Gore's reeling mind. He nearly choked himself with the silver chain, thrusting his cross at me. But I had no time to consider him too deeply. Warlock had come striding past him, similarly armed. My whole being was trembling with massive rage at their temerity. My eyes burned as never before and on the surfaces of everything facing me, a blood-red light began to glow.

"His eyes," cried Warlock, kicking aside the briars, "do not look at his eyes!"

He caught up a silver bowl and hurled it at me. He was being so careful to avoid looking in my eyes that he missed me entirely. His mind signalled that he wanted help. "Hugh," he cried impatiently. The old man began to approach me slowly. I fell back. Walls gathered behind me. Warlock caught up a cross of wood. Its foot had been sharpened. There was a mallet there also. Gore began to mumble prayers aloud. They closed towards me. My mind reached out in all directions, commanding the children of the night to help, but I feared I was too late.

Then abruptly there came a terrible scream. Rebecca stood at the head of the stairs. The two men turned towards her. I launched myself forward in one desperate dive, my fingers clawing the air as though I might take flight. Even as my scream echoed hers I was standing beside her at the head of the stairs.

"Quick," cried Warlock, but he was already too late. I swept her up into my arms and ran down the corridor. The window at the end was sealed with prayers, and although the sharp glass did not touch me, the prayers cut at me till I screamed as I dived through it into the welcoming night, keeping tight hold upon her as we fell safely to the ground.

In a few seconds of flight we were in my only refuge — Jane's home, and safe for the moment in the hall. But now they knew who I had been in life, it would take them only minutes — as it had taken mad Arthur Allen only minutes — to work out where my lair would lie in death. I began to cast about immediately for some sort of weapon which might stand against them. But they gave me no more time. The front door slammed open. Brightness washed over us, dazzling me. I staggered back, stunned. Warlock's voice bellowed the words of a prayer. He and Rebecca's father, each brandishing a length of wood topped by a blazing bundle of oil-soaked rags, advanced into the hall. The men were both festooned with charms and talismans against the power of the Dead. Their words chained me. Warlock had a leather satchel slung across his shoulders. The point of a stake and a mallet protruded from it. Gore's hand moved. Drops of holy water like molten lead rained on my arm, leaving holes in my flesh which smoked.

I turned away and would have raced towards the shadows, but one of them threw a tangle of blackthorn briars which bound my feet and held me. I fell forward, dragging myself across the littered floor to the foot of the dusty stairs. My taloned hands gripped banisters and steps. I began to pull myself up. But Warlock was on me too quickly. He grasped my shoulders and hurled me on to my back.

"Look after Rebecca," he called to the old man. His foot slammed into my belly. "Where is Jane Martin?" he shrieked at me. But I was too far gone in rage even to form words. Screams and hisses and roars bellowed from my throat as though I were some sort of cornered animal.

"Where is she?" he demanded once more. But even had I wished to fling the answer in his face, I could not find the words. For the briefest instant there was black bitterness in me as I wondered, *What sort of creature have I become if I cannot even speak?*

Warlock threw down his torch upon the tiles and lurched forward, his knees crashing into my arms, pinning them. His hands went to the satchel, to the stake and the wooden mallet. He began to pray again as he removed the engines of my final destruction. On the other side of the hall the old man was only just able to restrain his daughter as I summoned her to my aid with all the power I could muster. I was not strong enough to overcome the rituals and spells, or the force of a loving father's arm, but the Dead in me overcame something else.

In the blackest moment of my rage, I heard something moving in the shadows. A shambling step behind Warlock: he did not hear it. A floorboard creaked upstairs. He did not care. He had the stake out now. The head of the mallet was caught in the lining of his bag. Another step behind him in the shadows. Another. The mallet came free. He reared erect, his mouth drowning me in a wild torrent of prayer. Our eyes met, his aflame with fervour and victory. He did not fear my gaze now. The point of the stake rested on my

165

chest. The mallet swung up and back to the full stretch of his arm. His whole body tensed to drive it down . . .

. . . and the right hand of Richard Burke closed upon it, while his left arm, too bloated to bend properly, swung ungainly round the Brother's neck. Dead for weeks, he had yet been summoned to my aid. The faceless horror of his head caught the light for a moment, as his back straightened. It was a haphazard mess of putrid flesh. Then Warlock was lifted from me. Burke's dead muscles began to crush the life out of him. He struck back wildly with the stake. I tried to free my legs but the black thorns sliced my fingers, threatening to entangle them also. I looked around. Rebecca hung fainting in the arms of her father. Both were on their knees, the old man white as candlewax, watching Warlock's grim battle. Rebecca could not help me. And still I could not free myself.

I writhed, screaming in agony and frustration. Then, softly, a hand fell on my shoulder. White bloated fingers comforted me. Jane. She came down another step, her body massively swollen, her gait uneasy, for she could hardly bend her dropsical legs. She moved completely into the light of the torch on the ground. Gore gave a choking sound, dropped his flaming torch, and slumped forward unconscious. And at last Warlock had gained some inkling of what he might be fighting.

His eyes bulged. I could see his mind begin to crumble. He drove his stake in one more time and Burke's dead grip broke. Warlock sprang to his feet and swung to face his adversary. Burke, the stake through his chest, took one last convulsive step and crashed to his knees. As he finally toppled forward, the whole foul semi-liquid ooze which had been contained in the cavern of his skull burst forth and cascaded down upon the priest.

Warlock's reason snapped then. He staggered back, turned and fled, trailing a wild scream behind him. Burke's corpse rested on all-fours for a moment, shaking its empty head as though slightly puzzled, then it slumped slowly to the ground and lay still.

My feet came free. Jane looked up at me out of the blind, crusted sockets of her eyes, then subsided on to her right side. I rose, kicked her unresisting hulk aside, and ran across towards Rebecca. As I approached she began to stir and the movement roused her father. He saw me towering above him, my tall silhouette black as the night. He whimpered and began to crawl backwards, flushed with the red glow of my eyes.

He was beneath my interest. I turned away and raised Rebecca to her feet. This simple gesture was enough to halt the old man's flight. "In God's name," he yelled, imbued with new strength, "in God's name I bid you . . ." He grasped my shoulder, swung me round and waved his silver cross in my face.

But the full power of the Dead was upon me now, as it had been in the moment it overcame the Roman Ritual. My left hand closed even upon that most powerful of talismans and wrenched it from the old man's grasp. "Dear God!" he choked.

His feverish hands found a bottle of holy water. I carelessly knocked it aside. Overcome, he fell to his knees then, and held up before his face the white disc of a communion wafer blessed, no doubt, by the Archbishop himself. "Our Father," mumbled his terror-slackened lips, "which art in Heaven . . ."

Delicately, as any child prophesying love with a flower, I plucked the wafer from his fingers and crushed it into dust.

When I took him by the shoulders, he was actually crying. "No," he pleaded, the depth of his terror making him say it gently, as though to the child of a friend. I lifted him to his feet. There were no more prayers, no more crosses, wafers, garlic, silver or holy water. Only his flesh stood between me and his blood, and that was old, and tired, and very thin.

His daughter stood and watched me while I emptied his body. As his life-force died I turned to her and pressed my lips to hers so that her mouth was filled from my mouth with the last of her father's blood. Then we collected everything in the house that would burn readily, and piled it in the hall. We moved my narrow bed and this journal out into the garden. Finally I hurled her father's still smouldering torch into the pile we had made.

Long before we had reached the vicarage, where I had decided now to make my home, the flames from Jane's house were staining the sky with crimson.

167

STANA'S CHILDREN

Of course, Saturday's local newspapers were full of the fire and the tragic deaths of Miss Jane Martin, Dr. Richard Burke and the Reverend Hugh Gore, together with the mysterious disappearance of Brother John Warlock.

Rebecca had been disturbed early on that morning. She was, naturally enough, distraught at the news, but, no, thank you, she really did not wish a policewoman or any kind neighbour to keep her company. There would be much to do, yes: she would contact her family's legal advisers after Christmas. In the meantime, having given a statement to the police, she would prefer to be alone.

She spent much of the rest of the day fighting off well-wishers and one to two reporters. Late in the afternoon, just as I was rising from my narrow bed in one of the vicarage cellars, I heard her sudden laughter. I found her up in her mother's library, reading the doggerel which was the folk-memory of the words used by Stana to curse the Gore family:

> Women of blood, look to blood,
> Make of blood your bread.
> Feed on blood until your blood
> Feeds the Dead.

There was real joy in her laughter. The curse was worked out at last — but with none of her mother's madness. No horrors touched her now: only the weird joy of eternity. As she stood before me I searched through her mind for traces of sadness but there were none. She had been sufficiently educated in our dark ways for there to be no loss — least of all the death of her father — that could touch her.

The weekend passed in a distant bustle of activity. The whole village seemed to visit her at one time or another, their petty minds brushing the feather-ends of my sleeping consciousness. How was it that none of them suspected anything? The whole community should have been restlessly alert. Deep within me, I found their childlike innocence disturbing. Surely some race-memory, some collective unconscious should have warned them what was in their midst? The unsettling coincidences of the accident at Rebecca's New Year's party, the change in Underhill, the arrival of Warlock, the murder of Theresa Potter and her lover, Underhill's suicide, the change in Jane Martin, the disappearance of Andrew Royle, the deaths of Margaret Allen and her mother, the disappearance of Allen himself, strange doings in the Broken Woods, and now three more deaths. And Brother Warlock still to be accounted for . . . Surely someone must have suspected something?

But no. People today are far too sensible. How much more wise had been their forebears of four centuries ago. They had realised what was happening in their midst. But even Gore, who should have known so much better, had looked upon their ruthless self-defence as ignorance and blasphemy. How willing had been even Underhill, caught in the very middle of it all, to discredit the last strong barriers which superstition might have built. Oh, brave new world that has such sensible people in it.

On Sunday the vicar of Great Dunmow came over to hold services in Gore's church. He told Rebecca how well she looked, considering. In his mind, however, there was the deepest trepidation. She looked so thin and wan, and pale as death.

Ah, but at night, the sickly listless day creature was replaced by my vibrant, joyful companion. Stana's plan continued to work itself out surely and perfectly. We fed on each other's coldness. We used each other, passionlessly but to excess, as her senses died like mine and fulfilment became more and more elusive. The night was a dark shell around us during those haunted hours, as we extended the strength of our flesh and consumed each other, wildly, intemperately, madly. How our desire would have ended I cannot guess, had not tonight brought what it has.

After a day made oppressive even in my deep lair by Christmas and by the endless troupe of sympathisers and well-wishers about the house, I rose exactly on the point of sunset. The last old lady had been ushered away without an offer of tea, and Rebecca sat, dark-eyed, bone white and on

169

the edge of collapse in the quiet, dusty lounge. Her hair was in untidy rat's-tails, her cheeks had collapsed. The skin strained on cheekbones and stretched like tissue over jaw-line. Even her lips were thin and colourless. Then I touched her.

At once she sprang to life. Her eyes were deep and sparkling. A delicate colour suffused her flesh. Her hair became glorious, alive with red highlights. She rose and stretched like a cat. She yawned and suddenly her lips were full, her teeth, pale and sharp as the teeth of a cat, glistened in her coral mouth. The points of her breasts thrust passionately against the black wool of her dress. "Was I asleep?" she asked, her voice deep and vibrant.

"Almost."

"All those old women." She shuddered with the simple luxury of one observing a fate which can never befall her. "And they all say the same thing: so boring. 'How will we exist without the dear vicar?' 'What will we do for comfort.' 'Where will we go now for understanding?' All selfish, concerned only with how his absence upsets them or their little plans!"

Her mouth twisted in contempt. As she spoke of them, so for a moment I could feel them, the whole village, bustling around, each one self-importantly centred on his own little actions. The families of them, mothers, fathers, children, centred on the getting of gifts, on feeding, on drinking. Napier and his family above his butcher's shop, Grant the greengrocer sharing the evening with widowed Mrs. Browne above the papershop, he the more nervous. Pride the haberdasher with his unruly brood. Morris and his family above the farm-supply shop. Seven more in the dining room of the sexton's cottage, and all within a few hundred yards. Nearly a hundred more within the mile south across the village. Potter, recovered from the death of his daughter, is doing extra business at the George because of the notoriety. He has opened specially for the men in from the farms. All of it battered at the edge of my consciousness, stunning me for a moment with the sheer contemptible industry they put into being alive. Like ants teeming about a nest.

Then Rebecca said, "Look at me! I must get out this! Black is all very well for you, but I must have colour. Green! I will never wear anything but green."

170

"Green is bad luck," I said, uneasily. "The faery colour."

"Nonsense," she chided lovingly. "What have we to do with luck?"

After six we ventured out. The streets were quiet. The darkness had long since ceased to be clear crystal blue, and was at the moment thick under a heavy overcast sky. We walked through the village. I watched them hungrily behind bright windows beyond the flames of their Christmas trees. Never had the village seemed so close and vital around me. Any of the hastening little candles of life still abroad on the streets who chanced to brush close to our cold hunters' senses paused, surprised that the darkness should so disturb them on Christmas night, and then hurried on, not looking back. We walked south while I savoured Dunmow Cross like a hundred grains of salt on the back of my long tongue, then, opposite the black shell of Jane's house, we turned and retraced our steps.

It was after seven when we reached the skeletal trees of the Broken Woods. A movement in the shimmering under-growth caught Rebecca's eye. Her hands closed on my hand and I turned. Something was indeed there for a second, and then it was gone. Not a rustle, not a footfall, not a breath.

The woods remained silent about us as we prowled. At last our aimless steps led us to the Dunmow Round. Here too there was stillness, but a stillness tense with expectancy, as though every shadow were a panther set to spring. The pit beckoned to us so we scrambled down its side, the woman leading me. She dropped first into the tunnel and stood silently as I followed. I thought we would go to the chapel but Rebecca turned the other way. "Where does it lead?" she demanded.

When I shrugged she was off at once up a slight slope, past a crest and down again along the narrow twisting passage. I followed her along the dusty flags, brushing away the cob-webs and roots which hung in profusion from the roof. After a few yards the stale air became heavy with a strange smell which I did not recognise until too late, for it was an odour foreign to me now for many, many months. The aroma of cooked meat.

At the end of the tunnel was a huge stone wall, blackened but solid. We paused. I would have turned back, but my

171

companion suddenly threw all of her weight against one side of it, and it slowly began to grate open. "It's a door!" she exclaimed, her voice made guttural with the effort she was making to move it. "Help me. We'll open it!"

The smell of smoke lay on the still air and all at once I knew where the doorway would lead to. "No," I said, and would have turned away, but I was too late.

Rebecca gave a final convulsive heave and the stone swung fully open. Beyond it, was only darkness. Even my eyes could not probe the shadows, and so I paused. Rebecca did not. Her body followed the motion of the great stone door and she was gone into the cellar of Coul Hall, where the Dead had slept her days away in her great stone coffin, and where her children had been staked and piled around the walls.

No sooner had Rebecca and I entered the ash-filled chamber than there was light. I do not know where it came from, for I was too intent upon what it illuminated. More like bundles of wood than ever, the children were still piled round the walls. The heat of their burning had destroyed many, but others, more tightly packed perhaps, had survived — black, shrivelled, ill-formed. In the middle of this chamber Stana stood.

"My Lord, my Lady," she said, almost mockingly, "I bid you welcome. You must not mind my children." She flickered like a tall green star, the glow of her mounting power almost equal now even to the flame of Rebecca's fading life. "My children fear and envy such as you," she continued, gesturing to the roasted horrors piled against the walls. "So do we all. Fear your power and envy your *flesh*."

I thought I saw hatred in her as she said it. Her words flowed on like water. She directed our attention again to the burned corpses of the long-dead children. They looked like bundles of black rags loosely wrapped around twisted sticks of varying length. Some were surmounted by pocked black melon heads. "These of course are of no account now," she persisted. "They are like all good children, to be seen but not heard." I thought there was great sadness, in her voice, but she rounded upon us then so that her voice, had it actually moved on the the air like a human voice born of a muscled and gristled larynx, might have filled the room and echoed.

172

She gestured at our bodies with her unsubstantial, ghostly hand. "But you — " she cried, "you both have homes, castles, a safe refuge. How much more power can you exercise when you do not have to use so much spectral energy simply to *exist*!"

Rebecca had already grown impatient: I had put the blood of the beast into her veins and now it burned to be assuaged. She caught at my arm, turned her back on Stana, and without another word we left the burned-flesh stench of the place and followed the passage back down towards the chapel. Behind us Stana could be heard singing, for her children perhaps, a lullaby of hate.

I took Rebecca's hand in mine and led her in to the underground chapel. Everything in that strange place was as we had left it. We threw our clothing on the altar and there we made our bed.

She fed at my breast blood again, long and languorously, as a prelude to our copulation. When she fell back at last, she had drawn an excess of strength and passion from the night and from such cold blood as she had sucked from me. She was a fury to be ridden, controlled, mastered, in a battle which neither could lose or win, the waging of which was its own object. Tooth and claw we used, shouting our agonies and barren ecstasies. At one time I was master, then she — rising above me like a wild succubus.

But finally, at our last and cruellest coupling, when the most perfect ecstasy was frenziedly, futilely demanded, there had to be a further passage of blood. She lay beneath me, her hair afire with lust, her face — to my strange eyes which could not see water, pocked with perspiration, hollow eyes wild and red. The edge of the altar came across the back of her neck and she threw her head back, laying open to my burning lips the pale column of her throat. What more natural then for me that, as I thrust for the last time, I should lean down to slide my razor fangs into the waiting flesh? And what more natural also, since I had weaned her to it with such infinite care, that she should throw her ecstatic arms about my head to hold it there?

The blackness swirled in my mind as deadened nerves almost brought me to climax. Her cries fled from my ears. The only sensation my body held was the brushing of my needle teeth against the pulsing pipe of her artery. This was enough for me. Then her body allowed her one last shudder of fleshly ecstasy, and the arms behind my neck spasmed as her thighs rose beneath me. Thus, as she cried aloud again, the walls of the artery in her neck were split apart and her life sprang boiling into my mouth.

The ground shook around us. At the moment of her death the earth quaked. Nerves ran from my arched spine to every corner of the land. In that instant when her life throbbed under my lips and was gone I felt the land of Britain spasm and shake with her. *We* have done this, I thought. Our power is such that when she dies the earth quakes.

After a while I raised my head. Realisation of what I had done slowly came to me. Her head rolled to one side, a dead weight now, no longer at her command. How can I describe my feelings? Horror at first. Bitterness. Black rage. And yet what *had* I done? I had completed the final stage of Stana's plan. It was inevitable, after all. In order to join me as my eternal consort, Rebecca had to die. Wearily I climbed down from the altar and began to dress myself.

Then, with equal care I dressed my quiet lady. I gathered her up gently and carried the feather's weight of her out into the passage. A moment later we were back in the Broken Woods. In the centre of the Dunmow Round, my lips on her throat once more healed the wounds my fangs had made. Not even the most thorough autopsy would reveal how she had died now. The darkness cloaked me as I took her home. No one saw the tall black figure with the girl's corpse like a twisted rag across his arms, flitting from shadow to shadow. The church clock struck the half-hour of some small hour as I carried her across the green. I laid her cold corpse down beside her front gate, on the ground where it would be found in the dawn, then I returned to my narrow bed where it lies, here in its small cellar room which no one ever enters. I sat myself down beside it at a massively long oaken table, stored here for numberless years, and took up my pen, and this my journal of the night.

THE PIT

In the dawn when the monster within me is weakest sometimes I say to myself, Edwin Underhill did not die of gas. Jane returned and found him unconscious, his mind utterly destroyed. He is now committed to an institution for the criminally insane. He sits in a corner, semi-comatose, unaware of the passage of days. In his mind, in his mind *only*, his body is a vampire, host to the Dead. He has not risen from the grave and haunted the night. He has never sucked blood. There has been no death for Jane, Burke, Gore, Rebecca, the rest. There was no earthquake in England on Christmas night.

These things are all impossible.

Today as I lay sleeping I saw, as vividly as if I had been standing at the graveside, Rebecca's funeral. There was an air of desolation amongst the little congregation. They were poignantly aware of the tragedy: first mother, then father and daughter, dead like the Allen family. Afterwards, as they trailed away from the silent graveyard, I heard them agreeing sanctimoniously amongst themselves that it had been a terrible year for Dunmow Cross, almost as if some obscure curse were working itself out. Miss Simcox, bulked out against the cold by her best black funeral coat, shook her head as she lingered beside the raw earth mound, thinking of the coroner's courtroom where she had first heard the doggerel curse:

> Women of blood, look to blood,
> Make of blood your bread.
> Feed on blood until your blood
> Feeds the Dead.

Who — what — are the Dead? she wondered, and she looked around at the grey gravestones, as if expecting to see us waiting there to feed on her blood. Then she shivered, thrust her hands deep into her overcoat pockets and walked off laughing. But there was no humour in the laughter.

As the sun finally set, I sprang out of my narrow bed and moved out into the evening. In Jane's garden, undamaged by the fire or the firemen, the black-boughed bush that grew out of the stake stood stark against the scorched wall, its blossoms like great splashes of blood against the brick. I reached out carefully, selecting the stoutest of the branches. It felt cold and firm under my hands. There was power in it, but no bright surge of life, even though it was in full bloom for the second time this year. When I tore the limb away, the sap in the tear-shaped wound on the stem was red and thin.

I took my offering up to the graveyard. All the mourners were gone. Wreaths and bunches of flowers were piled on the bare brown earth. I kicked them away and laid my branch — three feet of it, straight, strong and laden with flowers — along the length of ground under which Rebecca's body lay. I stayed for a moment, eyes closed, head bowed, listening to her as she writhed beneath me and screamed in the coffin, experiencing the first panic moments of her re-birth. Eventually, I knew, she would appear out of a column of mist at the grave's head to be dazzled by the explosive glories of the night. I lingered only a few seconds, then walked away into the busy bustle of the village.

My head was a dizzy swirl of hopes and fears. The greater my emotion, the greater was my fight to hold the Dead still. Have patience, I told it. In a little while we will have a consort, a partner, a mate, and we will go hunting together like grey wolves in the night. We would take the country by the throat, find ourselves slaves to serve us, like Jane, mindlessly in all things. Such passion rose in me that I almost howled out loud. The Dead was like a force too great for my body to contain. I felt that I would explode.

When Rebecca would come to me I did not know, but I knew where she would look for me and I knew I should be there when she did come. I wandered on, slowly retracing my steps. Although she must acclimatise to the night on her own, she would come to me after that. She would come to me as her creator, consort, lover and master. The church reared over me again, the bright clock-face showing some unremembered hour. She would not rise until the streets were empty. I passed the black wrought-iron graveyard fence, looking across the misty ground. Her screams had quietened. I turned away and went towards the Broken Woods. I walked amongst the tall green flames of the trees. Many hours passed. The night drew in, thickening the air. Clouds rolled down from the icy north. A wind moaned. Distantly it bore the sounds of merriment as the creatures of Dunmow Cross wound up towards the celebrations of the New Year. I strolled back towards the vicarage, remembering this last week when I have wandered aimlessly abroad, waiting for the funeral, waiting for Rebecca.

The sky seems never to have varied during these nights — it has been overcast, always threatening rain. If the streets of the towns where I wandered were individually dazzling or dark, the clouds remained always bright. To my sensitive eyes, the dust in each invisible droplet that made up the great misty masses, caught and reflected the light from below, multiplying it until the whole sky always seemed to contain lightning. There was a wind from the north-east, wet and cold as steel, carrying something of the sea over the flat marshes and low banks of East Anglia. This wind, doubly wet with evaporation and the threat of rain, actually attained form, as though it carried a black mist within it beneath the strangely blazing clouds.

This vision remained with me, the sinister dead black fog sweeping towards me. No matter where I was, abroad or in my narrow bed, it came towards me and covered me.

It was with me tonight, as I paced restlessly in the bright hall of the vicarage. My mind strayed outside the walls of the old house, impatient for knowledge of my creature, questing, alone, defenceless. Suddenly a great spear of ice seemed to pierce my head. My hands came like white spiders clutching across my temples. A wall struck me on the back. I fell to my knees, and in my agony, the Dead took over, dragging me upright and unleashing such a fire of rage in me that the spear melted away and the agony in my mind faded. With the beast still in control, I raged through the house looking for the source of this unexpected attack, but there was nothing. Every nerve agonisingly alert, I finally fell back into an armchair downstairs. The wind began to whimper. The villagers' revelry continued in the distance. And in the graveyard something stirred.

As vividly as the spear of ice, a vision of the cemetery rose before me. The mist writhed tidally amongst the grave-stones. A column of darkness rose erect in the centre of the place and stood there, trembling with power. I stood up immediately and crossed to the window, looking down towards the church. The mist was there, black to my eyes, enveloping the tombs and gravestones. The clouds broke open and there was a little moonlight to make the marble monuments glisten coldly. It seemed to me that there were figures moving amongst them. I was suddenly struck with the feeling that I was in fact among the audience when I had thought I was on stage.

I glanced around, my hackles rising. Something was hap-pening down there to which I was not party. Something of great power and moment, about which I knew nothing.

At the centre of this strange shadowy movement rose the column of darkness and even as I watched, it fell away to reveal a pale figure standing in the moonlight. It turned towards me as though aware of my scrutiny, then it stooped, picked something up, and began to come towards the house. It was Rebecca and she walked like a queen. I moved back, unwilling to be seen waiting like an inferior. Emotion swelled in me and the beast stirred. I quietened it with a promise. Soon now, I told it, soon. I passed through the rooms alone for the last time, as I thought. My hearing stretched beyond the closed door, seeking her footsteps, but there was only the wind bearing excited chatter and laughter from the village. I settled at the foot of the stairs, drawing myself up to full height. If she was coming to me as a queen, I would receive her as a king. The waiting was not long.

The latch on the door moved, the tongue grating out of its socket. The hinges groaned. The door swung inwards and she was there, a flame of power before a wall of darkness. I stood silent. She moved forward, the brightness of her magic suddenly flooding the hall.

"Do you not bid me welcome?" she asked, her voice sweet and heavy on my ears.

"You are welcome . . ." I said. It had been in my mind to greet her by name: Rebecca; but something stopped me. The first icy awareness of the truth.

That this was Rebecca's body I had no doubt — the full

red waves of the hair; the pale vibrancy of the flesh; each curve, hollow and length of her described my lover. But the thrust of her teeth distorted her full, soft mouth. The cheeks were collapsed into dark hollows beneath the cheekbones. Something too fundamental had changed in the blood-red pits of her eyes.

"Am I welcome?" she taunted me. "Am I truly welcome, my little man?" She swept towards me, electric with power, burning with cold evil. I staggered back, stunned. She threw up her head and laughed.

"Stana!" I cried. "What have you done?"

She paused before answering, bringing her right hand forward to show me the bough I had laid on Rebecca's grave. As she answered me, she began to tear the flowers from it and scatter them at her feet until she seemed to stand ankle-deep in blood. "I have returned," she said.

The laughter died in her. Even that poor obscene relative of humour, stilled. She became like fire frozen in ice: utterly calm, utterly still, utterly evil. "I have returned that my will may be done."

I still did not comprehend the full madness of her plans, the evil of them. "But what is your will, Stana?"

"Freedom. Freedom and revenge."

"Freedom from what? Revenge upon whom?"

"Freedom! Can you be so stupid, so ignorant of our ways that you *still* do not understand? With this body . . ." Her hand moved, bringing the black stake she carried down against her thigh with a vicious *crack!* "I now have identity. I now have *power*."

"But how can it be?" I cried. "You are mine. I made you. I took you. I moulded you . . ." I stopped, realising that I was talking, not to Stana, but to Rebecca, who was dead. I had not moulded Stana who stood there, clothed in Rebecca's body. She had moulded me.

My mind began to work then, coldly. If I could not have Rebecca, why, then Stana might do to replace her. "Shall we sit down?" I asked her.

She nodded but I thought I saw the slightest of sneers at my lingering human ways. She followed me into the sitting room. She sat at one end of the settee and drew her legs up until she was curled like a cat, leaning against the arm. Her

179

crimson eyes were on mine. She waited for me to start talking. She was like an animal: absolutely still while you were watching her, moving only when you looked away. Power sat on her pale shoulders as easily as the cold silk of her faery-green dress.

"I came to you for help originally, because I am alone," I said. "I needed . . . *need* . . . a partner. A consort."

"Yes?" Without emotion.

"Will you be that partner?"

There had been little emotion in her from the second she came through the door, but now it exploded with terrible force. "You?" she spat. "Consort to you? If you are sufficiently humble, I might allow you to become my body-slave. You are fit for nothing else. Let me tell you something about yourself: I have controlled you, overseen your every thought and action from the moment a few ounces of your blood gave me a measure of release. You have felt your little surge of power and you think yourself a king. You are *nothing*. I am the Dead and you have never been anything but my *creature*."

I sat, stunned, the meaning of her words terribly at odds with everything I had come to believe about myself, about the Dead.

"What is it that you want then, Countess?" I asked at last.

"What I have wanted for centuries, little Edwin. Things you cannot begin to imagine."

But I could imagine. She had told me once herself. The one thing which had kept her in existence through the four hundred eternal years of total nothingness to which this village had condemned her: revenge. The desire for revenge beyond the bounds of reason, beyond the bounds of human imagination.

I sprang erect, my ears listening for the latest sound from the houses near and far around me. It was not yet midnight, yet strangely their revelry had ceased. The wind brought only the sound of its own wailing. In the houses there was utter silence.

She stood up. Her eyes dwelt on me for a moment, mocking and contemptuous, then she turned and crossed the room to the window. She threw it wide before I could move, and was gone into the greedy throat of the night. In a second

180

I was at the window, my eyes searching for her, but seeing nothing. A sense of terrible danger swept over me then. What monsters could she summon? What madness was she about?

In a matter of moments I had raced through the village down as far as the empty shell of Jane Martin's house, more than a mile from the vicarage. All the houses crowding the sides of the road were ablaze with electric light, but over the whole place hung brooding silence which stirred terror deep within me.

The nearest house on my left belonged to the Fullers. Father, mother, two boys and a girl. They always had a large noisy party on New Year's night. All the windows were bright. The door stood wide. Not a whisper, not a movement stirred. I ran through the dull garden and into the Fuller's cramped hall. There had been people here — I could smell them on the air. The lounge was cluttered with decorations. Glasses, tankards, pint-pots stood on the floor and tables, some still half full of liquor. More than one cigarette still burned in the overflowing ashtrays. A half-eaten sandwich lay on a plate. Upstairs and downstairs, the place was deserted.

Across the road at the Harveys' house the television played quietly to an empty room. The settee before it still glowed with the warmth of bodies recently removed. There was a smell of blood like iron on the air, and of something else which made my hackles rise.

Only in the George was there noise. I crept towards it carefully and looked through the windows before I entered. The bar was completely empty: only the juke-box played raucously, giving the illusion that the place was tenanted.

As I moved on through the empty village, my body grew so tense with its strangeness that I jumped at even the mindless whimpering of the wind and hunched forward, ready to spring into the attack at the slightest stirring of the shadows.

In the gutter outside the dark hulk of the Allens' house I saw the faintest point of brightness. My interest engaged, I crouched like a nervous predator on the prowl. It was the silvery brightness I associated with life. Something there was alive or held the memory of life, some tiny animal lying vivid at the dark curb's foot. As I crept towards it I scented once again the iron odour of blood and paused. Silence. Stillness. In the most shadowed part of the street it lay where the circles of brightness from two street-lamps did not quite overlap. The tension in me made my flesh crawl. I rushed out of the darkness to snatch up the bright thing and scuttle away to safety once more. It was a hand.

Curled in my palm, the fingers perfect and closed, the nails gleaming, the knuckles dimpled, still glowing with silvery life was the hand of a small child severed neatly at the wrist. I threw it away with an exclamation of impatience and the sinister shadows gobbled it up.

They closed around me then, those shadows, seeming to teem with evil movement, while I continued to search the deserted streets. As I reached the top of the village and the crossroads themselves, I experienced the deep conviction that if I swung round suddenly, I would find those shadows creeping up behind me in an unstoppable tide of dark evil.

I cannot adequately describe the horrific tension which gripped the whole of my body as I moved up above the green towards the vicarage and the Broken Woods. If the shadows in the village had seemed sinister, here they bred monsters beyond imagining. Nor were they silent any longer. They whispered wickedness and destruction, yet they were utterly impenetrable — there was nothing *living* in them. They pressed about me as I went up past the last houses opposite the green to the church hall, dilapidated and boiling with darkness. I found that I was walking in the middle of the road, far from the whispering hedges. Where was Stana? What was she doing? It required every ounce of the Dead's dark strength within to force my footsteps farther. The strangeness of the night closed around me like bars, and there, beyond the pool of the last street-lamp's shadow-ringed light I froze, caged by terror and the dark.

Then, suddenly, away on my right, came a roar of sound. I swung round. Beyond the first thin trees, beyond church, graveyard and garden, the vicarage was ablaze. For an instant I stood, watching the flames licking up out of the windows, the smoke already rising from the roof. Then I took a step towards it.

And a figure burst out of the hedgerow before me, bellowing with terror, running in a strange crippled manner. I saw the frog-face of Miss Simcox, strangely scarred with claw-marks. I saw the life-brightness of her made more vivid by her fear. I saw the wicked gleam of the carving knife in her right hand as it rose and fell, slashing at the darkness surrounding her.

I leaped backwards. She blindly staggered past me. At first in my fear I thought it was the shadows themselves which were attacking her, but then my mind cleared and I saw — I saw and shrieked aloud that what I saw might not be so.

Hanging all about her were Stana's children. Given a sort of monstrous life by their mistress, the blackened, crippled, all but limbless creatures, which had lately been piled like wood around the cellar walls, had come crawling out through the door Rebecca opened, along the corridor, out of the pit itself, through the shadows to begin the Dead's revenge.

One of these things — a black torso with stick arms but no legs — was fastened in her neck. Another hung like a bat on her stomach. The carving knife came down, cut through its crumbling, cindered flesh, buried itself deeply in the coroner's own belly, and was jerked up again. At her heels, like lizards, two more scuttled. They had arms to the elbow, legs to the knee, yet they kept pace with her on all-fours, their teeth snapping audibly on the air as she stumbled away into the dark woods, screaming and stabbing, screaming and stabbing.

The sight filled me with a great rage, and freed me from the bars of terror that had been caged around me in the dark. I broke away, and ran into the Broken Woods also. Here I crushed much underfoot — whether it was winter-brittle branches or fire-crisped flesh and bone I do not know. Such was the fury in me that I did not care. The village was *mine* — that she should bring her foul lunacy into *my* lair. The blind strength of the Dead within me rose with irresistible passion. By the time I burst into the circular clearing of the Dunmow Round, rage sat on my shoulders like storm clouds and I could feel the lightning of my power crackle away from my dead flesh to present the whole of my head and torso in a bright avenging aura.

183

The ground was a seething mat of the children, heaving like the sea. Here a twisted arm, flesh in black rags on stick-bone, would be thrown up, there a head, bald, earless, gaping pits for eyes and nose, hunter's teeth snapping, white against the cindered face. The stench was sweet, overblown, utterly sickening, and the sight so horrible that it was not until a warm rain touched my face that I looked up and saw what the children had done.

Like the picture on the side of the strange altar in the chapel buried below, there were bodies in the trees. The leafless branches of the trees had been torn back to make strong, sharp points, and on to these had been driven every living soul in Dunmow Cross that night. Through breast, belly, groin, head; through back, through front, from side to side; from shoulder to thigh, from fundament to gaping mouth, every one of them reared up there, impaled, and their blood rained down in misty clouds upon the soft night air.

She stood there, drenched from head to foot, the red blood clotting already and crusting about her. She swung to face me as I kicked aside the twisting offal on the ground. "A pretty harvest," she cried, throwing up her arms in a wide gesture at the trees. "Fruit in midwinter!"

She tilted back her head and laughed. Her hair swung, matted solid with blood. It cracked and flaked away from the ghastly flesh of her throat. It broke in a million wrinkles across the thick red mask on her face. Her beautiful face which was Rebecca's.

"And this is your revenge?" I demanded. "This is why you returned?"

"No!" suddenly her laughter died. "This is only the beginning. I will be revenged upon them all. ALL OF THEM."

So simple. So monstrous. All of them. Not all in Dunmow, or all in Essex, or even all in England. Just *all*: simply that. All who had a body while she did not. All who had a soul while she did not. All who had blood while she had none. All who had tears. All who had dreams. All who were alive, when she was not.

And she would do it, if I should let her. I kicked my way through the last of the circle around her. I held up my left hand. The spider-scar upon it blazed. Stana's hands fell to her sides. Her fingers brushed the top of the black stake from Rebecca's grave, driven into the ground by her legs.

"I cannot allow you to do this," I said.

"You're too late to stop me, Edwin. Far too late!"

She launched herself towards me as she spoke. I whirled aside. Her hooked nails whispered past my throat. She landed in a crouch, snarling. I threw myself towards her as she sprang erect and we met claw to claw, fangs bared, shrieking the purity of our hatred. Her head twisted and she went for my throat. My hands closed around her neck, pushing her back to arm's length, out through the circle to the very edge of the trees. She had expected to overcome me by the inhuman viciousness of her attack, but she had forgotten how well one of her own kind would know her. My fingers closed, sinking into her cold flesh. I could never choke her, of course. Even to break her neck would be insufficient. I would have to tear her head off. And this I was set to do. I felt the bones of her neck beginning to part when the man came stumbling out of the woods beside us, chanting in a voice like thunder.

At first I saw only the febrile brightness of his life-force in the corner of my eye and the blaze of his torch as it flared in the wind. Then his black-clad figure appeared, his eyes blazing with madness. In his right hand he held a great golden cross. "Lighten our darkness we beseech thee, O Lord," he was chanting. "And by Thy great mercy defend us from all perils and dangers of the night."

The sight of what he held so close, and the power of his words, caused me to sicken and turn aside. Stana twisted from my grip. I staggered back. The wild man came towards me, his hair flying. I recognised him then: it was Brother Warlock.

"Run, child, run," he shouted to Stana. In his desperation, blind to everything else around him, he saw only Rebecca's body wrestling with me. And I was the vampire.

He thrust the great gold cross closer, until I felt the flesh around my eyes begin to wither. "I have destroyed you," he screamed at me. "I have found out your lair, found out your coffin, your vile resting place, and burned it! Yes, and burned the whole vicarage around it!"

There was foam on his lips as he returned to his prayers.

"Thou shalt not be afraid for any terror of the night . . ." He was mad now himself, raving, but his words like blows to my head, the cross like fire before my eyes. I fell to my knees and then on to my back, wriggling and hissing. He arched over me, his prayers destroying all my strength, ". . . for the pestilence that walkest in the darkness, for the sickness that destroyeth in the noonday."

A hand brightly jewelled with claws came out of the darkness and fastened in his hair. His head jerked round, and he saw her properly at last: her red eyes, her teeth, the blood coagulated on her dead white flesh. And, beyond her, he saw the villagers arrayed upon the trees and her children creeping below them in the sodden grass. His face froze, eyes staring. One thin blue vein throbbed on his forehead. Of course he had yet another prayer — his last which was no longer his armour, but his epitaph.

"My soul is among lions," he cried, wrenching away. He swung around to face the clearing properly. All the children were still. "I lie among the children of men that are set on fire" he raved, and charged amongst them. I pulled myself to my feet. Stana watched him run amongst the little silent bodies. "Whose teeth are spears and arrows and their tongue a sharp sword . . ."

The Dead in the woman finally tired of the sport. She turned to her children and spoke a single, soundless command. The demented man in the midst of the clearing staggered now as small black hands closed on his leg. "They have laid a net for my feet," he howled, his voice breaking.

One of the children reared up, its little face level with his belt-buckle, its little fingers tearing at his breast. The mass of them heaved around him as more of them slithered up through the tunnel and out of the pit in the ground. More hands caught him, more lipless mouths, more little fingers. His movements slowed.

"They have pressed down my soul." He half turned and threw the cross, his last and only defence, at the woman he had come to save. She caught the thing and laughed. In her laughter there stirred such an excess of evil power that all the woods shook. "They have digged a pit before me," whispered John Warlock, defeated at last, falling to his kness, "and I am fallen in."

186

I was on my feet, stealing back, in among the trees. The children fastened on to the man and carried him silently, like ants, across the clearing. As the trees closed around me, I turned, obsessed with the need to go and check whether he had spoken the truth about my resting place, my narrow bed. But Brother Warlock's shrill scream drew me back, appalled, to the edge of the clearing. He was spread across a tree, higher than all the rest. The children hugged at his limbs, weighting them down as he convulsed in his death throes. Stana stood beneath him, her hands raised. He brayed his agony one last time, beyond prayers, and the point of the branch erupted from his black silk shirt-front. A great fountain of blood pulsed out into the air. And Stana stood beneath this scarlet cascade, and her laughter rang against the sky. The dead man convulsed, heels drumming against the tree, hands flapping, head rolling. I turned and left the Hellish place.

The vicarage was indeed ablaze. I stood before it, deafened by the roar of the flames, all but blinded by their massive light. Great billows of smoke carried sparks like shooting stars, whirling up into the sky, Overcome with frustrated rage, I raised my hands, and immediately wind came from behind me, a great gust of it pushing the hated fire back. What was left of the front door gaped. The hall was burned out, a hollow shell where there were no longer any flames. The wind fell. Smoke poured down again. I raised my hand once more, and once more the wind stirred, more forcefully this time, lifting the flames to the upper floors and blowing the smoke away. If I could trust the wind to remain steady, I might risk a moment or two in the hall, perhaps even in the cellar, to see if Brother Warlock had spoken the truth. My shoulders writhed uneasily at the thought of what would happen to me if I had nowhere to hide from the daylight.

The wind blew constantly from the south. Its strength began to increase slowly. As long as the roof-beams held I might risk a quick rush into the vicarage. I paused for only one moment longer as my friend, the south wind, carried the sparks and flames from the blazing house into the woods at the end of the garden and up into the Broken Woods, setting them instantly afire.

Then I was running forward, up the stone path, under the heavy lintel, into the house itself. Above me, the gallery was gone, and the second storey was a great dazzling cave. I looked for a moment at the roots of the flames which roared like a continuous thunder-roll. Sparks and glowing splinters of wood fell around me, my hands constantly busy brushing them away, the beautiful wooden parquet of the flooring had gone, leaving bare black boards that reached out to a ragged edge, torn away, I guessed when the landing and the stairs collapsed. Below, to one side, beyond the rubble, the cellar was relatively undamaged. Without further thought I ran lightly forward and leaped down. The terrible roaring of the flames was quieter here, the constant deadly rain of sparks less heavy, even the air was clearer. I began to search through the rubble. There were shrivelled planks of wood covered with blackened, blistered varnish — so Brother Warlock had not lied: these, then, were the remains of my coffin . . .

Only the old oak table remained and, beneath it on the stone floor, this book, pen still wedged between its pages as a book mark. I bent to pick it up.

Suddenly a great weight crashed into my back. Talons sank into my flesh, fangs stabbed down through my shoulder, grating on bone. The weight of Stana's body and the power of her leap threw us both forward on to the ground. Something clattered away under the table. Her grip broke as she scrambled vainly after it. I rolled wildly on to my back, caught at her hair. Through the gap in the cellar roof I could see that the wind was faltering. The flames were creeping back down the walls, smoke gushing out through the holes where floor joists had rested.

Then Stana's arm rose across the flames, weighted with a jagged brick. I wrenched my head away as it swung down, but I was not quick enough. The brutal piece of masonry crashed into the side of my face. I felt my cheekbone crack. There was no real pain, as there had been no pain from her fangs or her talons, but I was vividly aware of how such injuries would weaken me. My arms closed around her chest and gripped till her ribs began to crack.

The brick came down again, destroying more of my skull. Ribs split in her breast. We swayed like lovers in an embrace.

Claws flashed towards my eyes. I released her and she sprang away. I leaped to my feet. A great peal of thunder sounded over even the rumble of the flames. A blizzard of sparks whirled in the air. The beams were cracking. The roof was settling. In moments it would crash down upon our heads.

She caught up a smouldering lath of wood from my coffin and charged. I stepped back. My foot caught against a fallen beam on the floor and I fell. She leaped upon me, and the lath of wood plunged through my left shoulder, pinning me to the ground. I writhed wildly. There was pain at last, like boiling lead in my veins. She crouched astride me, twisting her makeshift stake. My collar-bone snapped. My upper ribs began to shatter one by one.

"You brought the wind," she hissed. "You caused the flames to carry to the Broken Woods. *You!* My revenge, my children: for the second time you have put the torch to them!"

Her knees crashed on to my belly. She hunched forward, her weight still fully on the stake which held me all but helpless. I could see that she was crying. Tears of blood wound slowly down her face.

Then her head reared up and her mouth spread wide. Her tears clotted on her icy cheeks and her eyes burned with triumph.

My right hand searched in the smouldering debris beneath the oak table for something to stop her fangs. My fingers brushed a hard edge as she struck. My hand closed, whipped it up in a blurr of speed, and thrust it across her mouth. Her teeth snapped shut like a mantrap, fangs sinking into it. It was the stake. The stake that Stana had taken to the Broken Woods. The stake that she had then brought here and with which she had intended to destroy me. It had been lying where it had fallen when she leapt upon my back.

She reared up, the black wood wedged tightly across her mouth, for the moment helpless. Both hands flew to grasp it, and I rolled free of her, the stub of lath still sticking from my shoulder. She tumbled forwards, fighting to get the stake out of her mouth. I knelt on one knee beside her, caught at it and dragged it from her grasp.

"No!" she screamed, "Edwin . . ."

189

I pointed the sharp end downwards, and brought it down upon her breast with all of my remaining strength. The faery-green silk of the dress ripped open. The white skin puckered and tore. The flesh parted. The ribs caught the point of it for a moment, then reluctantly spread apart, snapping away from the breastbone. Like the finest-pointed stiletto under the massive force of my strength, the long blunt piece of wood slid down into the red cave of her chest, seeking her heart. The blood which filled her body burst out then, and her wild convulsions sent the cold liquid in fountains on to my face. Her throat rattled. Her fingernails, clawing the concrete floor, split away and peeled back. The point of the wood slid past the inside of her shoulderblade beside the twisting column of her spine, and split like her nails on the cement beneath. Her mouth gaped wide, the rag of her tongue escaped her gleaming fangs and flopped obscenely on her cheek. The light in her crimson eyes dulled.

Abruptly by my side stood the twisted shape from Underhill's first nightmare. It had almost no boundaries, almost no will. I was briefly aware of its agony, and then it was gone.

The corpse staked there no longer held anything of Stana Etain, Countess Issyk-Koul. I looked down at her: she was my lady. She was Rebecca Gore, and she might have been lightly sleeeping, were it not for the black stump protruding from her breast. Her right hand lay upon the scorched cover of my journal, and I picked the book up.

How long I would have stood I do not know, but suddenly the roof beams sagged a little further and the blazing wreck of the building settled, showering bright death all around us. A spark or two flamed in Rebecca's perfect hair and Edwin, now strong in me, was revolted at the sight. I used the oaken table as an aid to climbing up out of the cellar with my quiet lady and my book, and then I drew it up after us and carried it all out on to the village green.

But the Dead had not died in me. As soon as I had laid Rebecca on the table, a new thought struck me, and the Dead threw back its head and laughed. "In my beginning is my end," quoted the faint working remnant of my schoolmaster's soul. I caught up a burning branch and carried it to the southernmost end of the village. In a moment that too was aflame. Laughing wildly, and cursing, I lit the outskirts

of the whole village. By the time the church clock told three
o'clock, entry to the village on all fronts was forbidden. Each
road was closed by fire, each pathway and garden was
ablaze.

I staggered back to the village green where it all had
begun, exactly twelve months ago. Rebecca lay on the table,
decorous in her death. The journal lay at her head. Wedged
in it still, its bookmark pen. Now, more than ever before, we,
the Dead and I, have light enough to write by. Idly I flicked
my journal open, and began . . .

Now, when the first ray of sunlight hits this body of mine,
it will turn to dust. But slowly. First the flesh will begin to
boil. Bubbles will rise to burst in gaping craters. I will swell
up, seething, thick with putrid gases. My bones will become
brittle, and long before oblivion comes they will splinter and
collapse. A thing without precise form, I too, like Stana, will
cry then my few burning tears of blood, before the lances of
sunlight shrivel up my eyes within my head. The bones of my
skull will fail. The great round of my brain will tear apart the
thin sac of my face to pour in a stinking mass on to the spongy
remnants of my shoulders.

And I, that part of me which is eternal and will abide,
will be aware of all of this, will watch it taking place, will *feel*
it taking place. And, after that, what horrors will remain?

For the Dead, for the damned, damned Dead, there will be
eternal nothingness. The failure of eyes, of smell, of taste,
touch and hearing. Only thought will remain, to madden, as
Stana was maddened. Thought, and identity.

Identity. I.

Edwin Underhill.

I fear, oh dear God, I fear that I too, like her, will abide. I
am this thing's identity. I will remain that part of the Dead
which knows *who*, if not always what, I am. I will exist beside
it, inside it, as blind and deaf and dumb and damned as it is.
Always.

I am the relentless hunter.

I am the stealer of souls.

I am the bringer of terror in the night.

You will know me when I come for you —

I am the Dead and I will abide.

Yes. I fear that is true, now. I am the Dead and I will

191

abide.

Even as I write these words I can hear it whisper to me.

The fire is dying and there is the first paleness in the sky. Not long. Dawn will come in its own time and catch me mid-thought, mid-sentence.

I can hear the monster whisper to me: Remain king of the night: the spider, the bat, the wolf, the stealer of souls . . .

That way I would become like Stana: utter and absolute evil. And I, Edwin Underhill, would be a part of it. And the choice, even now, dear God, is mine. Such conscience as I, Edwin, have in the dawn, is all the feeling there is left in me. What power will I wield if I hide from the ancient sunlight? The power, ultimately, to spend my eternity observing all feeling's degradation and final death in me.

Or, in anguish, I can cease.

It is so nearly dawn. A few moments more and it is done.

There will be little more remaining of my lady and me than of the place we have destroyed — dust, ashes, a few crumbling bones. Hardly enough to warrant even a modest monument.

How bright the sky is becoming. Through the pall of smoke below it drains the life out of the last low flames in the black house-shells around us. I had forgotten how lovely the sky can be, now at sunrise.

On such a monument as there may be, write this epitaph — I saw it once, in a prayer-book in Rowena Gore's library, and it is fit for such as we:

What profit is there in my blood,
When I

— light, Rebecca. I see day —

must go

— listen! Rebecca, a lark! I believe I hear a lark in song, there, high in the eastern —

OH DEAR GOD IN HEAVEN, GIVE ME STRENGTH.

Down
Go down

TEACHING MIME

TEACHING MIME

ROSE BRUFORD

HON. R.A.M.

**PRINCIPAL OF THE ROSE BRUFORD
TRAINING COLLEGE OF SPEECH AND DRAMA**

London

METHUEN & CO. LTD

11 New Fetter Lane, E.C.4

First published July 31, 1958
Reprinted 1960 and 1964

I·3
CATALOGUE NO. 2/6032/10
© *1958 Rose Bruford*
Printed in Great Britain by
The Camelot Press Ltd
Southampton

CONTENTS

PREFACE AND ACKNOWLEDGEMENTS

I have written this short text-book, hoping it will help the many teachers who have asked me to do so. The book sets out to guide these teachers, and others who want to make a beginning in mime. I hope, however, that they will add and develop their own ideas, using this simply as a starting point, so that their work does not become static and limited.

I would like to acknowledge kind assistance from my colleague, Greta Stevens, who has worked with such meticulous care on the proof reading of this book. Also to express gratitude to Helga Burgess for her advice and help, and to Jay Vernon, whose research has contributed much to the historical section of Chapter X.

I wish also to remember and thank Irene Mawer for her wonderful mime classes from which I learned so much when I was a student, and since then at her inspiring vacation courses, and I must also mention the work of Michel Saint-Denis whose artistry and teaching has always been a source of inspiration to me.

Barbara Lander's musical compositions, which are being published in a separate volume,[1] are an integral part of this book, and students and teachers who know her gift of

[1] *Music for Mime*, Methuen.

improvisation will be grateful, as I am, for her collaboration. Her book provides music for most of the examples needing accompaniment in this book, as well as for several of the Mime Plays in Chapter XIII.

I wish to thank Edith Scorer, and my brother, Lionel Bruford, for their constructive ideas, their kind patience and their continuous encouragement.

I am deeply grateful to Mr A. E. Dean, C.B.E., M.A., (formerly Warden of Goldsmiths' College) for so kindly writing a Foreword for me. During his retirement Mr Dean has given generously of his enthusiasm, his experience, and his great wisdom, and has been of the utmost help in developing the Education Department of the Rose Bruford Training College; I am proud that he is now one of its Governors.

Dr John Masefield, O.M. has specially written a poem to open this book, remembering the day in 1951 when he first visited the College in Lamorbey Park and saw some mime. I am very much aware of the honour he has done me, and thank him for his friendly and untiring help and guidance at all times over a long period of years.

ROSE E. BRUFORD, 1958

FOREWORD

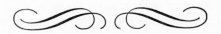

This is a book primarily for teachers and should be of great value, both to specialists and in ordinary classroom work, not only for the copious variety of the suggested practical exercises, but also for the thoughtful theory concentrated on these. It is not an easy book, for it sets its sights high, e.g. in Chapters IV and VIII, and in the last three chapters.

Miss Bruford is herself a fine teacher of great experience, and a fine teacher of teachers. For the last five years I have watched with admiration the gallant work she has been doing at Lamorbey Park, Sidcup. In the prefatory poem written for this book, the Poet Laureate recollects in tranquillity one of his visits to the extremely active training college of Speech and Drama which bears Miss Bruford's name. She has been able to work out a strenuous but well balanced dual course, covering in three years not only a whole range of specialized techniques in speech, mime, acting, production and all aspects of stage work, but also concurrently with this, a well devised scheme of training in class-teaching, comprising educational theory and organization, child development and teaching methods, together with extensive supervised teaching practice in Kent schools. At least half of the thirty or forty students who annually complete their three-year course of training take up full-time teaching posts, some in independent schools, but the majority in secondary and primary schools under Local Authorities. A dozen or more of them are now, to my knowledge, doing valuable work as qualified teachers in the county of Kent.

They have had a thorough, even a gruelling training, fitting them to meet with alacrity some of the recently increased interest in the oral side of English work in schools—in speech training, in spoken verse and prose and in dramatic adventures in classrooms and in school halls.

The basis of this specialist training, in Miss Bruford's view, lies in the thorough teaching of mime; and the potential scope of work in this field, as expounded in challenging detail in her book, will come as a revelation to many teachers. For all children the proper conduct of mime work, at a high standard, can be a source of joy and a lighting up of the imagination; and for some—as Miss Bruford shows—mime can have a therapeutic value, as a spur for retarded or handicapped children or as a lantern for those who have wandered into miry ways. This expert book should help in the good work.

A. E. Dean

Lines for Miss Rose Bruford's Handbook

This is the text-book that the scholars used,
The grammar, lists of words and exercises,
Pondered till struggle into order fused
And skill annulled suspenses with surprises;
These are the clues to joy in many guises
By which the happy learners won the power
To give the saddest heart a jolly hour.

I, who enjoyed the hour, offer praise
To this most patient but rewarding scheme,
By which delight is lured to human ways
Displaying other truth than what may seem,
Bringing the watcher to the land of dream,
Where Wisdom is, and Beauty, with her light,
Blesses, and makes the instant infinite.

This is the text-book: I have seen its fruit,
(Its first fruits) in the England now beginning.
The seed has taken soil and spreaded roots
While England's future still is in the spinning;
What Glory waits, what Laurel for the winning,
Are Youth's to win, as Youth imagine may,
When Hope and ceaseless effort show the way.

To all the unknown scholars who will learn
From these same chapters, let me wish the power
To tread the stony track and not to turn
Until the weariest heart possess its hour.
The barren stock, so long a mock, will flower,
Therefore, endure, for Conquest will ensue,
And England's Spirit waits on what you do.

Therefore, endure, like the heroic those
Who made our England Merry in the past,
Who made Her Symbol once a single Rose,
Though themselves starved in many a bitter blast.
However grim the way, be not aghast,
Endure, for darkness dies, the clouds disperse,
Beyond are Light and all the Universe.

JOHN MASEFIELD

I

THE NATURE OF MIME

Some of this book will deal with Mime as a useful and happy part of the education of children, especially of shy and backward children; another section will deal with it as a necessary part of training for the life of the theatre, in all its many forms.

Whichever aspect of it is our concern, certain fundamentals obtain. Teacher or performer needs not only to be physically prepared but also to be himself creative.

In training children a teacher should seek, with great care, what difficulties hinder and what exercises may reveal and encourage the talent that may be made manifest in the awakened and helped nature.

All the exercises mentioned here are designed to help such discovery. They should not be used, and cannot be helpfully used, without understanding of the purpose for which they have been imagined.

The teacher will have to use his imagination not only in thinking of new examples for mime, but also in such a way that the normal life of the individual is borne in mind and not overlooked. Usually the child of poverty will find great joy in miming richness and plenty, and so for a time experiencing this feeling by:

Being a King or a Princess
Receiving rich presents
Wishing, and the wishes coming true.

The more sheltered child of rich parents finds these suggestions dull, and would respond more readily to:

Being a beggar or a match-seller
Peeling potatoes and shelling peas
Opening a cupboard and finding everything stolen.

The example must be within the range of the child's
knowledge or imagination, and yet not uncomfortably near
to circumstances which are in themselves hard for him to
bear. This was acutely noticeable when teaching at a Borstal
Institution, where girls were allowed to attend classes as a
reward for good behaviour over a certain period; they were
not allowed to have any books, not even a pencil and paper,
so a mime class was exactly the right medium for them; but
if an exercise or example touched their own lives too
closely, it was met with lethargy and black looks, while if
asked to act a film-star or a successful professional woman,
instead of being on the defensive, they would use all their
energies to give a sincere performance.

The work could then be used as a power in the right
direction, not just an outlet into a world of fantasy. Ultimately they achieved some scenes of real beauty, largely concerned with nature; through these they became prepared in
mind to listen to great poetry. Their appreciation of the
classics was instantaneous, though the majority had never
read a poem before.

In working with mentally retarded children, examples also
need careful selection. Much patience is needed. It may be
necessary to sit quietly with a child for a long time. Perhaps
he may play with you at sitting by a fire, or at being in the

rain, or being in a tent, until at last he will have faith in your belief in the act; then he will enjoy and copy and in the end create for himself.

A child who had been entirely unco-operative for two years was one day seen to be moving her hands and arms rhythmically, as if turning a handle, and asked what she was doing, lispingly said "I sewing". These were her first articulate words, and marked the beginning of her general advance.

In normal schools the selection of examples can be more general and cover a wider range, and it will be found that good mime training gives poise and an ease in relationship, especially in adolescence when mime can serve as a legitimate outlet for a pent-up and growing emotional feeling.

The exercises in this book are not meant as systems for the entertainment of school-children, but as a means to a greater grace of life, or to skill in a complex and difficult profession.

Development from mime to utterance of sounds and from these to improvised speech and acting is clearly of value in the development of the whole personality or *person* of either child or adult. Activity is natural. Life is movement. A baby points or reaches to get what it wants; failing in this it utters cries and continues the movement: after this, speech follows. Primitive man's pain or pleasure was probably demonstrated by movement and gesticulation, quickly followed by sounds which were the beginning of speech. There is no doubt that expressive movement is spontaneous and natural; this is immediately apparent in watching animals or children. This is the basis from which we must build.

Watch a child—maybe he is waggling his coat to and fro —and telling you he is a goose flapping his wings; unless

we can see it as such, this is not yet mime, but only imaginative play. Children have infinite ideas, but only outlines of
expression, and often very little power to sustain. Control,
discipline, freedom, and relaxation can be learnt through
quietness and stillness, which are such essential parts of
acting, as well as of life.

Consider scenes like: "Little Miss Muffet" and "Bruce and
the Spider". In both there are moments of dramatic activity,
and moments of absolute quiet; but the quietness the
children will tend to neglect.

The same applies in group work; the rowdiest cowboys
can be encouraged to appreciate that absolute quiet and
stillness is of first importance while they are waiting in
ambush.

Or interest may be roused in Trappist monks who go
about their work without a word; to act this requires clarity
of thought, control, and discipline.

Working together in a group improves social relationships
and gives a great power of understanding as well as a chance
to consider other people and to co-operate with them. Each
individual in the group will consider what it feels like to be
someone altogether different and will experience the feeling
of, and the reason for, other people's reactions.

I believe that a teacher will find it helpful to begin any
classwork, either with children or with young people, by
giving them exercises that will make them feel at ease. To
give them this sense of freedom, nothing can be surer than
an exercise of noise and lively movement:

Let little children imagine themselves to be dogs barking
at each other, or at being chained up.

A moment later, let them imagine themselves to be the
same dogs suddenly released to be petted, fed or taken
for a walk.

Let the older class imagine themselves to be savages dancing and yelling to bring the rain.

A moment later, let them imagine that the rain has come, the heat gone: they are cool and happy, their thirst quenched and they are gathering their food for supper.

These are very simple exercises, and need not last more than a few minutes, but they will give to both young classes a feeling of restraint removed, and of happiness restored.

This mood is a precious mood in which both classes can and will profit from what follows.

II
STAGE FALLS

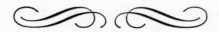

It is helpful to teach stage falls very early in any senior school or young adult course. Little children fall about easily and for fun without hurting themselves. Older children and adults naturally have not the same confidence; an element of fear has crept in, and to fall needs more and more courage as age increases. When, however, the technique is mastered—and after some practice the fall that appeared to be so difficult is really very simple—the achievement and mastery of it give a great feeling of confidence. Once you can safely throw yourself in any direction with abandon no sense of restriction remains.

It is often a help to start with exercises:

> e.g.   Droop the head and shoulders.
> Lift the head and shoulders.

Repeat these several times, gradually increasing the movements through the whole body and out to the extremities.

Probably some will droop nearly to the floor, or even sink down to a kneeling or sitting position; and reach up with the arms on the lifting movement.

> Then—Begin again and this time let sound grow, as the movement increases.

With suitable encouragement from the teacher, even a shy adult will respond, so long as the whole class are working together without onlookers. There may be groans of despair on the downward movement, and shouts of joy on the upward one.

Gradually movement and sound will grow more wild and frenzied and the feeling of freedom from restraint is gained, and from this moment the class progresses more easily and happily.

Even with a class of older men and women, this same feeling can be reached through emotional expression in sound, though the movement must of necessity be less. For them falls would be neither suitable nor advisable.

These simple exercises give the teacher the opportunity to begin to make the class aware of the difference between tension and relaxation: a greater consciousness of the full meaning of relaxation must of course be gained later.

Now the stage fall can be attempted, but it is important to have patience and avoid trying to do too much at once. Here follows a description of the process which should cover some weeks of work:

Technical Falls

In principle all falls are the same. The procedure is to kneel, to sit and to lie.

SIDE FALL

If falling to the right, kneel on the right knee, sit over it to the right, swing the arms in a sweeping movement from left to right brushing the floor all the way, and simultaneously lie to the right, with the arms extended to the right, dropping the head so that it is supported on the right arm. At the finish, the body will be outstretched to the right in a long line, arms extended, left leg extended, right knee bent and tucked under left leg.

It is important that the hands and arms sweep round silently to their destination and do not flop to the ground from above, which is noisy.

If the legs are not relaxed they will be inclined to kick up, which they should not do.

If falling to the left the instructions are reversed—kneel on the left knee, sit to the left, lie to the left, arms move from right to left.

BACK FALL

Kneel backwards allowing the foot to cross the line of the body, so that there is room to sit backwards over the kneeling leg (without sitting on the foot); sit backwards; then lie backwards allowing the arms to sweep along the ground on either side until they are nearly overhead. Again it is important that they brush the ground, rather than flop noisily. One knee is bent and tucked under the other leg at the completion of the fall. This should be practised, using either leg for the kneel.

FRONT FALL

Kneel forward on the right knee (keeping the weight on the left leg until the last moment, to avoid bumping forward on the knee). Bring the seat round to the right, and sit as far forward as possible. Sweep the arms round from left until they are extended forwards; lie forwards letting the head drop on the extended arms. Again the hands and arms brush the ground, rather than dropping from above. As before, this should be practised using either leg for the kneel, the directions being adapted accordingly.

In all these falls it is essential to practise slowly and accurately. The temptation to hurry will lead to leaving out either the kneeling or sitting stage, and the fall will never be easy. By degrees speed up, and relax more and more, so that the fall seems like one movement. The aim should be to fall almost silently, like a leaf rustling to the ground. When the technique is understood, the secret of a silent fall is to breathe in and lift on to the toes, also to lift the arms upwards *before* falling. It is almost a drift upwards, giving an impetus to the fall; a preparation for it—rather like a breath before speaking, or a preliminary movement before a tennis stroke. The fall and breathing out must follow the lift without pause.

COLLAPSING FALL

Do not try this until after the others have been thoroughly practised, otherwise it becomes a temptation to use the collapse for every type of fall, and the basic technique is never really mastered. Once relaxation has been fully grasped and practised, the collapsing fall is comparatively easy, but it is essential to have experience in relaxation to be successful with this fall.

Allow the head to droop, the shoulders to droop, and the knees to sag until they are nearly in a kneeling position; in fact, loosen every muscle until real relaxation is achieved, which means that everything crumples, and you gently fall to the ground in a heap, completely relaxed. In this fall the impetus of the drift upwards as used in the other falls would not be of any help. It is possible to vary falls for all purposes, and ultimately no kind of fall should present difficulty.

Dramatic Falls

The basic technique for stage falls given above, must be mastered before there is any attempt to do a fall with dramatic intention. Eventually, as with all other aspects of mime, having a reason for the movement makes it more convincing, as well as being easier to do.

e.g.   Right Fall as if jostled in a crowd.

Left Fall during a boxing match.

Forward Fall (using right leg to kneel) after having tripped.

Forward Fall (using left leg to kneel) after having been shot.

Backward Fall (using right leg to kneel) after a punch on the jaw.

Backward Fall (using left leg to kneel) trying to recoil from someone who is attacking.

Collapsing Fall as if fainting.

Any fall you like conveying that you have taken poison. Finish by rolling over on the ground as if you are in agony.

The drift upwards would now seem out of place and unnatural. In most cases, however, the same impetus of the lift can be used, but used dramatically, e.g. a spasm of pain, which would cause a moment of tension before relaxing into the fall.

III

EXPRESSIVE EXERCISE

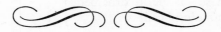

The body will be physically expressive only if it is able to be immediately responsive to any demand. This cannot be so unless it is well trained, well poised, and in tune.

Some good movement training is an essential part of good mime, but whatever the technique it must become habitual, so that in expressive work the technique is unconsciously used without having to be consciously considered. The type of exercise used will depend to some extent on the age of the class, the reason for the class, and the kind of children or students in the class.

Broadly speaking it would be safe to say that the younger child is so supple that exercises are seldom necessary. Rhythmical movements with some imaginative significance will do all that is needed in the way of bodily preparation.

Examples of Imaginative Physical Practice for Young Children

Mime skipping
Be a kangaroo
Be a frog in a marsh
Walk like a tortoise
Walk like a cat
Be a Jack-in-the-box in action

} These give a variety of movements for feet and legs

Show the neck and head of a giraffe
Show an ostrich looking about, and
   then hiding his head in the sand
Be a puppet on strings
Show a bird pecking for crumbs
Show a fledgeling in a nest putting
   up its beak for food
Be a Chinese Mandarin ornament
   with a nodding head

> These are largely for head movement, but the whole physique can be employed as well

Be a rubber toy—flabby at first—
   someone blows air into you—you
   are nearly bursting—then the
   cork is removed and you collapse
Be a worm
Be a seal
Be a brightly burning candle—
   gradually you flicker—and finally
   gutter away
Be a corkscrew
Be a golliwog; you are playing—
   you lose some stuffing—someone mends you again

> Mainly movements of the torso giving flexibility and freedom

Play with a ball
Wash some clothes, putting on an
   apron to do so
Wash your face and hands
Do some clay-modelling. Show
   what you are making
Be a butterfly
Be a dragon-fly
Hover like a hawk

> Mainly for use of hands and arms

As children grow older they seem to enjoy the security of some basic technique and feel happier if they have it.

Very few exercises would be needed in free mime or ordinary classroom work, as the purpose is not performance. Many teachers will find they can devise the exercises they need for this, and will prefer to do so in order that they may link them with the work being done in physical education. It is, however, important that any exercises given should lead to dramatic movement, so that the expressive work grows naturally from the exercise.

Examples

Appropriate shoulder action (swinging in various directions) might precede the occupational movement of *felling a tree*.
Waist turning might precede the movement of *scything*.
Stretching downwards and upwards of the body might precede the action of *flying a kite*.
Flexibility of the joints and muscles of the foot might be practised before *walking stealthily round a house*.
Rippling movements through the body and arms and hands might be practised before expressing movements *of fire and water*.

For those who know it, Greek dance would provide good basic movement, and so would the best form of modern dance.

For the artist in mime (just as for the ballet dancer) some technique must be learned and practised, or the work will never have 'finish'.[1]

All dramatic movement starts in the centre of the body: this is the seat of the emotions. It is advisable therefore to arrange exercises and expressive practice working from the

[1] For this type of student the exercises listed in Irene Mawer's book *The Art of Mime* are in my opinion the most satisfactory, and should be constantly practised, and linked with expressive work.

torso out to the extremities making a sequence named from the human frame in this order:

1. The torso, the main structure directing.
2. The feet and legs, that give the base.
3. The head and neck, that show the poise.
4. The arms and hands, that work.

Think to yourself what these four can show in mime and imagine how each 'age-group' may exercise and use each one.

Please remember that I only offer suggestions that may help you to invent others, not intending them to be slavishly followed. The teacher of mime needs a constant flow of creative ideas.

Age-groups have been classified as:

Infant
Junior
Senior
Adult

These are used in a broad sense, not rigidly representing the age-groups as recognized in the maintained schools of the country. Always remember that much of the work suggested can be done by any age-group. Some little children have unexpected gifts for mime: age has little to do with aptitude. In one school, I so arranged the classes that each included every age from 8 to 18, mixed together. It worked very well indeed, and the children welcomed the arrangement. Here follows a list of

Examples of Expressive Work

for each of the four body-parts, for all ages. The examples are designed to give a wide range of expression in each division.

INFANTS

Little ones will naturally be unaware which part of the body is being employed and why, but it is well that the teacher should know.

TORSO

Response   Feel hot
Feel cold
Sit in a pool at the sea-side
Play in the sand
Play in a hay-field

Clothes   Put on an imaginary dress—take it off—hang it up, or do what you like with it
Do similar actions with an overall, a jumper, a mackintosh, etc.

Character   Be: A lively puppy
A cart-horse
A baby
One of the Three Bears
One of your dolls
A bad goblin that becomes good
A mermaid
A flower-seller
A grocer—stooping under the counter and reaching up to the shelves
A dustman

FEET AND LEGS

Response   Walk: On soft sand without shoes
On wet sand without shoes
In pools at the sea without shoes
In puddles with shoes on

> On pavement, in the squares with
> shoes on
> Up steps

Clothes   Put on and take off shoes and socks for different
reasons, describe where you are going, etc.

Character   Be: A naughty elf in a wood
A good fairy
A dragon who hates everyone. (The three
can then work together.)
Little Red Riding Hood setting out
Little Red Riding Hood going through
the wood
Little Red Riding Hood going up to
Granny's door, etc.
Jack and Jill
Jack and the Beanstalk
Other fairy tale or nursery rhyme
characters

HEAD AND NECK

Response   Go to sleep
Wake up in the morning
Eat something nice
Eat something nasty
See a bird's nest in a tree
See a fish in a pool
Look into a wood and go and play with some-
one or something you see there

Clothes   Put on mother's hat $\left.\begin{array}{l}\text{Put on mother's hat}\\\text{Put on a sun-bonnet}\\\text{Put on a witch's hat}\\\text{Put on a fairy crown}\end{array}\right\}$ In each case become
the owner of the head-
gear

Character Be: A bird
A goose
A prince
Punch
Judy
Cinderella
Hansel and Gretel. Find the sugar house
and eat it

HANDS AND ARMS

Response Have cold hands—touch ice
Have fairy hands—touch gossamer
Touch a bird
Put hands in hot water
Hold a wriggly baby fish

Clothes Put on woolly gloves
Put on gloves and find a hole in the finger
Show the feeling in your hand when the gloves
are removed
Put on magic gloves. What do they do?

Occupation Pick flowers
Pick and blow a dandelion clock
Make sand pies
Draw and crayon a picture
Play with trains
Play with any toy

Character Be: The little match girl
A Djinn
A cobbler
A 'bus conductor
A witch making spells

THE WHOLE

Go for an imaginary walk across fields in the country, come to a stream, cross a plank, or stepping stones, paddle across; then come to a wood.

(Let the children continue as they like eventually arriving home again.)

*

Go into the fields and pick flowers and do what you like with them—making daisy-chains—giving them away—taking them home and putting them in water, etc.

*

Go for a day to the sea, get into the train, see the sea, go on to the beach, dig, paddle, have lunch, etc., etc., and finally go home.

*

Be a group of elves who make all sorts of magic shoes, give them to someone and show their magic by the effect they have.

*

This sort of practice can be done individually or in a group. Teachers are sometimes tempted to 'talk down' to the children, which makes the whole idea puerile. By all means use the the question and answer method, but let the voice remain natural and genuine, meeting the children as individuals, exciting their imagination, and adopting their ideas. Working in a community in this way, the children gradually learn to understand themselves better. By degrees simple scenes will develop, which can be mimed very informally, with some children being a group of trees or flowers or whatever background may be needed, so that everyone takes part. At this age there should be no audience, and it should not be regarded as serious acting, but as play.

In the same way stories and songs can be brought to life by the children, but they must be encouraged to develop their own ideas and not on any account to reproduce an imitation of movements made by the teacher, which will be quite meaningless to the child, and serve no useful purpose.

JUNIORS

TORSO

Response   Lie in bracken
A bucket of cold water is thrown over you
Someone is tickling you
You are pulled by a dog on a lead
Walk against a strong wind

Feelings   You are going to a party
You are not able to go after all
See someone crying
Listen to a funny story

Clothes   Imagine you are wearing best clothes
Imagine you are wearing a swim-suit
Imagine you are wearing a dancing-tunic

Character   Be: A coalman
A policeman
A typist   Contrast
A Red Indian   downward
A dwarf   and upwards
A Prince who is changed movements
into a frog and then freed
again

c

FEET AND LEGS

Response   Kick through fallen leaves, wearing shoes
Step over tree trunks, and walk along a fallen trunk, wearing shoes
Walk on rocks, without shoes
Walk on grass which is full of prickles, without shoes

Feelings   Walk: As if you are away on your holidays
As if you are going to see your grandmother
As if you have been told to go for a walk and don't want to
As if you are going to school
As if you are going shopping

Clothes   Wear: A pair of boots
Dancing shoes
No shoes
Walking shoes
Wellington boots
Bedroom slippers

Character Be: A giant in seven-league boots
A witch
A tight-rope walker
A highwayman

HEAD AND NECK

Response   Try to see something that is just too high for you
Feel too hot
Bump your head unexpectedly
Find you have sand in your mouth

Feelings   Show: You are very bored—show what it is
                     that is boring you
                     You look mischievous   ⎫ You
                     You are looking very guilty   ⎪ must
                     You are convulsed with laugh-   ⎬ know
                     ter   ⎭ why

Clothes   Wear: A mackintosh hat
                     A paper hat from a cracker
                     A cowboy's hat
                     A crown
                     A dunce's hat

Eye Focus   Look at: An ant-heap
                        A tall tower
                        A train
                        A worm
                        A ship leaving the quay

Character   Be: An old lady
                   Rumpelstiltskin
                   A dressmaker
                   A naughty child
                   A clown

HANDS AND ARMS

Response   Let dry sand run through your fingers
               Prick your finger
               Handle plasticine
               Show sticky fingers

Feelings   Show sleepy hands
               Show agitated hands
               Show idle hands

Clothes	Put on and take off fur gloves without separated fingers
	Show the difference between your best gloves and your oldest gloves
	Put a bandage on one finger
	Put a plaster on one finger
Occupation	Dig a sand castle
	Sew a seam
	Throw and catch a ball
	Paint a picture
Gestures	Express in any way you like:
	"Look up there"
	"Come here"
	"Go away"
	"I hate you"
Character	Be: A shopkeeper—packing up goods—taking money, etc.
	Peter Pan—trying to sew on his shadow.
	Alice in Wonderland—doing anything you like
	A shepherd—tending his sheep

THE WHOLE

Feel that you are a gas-filled balloon—you are anchored to the ground—suddenly the rope snaps, you sail away and away for miles. While you are gaily sailing along, a bird pecks you—the gas escapes—you collapse and fall to the ground.

*

Hold a wish-bone with a friend—make a wish—as you snap the bone your wish comes true—show what you wished for.

*

You are sitting on the top of a high cliff—at the edge of an immense hole—it is known as the Witch's Cauldron—the sea is coming in at high tide. You have been watching it with fascination, and now it is time to go home. Just as you are leaving you see an extra big wave fill the cauldron—it looks as if something is rising in the middle of the whirlpool—you have a strange feeling about it. Something happens—show what it is.

*

You are sitting by a window—it is summer and it has been a still day, but a gentle wind is beginning to move the trailing honeysuckle at the window. Idly you reach to touch it, but it is wafted away by the wind. Each time you reach, it blows further away, as if some magic in the wind were carrying it. You are determined to catch it and jump to do so—as it breaks off in your hand—something unexpected happens—show what it is.

*

Now let the teacher divide the class into four groups. Each group can be responsible for one of the four seasons, and decide for themselves how to show them—e.g. plant-life, bird-life, farm-life, reaction of humans to the elements, etc.

There can be infinite variety in this exercise and room for development into a play.

SENIORS

TORSO

Sensation Enjoy the wind on your body
Enjoy the sun on your body
Lie under a tree—a caterpillar falls on you

Be nearly asleep—you are worried by a wasp
Go into a very cold sea
Writhe in agony

Emotion   Show: Disappointment (failing an exam)
Delight (going abroad for the first time)
Fear (sleeping in a haunted room)
Envy (someone else's success)

(The suggested reasons are to ensure that emotions are not superficially imposed without reason. It is all too easy to do this, which leads to posing and falsity of expression.)

Show: Joy
Sorrow   (Let the reason first
Sympathy   be thought of by the
Amusement, etc   individual)

Costume   Wear: A smart afternoon dress
A sun-suit
A winter coat
A pair of shorts
A tennis dress

Character   Be: A sailor
A hunchback
A ring-master of a circus
A savage

FEET AND LEGS

Sensation   Walk: On heather wearing shoes
On mud wearing suitable shoes
On mud wearing unsuitable shoes
On pebbles without shoes
On springy turf without shoes
Through a mountain stream

Emotion   Show: Pleasure
                     Hesitation
                     Determination
                     Stealth

(Again it is important that the reason for the feeling is thought out by the individual or it will never ring true)

Costume   Wear: Shoes that are too large
                   Shoes that are too small
                   Skates
                   Fisherman's boots

Character   Be: An athlete
                 A burglar
                 An Eastern man or woman
                 A 'bus conductor on his 'bus

HEAD AND NECK

Sensation   Feel water trickling down your neck in the rain
               Show your reaction when something hits you on the head
               Feel an irritation
               Show that you have a headache

Emotion   Show: Shyness
                   Curiosity
                   Certainty
                   Enjoyment

(Develop reasons why)

Costume   Wear: A smart hat
                 A sou'wester
                 A bathing cap
            Tie a scarf round your head

Eye-Focus   Look at the stars
                Look at the horizon
                Look at a picture

Look in a shop window
Watch a jet aeroplane
Watch sea breaking under a cliff
Search in the sand for something you have lost

Character   Be: A Spanish lady
A Hockey International
An artist
A prim lady of 65
A gipsy

HANDS AND ARMS

Sensation   Trail your hand in the water from a boat
Mistakenly put your hand in a pot of jam
Mix flour
Pick roses with many thorns

Emotion   Show: Angry hands
Frightened hands
Imperious hands

Costume   Try to put on gloves that are too small
Wear: Gloves that are too long in the fingers
Fur-lined gloves
Silk gloves

Occupation Show: Knitting
Scrubbing a table
Hammering in a nail
Peeling and eating a banana
Peeling an orange

Gestures   Express in any way you like:
"You dare!"
"No, I won't"
"Please come with me"
"Help! I am lost"

Character   Be: A weight-lifter
             A dentist
             A draper's assistant
             A student
             A hairdresser

THE WHOLE

You are in a garden—show that a stream runs through it, that there is a high wall on one side of it, and that you can look across a valley below you to a mountain range. Live in that garden and, as well as showing the scene, convey the atmosphere.

*

Show that you are in a busy street crowded with shoppers; you are anxious to see what is in the shop windows. Show what you see and whether or not it pleases you. Finally, come across something you have been wanting for years—decide whether or not you will buy it—show what it is like.

*

Show that you are walking up a wooded glen following the river—you are surprised to find that it ends in a waterfall which cannot be passed, and which covers you with spray—you take pleasure in watching the salmon leaping to the upper reaches of the river.

*

Show that you are lying on the rocks near a lagoon in the South Pacific—the sun is beating down and you are enjoying relaxing in the water—or in your little boat moored to the rocks nearby—suddenly there is a cry from your companions of "Sharks!"

*

Show the way people move at different periods of their life—try to show what you imagine you felt like when you were just learning to walk and movement was rather perilous and uncertain—then show the same child firmly established in life at the age of seven—again aged fourteen, twenty-one, forty, fifty-five, seventy, ninety; or whatever ages you like to select. (The young will always fall into the trap of making fifty quite decrepit, and have nothing left for what comes after!)

Develop further by thinking of different types of people in each age-group; how do they feel, and therefore how do they move? (The reason for their mode of movement is all-important, otherwise the average student will develop a *facility* in expression which can be entirely superficial, and will never be convincing to any spectator.)

*

You are in a forest in a foreign country. A group of you set out to cross it, not knowing what you may meet. Show your adventures—crossing deep water—avoiding wild creatures—watching birds drinking at a pool—finally you reach habitation, and are glad of shelter. Night falls, your voices are heard round your camp fire, and the distant sounds of the forest die away.

(In this sort of scene some noise would be permissible, and some members of the class might be mainly responsible for it.)

*

A group sets out on a journey—show the excited anticipation, the catching of the train, the arrival,—then boarding the boat—the movement of the boat,—it pitches and tosses —there is a storm—you are wrecked. Show your adventures after that, and a final safe return.

OR

—the ending of the journey as originally planned and a safe return.

*

(Perhaps only one or two characters may begin a scene but gradually all members of a class will find themselves contributing to it.)

ADULT

TORSO

Sensation   Take a cold shower
Battle with a hailstorm
Lie in hot sun
Lie in gentle rain
Show you are being lashed with whips
Show you are at sea
Be a Spirit in torment (as in Dante's *Inferno*)

Emotion   Show: Despair—having lost your job and having no money
Confidence—having just left College
Anxiety—watching someone who is ill
Ecstasy—you are just engaged to be married

(Repeat all these—thinking of different reasons for the same feeling.)

Costume   Wear: A fur cape
Slacks
A long evening dress
A cloak
A sari
A Roman toga

Character   Be: A beggar
              A butler
              A matron of a hospital
              A slave
              A 'spiv'
              A street performer

FEET AND LEGS

Sensation   Walk over barnacles, without shoes
              Walk on hot asphalt, without shoes
              Walk in the sea—knee deep
              Try to get out of a bog—wearing shoes
              Walk in deep snow—wearing shoes
              Walk on heather—wearing shoes
              Walk over gravel—dressed for a dance
              Stand in the Underground after a day's work

Emotion   Show: Sadness   ⎫
                  Eagerness   ⎬ (Think of reasons first)
                  Doubt   ⎮
                  Jubilance   ⎭

Costume   Wear: Heavy boots
                  Sandals
                  Sandals with a buckle off
                  High heels
                  Sloppy shoes

Character   Be: A farmer
                  A thief
                  A dancer
                  A scrubber
                  A mannequin

HEAD AND NECK

Sensation   Show: Giddiness
                Drunkenness
         Avoid something that is going to hit you
         Carry a heavy basket of fruit on your head

Emotion   Show: Sorrow
                Freedom
                Pride   }(Develop reasons)
                Tolerance

Costume   Wear: A modern hat
               A picture hat
               A nun's habit
               A pierrot's conical hat
               A crash helmet

Eye Focus Watch: Clouds
                A snail
                Birds
                A tennis match
                A frog jumping
         Look for a book in a bookcase
         Look in a mirror

Character Be: A blind man
              A jester
              A general
              A short-sighted old gentleman
              Comus
              A Puritan lady
              Mephistopheles

HANDS AND ARMS

Sensation   Touch fur
            Touch muslin

Touch satin
Handle wood
Feel and find a secret panel in the drawer of
an old desk
Cut your finger
Put your hand on a jelly-fish
Receive an electric shock

Emotion   Show: Terror
             Menace   (Show your reasons for
             Gentleness   them)
             Exultation

Costume   Wear: Mittens
              Tight kid gloves
              Surgical gloves
              Gardening gloves
              Long gloves

Occupation   Saw wood
              Fish, in a river
              Prepare and cook potatoes
              Use a sewing machine
              Write a letter
              Go shrimping

Gestures   Express in any way you like:
              "Bring that here"
              "You naughty dog"
              "I love you"
              "Look, thirty elephants are coming down
the road"
              "I dress beautifully when I am going to
play the fiddle"

Character   Be: A sculptor
                    A household help
                    A lady of leisure
                    A porter
                    A bar attendant
                    A musician
                    An actress
                    A tramp

THE WHOLE

You are sitting in a cell in solitary confinement; you have been there for a very long time and are accustomed to silence—your mood is of despair. You hear a distant knocking—tension and excitement grow in you as you listen—it fades—you decide it was only a figment of your imagination.

*

Repeat the same scene—but the knocking is real—it is a signal which has to be passed on from cell to cell—you have been waiting for it—eagerly you join in the knocking and pass on the message.

*

Repeat the scene again—but this time the sound brings escape—you stagger out into the open dazed by the light and by the sight of the world beyond—react to it.

*

You are sight-seeing, visiting a beautiful castle—you look at all the antiques, pictures, suits of armour, etc.—then you come into a room full of mirrors and catch sight of yourself —you alter your posture and way of walking, again you catch a glimpse of yourself on the other side of the room, and find again that you do not walk as you thought you did! You forget yourself, and return to the magnificence of the room you are in.

*

Repeat this scene as someone else, who has different reactions from yours, and will therefore respond differently.

*

You are a fisherwoman gathering sea-weed on the shore, it is a sunny day, life around you is active, boats are putting out, the older men are mending the nets—you say good-bye to the men-folk who go out for their day's fishing.

*

You are the same woman but on a very different day. The sky is overcast and high seas are running. You are working in your house, but anxiety takes you out to the cliff-top to look for the boats. End the scene as you like.

*

Sometimes it will be noticeable that a performance is unconvincing, but the reason may not be apparent. It will then be useful to the teacher to be able to analyse the expressive power of each part of the body. He may well find that although the mood is expressed in face or body, the feet and legs are not in keeping with the rest. This frequently happens with beginners. Each individual will of course have his own particular weakness, but the power of the various parts having been established, they must finally be blended into a harmonious whole.

Consider for a moment the power of the hands alone.

Say to the class:
Put your hands out in front of you and look at them. The

use of your hands is very revealing and shows quite a lot about you. Imagine they are going to be photographed, and consider if you looked at such a photograph whether you would recognize the person to whom they belong. Hold them again in front of you. Without rushing, change from one feeling to another:

Examples

Juniors	Seniors	Adults
Strong hands	Greedy hands	Avaricious hands
Gentle hands	Kind hands	Be-ringed hands
Fierce hands	Cruel hands	Sorrowful hands
Flabby hands	Useless hands	Luxury-loving hands
Magic hands	Useful hands	Uncertain hands
Nervous hands	Angry hands	Artistic hands
Pleading hands	Frightened hands	Determined hands

(Do not trouble infants with such detailed work as this.)

*

When these expressions have been established in the hands, it is a useful practice gradually to add the other parts of the body, and ultimately from the feeling aroused, to build a whole character.

Example

Greedy Hands—add a greedy face, and the sort of body that goes with it—feel it in arms, neck, and shoulders; now add the legs and feet, and begin to move about—Do an occupation—Show where you are, and where you are going —whether anyone is with you, and whether or not you are happy—if not, what is your mood and intention?

Gradually in this way, the character will grow to be some-one you can believe in, provided you fill out all the real thoughts and feelings of the person, and don't leave only a

D

shell that is simply an outward appearance, with no motive force of spirit.

Having practised this, you will find that any of the examples listed for hands could equally well be used for feet, body, head, etc. Try some of them starting with another part, and gradually add the rest, perhaps bringing the hands in last.

All this will increase your awareness of the capacity of each separate part of your body and remind you that ultimately you must be a *whole*.

*

All the examples listed in this chapter are carefully selected so that there is scope for the particular part that is being practised. It is advisable to remind yourself of the heading all the time you are practising, so that the best use is made of the particular examples. Otherwise it is all too easy to treat *all* examples as free expression, forgetting the need to find your ability with each part first.

It is quite a good plan at frequent intervals to revert to a natural walk round the room without any thought of characterization. The practice and analysis will have given some freedom, new confidence, and poise.

Exercises—like vain repetition of prayer—will not in themselves be any use. It is the way they are done that matters. They need great concentration always, and there should be some improvement and greater freedom and finish each time they are performed. As with other Arts— ninety per cent of the students seem to think that running through the practice at great speed will have a magical effect, and having performed this ritual, they are surprised that their work is no better.

For any art, concentration and regularity of practice are needed; the true artist knows this, and brings all his energy and his being into his work. Only then can there be real results.

There is considerable talent to be found everywhere; there are numbers of people who can arrive at quite good standards by sheer hard work and tenacity of purpose. Alas, only very rarely is there a blend of real gift with complete concentration and persistent hard work. When this is found the result is inspired brilliance.

IV

RELAXATION

It may seem strange that I have not talked much of relaxation until this point, as it is so fundamental a part of all movement.

I have found, however, that classes are more able to grasp the full significance of relaxation and to make use of it, after they have done some spontaneous expressive work. Then they find that, if relaxed, they can do everything much more easily.

Unless there is this incentive, and understanding of the need for relaxation, there is a tendency for the young to turn from it, since activity is so much more natural to them. A simple way to illustrate the necessity for relaxation is to refer back to the stage fall, which will obviously be more effectively performed if it is completely relaxed.

The processes described here cannot all be achieved in one or two lessons; they will cover some weeks of work. The development will often be very slow, but always worth while. Strength of movement grows from relaxation, and in beauty of movement relaxation is always apparent.

The mind governs bodily movement: but if the body is really deeply relaxed, relaxation of mind usually follows. It is not easy for the average person to go through the necessary processes to achieve this state. The harder he tries the less he can relax; it is contrary to all other learning to be asked not to try, but instead to allow the muscles to be at rest, and in fact to loosen the reins of control. Also, the more he is in need of relaxation, the less he will want to discipline himself to achieve it, and relaxation does require self-discipline.

Often, rather than relaxing, people seem to find it easier to remain in a state of nervous tension and irritability.

In learning to relax, it is necessary first to appreciate the weight of each limb when it is not moved by muscular activity.

Lie flat on the back, feeling as if your limbs are heavy as lead. Let someone lift your hand or arm. The natural instinct is always to help by lifting it yourself. Avoid this—leave it as if without life. Then the limb will fall heavily and limply to the ground, without a moment's hesitation in the air; (any hesitation would be a sign of tension). Each of the limbs can be tested in the same way. Sometimes if the leg is lifted underneath the knee, you will be tempted to raise the whole leg—this again is a sign of tension. If completely relaxed, it is possible to lift the knee joint only, leaving the foot sliding along the ground.

These are merely initial tests as part of the first experience of letting go.

Now try to stretch as far as possible in every direction, just as an animal does before lying down by a fire; then let go; this helps you to release. Choose any set of muscles you like (e.g. wrist or neck or toe) and tense it for a period. You will want to release it; continue tensing beyond that point so that on releasing it you will become aware of the comfort of relaxation. Then enjoy that feeling of release. Feel consciously that you can enjoy the same looseness in your whole body.

Take a few slow easy breaths, and each time you breathe

out imagine that all effort oozes from you with the outgoing breath. Do not be afraid to move if you are uncomfortable; being uncomfortable will itself cause tenseness. Be as easy as you can, but remain on your back with your hands at your sides, not overhead. You will find in time that you can succeed equally well whether you are on a soft bed or a hard floor. Send a thought to each part of your body in turn. As you think of each part remember that you must not try to *do* anything—simply ask yourself "Is it relaxed?" It is quite a laborious process, and much easier to achieve if an outsider suggests the thought for you. If such assistance is available, the suggestions must be given sufficiently slowly and without any suggestion of hypnosis, though a calm quiet voice will obviously be a help to the realization of what is required.

When you have sent a thought to each part, return to any that may have proved to be too tense—perhaps the hollow of your back, the nape of your neck, the jaw and tongue, behind the eyes, and so on. Just let them sink, and imagine yourself to be floating away into a state of happy unconsciousness. Feel the blood flowing easily through your veins, and imagine sunlight pouring through them. Any images that help to give the feeling are valuable. If your mind is still centred on a conversation you will find that your speech muscles will not be relaxed; and similarly if you are seeing something vividly with your mind, your eye muscles will be too lively. Let go, and enjoy the lack of responsibility—and *rest*.

Even then you may need to anchor your mind if it is to be at rest. Choose a tranquil scene—a blue sky, a still lake, or a peaceful colour such as green. Some people prefer to think of black and find it excludes all else: others like to imagine they are lying still, almost floating, while nature moves round them. It is impossible to think of nothing, but it is not impossible to concentrate on one of these ideas. Choose the one that suits you best, and do not waver. Gradually and with constant practice, relaxation will come, but it needs concentration in the initial stages.

After deep relaxation of this kind, it is very unwise to jump up quickly, or rush back into activity, you may experience giddiness if you do. Sit up slowly, and stay sitting for a few minutes. Breathe and stretch, then stand and walk round easily, feeling that you are using the muscles that are necessary, and no others. Do not be distressed if you are sleepy, this will mean you have succeeded. By degrees your result will be achieved more and more quickly and after some practice, physical relaxation should be possible instantly—as is necessary in the stage fall.

Classes gain enormously from this ability to relax. The most undisciplined are often those who need and enjoy it most—and if they go to sleep do not worry, but be glad. The very fact that they do so proves that they have relaxed successfully.

During the war, working with groups of boys and girls in their late teens and in a place where discipline was unknown, and chaos and noise were perpetual, I found the only way of achieving any serious work in mime was by starting each class with relaxation. This was soon accepted as a natural situation, and it worked miracles. Late-comers (inevitable in those uncertain days) instead of entering noisily would creep in on tiptoe and lie down with the others. The result was that twice the amount of work was accomplished in half the time, and it was done with zest and interest, instead of the time being frittered away and treated as an opportunity to add to the general tumult.

In all movement or drama classes, discipline can be difficult, for sheer enthusiasm can create turbulence. Moments of quiet are essential, and as all the civilized world seems to need to learn to relax the practice can be beneficial from every point of view, apart from the fact that for good movement it is an essential basis.

Having developed the habit of relaxation[1] so that you can use it at will, it is necessary to appreciate that during all action some groups of muscles are relaxed while other opposing muscles are tensed; also that most people use far too much effort to carry out simple everyday actions—e.g. dressing, washing, and so on. This excess of effort is very noticeable if your hand slips while doing one of these actions and hits a piece of furniture! The impact is unexpectedly great, and you will usually find that you could have achieved the desired result with half the effort.

Movement will benefit from relaxation, and become altogether more free; naturally it must not be slovenly, but easy and well poised.

The word relaxation is commonly used, but it is still uncommon to find a real understanding of its meaning.

[1] Anyone who is sufficiently interested to wish to study the subject more deeply should read *Relaxation* by Maurice Jacobson.

V

OCCUPATIONAL WORK

Occupational work takes our minds back into the past and forward into the future. It covers any and every daily action and belongs to all generations of mankind. In itself an occupational action is not of particular interest. The reason for it, the surroundings, the people who make the action, their feelings—these immediately hold the elements of drama. This should be in our minds when we teach occupational action in mime.

So many classes seem to work away at realistic details which can be of no interest to anyone. When we paint a field we do not set down every blade of grass, we give an impression in which those who view the picture can believe. In miming an occupation we give an impression of an action which is accepted as truth by the onlookers although the mime may actually take much less time than the real action. Occupational mime has many practical uses. Children seated in desks, or working in a small space, can enjoy this work when other branches of mime might not be possible. With young children it is especially valuable and stimulates and disciplines their natural inventive powers and imagination.

With older children in their school plays, as indeed with all serious adult actors, there is obvious benefit. How seldom are the stage properties available before the last few rehearsals! How often one sees the timing of a scene, which has been carefully planned beforehand, completely upset, because an occupational action, such as pouring out tea, was not properly anticipated—the actor's mime having been inadequate!

Children are apt to attempt too much at once, which usually gives a blurred result. They should be encouraged to think on simple lines at first, and to make one action recognizable at a time.

A group of boys will decide to be highwaymen, riding, lassoing, sniping, stealing; they will make none of these actions clear, but merge them all into one, in their excitement about their story. They will, however, enjoy themselves very much more when they have given time to direct their imagination into the particular channel that is required. Let them express their feelings, and all that they personally want to express, but let them understand that they must be selective, and concentrate on the sequence of events, one at a time, and as if they were all true.

Here are some suggestions for practice:

Let the class begin by shutting their eyes, excluding everyone and everything about them. Then in their minds, without movement, go through the simple action of undoing a button. Then—quite slowly—again only in their minds, let them do it up again.

Now ask them to make the movements they have imagined, and they will find the doing strangely real, because the imagination has been used.

Treat another simple action in the same way, as for example, mentally tying up a bow or taking off a sweater. After they have done the action very carefully in the mind only, let them attempt to mime it perfectly.

This amount of concentration and absorption is needed in all mime, especially in showing an occupation.

Now try to develop a sense of weight and size.

Describe the size of an object to the class and ask them to imagine they are holding it. They must feel the weight of it, then be conscious of the shape of it, touch it as if they were holding it, look at it, think about it, come to know it and to establish a proprietary interest in it.

Try this with the following objects

Infants	*Juniors*
A ball of wool	A snowball
A big book	A glass tumbler
A silkworm	Two cherries on a stalk
A spoon	A sack of coal
A kitten	A bunch of flowers
An egg	A bucket and spade

Seniors	*Adults*
A pile of books	A cake
A garden rake	An electric iron
A paper weight	A cigarette
A puppy	A basket of potatoes
A cricket ball	A horse-shoe
A mail bag	The week-end shopping

Then having experienced the weight, shape, and feeling of the different objects, let them each fetch one (still in mime) from a suitable spot, give it to someone else, and let him put it down. Let them get used to handling and exchanging these objects. The children's success will be gained by their own belief in what they are doing.

Now pass on to other objects which are of such a nature that action is indicated. If the articles are of a sort that can be opened, let them do so and show what is inside; ask them in each case to *use* the object in any way that seems suitable.

Examples

Infants
A handbag
A bag of sweets
A sunshade
A box of bricks

Juniors
A parcel
A work box
A garden hose
A bottle of ink

Seniors
A wooden box
A bucket of water
A change of clothing
A candle

Adults
A suitcase
A coal scuttle
A pair of skis
A mower

It is sometimes a good plan to divide classes into halves, and allow one half to watch the other half, taking it in turns: or to divide into couples, so that each person has his own partner, and one can watch the other, and say what is clear and what cannot be understood.

Then it is useful to analyse which part of the arm is mainly used for certain actions. Although it is true that more often than not all the muscles are used in some degree, yet the concentration of the movement may be in a particular part, as in these examples, which are worth trying:

FINGERS AND HANDS

Infants
Threading beads
Playing with toy soldiers
Making a daisy chain

Juniors
Writing
Winding a watch
Plaiting

Seniors
Sewing
Playing cards
Counting coins

Adults
Painting a miniature
Examining jewels
Shelling peas

WRISTS

Infants
Turning on a tap
Playing 'tiddly winks'
Stirring a mug of cocoa

Juniors
Using an indiarubber
Hammering with a small hammer
Cutting out a paper picture

Seniors
Sharpening a pencil
Winding a small clock
Using a pair of compasses

Adults
Pinning up a hem on the wearer
Typing
Using a small screwdriver

ELBOWS

Infants
Ringing a bell
Weighing and putting sweets in a bag
Spinning a humming top

Juniors
Bouncing a ball
Beating a gong
Playing draughts

Seniors
Polishing shoes
Turning the handle of a sewing machine
Arranging large flowers in a vase

Adults
Wringing out a wet sheet
Winding a large ball of wool
Cranking up a car

SHOULDERS

Infants
Making a 'snowman'
Digging
Beating time with music

Juniors
Stirring a Christmas pudding
Pumping a bicycle tyre
Pulling a sledge

Seniors	*Adults*
Polishing a floor	Hanging washing on a line
Playing tennis	Pushing a car
Using a pick	Hauling a sail

Once again the classes will no doubt supply other ideas and there may be plenty of argument about the way in which all these things are done. All this is healthy, and the argument can only end in whether or not the general effect is one in which an onlooker can believe.

Some accurate practice in varying occupations should then follow. Take the simple example of *using a hammer*. *Try to knock a nail into a wall*. Nine out of ten people will hold the hammer normally in their right hand and the nail in their left, and will then make the mistake of letting the right fist contact the nail, not judging accurately the length of the hammer or allowing for the head of the hammer to reach the nail—which means the right hand should be well below the left. This sounds so elementary when it is written, but the mistake is a constant one! Similarly, ask someone to mime *scrubbing the floor*. The main action will often be realistic, but frequently the hand will be found to be clenched so that it could not be holding a brush, the imaginary brush being on the floor with no allowance for the length of the bristles! In the simple action of *sewing*, everyone will push the needle into the material, but the majority will then make a continuous movement instead of releasing the fingers to take up the point to pull it out! Asked to *handle a bucket of water*, nearly always the distance from the ground will vary each time it is put down, the action of the handle will be exaggerated, and the difference in weight when it is full or empty will not be clearly shown.

In the case of small articles, as for instance reels of cotton, they will start one size, but will shrink and expand in use!

When illustrating these points to a class examples could be quoted indefinitely, but the teacher must beware of spending too much time on detail and so making the class dull. It is sufficient that the difficulties be grasped in such a way that the principle of the work is established. Interest in the work will automatically follow.

The next stage then is to consider who is doing the action and why. Much the best way is to gather ideas from those who are carrying out the occupations, but, by way of illustration, I will indicate below the sort of suggestions which might apply, basing them on some of the earlier examples.

INFANTS

Ringing a bell as:
> Mother letting you know it is dinner-time
> A man selling old clothes in the street
> Teacher ringing the school bell

Turning on a tap as:
> A gardener who is going to fill a watering can
> A naughty child letting it run for fun
> A washerwoman at the kitchen sink

JUNIORS

Playing draughts as:
> Someone who is learning the game
> A small boy who hates playing
> A very earnest old gentleman who has played all his life

Stirring a Christmas pudding as:
> Father of the family, just home from work
> The cook who is making it
> A visitor who has just called

SENIORS

Using a pair of compasses as:
> A lethargic schoolgirl doing her homework
> A neat, very short-sighted little boy
> A clever architect

Polishing a floor as:
> A very fat elderly lady who is very hot
> A child who is full of energy
> A rather affected young man

ADULTS

Typing as:
> A head-mistress whose secretary is away
> A young person who is struggling to do it with one finger
> A very efficient secretary.

Pinning up a hem on the wearer as:
> Mother, having made the child's dress
> Younger sister, trying to satisfy an older sister who is going to a dance
> An old dressmaker, who is well accustomed to it.

As character is added in this way, the pupils will immediately begin to show more individuality and vitality, and enjoyment will grow; the difficulty often arises that in their excitement about the character, the occupation becomes vague and indeterminate and a reminder is necessary.

A good deal of work can be done on these lines which will lead naturally into scenes using occupational movement. Before developing these it is well to appreciate that in a play all characters are expressing some sort of feeling. At any moment in life, any person, or a group of people, may be doing ordinary everyday actions—washing up, digging the garden, smoking a pipe, eating lunch, and so on, but at *all* times these actions are accompanied by some emotion, however slight. The mind is not always occupied with the action, but may be centred on some other more absorbing interest, which means—in acting—that the occupation is being done, by a particular character and with a particular feeling or emotion which may or may not be related to the occupational action. In a play or a scene so much happens in a short space of time that the emotion is a very important part of the situation, and usually the occupation alone would seem dull. Therefore the occupational action must appear to be so natural that the emotion of the imagined situation holds the audience. With or without stage properties, this naturalness requires a good deal of practice.

A further good exercise, therefore, is to use the foregoing examples of occupation and character adding emotion to them, making quite sure that occupation and character are not lost when emotion is added.

For example

SENIORS

Using a pair of compasses as the three characters already given. Act all three first expressing the emotion of *despair*, and then all three expressing the emotion of *hope*. Similarly *polishing the floor* as the three characters already given first expressing the emotion of *sorrow*, and then all three again expressing the emotion of *happiness*.

Be watchful to see that these emotions are not put on artificially. The test for this is to question the class individually to find out what reason was behind the expression of that emotion.

E

Many reasons may be given; one might expect, for example, that the *lethargic schoolgirl* might easily be in *despair* about her work, on the other hand her lethargy might well be caused because she had been to a dance the night before and was daydreaming of the handsome boy; her expression of *hope* could equally easily spring from either. The *short-sighted boy* might be in *despair* because he had failed his examination which would affect his future career, or the emotion might be quite unconnected with his work,—perhaps because his dog had been run over. Equally *hope* could spring from the opposite of either of these thoughts. The *clever architect* might be doing his job perfectly, but the emotion of *despair* could be caused by his wife's serious illness, and equally the emotion of *hope* by her recovery.

In the same way the *fat elderly lady,* the *energetic child* and the *affected young man* would most likely be suffering *sorrow* about something quite unrelated to the polishing of the floor, but their work would probably be slower as a result; the feeling of *happiness* would bring activity to whatever they were doing, and perhaps a song or a whistle!

ADULTS

Typing as the three characters already given. Act all three, first expressing the emotion of *doubt*, and then all three expressing the emotion of *confidence*.

Similarly—*pinning up a hem* as all three characters already given. Act all three, first expressing the emotion of *fear*, and then of *relief*.

Again it will be advisable to ensure that the emotions have been real by questioning, and remember that the occupation in question is often quite secondary to the feeling and emotion hidden in the mind. When acting, however, these emotions which in real life are hidden, must be clearly shown in the way that that particular character would show them. It is not easy to keep occupations, character, and emotion all in unity. An actor in performance must keep to the character he is acting, and if a lady drops her fan or handkerchief, he must pick it up and return it *in character*, at the same time showing his *emotion* towards the lady.

Another point to be remembered in connection with all acting, and with occupational mime in particular, is that it is sometimes necessary to magnify what is being done in order that the audience may be able to follow it.

This does not mean being untrue, it merely involves some slight emphasis in the exhibition of the act being performed, e.g., if miming darning, let it be seen, by putting it in a better light as if it is difficult or dark; this looks and is natural and an audience can understand the reason for it.

Examples for Infants and Juniors have not been listed in this 'emotional' work as it is not really suitable for them, though, of course, there can be no harm in asking them to show whether they are enjoying or disliking what they are doing, or whether the person they are acting is enjoying or disliking it.

Up to this point, my remarks on occupational mime have been kept to hand and arm movements. Try now to show the strains and stresses of the body during work. Try all the suggested movements with the natural reactions of all the body. This can be felt in an action such as *pushing* or *pulling*: the same applies, naturally, in all *lifting* or *winding* movements, and strength of action will be gained by a concentration on the Torso. Feel also that with a big movement like *swinging a roadmender's hammer* or *pulling a heavy rope* the feet and legs and back are very strongly employed; in a lesser degree this also applies to the smaller actions; but always the base must be firm, and the spine is usually active.

Perhaps the reaction of the head to occupational movement may not seem so obvious, but in fact, there are very few actions which do not bring a strong reaction from the head, and a very vital lesson could well be devoted to this subject alone. Think of *knocking in a nail, catching a ball, digging, cranking up a car,* and many other obvious instances. In a lesser degree with even small actions, the reflex action of the head is present.

It is important in mime to know what each part can do separately, but it is equally important to realize that no part works in complete isolation. Movement is rhythm, involving the *whole body.*

This reaction of strain and stress of the whole may be more noticeable in some of the heavier examples. When carrying a *bucket full of water, a very heavy suitcase,* or a *sack of coal,* some muscles are working against others, reacting to the strain. In the actual doing of these things the more muscles that can be relaxed the easier the job will be. In miming the action it is necessary to feel which set of muscles will be tensing, which relaxing. If the mime is good, on finishing the action it will be felt as if it had been real, and the muscles will have worked in that way.

Schoolgirls and boys enjoy miming every kind of sport. To begin with, let them mime the separate actions that may be needed, e.g. throwing and catching balls of varying sizes and textures, handling the tennis racket, cricket bat, hockey stick, etc.—then let each join with a partner and mime passing the ball between them, watching carefully the weight, speed, and power of the pass so that it is suitably received. A good preparation is to divide the class into small circles and to let them mime throwing a ball across and about the circle, noticing carefully when it drops, how it is thrown, and giving a real reaction to it. Ultimately set the whole game as if on a real field, and let them try to play it.

Accuracy, a sense of weight, a response to other people, and a great deal of pleasure will be gained from this practice.

This can lead into a form of team-race, which differs from the normal race in that it will be judged, not by speed, but by accuracy of definition. Set the leader of each team an imaginary object to carry up and down the room—e.g. a rabbit, a bicycle, a vase of flowers, a bottle of wine, etc.— according to the age of the group. The leader having carried it back to his place passes it to the next who carries it up and down and so it passes on through the team. The rest of the team turn their backs until the one before them is performing, which ensures that they must take what they see, without having witnessed the original performance of the leader. The team which finishes with the same object as that with which it started is the winner—and it is not so easy as it sounds! The game can also be played from other angles: instead of using it occupationally it can be used similarly for character work, costume work, or any other aspect of mime.

Another test for a group at work:

Let a group carry any object, such as a piano, an instrument of an orchestra, fire appliances, or a folded tent,—and set it down. Another group recognizing what is placed there will immediately go forward and use it. If the mime has been satisfactory, there should be no moment of hesitation, no need for explanation.

Here are some suggestions which would provide opportunities for group practice in occupational mime. Scenes should not be attempted until there has been some careful practice of individual work.

Suggestions for Group Occupational Practice

INFANTS

It is Christmas morning. The children are divided to represent families in different houses. In one house each child has a stocking to open; in another the postman brings parcels to the door for each one to unpack; in a third the children are giving presents to one another and show what they are. After this they all come to a fourth house to a party, and there is a big Christmas tree; toys of various kinds are taken down by the host and hostess and given to the visiting children; finally Father Christmas himself arrives with a sack of things to add to the others.

*

It is a lovely summer day. The children get up in the morning, wash, dress, and prepare themselves for a day by the sea. They go down to the sands, some dig, some paddle and some try to catch fish in the pools, others sail boats. Presently mothers and fathers bring out picnic lunches, and all sit down to eat. Some men come along, one is selling balloons, another ice-creams and some of the children have one or other. After a little more play they will go home, undress and go to bed.

*

There are Mother pig, Father pig, Auntie pig, Uncle pig and a large family of baby pigs. Father and Uncle decide that they are not very comfortably housed. They call all their friends to help them, and together they build a wonderful house, so strong that no wolf or any other creature could destroy it.

Tired, they all go to sleep contentedly.

*

A naughty little boy is left alone in the house while his mother goes to the shops. He calls in two families of friends who live on either side of his house, and they decide to have some fun; they tie all the furniture together with string, and barricade the dog in the middle of it.

When mother returns she is naturally very much upset.

*

It is winter, the snow is on the ground, the children are allowed to stay out-of-doors instead of going to school. Some make a snowman, others play at snow-balls, others drag one another on sledges, etc. Then it begins to get dark and they are called in to bed.

JUNIORS

The scene is the Doll-Maker's shop. The children are his workmen, and he is in charge of all that happens in the shop. Some are the dolls of various kinds—boy and girl dolls of every nationality, some china, some sawdust, etc. The doll-maker and his helpers finish making the dolls, sewing in the sawdust, painting the faces, putting on their clothes, etc. Others are still busy chopping and carving wood to make wooden dolls, and some are making clothes for these.

When the day's work is done, and the old man and his workers leave the shop, the dolls come to life, but quickly go back to their places when they hear him coming back.

*

The scene is a large kitchen, the cook is busy baking a cake, a woman is washing-up, a boy is scrubbing the floor, a girl is preparing the vegetables, and others are occupied in similar ways. Suddenly there is a disturbance outside and everyone runs out to see what it is. Two children who have been a nuisance to everyone all the morning, stay behind, steal the cake and run away with it. When the cook and the others return there is great trouble.

*

A party of children take a walk in some woods. They come across woodcutters felling trees in a clearing, who let them help with all their jobs. Some make a fire and cook over it, and have a meal with the woodcutters before being taken home by them in the dark.

SENIORS

The scene is a fish quay. Men and women are occupied bringing fish from the boats in boxes, nets, barrels, etc. Some clean fish, others sell them whole. Everyone is busy. Dealers come to buy. Some boats come in laden, others nearly empty. Argument can cause a dramatic incident, or a boat might not return.

Alternatively, the scene could be set on a beach, and the boats would be drawn up by winches.

*

The scene is the fitter's workroom in a big London store. There are a variety of dressmakers at work, pinning, sewing, machining, measuring, etc., according to their particular grade in the workroom. News comes through that no one is to leave the workroom until a search has been made, as everyone is under suspicion for theft.

*

Noah is making his Ark. Various neighbours come and help for a while, but in time each one gives up, and tells Noah he is mad. His three sons, their wives, and Mrs Noah also come and help with finishing touches, though no one

works as whole-heartedly as Noah does. He finishes and
then the rain comes.

*

A caravan is set by a river. The women of the party are
busy with their domestic jobs inside and outside the van.
The men are fishing in the river. They have an amazing catch;
a fish that needs several of them to help to land it. Some of
them fall into the river,—but it was worth it!

ADULTS

The scene is a removal of furniture from a large house into
a small one. Four removal men continually bring in furniture; members of the household try to polish the pieces
before placing them. Some are washing china, others polishing the floors, others brewing tea. A man is laying carpets
and another dealing with electric wiring. Evening comes.
Only the darkness causes everyone to stop working.

*

A number of ladies are gathered together at an afternoon
bridge party. They play happily; there is an interval when
they all have tea. Just as they are resuming their game the
party is disturbed by a mouse, which causes such confusion
that they give up the game.

*

The scene is a factory. Workers are busily engaged tending
the machines. There is a mid-morning break for cups of
coffee which they buy from the snack-bar. Work is resumed;
there is an accident and the machines have to be stopped.

*

Roman soldiers are throwing dice and gambling round a fire. Some make up the fire, others pour drink, in turn they gamble with cards and dice.

*

The scene is a post office. Behind the counter the officials go through the usual routine with stamps, forms, change, writing, etc.—and on the other side of the counter impatient customers write their telegrams, put their parcels on the scales, go into the call-box and telephone—but nothing hurries the officials.

*

These suggestions are only outlines, anyone of them could eventually be built up into a scene; as they stand they are intended to be for group occupational practice. A scene needs more than this, it must have conflict, and have a climax. It will not be difficult for the group to develop these settings and situations into scenes that have these elements. Let them first work them out clearly as set. They will quickly create characters, and the need to make the drama more powerful will be felt.

VI

ANIMALS AND CHARACTERS

Let us now assume that the pupil has a sure technique, almost second nature. Let the pupil now concentrate on interpretation. This is a more difficult matter than using a set of tricks. It is a focusing of the entire nature to become the thing or person mimed. In this way he will be able to transform and transcend himself and become someone else. Only this is true characterization.

Actors are often tempted to employ 'stagy' tricks: to stoop to represent old age, to hold the lapels of a coat for a Victorian father, to use any superficial act to *represent* a type; but great actors renew their minds continually and use their imagination so fully, that their drama seems to be as true as real life.

In imagining, few exercises help the young and adult pupil more than the pleasing, but not easy, exercise of imagining himself or herself to be an animal. All have observed animals, none can really know them, but pupils who have gone through the preceding exercises will find that they have attained the power of seeming like one when called upon to do so. The body being by now well prepared for this, all we need to do is to concentrate so deeply that the outward showing is like sleep-walking in that the feeling seems to take possession of the movement.

ANIMALS

Let the class sit well-spaced on the floor, no one touching another, and follow these instructions:

Shut your eyes excluding everyone and everything about you; as far as is possible in a sitting position, relax and empty your mind. Now think *cat*. Feel as you sit there that your spine is becoming supple, that from the top of your head all down your spine to the tip of your tail you are sinuous and lithe. Think round your body. Feel as you sit and stare at the world that you are a rather superior being; blink, half-close your eyes, and stare sleepily into the fire. Feel conscious of the top of your head as someone strokes it and you move slightly. Feel the change in your ears when they listen or relax. Your whole face expresses your feelings, even your whiskers, and when you yawn we see your teeth and that tongue that laps milk so easily. Be aware of the soft fur under your chin, and all along your back, your flanks, and underneath you. Again mentally follow your tail to its tip and know its strength. Then think of your legs, back and front, and the soft pads on your paws, and your claws that show themselves when occasion warrants it. Feel the enjoyment of padding round and round on a soft cushion before you sit down in the best chair, or in another mood the pulling at the table cloth, or playing with a ball of wool. Feel pride in yourself as you busily clean yourself with your tongue, and the way at times you arch your back in anger. The stretching movement you do before you prowl away after being relaxed, and the twining of yourself round either human or table leg. Feel sounds growing inside you, maybe a satisfied purr, or an appealing but timid miaow. You may be angry or excited, you may be hungry or happy, we shall know your feeling by the movement and sound you make. Each of you is a particular cat, a particular colour, and temperament. Go on quietly concentrating on *cat*—and when you feel it taking possession of you, begin to move, and make a sound if you feel you must.

Some of the pupils will probably want to move during the description, *this should be avoided*. The result of it can only be that with part of their minds they will be listening and trying to follow the instructions, and with the other part they will be trying to absorb and act.

Class and teacher will gain more if the description is used as a setting of mood and feeling while the class remain seated, possibly moving the body slightly as the feeling grows. Then when the teacher has finished the description, he should encourage some minutes of silent thought, and let each member judge for himself when he is ready to move; some will naturally want to think longer than others. Do not let them open their eyes until they are just beginning to move, thus they will not be made self-conscious by being aware of what others are doing. It is unusual to find a class that does not respond, and often the feeling will be so strong that the impression is truly a room full of cats!

There will probably be among them one who dislikes the cat or any other animal you may choose. Handled gently, this work can help and not frighten such a child. Explain that he *is* the cat, so there is nothing to mind, except the fact that others may fear him, which is a pity since he has no wish to hurt.

This work is suitable for *any age group* provided it is used at the right moment in the training, when there is a readiness to attempt it; it is not a good idea to start on it until the technical work for the whole has been practised. If there is self-consciousness in the class it arises either because this stage has been attempted too soon, or because the presentation has been faulty. Little ones will of course treat it as a game quite readily. Adolescents will find pleasure in it at the right moment. Adults will be shy at first, but will nearly always find great release and help in it when they have grown accustomed to it. An important point for them to realize is that to feel like a cat it is not essential to start on all fours. The sinuous muscular movement can be imagined in the spine while sitting upright in a chair; the face and neck will alter as the mind works, and with older people this feeling through the body is all that should be expected, though almost invariably there will be among them a number of bright spirits who will want to do more.

The action must be governed entirely by *feeling*; directly the intellect begins to work there is a realization that the legs are the wrong shape and that the human body can never appear like an animal body: once these thoughts have arisen it is difficult to revert to feeling only. The thoughts themselves would, of course, be true, but they are not relevant: the facts could not be disputed, but we are concerned not with facts, but with instinctive feeling. A right feeling will always prompt a right movement. This is so true of acting, too: while we admire a good brain behind characterization, too much 'intellectualizing' often makes instinctive feeling impossible.

Now let the class once again sit well-spaced, and prepare mind and body to be relaxed sufficiently to be possessed by any new impression.

Choose another creature—it may be animal, bird, insect or reptile, wild or domestic—and treat similarly to the cat. Take time, and speak to the class in terms of "You are . . ." rather than "It is . . ."; this helps them to become the creature, instead of being, as it were, an objective onlooker. If a wild creature has been selected it often helps to describe the setting—jungle, swamp, river, or whatever it may be; but avoid the temptation to turn the class into a natural history lesson, or you will again impede the flow of feeling. The description is all-important and will make or mar the class.

After the idea has been absorbed and two or three animals have been 'felt' in this way, give the class the opportunity to concentrate in their own time, and without direction from the teacher, on any creature they choose. This gives a sudden feeling of freedom, and nearly always there will be surprisingly interesting results. Do not worry at this stage if you are not exactly clear what they are all representing; it does not necessarily mean they are bad, and if they are bad, no good will come from drawing attention to it. The important factor is that they are now developing their own ideas with intense concentration of the right creative kind, and there is no attempt to copy other people.

Later, when the class is more used to this work, no harm will be done by guessing what each one has become. They in turn can quickly join in and help to speed up the guessing of the last few; do not leave one or two struggling alone at the end.

It should be understood that this development will take place over a series of classes; it would be tiring to work on these themes for too long at a time.

The next development is to ask a member of the class to do the describing. This will refresh everyone, and if you select one with capacity in this direction first, it is sure to succeed; then ask others. Very soon members of the class will themselves suggest that they would like to try. In time let them all have a turn. Individuality will keep the interest of the class alive, and they will become rightly critical of one another's efforts, and will know what constitutes a helpful description and what kind of description presents them with a difficulty. Co-operation and general discussion help a group to work constructively together, and much freedom is gained by them. Even those who have not so much gift in performance may be able to come into their own in discussion or through their descriptive ability. Quite apart from mime itself, this work is of immense value with children, since directly there is desire and competition to be given the chance of describing an animal, the child frequently forgets personal difficulties and inhibitions about speech, and eagerly takes the chance of leadership,—the fact that words are now the medium is forgotten, and a great advance in personal expression is made. This then is of real value in education; helping to make the child expressive and vital.

Thinking again of dramatic expression, it will soon be realized that being a particular animal is not enough. Animals vary even as humans vary, though in a lesser degree. The reasons for their variability are often found in circumstances just as ours are. Another exercise then will be to select a particular animal that the class would like to be. Being this animal let them first try walking slowly, and then move more rapidly, so that they find what difference in feeling there is in the same creature when the rate of movement varies.

Imagine they have selected a Fox:

Let us see the fox lying at rest in his lair, unmolested and content.

Now let us see the difference when he is young and playing, almost like a big dog, happy and free.

Now let us see him running for his life, hunted by the hounds, frightened and alone, looking about for a hole in which he can hide from the huntsmen.

Now again he is close to his home, but he is guarding the vixen and the young cubs, suspicious if anyone comes near; ready to be fierce in being protective.

In another mood, he is alert, ready to attack, scenting danger.

Now it is late evening, he is out hunting, stealing fowls from the farmyard, looking for food everywhere.

Now he is wounded, and struggling because of his wound, trying to get to safety in a miserable plight.

Let us see him now when he is fascinated by something he is watching. Perhaps he is watching a man or, maybe, a snake, and he is afraid. Maybe it is a fire made round a camp to keep wild creatures away. It could be another fox, a stranger to him; or another animal, larger or smaller than he is.

Other moods and reasons for these moods will no doubt be suggested by the classes themselves; the variety in choice of creature will of course affect the chosen mood, but there is plenty of opportunity for development on this theme.

Finally, it is worth trying some scenes introducing animals.

Examples

INFANTS

Mr and Mrs Lion—being King and Queen of the forest decide to have a tea-party. They invite all the birds and beasts to join them. Some are rather timid, others flattered, but they all come. The tea-party starts off well, all are on their best behaviour because they are the guests of Mr and Mrs Lion—but . . .

(Let the children finish it in their own way.)

JUNIORS

It is the middle of the jungle, the antelope have come down to the water to drink; they are startled when they see the

F

vultures flying overhead, and, with a great stampede, they move away back to their mountain ledges. There is a soft padding in the leaves and two tigers meet, under their feet insects scuttle to and fro, and in the distance they hear the movement of a herd of elephants. . . .

(Finish as they like.)

SENIORS

The London Zoo. Cages of animals of every kind. Houses for reptiles and for lions. Water for sea-lions. Elephants and camels meekly carrying children up and down, always covering the same track.

Visitors come and peer and throw buns to them all. . . .

(Finish as they like.)

ADULTS

It is a circus ring. Here is the equestrian with his beautiful prancing ponies who react to his command; then comes the bare-back rider, the performing seals and elephants, the lion tamer with his lions, as well as the clown who will, of course, be there. . . .

(Finish as they like.)

*

There are plays like *The Wind in the Willows*, *The Insect Play*, *Noah*, and *Under the Sycamore Tree*, with ample opportunity for animal characterization, and they are so often played 'straight' with no real attempt at animal quality.

Mime plays could well be adapted from Kipling's *Jungle Books* which give infinite character work in animal life, and provide all the conflict and climax which drama needs.

It will now be found to be quite a good plan to let the

class have the experience of concentrating on nature and inanimate objects, and see if they can feel them so strongly that they convey something of their character. Tell them that it was said of Garrick that "he could act a grid-iron"!

Let the student concentrate and try to feel as if he were being transformed into *a tree*. This does not mean that he raises his arms to look like branches—nothing as external as that—although if he wants to do so ultimately there is no reason why he should not. It does mean that he must think and feel and use his imaginative powers, so that the translation seems to take place, and he is possessed of the feeling without knowing how.

Let him feel in the same way:

> a bush
> a fern
> a blade of grass

feel their vulnerability to the sun and the rain, the wind, the storms, cold and heat, dark and light, as well as to people and animals around them. In the same way he can feel himself being transformed into:

> the sun
> any of the elements

Then inanimate objects like:

> an ancient moss-covered wall
> a rocky cliff

Develop into scenes that introduce all these ideas mixed with human life.

A good setting for infants and Juniors would be

> Under the Sea

Some would choose to be rocks, some sea-weed, others star-fish, crabs, octopus, fish of all kinds, or even mermaids and mermen.

Seniors could set their scene in

An old castle

giving opportunities for ruins, relics, plants, ghosts, knights in armour, mists, etc., as well as the modern tourists.

The average adult will be a little shy of this imaginative work, and should be led to it by gentle degrees, not rushed. Dramatic students will be quite at home in the medium.

A further exercise in the same range of expression is for each member of the class to imagine he is a *sculptor* and to create his work of art. As he does so, the work should become clear. The development is that each one should then

Be the statue he has modelled

He must again feel and concentrate as intensely as possible, and then imagine he is given life. Let the statue grow and be; let it have the soul and life the sculptor had thought of in his imagination.

Here is the feeling first of an inanimate object followed by that of the same object infused with life.

CHARACTERS

When sufficient self-knowledge has been gained through acting the life of the animals, plants, and inanimate objects, then it is time to develop the process further, and use what has been learnt to build up human characterization.

Before doing so, the obvious stepping-stone is to think of two-legged creatures, and, in particular, the monkey—being nearest to man! This is comparatively easy to most people, and a scene in the monkey house is always the greatest fun.

The same way of working can now be applied to human characterization. Instead of descriptions, it may be found to be more valuable to ask a series of questions, allowing time for the pupils to answer themselves mentally, but they must not answer orally. In this way character can grow from individual thought and feeling and will not be dependent on imitation, or on type representation.

Again let the class sit, or be comfortable in any way they like, and prepare themselves to concentrate so that they can become submerged by some character other than their own. The chosen character-type must, of course, suit the age of the class, but I think that this is so obvious that it is unnecessary to give different examples for each age group. Here is an example of the sort of help that the teacher might give. (Dots indicate pauses for the class to think and feel silently.)

You are a *beggar*. You are in a busy city; your age is forty. . . . . . Are you male or female? . . . . . . Are you disabled in any way or are you perfectly well? . . . . . . Or do you act a part, and take on another when you leave your begging behind? . . . . . . How long have you been begging? . . . . . . Do you make much money? . . . . . . Where do you live? . . . . . . What are your likes and dislikes? . . . . . . What do you like to eat? . . . . . . What do you do with the money you have? . . . . . Have you any friends . . . or relations? . . . . . . Think more about yourself and your present life. . . . . . Now cast your mind back to when you were a child, think of your home and family, your school, your young life, your dreams and ambitions. Did you do a job? . . . . . . Think on to the last ten years, of all that has happened until today. . . . . . Now look ahead . . . . . . what lies there? . . . . . . Imagine for a moment that you can see your future lying before you until the end of your life. . . . . . Back to the present again. There you are in your city street. How are you dressed? . . . . . . Where did your clothes come from? . . . . . . What form does your begging take? . . . . . . What is the weather like? . . . . . . What success are you having? . . . . . . What sort of people are passing by and how do they treat you? . . . . . . What do you feel like—is your life a happy one, what is your attitude to all the folks around you and to life in general? . . . . . .

Think quietly for a while; when you feel you are a beggar, begin to move, and make any appropriate sound if it helps you.

*

An exercise such as this helps the class to think constructively, and usually brings good results. Some may object and want to be told more definitely what to think, as they were in the first instance with the cat. By this time, that initial practice should have made the class ready to welcome the opportunity to develop their own ideas, but if some are not yet ready, it is easy to give a fuller description and then to return later to this more advanced method.

Characters such as beggar, a blind man, a typist, a giant, a witch, etc., can be filled out and developed by the individual in this way. Another development can be to describe more specific characters which the class might know, having studied or read the play from which they are taken. Here is an example:

You are a mischievous sprite; your name is Puck. You are the chief attendant spirit on Oberon—the King of Fairyland. You take pleasure in practical jokes, and love to laugh at people's confusion and misfortune, which you yourself have usually caused. You can cover hundreds of miles in a second, passing invisibly through the air faster than any 'jet'. You can disguise yourself as you choose, sometimes as a flower or a leaf, sometimes as an animal,— but at heart you are a mischievous little boy, and often have to be kept in order by your master. No one knows what you eat or how you live; you are of the fairy kingdom and the forest is your hiding-place although the whole earth is yours. You live for ever; you play with the fairies and with other elves when you are not busily employed by Oberon. You are sometimes sorry for your pranks, and you really like the people whom you tease. Oh! the joy of your feelings! The fun of being able to spring into the air and stay there, to settle on a bird's back and whisk over the sea, and then to dive down among the mermaids, until you are caught by Neptune and sent flying back to your own kingdom and your own master! Then perhaps, you trudge the last part of the way pretending to be an old cart-horse until you meet a poor old lady who needs help, and you guide her safely home at night; then off again for some more elfish nonsense. You little green spirit! You are Puck!

*

Again a few moments of silent thought, and then they will start with their own conception of this well-known character. We need not, of course, be limited to Shakespearian characters. Innumerable plays, suitable to every age, lend themselves to this treatment. This way of working will avoid stereotyped imitations, and any danger of the teacher's ideas being implanted, therefore the acting will be sincere. It will also mean that the method can be used by the pupil when he is left to himself. Thus he becomes independent in thought; a very important point. No teaching is good if the pupil in the end relies on the teacher.

The teacher will follow the same process as was used with

the animals. He will describe various characters and then more specific people, from play or book, sometimes giving a detailed description, more often making use of the questioning method. Then still following the same idea, ask members of the class to describe or question, which will again develop thought, interest, and discussion, and benefit everyone.

A further development will be to choose a character and to consider differences of mood related to circumstance, and the effect of other characters on this one—the pupils always trying to translate themselves with truth into the physical and mental feeling of the person.

Finally, scenes which provide opportunity for characterization are a useful practice.

Examples:

INFANTS

The scene is a park; it is a sunny day and many people are passing to and fro. There are seats and chairs, litter-baskets, grass where games are played, and a large pond for those who want to sail boats. All sorts of people congregate there because of the sunshine.

(Give this setting to the children in whatever way they can best follow it—let them decide what kind of person they will be before they begin, so that they can think about it, then let them meet one another and play together, and quite probably some climax will occur. For them it should be just a game, so the performance side doesn't matter at all.)

JUNIORS

You have all gone by coach for the day to Windsor Castle, and you are queueing to see the Queen's Dolls' House which is in one of the rooms. You may be any person in the party; grown-ups and children of all sorts go to see this beautiful dolls' house. When you finally get in, you walk all round four sides of it, and then come out again; then all sit on the seats looking at the view, and have a picnic lunch. Show your reaction to the people around you. Finally board your coach for the return journey.

Take time to think about your characters before you begin the scene.

SENIORS

The characters in this scene are the parents and friends of a young couple at an elaborate cocktail party given in honour of their engagement. At the end of the evening, just as the announcement is to be made, it is discovered that the young man is missing.

ADULTS

The scene is the foyer of a theatre. The play is a modern comedy. This is the moment before it opens, when some are still buying tickets, others hurriedly finding theirs; some wait patiently for late friends; some arrive together—an excited or a bored party; some unexpectedly meet people they know, and so on. Behaviour varies a little according to the clothes being worn, which again depends on where their seats are in the theatre. After a time the bell rings, and there is a general sense of hurry not to miss the opening of the play.

The teacher will find that all sorts of incidents crop up in such a situation. He can encourage them to come about as a result of character and circumstance, without forcing.

Insist that the pupils think about the characters inwardly before starting the scene.

All these scenes could be pure mime if there has been sufficient practice in it. For those who have not done so much mime, it may be easier to improvise words; provided they come readily, there is no harm in using them. The danger is that the speech may become more important than the movement, which, at this stage, would be a pity.

An amusing experiment in this branch of the work is to compare animals and human beings. I would urge, however, that this should only be used sparingly and not be done until after the rest of the work I have suggested here is to some extent mastered. If this other development comes too soon, serious study will be interfered with.

Scenes will grow from this too:

A group of twittering little birds will develop into a gossipy *women's meeting*. Lions and tigers, with an occasional laughing hyena will be perfect in a *gentlemen's political club*!

To some extent all of us behave differently in differing circumstances and with different people: the psychological effect of one person on another must certainly be considered in building a character. This point is fairly obvious. It is perhaps not quite so obvious that people are different at different *hours of the day*. Part of this difference is dependent on their occupations, part on their habits of eating and drinking, part on their leisure-time occupations, and part on innate temper and temperaments.

An exercise then to add to others that have already been used (not to replace them) is to build a character as far as possible, then show the same person at:

7 a.m.   11 a.m.   3 p.m.   6 p.m.   9.30 p.m.   11.30 p.m.

or whatever hours you prefer to select, or possibly also on different days of the week. It will often be quite revealing, and can be applied to any and every character. Possibly it might even be more real to a group if they first analysed themselves in this way.

There is also usually a difference between people who are doing a job, and the same people off-duty.

Examples:

A waitress	A Member of Parliament
A clerk	An engine driver
A chauffeur	A saleswoman
A queen	A hairdresser

The class will no doubt have other suggestions.

To little ones, character work can only be a game of 'let's pretend', and although they have an infinite capacity for pretending, they do not normally show a great deal of difference in movement; their knowledge is slight, and their imagination is sufficient to satisfy the needs of the game. One will say "I'm a bee", and you will hear him buzzing and there will be some movement. A few minutes later the same child will say "Now, I'm a crab", and the other children will accept him as a crab whether his movement changes recognizably or not. There is no reason to intrude on this natural play, only to add to its pleasure by suggestion; but it is clear that actual 'character' work is not desirable at this level, although animals may prove valuable. Children who are a little older are more aware of people and circumstances, and can work slowly along the lines I have indicated.

It is of even greater importance that seniors and adults should be trained by these slow, simple, honest methods, to ensure that the character shall not be externally put on, like a cloak, but shall be truly created from within.

VII

REACTION

Until now exercises have been chosen in order to give the individual a control of body, mind, and imagination. But no one can live in complete isolation: there is also relationship, which implies action, and what we may call re-action; the clash or agreement that comes from the meeting of wills or minds.

It is a good thing to cultivate natural response through the medium of mime, and for drama it is essential.

Care is needed in dealing with response; to be over-responsive is to over-act. The key-word that all actors and all mimes must remember is *economy*, and if another word should be remembered alongside it, I would say it is *stillness*. As life is movement, and mime is movement, this may seem to be a contradiction, but it is not. Stillness does not mean deadness; there is still breath and life, and in stillness a character may be intensely expressing with every muscle and feature. This is one of the most difficult parts of this art to learn; people are so afraid to take enough time over a movement, and are afraid to conclude one movement and let its effect be 'telling', before passing on to another; then their expressions become blurred instead of having a clear line. They tend to feel that they are not miming if they are not moving, but only that inner urge through the whole body will make the stillness *speak*.

This does not mean that *slowness* must come from stillness. The silence must have the tense purpose of the tiger or snake, not the sleepiness of the sloth or Koala bear.

Breathing has a major part to play in this, as it inevitably follows the emotion and changes with every mood if the feeling is real.

Inexperienced mimes will almost always make the mistake of doing two or three small actions, where one decisive one would have been enough. It takes time to appreciate the need for economy, but it is necessary to realize it, and to feel that every movement, however small, matters. The raising of an eyebrow, the movement of one finger should be telling in themselves. Stillness in the midst of movement has the effect of silence in the midst of noise.

Response can be made to an inward feeling or to an outside stimulus; to something expected or unexpected, to people or to circumstances. The five senses, touch, sight, smell, taste, and hearing will almost always bring a natural response. Many valuable exercises for any age-group can be evolved from this theme.

e.g.   Touch something and respond in feeling or action
      See something and respond in feeling or action
      Smell something and respond in feeling or action
      Taste something and respond in feeling or action
      Hear something and respond in feeling or action

Examples:

TOUCH

Infants	*Juniors*
A teddy bear	A Cat
Prickles	Honey
A worm	Chocolate melting in the sun

Seniors
A sharp knife
A canary
Sticky adhesive tape

Adults
A road drill
A fur coat
A wasp

SIGHT

Infants
A bunch of balloons
A car
A baby sister

Juniors
Waves
A monkey
A new dress

Seniors
A ghost
A whirlpool
A head-mistress

Adults
A football match
A cigar
A mountain

SMELL

Infants
A bunch of roses
Soap
New-mown hay

Juniors
A field of clover
The sea
Newly-baked bread

Seniors
A cow-byre
Gas
Fresh paint

Adults
Burning
Scent
A rotten egg

TASTE

Infants
A banana
Chocolates
Milk

Juniors
Liquorice
Coca-Cola
Rice pudding

Seniors	*Adults*
Raspberries and cream	A caramel
Medicine	Champagne
Peppermints	A fish bone

HEARING

Infants	*Juniors*
A kitten miaowing	A waterfall
Thunder	A cricket
Someone calling your name	Distant guns

Seniors	*Adults*
A dog barking	Seagulls
A gramophone playing	An aeroplane breaking the sound barrier
An explosion	Schoolchildren in a playground

Quite a number of examples that will evoke response in all parts of the body have already been given in Chapter III. Many other examples could of course be added, as almost everything one does is in some measure a response.

Other Exercises for Response

INFANTS

You are playing in a sand-pit—a strange dog comes and sniffs around, but he goes away and leaves you in peace.

You are watering your garden with a big can, and you soak yourself as well as the garden.

You are enjoying yourself, and you are told to go to bed.

You break one of your favourite toys.

You see a spider on the wall.

JUNIORS

You have built a sand castle with a moat and you are hoping the sea will come into it. You stand on the top and wait,— it comes in more quickly than you thought, and nearly washes it away.

You are looking for fish in a pool, and you find a crab.

You have gone out when you were told not to, and it begins to snow.

You are away from home, and you receive a letter from your mother, or from a member of your family.

You see a caterpillar crawling over your foot.

SENIORS

You have just started in your first job, and you are sent for by your employer.

You are on your way to a garden party in your best clothes, and you are caught in a sudden cloud-burst and thunder-storm.

You are staying with a relation who collects beautiful china. By accident you knock a piece off a shelf and it breaks.

You receive a letter telling you that you have passed an examination.

You see the door open silently, and no one behind it.

ADULTS

You are lying on the beach on a very hot day; you go to sleep and when you are awakened by the waves reaching you, you find you are cut off by the tide.

You are out to dinner with someone of importance, and you burn your mouth badly with your soup.

You are waiting at the station to meet someone whom you dislike; the train is held up by fog, and while you are waiting, a great friend arrives whom you haven't seen for some months.

You receive a telegram,—show whether the news is good or bad.

You hear footsteps and you thought you were alone in the house.

I will now suggest some *phrases* which should come to life through the natural mimed response of the individual. The same phrase will lead to a different reaction with each person who hears it, because each has his own response to give. Let the responses be slow enough to show real thought. A quick facility and forced reaction sometimes occurs in this exercise, which is quite opposed to the intention of this teaching. They should sit quietly and slowly let the thought have its effect—and on no account introduce speech gesture.

The phrases will begin with one of the following:

"I hear . . . "
"I think . . . "
"I know . . . "
"I am given . . . "

Let the class listen to the phrase, then make their own reactions in movement.

Classes will enjoy thinking of phrases to set their companions for reaction, but here are some examples to set them on the way:

INFANTS

I hear a little mouse talking to its mother.
I hear a cuckoo.
I hear a band.

I think my mother is going out, and I am going too.
I think there is an elf under that tree root.
I think you are a naughty boy.

I know you have my doll.
I know there is some jam in that cupboard.
I know what I'm going to do!

I am given a present I don't want.
I am given a rubber ball.
I am given a slap.

JUNIORS

I hear a ship's siren in the distance.
I hear someone talking about my birthday present in the
next room.
I hear drums beating in the distance.

I think you are cross with me.
I think I have sprained my ankle.
I think they have seen us.

I know that is an owl hooting.
I know! I am going to draw a picture.
I know you don't like me.

I am given a piece of cake, but it has a dead beetle in it.
I am given a lovely iced drink.
I am given a baby to hold.

SENIORS

I hear wolves, and they are coming closer.
I hear a tap dripping in the bathroom.
I hear someone singing under the window.

I think that is the murmur of a running stream.
I think that you spent a long time doing this.
I think they are coming to take me prisoner.

I know he was innocent.
I know we must go and cut the corn while it's fine.
I know my dog would not bite yours.

I am given a letter from someone I thought was dead.
I am given a hundred lines to write as a punishment.
I am given a horse and harness.

ADULTS

I hear by telephone that my wife has twins.
I hear the silence on these hill-tops.
I hear the rats in the wainscot.

I think there is a snake in the grass.
I think this meat is bad.
I think you are guilty.

I know you meant to meet her here.
I know that was an avalanche.
I know it was very cold in the sea.

I am given news of my son's imprisonment.
I am given a letter of apology.
I am given a part in a play.

Another development, which is the absolute opposite of the inward concentration learned in Chapter VI but none the less valuable as an *additional* practice, is to react in movement *immediately* without a second's pause, to whatever enters the mind when a word is spoken.

e.g. *Fire*

Everyone has an immediate reaction; to some the movement will be an abstract interpretation of flame with rapid rippling movements; to others it will be the character in 'The Bluebird'; another will move quickly manipulating imaginary hoses, etc., as if a house were on fire; or again, someone will visualize sitting by a fire at home, and another will think of a camp fire, etc. The point of interest is that with every fresh word, there will be a number of individual reactions, no two being alike.

Here are some examples to use:

Infants	Juniors	Seniors	Adults
Dormouse	Cosy	Plague	Rumour
Ball	Cook	Lightning	Fever
Slowcoach	Water	Freedom	Misfortune
Bedtime	Adventure	Jester	Courage
Sunday	Gipsy	Fate	Love-lorn

It matters very little what the word is, as almost any word brings a response, but to start with a word having definite and clear possibilities is a good idea.

Then there is the reaction of one person to another to be considered.

Divide the class into pairs

Let each couple start as far from one another as possible, then let them walk until they meet, and react.

Probably the teacher may have to suggest at first whether the meeting is unexpected, pleasant, unpleasant, awkward, opportune, exciting, amusing, nerve-racking, dangerous, etc.—but here is opportunity for spontaneous feeling in a given situation.

It should ultimately be possible to meet without preparing the way, one of the two reacting to the behaviour of the other. This makes for flexibility and alertness in response.

The same exercises can be played as characters; the characters will have to be clear if the partner is going to be able to react suitably. This is quite an advanced exercise, and comes almost out of the realms of mime into acting exercises and spoken drama—and almost certainly a mime scene can develop freely out of the characters evolved by the class.

It will be found that when a reaction is made, of whatever

kind, the whole body momentarily changes. Whether the cause is happy or sad, there is actually a physical reaction which affects breathing, the surface of the skin, and the temperature of the body. The amount of change will depend on the physical state of the person, and the degree of the emotion, but some change is bound to take place.

The understanding and acceptance of relationship give the student greater flexibility, easier readjustment, and quicker response. This is true of all life, and for that very reason is essential in mime, for mime must have basic truth.

In working out reactions and relationships the pupil will discover his own motives, his own thoughts, and this knowledge will help him to liberate himself so that a transformation can occur at will.

VIII

CROWD WORK

We can assume that the classes have now absorbed some basic technique, some ability to concentrate, and have learnt through concentration to feel their way into characters other than their own; then to feel those people's reaction to, and relationship with, other people and things around them.

All this is essential before they can make any contribution in a crowd.

If any imagine that they can hide in a crowd, they are wrong; each individual has to play his part with integrity, and one person not doing so is a drag, and can ruin the whole.

There must be a common purpose and a unified will. This does not smother individuality, but achieves collective relationship.

Technically, it is important for each person to realize that the onlookers will find the picture dull if the same group of players use the same positions on the stage every time they reappear. This sounds very obvious, but it is surprising how often it will happen. People are apt to take the easiest way, and use the space nearest their entrance, and it calls for quite considerable courage to move across a stage to the far side! Each character, therefore, should be given some training in covering as much space on the stage as possible. Then, if a number of people all do the exercises together—covering space, going in several directions, having the courage to leave their entrance and their favourite spot—there will be a natural criss-cross effect which gives an appearance of the natural movement of a mass of people. This sort of exercise must quickly be given some purpose, or none of the players will feel it is sensible.

For this, a scene at Marble Arch on a Sunday evening, with crowds moving from one orator to another, would give a fulfilment to the technical movement. It will be observed that if it is to appear natural and realistic, there will be a varying rate of movement; this is quite an important point.

This mass exercise will probably demonstrate that within every large group there are a number of smaller ones, and that within these smaller groups the relationship between the individuals must be very real, since it is from this nucleus that the whole scene develops.

If it is to develop successfully there will be need for great concentration and understanding, great economy, and real selflessness. It is so easy to steal unintentionally the attention of the audience at a moment when it should be focused on someone else. A sudden swift movement, a big gesture, or a look in the wrong direction, will all serve to do this. The eyes, especially, are so telling in mime and in acting, and the player who knows how to receive an impression, and hold his thought in his eyes, *before* either speech or movement, has great power.

Eye-direction is too important to be misused and must help to focus the attention of an audience wherever it is needed. If a crowd all rivet their eyes on one person or object, or in one direction, the audience looks at that point without knowing why. In the same way if the crowd looks at an entrance before a character arrives on the scene, the audience will look there also, and the character about to enter is greatly helped. The same device is often used to 'build up' an exit. If one member of the crowd isolates himself and does something entirely different, perhaps looking in quite another direction, he will immediately focus attention on himself. A producer of crowd work must be continually on the watch for these points.

A swift movement in a slow-moving group will always attract attention, and so will a slow movement in an excitable and swift-moving scene.

Another way of giving variety of interest and focus to the scene is to arrange steps or rostra in such a way that the characters can make use of the differences of level.

In a set mime play, the producer will probably direct the movement of each player; but much less direction will be required if the players have had some experience in impromptu group work. Then, when it comes to the play, they will be accustomed to free and unconstrained movement, filling the stage well, 'giving' to one another, helping the focus when needed, and making suggestions themselves, (which always helps the life of the production).

When practising impromptu scenes, the classes should still be able to notice whether or not they are part of a good design. Naturally, the character-work and the general impetus and truth of the feeling must not be lost because of this technical point; but as the attention and expectation of the crowd grows, the audience must not be distracted by the awkward appearance of a poor group. The Proscenium Arch (while we still use it) is like a picture-frame, and, as with any picture, the design within it must be satisfying to the spectators. Sometimes, in a crowd, a big sweeping movement may be needed to fill a corner which has become empty because excitement has drawn the group to one side, but no movement should be made without purpose.

It is sometimes useful to stop a scene quite suddenly, asking everyone to hold as a 'still' whatever they were doing or registering at that moment, so that the group realize that no movement can afford to be without intention, and that they may be caught in a 'still' at any time. It is revealing both to the group and to the producer, but this practice should be used sparingly.

Change of mood is difficult to govern in crowd work. It should come from a genuine feeling which runs through the group and is felt and followed. The actors in the crowd are like the members of an orchestra, each of whom must play his part at the right moment, individually vital yet subservient to the whole, not being led away by personal feelings or lack of control to play out of time, out of turn, or out of tune.

Here are some suggestions for practice—starting with reactions between two or three people, following on with small groups, and then larger groups or crowds:

INFANTS

TWO OR THREE TOGETHER

Peter Pan searches everywhere for his shadow. Wendy wakes up and sees him, finds the shadow and sews it on for him. They fly off together.

Cinderella prepares her ugly sisters for the Ball.

SMALL GROUPS

Cinderella tries on the glass slipper; there is great rejoicing from the Prince and annoyance from the ugly sisters.

Buying a pair of shoes at a shop.

LARGE GROUPS OR CROWDS

A childrens' party—refreshments—games, entertainment, etc.

A school picnic—setting out—arriving—eating—playing —returning.

Snow White eats the apple given her by the witch—the Dwarfs arrive and find her, and all their forest friends come too.

JUNIORS

TWO OR THREE TOGETHER

The little mermaid longs for legs. The witch gives them to her, but every step she takes is like walking on knives.

King Midas is given by the gods the gift of the golden touch. He is delighted that all he touches turns to gold. By chance he turns his daughter to gold, and he is grief-stricken. The gods give him the power to undo the spell.

SMALL GROUPS

Sleeping Beauty, surrounded by some members of her Court, wakes up after a hundred years.

Rumpelstiltskin asks the people round him to guess his name and is angry when he finds someone knows it.

Urchins play at hopscotch, also at marbles, in the street. They are given some ices and eat them.

LARGE GROUPS OR CROWDS

Waiting in a queue outside a cinema or children's theatre on a Saturday morning.

A child has run away from school, and suddenly comes in among his friends, having been found in a wood.

A Scene 'At the Fair'.

SENIORS

TWO OR THREE TOGETHER

A mother and father are at breakfast. Their daughter arrives very late, and is reprimanded by father from behind his paper. The daughter opens a parcel and finds it is a lipstick sent her by a friend. Mother disapproves and confiscates it; the daughter is angry, smashes a piece of crockery and leaves the room.

A peasant girl is gathering sticks with an old woman. The girl's arm is paralysed, and she cannot work fast enough to satisfy the old woman, who leaves her. While alone, the girl sees a vision, her arm is restored and the old woman on her return is converted to kindness.

SMALL GROUPS

A lady insists on completing her purchase and buying a hat just after closing-time; the assistants are trying to clear up, but the customer keeps them busy.

In a railway carriage. On one side of the window is a fresh-air fiend. Opposite is a very smart well-dressed lady; there are other characters in the compartment who take sides in the battle between these two.

It is rehearsal night for the village orchestra. There are only a few instruments; they are enthusiastically practising for their concert.

LARGE GROUPS OR CROWDS

Waiting to see the Queen in a large crowd outside Buckingham Palace. There are police, of course, and a mixture of people from far countries in the crowd.

It is the 'rush-hour' in a little café close to a station and people are anxious to catch trains. The waitresses are very overworked and their tempers are frayed.

A suburban 'bus-stop. Several full 'buses have passed, and a woman in the queue decides to hail a taxi. While she is doing this, another 'bus appears, the rest of the crowd board the 'bus, and she is left behind, for the taxi was occupied.

ADULTS

TWO OR THREE TOGETHER

A scene at the hairdressers, or the barbers.

A newly-wed couple go to have their photograph taken. The photographer takes great pains setting them in position, etc. Just as he is about to take the picture, one of them sneezes and upsets the pose. He starts again. When all is again set, a wasp buzzes round and disturbs them. They are so upset that they rush away without having the photograph taken.

SMALL GROUPS

A prisoner is in his cell. Gaolers outside his door drink and gamble. He is called to his trial.

Hollywood managers are auditioning chorus girls and variety artists. Some are chosen. The former leading lady is jealous of the new one, slaps her face and walks out. The new one makes herself popular with the leading manager.

Two nursemaids are in a park, each with two children, one of which is a baby in a pram. One of the children teases the baby, dangling a worm in front of it. The nursemaids quarrel.

LARGE GROUPS OR CROWDS

In a fashionable shop there is a fashion parade. Men and women are having tea and discussing the dresses, and the models.

A big liner is reaching its destination. Most of the passengers are on deck. It is apparent that they have mixed feelings, according to whether they are reaching home, or arriving in a foreign land.

In a Bar Parlour, a barmaid is serving drinks—and flirting. Following a commotion outside, an injured man is carried in. She makes her way through the crowd to give him brandy, and recognizes the husband she had deserted years before.

A Slave Market. Slaves are being bought and sold; one girl is separated from the master she had loved for years.

*

So far attention has been given to group feeling concerning normal people in a crowd. Now it will help the mass feeling to practise abstract mime in group form.

Quite a good way to begin this, is to ask the class to react spontaneously to sounds and rhythms, either human or instrumental. They become accustomed to their bodies following an impulse of feeling, and with the mind controlling what they are doing, they allow that feeling to direct the movement of the body.

For this exercise all the percussion instruments will be valuable, but perhaps the simplest is to beat a large tambour and occasionally to use cymbals to heighten the effect. The rhythm should be varied. Probably at first the effect will be primitive, but by degrees other feelings will emerge, and quite frequently each individual will develop his own little scene. Often there will be something grand and elemental in conception, which can readily be developed into a subject for mass movement.

When there is a feeling of freedom, direct it by asking them to be conscious once again of the pattern of the whole group and the pictorial effect. When this has grown to be a habit, select some elemental themes, and see if the whole group can react individually in their own way, while yet giving a collective whole:

Examples

> The Planets
> Storm
> Clouds
> Earthquake

It may be that good musical accompaniment will be available, which is naturally a great help, but rather than use poor and inadequate music, let the players make their own noises. If there is any feeling against this, do not force it upon them; if you do, they will not then be free. But some classes will be grateful to be allowed to express themselves in sound without restraint.

Another example that will be suitable at this stage is an abstract expression in group form called:

The Evolution of Man

The group huddle together in a heap on the floor, trying to forget they exist, trying to be nothing. Then by degrees they become something else: a moving mass, from which some will become rock, others primitive animals, birds or insects, others plants, until man himself emerges. Good grouping and good feeling will nearly always grow from this exercise, which seems to have a general appeal to all humanity.

Very often classes will themselves suggest starting at an earlier stage and ending later—e.g. by being Ether, and then after having reached man, becoming spirit only. This produces a sense of lightness that is gained in no other way.

Now divide the class into half, and ask one half of the group to express *war*; ask them to move freely and become a still tableau. Then ask the other half to move and mingle among them expressing *peace*, these also becoming eventually a still tableau. Finally, ask them all to move again—preferably without touching one another—and let the conflict arrive at its own conclusion; it may go either way. Having grasped the idea through this rather obvious choice of *war* and *peace* experiment with other abstract conflicts:

Interest and Boredom
Order and Confusion
Stillness and Movement
Serenity and Worry

Next divide the class into three groups. This time the idea is not one of conflicting emotions, but of progressing from one emotion to another. One group begins by expressing a feeling; a second group enters expressing a second feeling which influences the first group. A third group enters with a third feeling, and the whole class follows this third feeling.

Similarly, divide the class into four groups, and choosing four emotions, follow the same process of progression of feeling. At this point the feelings should be entirely abstract expressions. For example, the individual may represent 'sorrow' *itself* not someone who *is* sorrowful.

Examples

Sorrow changes to *hope* then to *joy*.
Uncertainty changes to *fear* then to *anger* then to *lethargy*.

Now, allow the class to work together again as *one large group*. This time suggest a succession of five or six emotions or states of mind which follow one another, for the whole class to interpret. They will know the order, but will not plan the movement from one emotion to the next. This should happen naturally if their feelings are genuine.

Examples

> Freedom, anxiety, bewilderment, captivity, despair.
> Tranquillity, humour, anxiety, terror, grief, resignation.

Music again will help very much, but it is more than likely that by this time the students will be wanting to express themselves vocally and it may help their feeling to do so. Do not mix the two kinds of accompaniment. It would be futile to suggest sounds to the class, but here is an indication of the kind of sound that might be expected from:

> Tranquillity—a vague serene humming
> Rumour—a hissing or buzzing of voices
> Anxiety—questioning or doubtful inflection of sounds without words
> Terror—screams
> Grief—sobs
> Resignation—a slight sighing

Now is probably the right moment to allow these abstract emotions to become personal, and be given reasons.

Ask the class to suggest a theme and a possible development for some of these emotions. There will be many and varied ideas.

Here is a possible suggestion:

Tranquillity—A small village in Central Europe is happy, and the people go about their daily work without fear or trouble.

Rumour—News comes that troops have been seen gathering on the borders.

Anxiety—If it is true, what are they to do?

Terror—Without further warning, armies arrive and invade the village, burning and pillaging as they go, leaving destruction behind them.

Grief—Homes and loved ones have been lost in the invasion.
Resignation—Time passes, life must go on for those who are
left, and the village be re-built for the next generation.

Now here are some suggestions of abstract scenes for
practice.

INFANTS

A group of trees. When night comes and the moon is high,
they come to life and dance together; but no human ever
sees them or discovers their secrets.

One evening a little girl is playing on the sands when
everyone else has gone. She is delighted to find that the
waves each have a spirit, and that they rush out of the sea
and play with her. Some are rollicking and boisterous,
others are more timid and slow. They run back to the
sea when she goes, promising to meet her again another
day.

(A similar idea could be applied to other aspects of nature,
provided it is not over-used.)

You are what is called 'still life'. A potato, an orange, a
silver tray, a Dresden statue, a jug, and a dead fish. Someone
is painting you in a picture; when the artist goes, you all
come to life.

Half of you are a smouldering fire which is gradually
spreading from bush to bush. The other half are a waterfall
which is running swiftly into a river. The fire and the water
meet and clash, and the fire is vanquished.

JUNIORS

One of you is a witch. She is brewing a spell in her cauldron.
The rest are the spell, which gradually grows and shows
itself.

H

Clytie, the nymph, is in love with Apollo, the Sun-God. Daily she watches his journey across the sky and hopes he will notice her. He does not. The spirits of nature are kind to her, and she becomes a sun-flower.

Express what you feel in movement when a sound is suggested to you and create a scene round it. E.g. drums, a bell, breaking glass, a bleat, guns.

The God Mercury brings Pandora a box and instructs her not to look inside it. When he has gone, the temptation is too strong for her, and she peeps in. At once all the Evils spring out of it and flood the world. She struggles to shut it, and just before she manages to do so, Hope has escaped also.

SENIORS

Spirits are in torment of every kind. They work together and manage to triumph over the Devil.

Base a scene on any of the following words:
Conscience. Achievement. Sleep. Hostility. Self-aggrandizement.

One of you represents your brain. The others are evil thoughts that come from various places and enter your mind. The brain quells these thoughts.

The spirits of the dead are in Hades. Death enters, then Pluto and Persephone. Orpheus comes to find Eurydice, and she is given to him on condition that he does not look at her. As she follows him she entreats him not to look, but he cannot resist the temptation, turns and sees her. She fades, and he is banished from Hades.

Express what you feel in movement when colours are suggested to you: red, black, blue, purple, green, yellow.

ADULTS

Life and Death struggle for the possession of a beautiful girl. Death triumphs over her body, but Life possesses her soul.

A woman is in misery. Temptation comes to her and tries to persuade her to commit suicide. She struggles and nearly yields, but finally overcomes Temptation.

The scene is a churchyard. It is a moonlight night; bats and owls and the church clock are the only inhabitants. Men gather for a clandestine meeting, and as they are leaving to fulfil their purpose, they are haunted by their guilty consciences.

An artist is starving; he works, but no one wants his pictures. He is visited by Material Necessity, and later by Inspiration. He struggles between the two.

Immanent Will creates the Iceberg. It also creates the *Titanic*. At a given moment in time they come together. The ship sinks, the Iceberg moves on.
(Suggested by Hardy's poem—'The Loss of the *Titanic*'.)

*

In any of these suggestions the abstract concepts may be suggested by one person, or a group of people.

By this time classes will have appreciated that to be part of a crowd is as exciting as any solo performance, that the work is just as arduous but equally rewarding. Each individual contributes to the mass feeling.

IX

IMPROVISATION WITH UTTERANCE

Teachers will find that improvisation with utterance or speech can give their pupils both confidence and control. The actor must be ready to make use of it on occasion when he is faced with an emergency; practice in it will be an addition to all previous mime training, but will never take the place of it.

In improvisation, mime and sound should spring spontaneously as from one source. There can be no success in miming, and then in adding words to fit the mime, nor yet in speaking, and then adding mime to fit the speech. There can be satisfaction only if both happen together, or if one is the inevitable outcome of the other.

This does not mean that all movement must be accompanied by utterance or speech. The situation must be natural and therefore sometimes silent. Most people, when alone, refrain from talking to themselves, though they may occasionally let forth a sigh, a grunt, or an ejaculation.

It is necessary to remember this when improvising solo scenes. I have seen people try to improvise, who—feeling that they ought to be talking—have either uttered all their thoughts aloud—in the form of a soliloquy—or talked to imaginary characters around them. Certainly some have the gift of 'peopling' an empty stage, but these are rare artists, and in scenes where this technique is required, the words are usually of primary importance and the mime becomes secondary. The result will then be a prepared monologue or sketch; this is no longer improvisation.

Improvisation does not need to be taught in the same way to infants and juniors. They talk freely in their natural play, and will be quite ready to express themselves in sounds or in words without feeling awkward or self-conscious.

With these younger children it is important that the mime already learnt should bear fruit and be developed into play-making.

Generally speaking, small children are much more successful in their plays when they have been allowed to improvise their own words. A useful beginning is to suggest to a few children who are quite good at mime that they act particular characters, and let them begin a scene, using sounds or words if appropriate; the rest of the class will listen, and directly they see an opportunity for the entrance of another character others will in turn join in and add to the scene.

Examples:

> One child will be a witch
> One child will be a princess
> One child will be an owl

Here are our first three characters. They will probably know how they want to start the scene;—if not, suggest that it is set in a forest; the owl is perched on a branch hooting occasionally and the witch is stooping over her cauldron, muttering to herself as she brews her frightening spells (for she is a wicked old woman). After a few minutes the princess comes along, speaks to the witch and tells her how she climbed over the palace wall to find the golden ball which she had thrown too far, that it was so fascinating outside that she has lost herself and is tired.

Childen will soon develop the theme, and all sorts of characters will join in—fantastic, animal, and human.

The improvising must be very free, but if it is to become their own play the teacher will no doubt need to help by pruning here and developing there, and finally deciding the exact order of entrance, the timing, climax, and conclusion. Having thus reached the form of a play, improvisation must be put aside, and, however young the children, the discipline of the theatre must begin. They have selected their own words, the words must now be accurate; the movement becomes planned to their own design, and must not change, —unless to make an agreed improvement.

Acting now becomes quite a serious business, and they will enjoy it all the more because of this. Teachers are some-times apt to be carried away by free work, improvisation, and what is called 'the play way', so that nothing ever reaches a satisfactory conclusion or makes an artistic whole, and no one learns the meaning of control. In all good dramatic work freedom and control must go hand in hand, and while improvisation is the perfect way for infants and juniors to learn, we must not be content for it to end in a rather poor charade. If we are, then we might as well leave the children to play happily in their own way and without guidance.

The main difficulty in this work however is experienced by seniors and adults, and therefore much of this chapter is written with them in mind. The difficulty seems to be in the transition from mime to words. Explaining to them that there really is no transition does not always help.

I have found that the easiest method is to ask them to think about their own natural behaviour when alone, and after that to suggest the right kind of examples for practice, asking them to do them perfectly naturally, making a sound or saying a word if it would be normal to do so, and not otherwise.

The examples selected should be of such a nature that they will call forth a natural response in sound, probably demanding at first only an ejaculation; then developing others, which bring the natural response of a word, or words. In this way, the class will realize that quite a considerable amount of time may be spent in silent acting, that nothing should be forced or unnatural, and that utterance of some sort, whether in sound or speech, will happen in its proper place.

The teacher will soon find that the examples develop into little scenes. He must realize, that more particularly in teaching this branch of the subject, the selection of example matters. It must be suitable for the class, and must be graded so that the development is sufficiently gradual, and so that they are never made to feel silly, awkward, or self-conscious. Once this happens the work is valueless.

I would, therefore, advocate very strongly indeed that in the early stages (even though we must call them 'solo examples'), the whole class should work together without onlookers. This applies to all mime classes; only gradually, as confidence grows, should any solo work be asked for.

In improvisation there will naturally be exclamations and sounds of all kinds springing from all quarters of the class at different moments; this does not matter, let them go ahead in their own time regardless of one another, thus any foolishness they might have felt if left alone is lost, because the individual movements and sounds appear to merge into one. The experienced teacher grows accustomed to looking at and seeing the individual within the group.

Presently the moment will come for two to improvise together, and then for small groups. It will still be well, to begin with, to allow all the groups to act at the same time. Gradually they will suggest watching each other's scenes, and interest will take the place of awkwardness.

Eventually the whole class can join in a concerted group scene, and having worked from solo scenes, through the small group to this point, they will all be ready and able to contribute to such a scene. Some of the crowd scenes suggested for mime in Chapter VIII could equally well be used for improvisation.

When the class is quite at home in this work, refer back to some of the solo improvisations and ask some members to repeat them alone. If this seems too great an ordeal, do not force it, but let half a dozen do the same scene at one time, then gradually reduce the number until all grow accustomed to the idea. Then allow those who have gifts in this medium to use them for the enjoyment of others, but quick thinking is needed, so some will excel in this, and others will succeed more easily in prepared work. Rightly handled by the teacher, as with all mime, confidence and ease will develop, but wrongly handled, no good will come of any of it, only acute discomfort.

Here are some suggestions of examples that are likely to bring response in sound or word as well as in movement:

Ejaculations

You are: sewing, and prick yourself.

trying to read, but are constantly disturbed by a fly.

putting the finishing touches to your toilet, and just as you are ready, you ladder your stocking.

asleep, and are wakened by an alarm clock.

opening a tin and you cut yourself.

doing up a shoe-lace, and it breaks.

listening to a play, and someone in the row behind rustles sweet papers.

cooking, and you burn yourself on a hot pan.

walking, and you trip unexpectedly.

taking a cold shower, against your will.

watching a clown at a circus.

seeing the top of a snow-mountain for the first time.

watching a village cinema show, and the projector fails.

out to tea, and you upset your cup in your lap.

dozing in a train, and wake up to find you are moving out of the station where you wanted to get out.

preparing a meal, and the milk boils over.

watching a trapeze artist, and he falls but is caught by the safety net.

watching motor-racing.

sitting quietly, and a mouse runs across the room.

standing on a pavement, and a car nearly runs you down.

walking into the sea on a lovely hot day.

carrying a suit-case, and it opens in a crowded street.

waiting for the curtain to go up on the opening night of a show, and a 'prop' is missing.

Let the class take plenty of time to get into the scene, and build up to the moment of ejaculation. Some examples may not bring an audible response, but the class will be quick to suggest others they like better. Sometimes it works well for them to set exercises of this kind for one another to do.

If some pupils suggest that they never make audible response under any circumstances, let them act the sort of person who might do so; very often the people who make this sort of objection are those who need the freedom that this work gives, more than the rest.

IN TWOS

Two people are:

sitting reading quietly, and there is a sudden clap of thunder.

walking arm-in-arm and one trips.

going into the sea on a cold day; one who is already wet splashes the other, who is not.

pulling a cracker together.

listening to the radio; one smells burning, the other remembers the cake in the oven.

in a street, one is on a ladder cleaning windows, the other walking underneath; the wet cloth drops on his head.

trying the bumper cars at a fair.

standing on the edge of a swimming bath, one pushes the other in.

in a restaurant; one is a waitress who spills the soup down the customer's neck.

SMALL GROUPS

You are watching television—Decide before beginning what the programme is, and remember it is not likely that there would be much talk from you, but sometimes an ordinary reaction that might be audible as sound or words.

You are a family:

at home	at the races
in a tube train	or in any other circum-
at a party	stances you prefer

BIGGER GROUP SCENES

You are waiting in a queue. Let us see and hear the difference in the following circumstances:

> a 'bus queue
> a shop queue
> a theatre queue
> outside a zoo
> a cinema queue

In each case end the scene by passing through a turnstile or door and going inside. It could, however, be equally effective without the entrance, if the characterization is strong enough.

Now other group scenes with utterance should happen quite naturally, following on the suggestion of a title.

Examples:

Before the wedding	Budget day
Bank holiday	On the brink of disaster
Departure	Planets
Nonsense	

Whatever the title, no two groups of people will ever react in the same way, so there will always be variety.

Another idea is to divide a large class into a number of small groups, making each group responsible for part of a continuous scene. Those not taking part can be watching but ready to take their part at the right moment, without any pause.

Examples:
The scene is:

A Snack Bar

Two or three waitresses will remain in the scene throughout—the other groups of different people will arrive at different hours of the day, and with no lull between each. The scenes will be at:

>   8 a.m.—on the way to work
>   11 a.m.—people of leisure
>   1 p.m.—lunch break
>   4 p.m.—tea time
>   7 p.m.—supper
>   11 p.m.—after the theatre

Several different groups can of course enter at one period; this just depends on the numbers in the class.

Similarly, the exercise could be played

a) In an ice cream kiosk
>   or
b) On the first day of the sales (the same department throughout)
>   or
c) In a hotel kitchen (various shifts of workers)

Now, thinking back to the original ejaculations, some of the class will perhaps be inclined to develop them into little personal scenes. Others may like ideas which are more formed, but which still lend themselves to improvising with utterance.

Here are some suggestions:

1. You are trying to put up a camp bed; it is awkward and stiff and you find yourself doing ridiculous contortions before your efforts have any success.

2. You are sitting in a haunted room just before midnight. You have been told that terrible happenings take place as the clock strikes twelve. Midnight strikes, and you show what happens.

3. You take your little pug dog on a 'bus. You hoped to travel inside but are forced to take him on top, much to your disgust.

4. It is Hallowe'en. You are sitting looking in the mirror imagining you will see your future husband. You see something you didn't expect in the mirror. You show what it is.

5. You decide to lay some linoleum in a small old-fashioned bathroom. While you are struggling to fix it, someone opens the door, and you find yourself entangled in linoleum, half under the bath.

6. You are a maid taking early morning tea to your mistress in bed. You are surprised that she does not wake when you draw the curtains and light the fire. When you go to the bed you find she has been murdered.

7. You are very poor, and are tempted by something you see in a shop, which you know your mother badly needs. Finding you haven't the money, you slip it into your bag. You leave the shop and you are stopped by a detective.

8. You are listening to a gramophone on a verandah in a hot country. Suddenly you see a snake close by and realize it is a cobra rearing its head to attack you.

9. You take a turkish bath for the first time—starting off very gaily. Deciding it's not worth it when you arrive at the hottest room, you return rather crestfallen.

Once again after these solo scenes I would end by bringing a whole class together. The practice should have strengthened their feeling of freedom, and they should be able immediately to make an amusing improvisation with words on a subject like:

Camp

starting with the arrival—erecting tents—cooking—fetching water, etc.,—introducing every aspect of mime and coming to the beginnings of play-making. Directly groups begin to invent scenes or plays it will be necessary to add the other ingredients of drama; i.e. not only character, which will be there, but circumstance, conflict, and climax.

X

OTHER COUNTRIES AND
OTHER TIMES

Mime can be of benefit to most subjects in the school curriculum, and the mime teacher should help by trying to correlate his illustrations with the year's work. He will be unlikely to set out to teach a scientific subject like geography which requires vast specialized knowledge, but he may help to interest the children by asking them to imagine and mime some of the conditions of life in other parts of the world.

Correlation with the Geography Lesson

Climate will usually be of immediate interest, and the class could well begin with some discussion of heat and cold and their effect on body and movement. They will generally conclude that cold creates contraction and tension, while heat induces expansion and relaxation. Also that cold often brings about brisk movement in order to keep warm, while heat tends to make gentler movement and leisurely action more comfortable; but that the extreme of either might bring life to a standstill.

Here are some exercises developing this theme. They

could be used with any age provided they were appropriately introduced:

Move about imagining that it is:

> a pleasantly warm English summer day
> an unusually scorching English day
> a hot dry day somewhere near the equator
> a day of humid moist heat

Take time feeling the difference between these varying kinds of heat and the way you would react. Then repeat the last two as someone who is accustomed to live in those conditions, and notice if the reaction is different. It almost certainly will be.

Now move about imagining that it is:

> a damp English November day with drizzling rain
> a thick English fog in a city
> a sunny day with snow on the ground and crispness in the air
> further north, colder, greyer, with snow, but no sun.
> nearer the North Pole where nothing lives

Repeat the last two as if you were fully prepared and equipped for such cold, as the members of a polar expedition might be.

Now imagine the effect of other kinds of weather or climatic conditions.

Move as if you were in:

a very strong wind	a sandstorm
a hail storm	a gale
a snowstorm	the terrifying wind at the
a thunderstorm	top of Mount Everest
rain	

Let the class now divide into small groups. Each group will now be responsible for making a mime scene which will show a climatic condition or temperature. The scenes should cover as many different parts of the world as possible.

Watching each other's scenes, the class will soon begin to observe how temperature and climate affect behaviour, and as the characters in the scenes begin to emerge an understanding of national characteristics will grow too.

If the children begin to think of too many ideas at once, the mime will become untidy and the results will not satisfy them; that is why this sequence should develop slowly, and concentration on climate and character will be as much as can be carried out satisfactorily at first.

They might then learn something more by considering the countryside in this way:

Show the difference in your feeling as you walk:

on a mountain track	on downs
on a tarred road	on rock
on quicksand	through jungle
on desert sand	

It may be a good plan to repeat some of the scenes which illustrated climates and see if enough consideration had been given to the surface of the earth.

This brings them immediately to modes of transport, always an exciting topic for children:

Imagine you are travelling:

on a horse	in a boat
in a rickshaw	on skis
in a car	on a bicycle
on a mule	in a lorry
on a camel	on a sledge
in a jet airplane	

I

These need considerable skill in mime, but the feeling can be conveyed quite well while remaining on one spot. Consider again if any of these would have helped the scenes, and try to see the sort of countryside in which they might be.

What kind of shelter will these people have? Where do they live?

Show that you are in:

a tent	an igloo
a house	a caravan
a mud hut	a castle

Immediately, in order to show this, the children will want to begin 'doing', so the sort of occupation will become an interest.

Show that you are:

fishing	cotton growing
wine-making	doing factory work
fruit-farming	tea planting
doing basket work	rice picking
sheep shearing	

They will also want to think about the food and drink of other peoples. So they can try examples to show this:

Show that you are eating:

figs	pumpkin pie
macaroni	rice
avocada pears	pickled herring
bamboo shoots	

Show that you are drinking:

vodka	tea
Coca-Cola	sherbert
goats' milk	

What will they wear in other countries and climates while doing various occupations?

Show that you are wearing:

a sari	a mackintosh
Hawaiian straw skirts	a kimono
an Arab's head-dress and robes	a yashmak
an Eskimo's skins	a coat and skirt

I only give examples of variety; naturally the lessons could be directed along particular channels, depending on whether the ways of a special country will be more useful, or a wide variety to set the classes thinking for themselves. They can be encouraged to bring fresh scenes to illustrate various points, and in doing so they will often have to look up and find out information for the scene, which is valuable. They will also become more aware of the different ways of thinking and acting in different parts of the world.

Correlation with the Scripture Lesson

Many of these suggestions can be used as a contribution to the scripture lesson.

Climate, countryside, transport, shelter, occupation, food, and clothes are all applicable. The method of working can be much the same, only in this case the bias will be in a different direction. Characters will now have to stand out strongly against the appropriate background; the people in the stories matter more than their surroundings. The exercise of acting scenes will now be less of a study, the purpose being rather to make the stories more memorable. Perhaps this may not seem to be necessary, but I think it is comparable with little children drawing pictures of stories in Sunday School; only in this way the pictures come to life. Most teachers will have their own ideas about which stories to mime, so a lead is probably unnecessary, but here are a few suggestions:

INFANTS

Noah building the Ark with his family. The animals are collected. The rain comes.

The Nativity. Shepherds and kings visit Mary and Joseph and the Baby in the stable.

JUNIORS

On the Ark. The sending out of the dove, and the return with the olive branch.

Pharoah's daughter, Princess of Egypt, goes down to the Nile with her ladies, to bathe. She finds Moses hidden in the bulrushes, keeps him as her son, calls an Israelite to be his nurse; the child's mother offers herself and is accepted as his nurse.

SENIORS

The return of the Prodigal Son. There is great feasting and great rejoicing.

The parable of the Good Samaritan.

The feast of the Passover, and the Israelites journeying across the Red Sea.

David slays Goliath. Saul is jealous. David plays to Saul. Saul throws a javelin at David, but he avoids it.

ADULTS

The healing of the blind beggar by St Paul.

Adam and Eve eating the apple and being banished from the Garden of Eden.

Two mothers make claim to one baby before King Solomon. He offers to cut it in two. The true parent is recognized because she would rather give up the baby than have it destroyed.

Salome dancing for Herod and demanding the head of John the Baptist.

Correlation with the English Lesson

The English lesson offers such obvious opportunities for mime that there is little need to give space to it.

Most teachers will, I think, agree, that episodes from 'set books' are likely to live more fully in the mind of the young person after being acted. For this purpose it will be wise to concentrate largely on characterization; then revert to the book and re-read the description given by the author, so that there is an incentive to read and an enjoyment in doing so. To the scholar or the more literary child reading will be a habit, but not to all. Here again are some suggestions for scenes:

INFANTS

The story of 'The Tailor of Gloucester' by Beatrix Potter (or others in this series.)

The story of 'The Three Bears' or other fairy stories.

Some of the adventures of 'Tom and the Water Babies'.

JUNIORS

The story of the poem 'Goblin Market' (Christina Rossetti).

Some of the adventures of 'Alice in Wonderland'.

Ulysses and his men land and find the lotus-eaters—some eat the lotus and fall under its spell—Ulysses drags the others back to the boats.

Perseus is sent by the King to slay the Gorgon and bring him its head. He meets Athene who gives him a sword and shield and warns him not to look at the Gorgon. Perseus slays the Gorgon and brings the head to the King, who looks at it and is turned to stone.

SENIORS

The Lady of Shallott sees 'the mirror crack from side to side'.

From *The Pickwick Papers*—Mr Winkle and Sam Weller with their companions on the ice.

'Vanity Fair' and other episodes from *The Pilgrim's Progress*.

An Elizabethan tavern—the death of Christopher Marlowe.

ADULTS

Episodes from the life of Samuel Pepys.

The death of Cleopatra—from *Antony and Cleopatra*.

Mephistopheles shows Dr Faustus the wonders of the world and the beautiful Marguerite—tempting him to sell his soul. He agrees, but when he would keep Marguerite for ever she has to return to Mephistopheles, and Faustus becomes an old man.

Comus brings the lady to his palace and introduces her to Greed, Avarice, Pride, and his other followers. She is made to drink and turns to stone, but is rescued by Sabrina and her brothers.

Correlation with the History Lesson

The history lesson naturally takes us away into other times, and here mime can offer an important contribution.

Infants and Juniors will be interested and excited in the subject because they love stories, and love acting stories; these they should be allowed to mime freely, or develop into their own plays. If some are good story-tellers, a narrative could string together a series of episodes, some of which could be told, some mimed, some acted, or told in verse.

Seniors and adults will need to do (and will enjoy doing) some detailed study of the modes and manners of the times, so that the movement in the scenes is appropriate. In doing the necessary careful study or research, their own knowledge of social history must increase. There are interesting reasons to be found for changes of costume and these are linked with changes of movement. Without at least some knowledge of the social background of the times, 'period' or historic movement is bound to look mechanical and unreal.

Look at the pictures and you will realize that although the human shape always remains the same, it is astonishing how humanity has contrived to alter it by variety of costume. Compare the outline in pictures of:

Julius Caesar, Dante, Richard of Bordeaux, Henry VIII, Charles II, Napoleon *or*

Helen of Troy, Cleopatra, Joan of Arc, Queen Elizabeth I, Nell Gwyn, The Empress Josephine, Queen Victoria.

Studied chronologically, the infinite variety of costume and shape explains itself; one thing evolves from another. Generally speaking, a period of war brings little change except that the clothing becomes more practical or more military; while a period of peace usually brings an interest in dress and more elaboration. Very often the personal foible of a reigning monarch or someone of importance sets a fashion. For example, in James I's reign fashions changed little, because he and his wife were thrifty. The men wore padded clothes, largely because the Scots king (feeling he was in a foreign land, and having the fate of his Mother, Mary, Queen of Scots, well in mind), adopted padded clothes—his courtiers following suit, and so the fashion was set. The weight of the costume obviously affects the movement, so a detailed study of costume is bound to be a help.

Books on historical costume are legion, so I shall not enlarge by giving full costume notes here; but naturally it would be advisable to show pictures of the period to a class, and consider in which way the clothes would affect movement, before starting to build up the atmosphere.

The notes that here follow are no more than a skeleton for further study, but include some points of interest about each period that might be helpful, because of their dramatic significance, in building a historic scene in mime. It will be found, too, that these beginnings will tempt the children to continue research for themselves.

MEDIAEVAL PERIOD
A.D. 1000 *to roughly* 1450

There are few contemporary accounts of the early part of this period, but much information can be gained from the study of carvings, effigies, tapestries, and illuminated manuscripts, and later from stained glass, brasses, and pictures.

By the twelfth century there were books called 'Herbals' which were about plants, also 'Bestiaries' about animals and insects, as well as religious books; all these show illustrations of people at work.

Generally speaking the people were greatly influenced by the Church, and most of them had complete faith; the

Church was part of their daily life; pictorial representation on the whole is grave and thoughtful.

The Crusades, later, had a great influence. The country was divided into small estates, each manor with its lord, its freemen, and serfs; the dependents of each manor regarding others almost as if they were foreigners.

The feudal system stands roughly for castles, open halls, and rather public living. There are many pictures of banquets, which are a great assistance in showing us small points of etiquette.

Some of the customs are of particular interest from the dramatic point of view. For example:

In Norman times the *mantle* was very important; boys would not be allowed to wear the mantle as it symbolized manhood.

To throw a mantle was a challenge.

In presenting a petition, the petitioner knelt and touched the mantle of the overlord.

A newly created knight was presented with a rich mantle by the sovereign.

If a messenger brought good news, he might be presented with the mantle then being worn by the receiver of the news.

Troubadours who pleased by their singing were similarly rewarded.

Norman scenes should be dignified and slow because of the clothes. The wearing of the mantle meant that a typical attitude had to be one hand on the hip, holding the mantle away from the body, preventing it from impeding the movement.

In Henry II's reign the male courtiers needed easier clothes to fit themselves to compete with Henry's energy and constant moving round his possessions. On occasions they hardly had time to sit down, even to eat, as no one could sit in his presence until he was himself seated.

There was more etiquette at this time than most people imagine.

It was the practice to eat with the fingers, but it was stated:

Hands should be clean.

Only three fingers to be used for helping oneself, the others to be gracefully extended.

The mouth should be wiped before drinking.

Ladies must not cram their mouths too full, or try to deprive their neighbours at table of the choicest bits.

In the twelfth century gloves took on the significance held by the mantle in the previous period.

To throw down a glove was now a challenge to mortal combat.

To give a messenger a glove was a sign of authority.

The right glove was always removed before greeting a friend or addressing a superior.

It was irreverent to enter a church without removing gloves.

Poisoned gloves were sometimes given.

The sleeve, too, held an important place:

Ladies liked to bestow them as love-tokens on their knights. Sometimes even a whole garment was given, which the knight would wear over his armour at the tournament, and come back with it gashed and rent, showing the rents with pride.

Sleeves were often detachable; it was a custom in the

tenth century for a queen to bestow her stylish sleeves on the poor.

In the fifteenth century we read of a costly sleeve being stolen from her arm, while a queen sat watching a miracle play.

A man would move freely, probably carrying one or both hands in his belt, his legs (when not covered by a cloak or robe) would be particularly noticeable because of the long tights; there would be no turn-out in the leg movement, and the feet would be parallel.

When he bowed he would slide one foot back leaving the weight on the front foot, both knees bent, the back heel off the ground, and again no turn-out. His body would tilt forward slightly as he removed his hat and brought it down to his side. He would then bring the foot forward again and replace his hat.

A lady's movement would be affected by her closely moulded gown with its very long voluminous skirt, often with a train and coloured under-skirt, so that she would find many ways of lifting her skirt for practical reasons, and always we see her holding it in decorative positions, also showing her hands to advantage, her body tilting back slightly as she walks. A widely varied range of elaborate head-dresses were worn.

In the later part of the period the mantle became a significant part of the woman's attire, because it was only worn by married women.

When the lady curtsied she would slide one foot back, dropping down on to the back heel, with her head up, and her hands by her sides; on rising, the back foot would come forward to the front one. The essence of the movement would be simplicity.

There are some stories about the women and their

clothes, which might well be developed into mime plays:

One story is about the women's trains:

That a woman with a long train passed by two monks; one monk saw a devil sitting on her train, and when she turned to the monk the devil fell off into the mud. Therefore we know that the devil hath power over women's long tails!

Another is about the elaborate head-dresses:

A famous monk travelled from place to place, preaching against these head-dresses, often collecting a congregation of 20,000 people (men one side, women the other),—the women 'like a forest of cedars with their heads reaching to the clouds'. He succeeded so well that 'many of the women threw down their head-dresses in the middle of his sermon and made a bonfire of them within sight of the pulpit'. For a time the monstrous ornament was pelted down by the rabble and stones were flung when people wore it. But the effect did not last long, and it is said that—'the women that, like snails in a fright, had drawn in their horns, shot them out again as soon as the danger was over'.

This, I am sure, brings to mind a number of interesting scenes for the classes to act, and in doing so, become accustomed to movement suited to mediaeval clothes.

It may be helpful to them to know a few more points of *etiquette of the early fifteenth century*.

If a gift was to be presented at a shrine, the hat was either held, or removed and placed on the ground beside the wearer, who knelt on both knees.

If a gift was to be presented to a human personage, the hat procedure was the same, but the giver knelt on one knee only.

If approaching a noble, the hat would be taken off, and the wearer fall on the right knee two or even three times, not replacing the hat until told to do so.

If two men met and greeted each other, each pushed off his

hat, so that it fell behind his shoulder. (This was the period when the liripipe was attached by a brooch.) The two men clasped right hands, but did not 'shake' them.

On entering the house it was customary to remove hood or hat, and gloves.

The lady knelt to God and high dignitaries on both knees. She often sat on the floor.

Two extracts from Books of Courtesy of the fifteenth century will assist in making scenes or plays:

The first one might make a children's scene.

'A schoolboy must bring pen, ink and paper with him, and on the way politely take off his cap to those he meets and give way to them on the road. At school, he should salute his master and the scholars, go straight to his place, undo his satchel and begin his lessons. He must work hard at his books if he wishes to be thought worthy to serve the State.'

The second gives a lovely banqueting scene:

'When you come to a feast, greet the steward who shows you where to sit—you will find bread laid for you and perhaps a platter also for soft food. There will be drinking cups upon the board and a salt cellar, but bring your own knife and spoon, the best you can afford.

When the food is brought around you will be served on to your trencher of bread or platter.

Eat quietly, and, as you share plates and cups do not leave your spoon in the food—or drink with your mouth full—lest you soil the cup.

Don't stroke the dog or cat under the table but keep your hands clean. Don't blow upon your food—but talk awhile pleasantly to your waiting friends while it cools. Don't put your elbows on the table or turn your back on

your neighbour—do not inconvenience your host by calling for unserved dishes. Be sedate and courteous if you
sit among gentlefolk—and tell no tale that would harm
or shame any guest that so the feast may be pleasant to
all.'

Perhaps one more extract may add flavour to the scenes.
This is a foreigner's opinion of English people of the time;
only helpful for senior or adult classes:

'The English are for the most part, both men and women
of all ages, handsome and well-proportioned . . . great
lovers of themselves and of everything belonging to them;
they think that there are no other men than themselves,
and no other world but England. . . . They all from time
immemorial wear very fine clothes, and are extremely
polite in their language. . . .

In addition to their civil speeches, they have the
incredible courtesy of remaining with their heads uncovered with an admirable grace, whilst they talk to each
other.

They are gifted with good understandings, and are very
quick at everything they apply their minds to. . . . I have
never noticed anyone, either at Court or amongst the
lower orders, to be in love; whence one must necessarily
conclude, either that the English are the most discreet
lovers in the world, or that they are incapable of love.'

With some background of information from the teacher,
the classes will certainly be able to develop scenes on the
themes already given; on ladies and gentlemen banqueting
in their great halls; troubadours bringing their songs and
tales of love and war; or a romance between the troubadour
and the young princess who may not realize her dreams;
of gentlemen hawking, ladies on their way to Church,

meeting one another; or ladies at home embroidering their tapestries, and receiving news or arrivals from the Crusades.

TUDOR PERIOD
End of fifteenth and whole of sixteenth centuries

To learn about the people of this period and the clothes they wore, we can still turn to sculpture and all forms of effigy, also to brasses and tapestries, and illustrated manuscripts which are often very beautiful; by now wood-cuts and metal-cuts, too, are a valuable source. We can look to the portrait painters—Memling, Dürer, Botticelli, Leonardo da Vinci, Titian, Holbein, and Raphael and, later in the period, at El Greco, and Rubens. There was at this time in England a spirit of enquiry and adventure, and more interest in travel; as a result there was less feeling of serenity than in the earlier periods, and the fashions of France, Holland, and Italy influenced England very much. As a result there was more breadth of outlook, and buoyancy of spirit, more learning, and more mental equality between the sexes, although Luther said:

'When women are ready in speaking it is not to be commended—there is no gown or garment that worse becomes a woman than when she will be wise.'

The girls' education was still deplorably low at the beginning of the period, but improved as time went on and Queen Elizabeth came to the throne.

The farthingale brought with it the fashion of sitting on a pile of cushions on the floor or on a joint stool; but towards the end of the century, specially made wide chairs were introduced, to accommodate the farthingale, though cushions were still quite popular.

Boys still waited at table, and a book on elegant deportment says:

'Boys of gentle birth when waiting at table must not scratch their heads or any other part of their persons, nor must they sneeze or cough into the dishes or drinking utensils.'

and again:

'Princely establishments must be conducted on different lines from common pothouses—all tin and pewter utensils to be scoured every Saturday, or at even shorter intervals if company was expected.'

There seems to have been a complete lack of cleanliness and hygiene from the sixteenth century; for public baths, which had been available in the fifteenth century, were then closed down as being breeding places for epidemics.

Outwardly, there was much luxury and pomp, and much use of perfumes, often in ball form, called pomanders.

Queen Elizabeth sent for a Flemish woman—Mistress Dingham Van der Plasse—who knew the secret of starch, and this lady earned great wealth giving lessons on ruff making and the secret of starch.

There was a story that amused Queen Elizabeth that might be made into a macabre mime:

'A lady of Antwerp who was in a great state because she could not get her ruff to set aright, in a passion called upon "the devil to take it". A handsome gentleman appeared. Together they tried to set the ruff; the gentleman strangled the lady and vanished. When they came to carry away the coffin no one could lift it, and when they opened it they found—a great black cat setting a ruff!'

In this period:

The man would walk easily, though his waisted tunic made his poise a little stiffer, and his feet were more turned out. Often he carried one hand on sword or belt, and before giving his hand to a lady he would kiss it. He also adopted the charming habit (probably French in origin) of kissing any article before handing it to a lady.

In *his bow* he would slide the right foot back, transferring his weight on to the back leg and bending the back knee. The front knee would be kept straight, and the body bowed. His hat would come down to the side with a curved arm position.

The lady's movement would be affected by the heavy materials of her dress, velvet, brocade, etc., often covered with quite weighty jewels. The wearing of the ruff or starched collar would encourage a well-poised head, and it was not considered correct for the farthingale to sway too much—so she would 'sail' as she moved, her hands on farthingale or stomacher.

Her curtsy would be much like the mediaeval curtsy, but looked very different because of the difference of timing: a quick drop and a slow rise; the hands on the skirt at either side at the beginning and coming up to cover the low-cut top of the dress on the downward drop.

Let the class now develop scenes for these times. Some of the most well-known happen to be the most dramatic:

Queen Elizabeth signing the death warrant for the Earl of Essex, *or*

Sir Francis Drake finishing his game of bowls as the Armada approaches.

The children will have plenty of suggestions of scenes about people in this period that they would like to act, and

K

will grow gradually more accustomed to moving as if wearing the clothes shown in pictures.

THE SEVENTEENTH CENTURY

Again it will be necessary to make a study of the costumes, and consider how they would affect the movements of the people who lived at this time. There are now many pictures available, and Van Dyck gives us an exact knowledge of the costumes that were worn. For a description in words, look at the pastoral called 'Rhodon and Iris', first acted in 1631, which contains a long and curious speech about the ladies of extreme fashion; or in Massinger's 'City Madam', the passage about a merchant's wife.

An interesting touch is that ruffs went abruptly out of fashion, because a physician's wife—condemned for her part in a poisoning case—went to her execution in a ruff; so they became unpopular.

Charles I had ideas about cleanliness that were ahead of his time, and he regarded fresh linen as being of great importance.

A book of rules in 1640 says:

'An occasional bath should be taken, the hands washed daily, and the face every day or so.'

A book of rules in 1624 refers to table manners in this way:

'Gentlemen to come sober and decently dressed to table, to refrain from sucking their fingers, using the table-cloth as a handkerchief, spitting into plates, throwing nibbled bones and crockery at each other, or "absent-mindedly" slipping their napkins into their pockets.'

In movement this was a rather pompous and affected period; dancing was much taught, and the 'turned out' line of the ballet was so much in vogue that it was said of Charles I that he 'walked as if he were dancing a measure'.

Deportment was learnt from these dancing-masters, including the use of the fan, and how to talk with it. There was a continental influence, and the women were treated like pretty dolls and in no way the marital equal of man.

'Bucket boots' were fashionable for a short time; the most extreme were as wide as a yard round the top, and tracts and pamphlets were written about the useless flapping tops of the rich:

'wasted leather that would serve the bare-foot poor'

which they said required their wearers

'to swagger like a bandy-legged duck'.

So this fashion did not remain long, but undoubtedly had some effect on the walk.

The Cavalier man would walk with a very turned-out hip line, almost doing a circular ballet movement on the ground with each step, his shoulders swinging in the open line with his foot, giving a swagger. In bowing he would sweep his hat off with a flourish, and hold it under his other arm, extending one foot forward, bending the back knee and tilting forwards, the empty hand remaining at his side. He would then take the hat again and replace it as he stepped forward to complete the movement.

The Puritan man had a much straighter line, and, of course, less swagger. His bow was much less elaborate; the step and inclination of the body being less, and the hat held with both hands in front.

The Cavalier lady would walk in the same way as the man, her full skirt (slashed down the front and looped up at the sides) swaying as she walked, and her bold eyes 'inviting'.

The Puritan lady would sway less as she walked, and her eyes would be downcast.

The Cavalier curtsy would be a step to one side, a closure of the feet, then bending both knees, she would look round at everyone in the room, as she dropped and rose again.

The Puritan curtsy would not be so deep, and would be more modestly carried out.

There are again plenty of opportunities for development of scenes based on this period:

—Cavaliers and Roundheads waiting for the Post to gallop into the village and bring news of the Civil War.

or

—Nell Gwyn—the orange girl—meeting Charles II.

A few other points of interest that might give background or suggestion for scenes are that:

—fish oil was used to make soap, and special soap was often made at home; seventeenth-century people washed in their own rooms.

Pepys, in his diary, says:

'My wife busy in going with her woman to the hot-house to bathe herself after her long being indoors in the dirt, so that she now pretends to a resolution of being hereafter very clean. How long it will hold I can guess.'

Then with regard to food, he says:

'Home from my office to my lord's lodgings, where my wife had got ready a very fine dinner, viz: a dish of marrow bones, a leg of mutton; a loin of veal; a dish of fowl; three pullets, and a dozen of larks all in a dish; a neat's tongue. A dish of anchovies; a dish of prawns and cheese.'

Coffee and chocolate had come into fashion, and doctors discoursed on the good and bad effects. To coffee they imputed moral effects, to chocolate the reverse!

Tea was also new enough for controversy. Amusing mime scenes could surely evolve round these discoveries.

THE EIGHTEENTH CENTURY

As in every period, some reading is necessary to feel the life of the time before thinking of the movement; and there are many authentic pictures of this period which can be of great assistance.

Dancing masters were even more famous than before. Everyone in society would learn to dance; all were slaves to rules of deportment, poise and elegance were of real importance; a man who wore the wrong kind of wig, or who behaved in an unfashionable way would immediately be an outcast from society.

A superficial wit was almost a necessity, as we see in the plays of Congreve and Sheridan. This is the peak of artificiality and of external effects. Underneath all the outward show of perfume and beauty, there was an incredible amount of dirt. Snuff was used, but not as often as is commonly supposed.

The man would carry his head well, and walk with his foot well turned-out, 'making a leg' showing his calf and red heel. His shoulders would be erect, chest well out showing his beautiful coloured silk waistcoat. His hands would be held gracefully, sometimes one on the hip, one perhaps carrying a handkerchief; the hand would never be on the sword unless to provoke a quarrel; if this happened even by accident, there would be a duel rather than a confession of a breach of etiquette.

To bow, he would remove his hat, placing it under the opposite arm and releasing the hand as in the seventeenth century. He would slide one leg forward—neatly turned out—then step forward closing the feet and replacing the hat. Sometimes the hat would be held in the hand with a good arm line. The hat was never placed on the heart.

The lady walked with the same feeling as the man, and of

necessity she had to carry her head well because of the size of her wig; at the height of the period the wigs were colossal erections covered with lace, ribbons, flowers, jewels, and all sorts of ornaments; the width of the skirt meant that the hands and arms were considerably used; they could not naturally fall at the side, and fans were greatly used and had significance.

The curtsy was much like that of the seventeenth century, with more ballet curve in the arm positions and some use of the fan while curtsying.

This period lends itself to many mime scenes:

An amusing scene would be of a dancing master and his pupils, watched perhaps by dowager parents who register their disapproval when necessary. The dancing master might perhaps invite his favourite pupil to remain behind.

A very different, but equally suitable subject might be that of:

The aristocrats being taken from their great houses to the guillotine in the French Revolution.

REGENCY OR EMPIRE

In 1810 when the mental state of George III made him unfit to rule—George—Prince of Wales became Regent. He was much more interested in dress than in affairs of state, and preferred the company of Beau Brummell to the company of his ministers. The word 'dandy' (applied to Beau Brummell) was first applied at this period.

Looking at pictures of the time reveals what an amazingly sudden change in costume has taken place. At the end of the eighteenth century people had grown so tired of all the rules of deportment, that bows and curtsies disappeared and they began to use the hand-shake. The leg-line which had developed from being straight forward in the mediaeval times to being completely turned out in the eighteenth century, diminished, and a natural simplicity returned, with classical draperies, very flimsy at first, later becoming more substantial.

The man, influenced by a long era of warfare, walked with an upright bearing, using his legs well, conscious of his very tightly-fitting trousers.

In the bow he would push one foot slightly forward, bending the back knee, inclining a little forward.

The lady now walked with her arms at her sides, sometimes holding her skirt, using small steps, and occasional little runs.

The curtsy was not used so often, as shaking hands had become fashionable, and often the women kissed on both cheeks. If they curtsied, one foot would slide forward, the back knee bending, and as they stepped forward from it there would be a very slight waggle of the hips.

Appropriate mime scenes are again easy to find, based perhaps on the lives of Napoleon and Josephine, or of more simple folk—ladies sitting at home bored and dull, waiting for romance, while their young men are at the wars; then the excitement and intrigue among them when they go to the balls.

EARLY AND LATE VICTORIAN

As we move nearer to our own time, pictures become less necessary, family portraits and photographs, old-fashioned books and advertisements, can help us considerably, but it is important that the same respect be given to them; there always seems to be a tendency to burlesque this period.

Queen Victoria's influence effected a diguise of the natural line of the figure, feelings were hidden, modesty was predominant, and the back-board was the order of the day.

The influence of the Industrial Revolution seems to have been felt in the clothes also, and the men looked rather like black chimney-pots.

The mid-Victorian man was stiff (he wore corsets) and pompous, very conscious of his dignity as 'the head of the household'.

The bow—when used—was over the hat, which was placed in the middle of the chest, but shaking hands was common also.

The mid-Victorian lady was taught to cast her eyes on the ground and look demure, but her poke-bonnet would affect the way she looked about her, and indeed often encouraged a rather coy expression as she peeped out of it. As the crinoline was not allowed to bounce, she had to take very small steps, and her hands were often resting on it. It was a matter of art:

   to sit without steel hoops getting out of place
   to step into a carriage without crushing the tulle
   to travel
   to lie down
   to play with children

and it gradually went out of fashion for a man to offer his arm to a woman when accompanying her.

Handkerchiefs were always carried in the ladies' hands;— and it was said that 'the character of a woman could be ascertained by the way she held her handkerchief'.

The curtsy—when used—was a little bob inside the crinoline, one foot just behind the other.

The late Victorian man had a more debonair appearance, being no longer corseted as his father was. His cane gave him an air, his hat swept on and off as he passed by.

The late Victorian lady made the most of chest and bustle, and had a rather hollow-backed appearance. The wearing of a little 'pork-pie' hat perched on a mountain of hair, gave her a rather 'inviting' expression. She would shake hands rather high in the air, and her curtsy would be reserved for Court.

It would be good practice and amusing to mime two scenes—say in Hyde Park—one in early and one in late Victorian times.

The dramatic incident of the young Queen being shot at might be used for the first scene.

The second might be a domestic incident between two nursemaids with their perambulators (commonly seen in those days), quarrelling about the attentions of a passing soldier.

The history lesson may not gain very much from acting scenes from modern times, but classes will no doubt be interested to mime them and compare the difference of movement. The fact that there are such marked differences in the last hundred years makes it obvious that my earlier remarks covering whole centuries are only very broad generalizations.[1]

Here are some additional scenes which have dramatic incident and are likely to prove popular:

INFANTS

King Alfred burns the cakes.
King Canute tries to command the waves.
King Bruce and the spider.

JUNIORS

Romulus and Remus each decide to build a wall. Remus scoffs at Romulus' attempt and jumps the wall. Romulus kills him as he jumps.

[1] Excellent pictures illustrating costumes and customs of the different periods can be found in the following books which will be of great assistance to the classes: *Modes and Manners* by Max Von Boehm. (Translated by Joan Joshua, published by Batsford.) *The Life and Work of the People of England* by Hartley and Elliott. (Published by Batsford.)

With the help of these books, and the lead given in the notes above, some fresh and authentic work could be done.

Saint Joan leading her French troops.

Robin Hood, surrounded by his followers, Friar Tuck, Little John, Much etc., competes in an archery test and wins. As he is presented with the silver arrow he is recognized and taken prisoner. His followers help him to escape. King John and his yeomen and sheriff are left raging.

Florence Nightingale nursing in the Crimean War.

SENIORS

The murder of Thomas à Beckett.

Ann Boleyn hears news of her impending execution.

Christians in prison waiting to be thrown to the lions.

Old hags knitting, and watching the heads of aristocrats fall at the guillotine.

ADULTS

Hecuba hears of the fall of Troy, of the captivity of herself and her daughter.

Marie Antoinette saying good-bye to her son.

The Pump Room, Bath, 1720. Ladies and gentlemen meet to take the waters. The Duchess of Queensbury arrives wearing an apron costing 200 guineas after the fashion of the German woman. Beau Nash arrives, tears off the apron in disgust. She leaves in dudgeon.

*

Some knowledge and practice of historic movements are necessary before performing any period play, or the characters will look like people of today in fancy dress. For anyone who is hoping to make the theatre his career, considerable experience in this subject is essential.

XI

MASKS AND TRADITIONAL MIME

With classes of almost any age it is a useful experiment at some time to find out to what extent expression comes through the use of the body, and to what extent it is dependent on facial expression only.

As a test, ask the class to hang a handkerchief or scarf over their heads, letting it fall so that their faces are obscured. (The material must be sufficiently transparent for the actor himself to see where he is going.)

Suggest certain feelings to be shown in mime:

e.g. sorrow, fear, anger, happiness.

You will probably be surprised to find how little emotion is shown. The group will need to be convinced of this and will probably say that they were feeling deeply.

Let them repeat the exercise half at a time with the others watching; almost invariably the watchers will be amazed to see that although the groups were feeling so strongly, the expression had been largely confined to the face and that when this was covered the body described nothing. Once they have grasped this fully, they will soon improve.

Now ask the class to repeat the exercise realizing that the whole of the body must, as it were, take the responsibility. The movement and the expressive power of every part of the body will increase and strengthen through this practice, and it is quite a good plan to revert to it from time to time as a reminder.

I would do the exercise described above before starting any work in masks.

Infants and juniors are not so likely to do plays in masks as the seniors and adults, but the practice is still useful to the younger ones, for, apart from helping them to realize how much the body is capable of showing, the wearing of a mask gives a chance for the shy child to hide behind it and become someone else—like a puppet. This sometimes gives good results, and has a very good effect on the child.

Seniors and adults will become very interested in the different technique that is required for working in a mask.

It will be found that a good mask, or half mask, can be, and should always be, a work of beauty in itself, and when worn, the light will fall on it in so many ways, that it appears to take on different expressions. To make the most of this all the movement must be bigger than normal, it must be slower and more prolonged and there must be striking and often arrested positions. The gestures need to be wider—often with straight arms and legs, moving in big sweeps. A small movement of the head which would be quite effective without the mask would not show at all when masked, and a great deal of neck movement is needed to convey that the masked head is looking down or up or to the side: what may feel an exaggeration will probably be just right.

Most serious students of mime find this work absorbingly interesting, and love to watch one another and delight in the strange effects.

For some of them it will help if they are given a character

mask, and asked to wear it at every possible opportunity for a week, and then come back having developed the whole movement and character to fit the mask.

The same can be done with animal masks if they are to be used in a play, so that the actor, the character, and the mask grow together, and become one.

Four Plays for Dancers by W. B. Yeats are written specifically to be played in masks. They are most beautiful, and students will always be thrilled and excited by them; but they require experienced and expert speakers and movers. In these plays the technique I have just been describing could reach its culmination and fulfilment.

Some Characters of the Commedia dell' Arte

Students who are training for the theatre will no doubt be interested in studying the history of mime and will read widely to do so. An important part of that study will include the impromptu acting that was at its height in Italy in the sixteenth and seventeenth centuries.

This style of acting was known as the Commedia dell' Arte, and was a revival of the ancient Latin mimes who first performed comedies in Rome; they, in turn, were derived from the satirical buffoonery of the Greek comedies. Mime evidently provided a language that could be understood and appreciated by many nationalities and so had a universal appeal to all audiences; this was a great advantage with the widely varying peoples of the Roman Empire.

In the sixteenth century Ruzzante presented some comedies in which many parts of Italy were represented, each with its own dialect; from this, certain character types developed, and were acted all over Italy and France; some of these are still popular today, and should certainly be practised by adult students of mime, though they would have very little significance or value for children or in average classroom work.[1] Here, I will only attempt to outline the more obvious features of the major characters, and the way in which the companies worked.

The Commedia dell' Arte actors must have been highly skilled for they memorized no parts and acted impromptu. They were given the outline of a story, which was usually nailed up in the wings; the rest was invention. The good actor had to be capable of using his imagination, of reacting quickly and spontaneously to a given situation, and able to support his fellow players so that it all appeared to be rehearsed and prearranged. No amateur could hope to succeed in such conditions. Sometimes actors would change parts, and the same audience come again and again to enjoy the ingenuity and variety of the performances. Most of the actors were skilled in movement and even acrobatics, and descriptions of the plays of the time often include dancing, interpretation of animal movements, and mime as we know it, as well as improvised spoken scenes.

In our improvisation nowadays we are not really creating anything new, but are simply trying to renew an art that was very beautifully developed three or four hundred years ago.

The notes that now follow about some of the characters do not set out to be in any way a complete description, but—as those in the chapter dealing with historic movement—they hope to provide a lead which may encourage further study.

HARLEQUIN

As with all these characters, both the costume and behaviour of Harlequin have changed with the various actors who have played the part. He was originally just a lackey in tattered garments, using his wits to make a living. Many changes

[1] Those who intend to make a comprehensive study of this branch of work should read, *The History of the Harlequinade* by Maurice Sand.

took place, but it was the acting of Domenico that made Harlequin into the attractive character he has become. He is now recognizable by his many coloured diamond or lozenge-shaped spangles which cover his skin-tight garment, also by his black skull cap, his half-mask, and his baton which has magic powers. Harlequin is insolent, lively, and confident; popular with women, always successful in love, but often fickle. His mood changes like quick-silver; one moment he is petulant and childish, the next he is full of wit and he has flashes of brilliance; often he is a romantic lover with great personal magnetism. Sometimes he is in great poverty and difficulty, but he usually finds a way out for himself quite readily. He is essentially an acrobat and a dancer, amusingly supple and lively; his capers make him seem to be as much in the air as he is on the ground. Always he has an irresistible charm.

PIERROT

Pierrot also was at first a stupid lackey, who suffered from beatings and other indignities which made his audiences laugh; he was, in fact, originally a clown, but he became transformed by the acting of Deburau.

Like Harlequin, Pierrot can be petulant and childish, or a gay confident boy; but more often now we think of him as the poetical and romantic lover, usually dressed in white, or in pale sad colours. His completely white face and his black skull cap heighten his artistic and expressive powers. He is often the rival of Harlequin, but not often successful in love; at his moment of triumph, his loved one is usually lured away by someone else. More often than not, both are in love with Columbine, and while Pierrot is lost in a dream of the poetry that he may write to her, the more buoyant and confident Harlequin will whisk her away, and Pierrot is left more sorrowful and romantic than ever. His eyes stand out sadly in his mask-like face, and the lively supple dancing movements and beautiful vivid gestures seem to collapse in a moment, until he looks like a heap of garments on the floor, surmounted only by his black skull cap.

COLUMBINE

The nature of Columbine's part has varied with the many actresses who have played her, but certain characteristics are always recognizable. She is essentially a dancer, she is always young and attractive, usually very well aware of her charms and very ready to flirt. She would never hesitate to cast aside a former lover if she found another who would provide her with more wealth and luxury. She is fickle, and her fondness for ribbons, jewels, finery, will nearly always win her, and she will betray her master, or her lover, for these.

She may love Pierrot and Harlequin both at the same time, choosing first one and then the other to flirt with; she finds it fun to 'play-off' one against the other. Sometimes Columbine is the daughter of Pantaloon; she may be a heroine, or a waiting-maid, but whatever her part, she is still a dancer and a coquette, and she always wears a little apron by which we know her.

CLOWN

Clown is known to all, though we may still see him in many guises. He can usually be recognized by his traditional black wig with its long queue, his black corkscrew eyebrows, and his white cheeks with their cart-wheel of red and his large red mouth. Nowadays he frequently carries a string of sausages and lives in fear of the Police Constable.

Clown invokes laughter wherever he goes by his mistakes, his stupidity, or his tumbling. He possesses nothing, so may often play the part of a servant; he is always making jokes, and laughs more at his own jokes than at other people's.

Joe Grimaldi was the most famous of clowns of the eighteenth century, and he was much loved by his public. Another who has been greatly loved in our own time is Grock.

PANTALOON

Pantaloon is always an old man. Sometimes he plays the part of a doctor who may be clever and ingenious, but more often he creates trouble, or fun, by his lack of knowledge and the situations he causes. He is usually rather ridiculous in his desire to please, and is exploited by everyone. He is a good foil to Clown when they play together; Pantaloon himself is always duped, mocked, and unhappy. Sometimes he is represented as a father, and he is often an old miser.

His costume will vary with the part; but he will frequently be seen in a gaberdine and carpet slippers, with a woollen cap, and, of course, breeches and stockings all in one piece (pantaloons). Traditionally he has a grey moustache and beard, and very often a mask; sometimes he causes amusement by his knock-kneed gait, while Clown, in contrast, may walk with his knees turned out.

ISABELLA

In every comedy there must always be a beautiful heroine; no doubt there always has been. In 1578 Gelosi had in his troupe a leading lady whose name was Isabella; and ever since, the heroine in these plays has been Isabella. She is always exquisitely dressed, usually witty and vivacious, as well as being virtuous and beautiful. She is outstanding among women, and has real charm. Often Isabella will be the heroine with Columbine as her waiting-maid.

L

LELIO

Every play demands a hero as well as a heroine, and Lelio
is this. He is always handsome, always immaculately dressed
in the height of fashion, and nearly always favoured by
parents because he is so rich and elegant. He usually plays
suitor to the beautiful Isabella, although he may in some
plays be in love with Columbine.

In the Italian comedies he is often maliciously placed in
an awkward situation, for, although he looks so important
and dignified and holds himself so proudly and stiffly, at
the first sign of being caught in an intrigue or awkward
situation not suited to his purpose he runs away! The hero
humiliated in this way seems to have pleased the Italian
sense of humour, and is far from our modern conception
of a hero.

PULCHINELLA

Pulchinella is a character whose name has varied considerably with actor and period, and for years he was known as
Polichinelle in the Italian troupes. In England he grew
from Pulchinello through Punchinello to Punch. In
France he was a famous marionette; and even as we
know him now, both in our Punch and Judy show, and
in our English magazine, we find many of his original
characteristics:

He is ugly, he has a hooked nose and a hump; he laughs
at life, but laughs with a certain cruelty. He carries a cudgel,
and sometimes makes raucous cries like a bird of prey.
He may look good-humoured, but underneath he enjoys a
certain ferocity, and when you hear him laughing you
should beware, for he has vicious qualities.

He has an easy conscience, and believes only in the
futility of life's struggle, and objectively observes and takes
advantage of humanity, amusing himself at the expense of

others. He may play many roles, but his hunchback, and his coarse laughter will be present in whatever part he takes.

THE CAPTAIN

The Captain is always dressed with great grandeur; a hat with plumes, large moustache, a rapier at his side, a huge ruff, and brilliantly coloured doublet and hose. He is essentially a boaster, who struts about the world claiming credit for great feats that he has never performed.

At heart the Captain is a coward, but he boasts that there is nothing he cannot do; that women fall at his feet, that he can demolish a mountain as easily as fight a duel. Some people fear him, because they believe him, but many know that if he is attacked he will run away, and that he is all bravado, even though he looks as fierce as a tiger.

SCARAMOUCHE

Scaramouche is the son of the Captain, and he inherits some of his father's qualities, boasting of his conquests over women. Most of them instinctively fear him because of his sinister appearance—dressed in black from head to foot, with a very white face—but are captivated by his gifts of music and imaginative and enthralling talk. He plays a guitar, whiling away the time to cover up his intrigues of deceit and theft.

SCAPINO

Scapino is another intriguer, and another that has artistic gifts, for he is musical, he can sing, and he can dance; but he is much to be feared, and represents 'the mailed fist in the velvet glove'. He is ready to perform any service for money, takes on disguise easily and often he seems to be a trusted servant, but actually he is a clever thief and a liar. His costume varies but is frequently a rather showy livery of white, laced in green. He is dangerously attractive, and greatly favoured by young girls.

Lesser personalities

TARTAGLIA

The stutterer, always in a state of exasperation because he cannot complete his words, a figure of fun, accentuated even more by his enormous spectacles.

COVIELLO

A simpleton, famous for his grimaces, though he sometimes is played as a wit.

THE POLICE CONSTABLE

In various guises he was always part of the Italian comedy, representing justice.

THE CANTATRICE

She was used as a pretty singer to fill in any interval and keep the continuity of the performance.

THE BALLERINA

She would dance during intervals in the performance. Both singer and dancer might be asked to fill other roles such as Isabella or Columbine—but, as in the theatre nowadays, the size of the company depended on circumstances.

There are countless other characters not mentioned here and there is much more to learn about them all, and anyone who wishes to become a serious student of mime should study this history in greater detail and treat these notes only as a beginning. It is interesting to realize that these characters are really applicable to every play and to every age:

the hero, the heroine, the successful and unsuccessful lovers, the mistress, the maid, the old gentleman and the servant, the maker of fun, the braggart, the evil-doer;— none of them is new to us, but the style of acting in the sixteenth and seventeenth centuries was particular to the Italians of that time.

Any senior schoolchild, or any advanced student, might find it of value to use these notes about the characters and to go through the process I described earlier, of concentrating and thinking himself slowly into a character, to see if he can bring to life in the same way these characters which were so vital a part of drama three hundred years ago.

Traditional Gestures

It is certain that there was a convention of gesture, and that it made a language significant to and understood by the audiences. We are indebted to Irene Mawer for her research and the revival of these speech gestures.[1]

There are charming gestures for:
'A lady', 'A gentleman', 'Money', 'No money', 'Exquisite', 'A letter', 'Look over there', 'Hungry', 'Asleep', 'Hark', 'Listen', 'Will you marry me'—and others.

These are only suitable for use in a traditional mime play —for example, one in which the traditional characters of the Commedia dell' Arte appear, or possibly in certain period plays of a rather stylized kind. They are *quite unsuitable and out of place* in a modern mime play.

The gestures themselves are valuable practice for most ages (not infants) because they give a neatness and precision of movement that it does not seem possible to induce without this kind of practice. They are, however, so 'continental' in flavour that their style is not easy for the average

[1] In her book *The Art of Mime* Irene Mawer gives a full description of the speech gestures.

Britisher; but the very fact that they do present this difficulty makes them, I think, all the more useful as a practice. Everyone seems to enjoy doing them, whatever the age, and although there can be no logical reason for teaching them in schools where mime plays of this particular kind are not likely to be produced, yet, I would occasionally allow the children to attempt them as a special treat—rather than a regular routine—just because they are invariably so interested in knowing about them.

L'Enfant Prodigue

This chapter cannot end without some mention—however brief—of the great three act mime play L'Enfant Prodigue. The music is by Wormser, and every bar of it is interpreted in the mime; the music and mime are one.[1]

The music is available, and the story is clearly written above the musical line; but much detail is left to the individual interpretation of the artist; there is sometimes a page or two of music to cover one simple instruction, such as—

'He writes,' or
'The reading of the letter.'

—it is necessary for producer and players to realize that every bar of the music has dramatic significance and should be used.

The play is only suitable to work with advanced students, but they will certainly find it an exciting study and a great experience.

---

[1] Irene Mawer speaks fully of the play in The Art of Mime.

XII

MUSIC AND MIME

Any mime class can be helped very greatly by a good pianist, but unless he is a real musician and capable of improvisation of the right kind, it is usually wiser to do without music altogether. If he is not able to improvise it is certain that the speed and impetus of the class will suffer, and then little will be gained, unless possibly he is able to be of use for the rhythmic accompaniment which is always helpful for physical exercises.

To be of real use, the ideal mime pianist should himself know something about mime. This knowledge can of course grow, with the experience of playing for mime, but his thought has to be very concentrated, since he is really composing all the time. He needs to be able to imagine all the moods or characters the class are asked to convey, and to translate these into music; the music cannot be just expressive, but must also have the quality of the movement in it. Some pianists are able to improvise well, but are apt always to use one key, and fail to grasp the change of character or mood that is given by the change of key. If, for this, or any other reason, all their improvisations sound alike, the classes quickly lose vitality.

Few pianists, however good as performers, seem to have all the qualities that are needed for accompanying mime;

perhaps they really need all the instincts of both dancer and actress in addition to their musical abilities. Playing for mime classes needs much greater skill than playing for dancing classes, as there can be almost no routine, and the pianist must be entirely creative.[1]

I am often asked to give advice about pianists for mime, and I would say that a very great deal of mime can be entirely satisfactory without accompaniment, and the teacher will find that it is happier to be without a pianist than to have the wrong one!

The teacher can, however, decide either:

To use rhythmic accompaniment, such as drums, tambour, cymbals, bones, etc., or:

To learn enough about music himself to be able to describe briefly to an inexperienced pianist what his need is. He should be able at least to indicate time-signature and tempo of whatever he requires.

My hope is that *Music for Mime* will help to solve this difficulty for teachers.

Another important point to realize is that it is very bad for a class to become too dependent on the pianist and perpetually look to him for a lead; so it is all to the good that some of the work should be unsupported by music.

Certainly it is a great help to have accompaniment for physical practice, also for imaginative or abstract work that is dependent on a mood and atmosphere. Music also helps to cover the self-consciousness that sometimes grows in

[1] I have been very fortunate in having an ideal partner to play for my classes, and Barbara Lander in filling this role has made a great contribution to our work together. At my request, she has composed short pieces of music to accompany many of the expressive exercises in this book, and also music for some of the mime plays. We hope that it may be a help both to mime teachers and mime accompanists, as it gives them a starting ground, which may be a guide to improvisations of their own.

The music is published by Methuen & Co., Ltd., under the title of *Music for Mime* and the price is 19s. 6d.

silence. The teacher will find himself talking much more, and building the atmosphere by means of speech, when he has no music; but for the main bulk of the simple practice demanded in this book music is not in any way essential, and most general teachers who introduce a little mime into their other classes will certainly not want or need music.

Animals, characters, occupations, improvisations, all these can be taught equally well, if not better, without any music at all. It is in traditional mime, and speech gesture leading to conventional mime plays that the need for music grows.

Much depends on the circumstances; if mime is going to be developed seriously as an art, accompaniment becomes an almost essential part of it. If it is a small part of other classroom work, or an addition to Speech and Drama classes, music would be quite unnecessary.

If mime is in any way linked up with music teaching in a school, the art of musical interpretation becomes important; this should not be confused with dance interpretation. A good mover can fairly easily interpret music at any rate to some extent in a dance form. It seems to need a different approach to interpret the music in dramatic form.

Mime is one of the most exciting subjects it is possible to teach, but it is also a subject which can fail completely if it is allowed to do so. It is so pitifully easy to go on teaching old material that has been successful. Although the classes may be fresh ones, the teacher himself loses vitality and interest unless the repetitions are renewed in spirit and brought to life again.

Remember too, that the young are living in advance of us and that we must keep abreast of life with them. If we believe that our work will contribute in any way to the betterment of man, we must strive to do it with inspiration.

XIII

MIME PLAYS

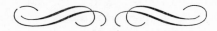

I have always found in working out mime plays that it is easier to produce a good result if the play is made especially for a particular group of people. I think many teachers find this to be the case, and so prefer to make their own. Some teachers may feel that they are not very inventive, but they need not be dismayed, for there are so many sources to which to turn for plot.

Think of all the stories there are in the world—great stories of all generations and all nations, legends, folk tales, fairy stories, stories from Greek mythology, Bible stories, poems, ballads, songs, operas—a supply without limit.

Select an episode or tale that is likely to be suitable for a mime play; which means that if possible it should be complete in one scene (although this is not a necessity). It should be pictorial, with dramatic incident that will bring it to a climax, without being too dependent on dialogue. I should perhaps mention that it is a legitimate and normal practice to print a brief synopsis in the programme when a mime play is being performed.

Those who have creative gifts will probably want to use their own plots and will not want to depend on other sources, but in either way good mime scenes and plays can develop.

This method pre-supposes that you will make your play and find your music afterwards; unless you are fortunate enough to have it composed for you as the play develops, which of course is ideal; but set accompaniment is essential; improvised music tends to lengthen each episode, and style is lost.

Some people, on the other hand, find that listening to music and allowing their imagination to roam is as profitable a source of inspiration as any.

As long as the final result is a good mime play, the method of creation matters very little. Here follow some suggestions of plays which I have evolved, tried out and proved to be successful. Most of these are free mime, and traditional gestures would in these be quite out of place; where they would be appropriate I have mentioned the fact. I have made notes about music or sound effects which will, I hope, be helpful. Barbara Lander has composed music for a number of the plays—this is included in the publication *Music for Mime*.[1] I shall be very happy if some of these plays are of use to other teachers and their classes.

[1] In order not to burden this book with details of every move in *Prometheus, The Wicked Piper, Ten Little Nigger Boys, The Young King* and *The Village Concert*, Barbara Lander has given directions above the appropriate phrases in her music.

PROMETHEUS

A mime play based on Greek mythology—with music composed by Barbara Lander. This is suitable for seniors or adults, but could be simplified for work with juniors.

Characters

Zeus (King of Heaven)
Ares (God of War)
Hera (Queen of Heaven)
Pallas Athena (Goddess of Wisdom)
Artemis (Goddess of the Chase)
Hephaestos (God of Fire)
Hermes (Messenger of the Gods)
Eros (Child God of Love)
Other Gods and Goddesses as numbers allow
Prometheus (who stole Fire from Heaven to benefit Mankind) ⎱ Both originally among
Epimetheus (Brother of Prometheus) ⎰ the Gods
A Vulture
Hercules (the strongest among mankind)
Mankind (at least a dozen, preferably about twenty, according to space)

Costumes

The Gods should be dressed and made-up with great beauty, following for their pattern the finest statues and pictures.

The Vulture should be dressed to suggest the bird.

Mankind should look as wild and primitive as possible. Hessian tunics are quite effective, with bare limbs made up darker than usual, and unkempt hair.

Set and Lighting

The skycloth or cyclorama must be lit to represent the vault of heaven.

Up stage right there should be rostra of varying levels, up to about 6 feet if possible, so that we can open with a fine group of the Gods on Olympus. Zeus and Hera will be enthroned at the top, and the others decoratively grouped below them at different levels almost to the ground.

Down stage centre Mankind will be grouped on the ground, looking like a dark mass that might be mistaken for rock.

Up stage left there should be a rock-like formation on which Prometheus can stand when he is chained on the side of the mountain. He must be raised above Mankind, but not as high as Olympus.

At the opening the Gods must be in a flood of light, and Mankind and the mountain in shadow. As Eros comes to earth there should be a gradual increase of light on Mankind for the Creation—the Gods still being just visible—but not 'flooded'.

As the play proceeds, there should be alternating light on Mankind and the Gods for their particular scenes.

Hercules must of course be well lit for his battle with the Vulture, and there should be a 'spot' up stage left on the mountainside which can be brought on to Prometheus when he is being tortured by the Vulture.

The lighting of Mankind can vary to help the mood; for example, during the scene of war, Mankind can move in silhouette with a red glow behind, whereas in the scene of hunger a much colder light will be effective.

At the general rejoicing on the final curtain, everything should be brought 'full-up'.

Theme of the Play

The Gods are on Olympus feasting and content. Zeus

desires that there shall be life on earth, and sends Eros to earth to create life. Watched by the other Gods on Olympus, Eros floats down to earth and begins by creating plants, trees, birds, and animals; then pleased with his work he returns to Olympus, and all the Gods watch the earth with pleasure. Zeus is still not satisfied; therefore he sends Prometheus and his brother Epimetheus to mould man from clay. They make their way to earth, and from the dark mass of rock they weld man; he is made in the likeness of the Gods (the only model they have), but even though he is well-shaped, he is still rigid and without life. Eros is sent again from Olympus and floats among Mankind giving him breath, so that he begins to live and move. Still Zeus is not satisfied with his creation, so with great power and majesty Pallas Athena comes to imbue man with soul. Mankind sees the Gods, realizes he is created in their likeness, feels the moving spirit in his breath and soul, is over-awed and kneels in gratitude to the Gods.

Time has passed on the earth: Man must eat and drink, he looks around to find food and water. He is primitive, he is hungry, he grabs what he can get at, and eats ravenously. He feels cold, he shivers and huddles with others, instinctively knowing his needs. Only Prometheus, who has not returned to Olympus with the other Gods, is watching mankind closely. He sees their plight, and sees Hephaestos holding the torch of fire in Heaven; without further thought, he leaps towards the fire, snatches it and runs with it to Earth, where he stands holding out the flame happily, as Man clusters round taking pieces of fire away to serve his various needs. Man is grateful and warms himself contentedly. But Zeus is jealous and angry at this theft and gift, and as we turn back to Olympus we see him rise on his throne to punish. He orders Ares and Hephaestos to capture Prometheus and chain him to a rock on the mountainside. There for years he is to be tortured by a vulture who will devour his liver all day, and each night it will grow again while the Vulture sleeps. Prometheus is chained to the rock and left to his fate. Zeus commands the Vulture to attack and it does so.

Ares is now ordered by Zeus to punish Man also for taking Prometheus' gift. Unaware of the dissension between the Gods, Man is contentedly warming himself and cooking the food he has found. Ares goads one man to snatch food from another, a third to snatch fire, and quickly he has incited War; and fire that was to be man's comfort has become a weapon of War. All we can see now is primitive fighting; until, inevitably, War has exhausted the world, and Mankind lies panting and waiting for death; while the Vulture again visits Prometheus who is suffering for Mankind. Then from out of this heap of desolation the great hero Hercules arises; he sees Prometheus in torment, and watched by the Gods and all Mankind, he struggles with the Vulture just as it is about to approach Prometheus again. The conflict is terrifying, but finally Hercules kills the bird, climbs to Prometheus, releases him from his chains, and Hercules is welcomed by Zeus on Olympus as a great hero, and invited to drink of the nectar of the Gods; while Prometheus remains on earth beloved of mankind.

ABU-HASSAN

A mime play based on a story from *The Arabian Nights*. The comedy of this makes it suitable for Seniors and Adults; but Juniors would no doubt enjoy it and play it with a deadly seriousness, which might be quite successful, though I envisage it as light-hearted comedy or farce for more mature students.

Music

I would suggest melodies from well-known songs. Choose a different theme for the entrance and action of each character. This I think will heighten the fun, and can be arranged quite simply by a good accompanist—e.g. 'The Teddy Bears' Picnic' for the Creditors or 'The Temple Bells' (Indian Love Lyrics) for the Caliph's Ambassadors.

Characters

> Abu-Hassan
> His Wife—Fatima
> Kayah—their faithful Servant
> Omar—the Banker
> The Three Creditors
> The Caliph
> His two Ambassadors
> Wife of the Caliph
> Her two Ambassadors
> Attendants on the Caliph
> Attendants on the Caliph's Wife

If further characters are desirable, it is possible to follow the Caliph's procession into the house with a street crowd.

Costumes

Eastern flavour. Can be very simple—baggy trousers, wide

waist-bands and turbans for the men—veils, robes, etc., for the women.

Set and Lighting

The lighting for this can be very simple as it is an interior scene without need for variety. The time can be morning or afternoon; if a change of light is simple and desirable a window could be imagined right, and the brilliant afternoon sun throwing its beam across the room, could change as the sun sinks towards evening.

The room must be Eastern in style, though not wealthy; some cushions about the floor, a divan diagonally placed stage right, and a table with bowls of tea or iced drinks towards the left. A door down stage left leading to Fatima's bedroom, and double doors up stage centre which lead to the street; in these doors there should be a little flap or grill through which the servant can peep and give warning of the people who are approaching the door.

Theme of the Play

Abu-Hassan and his wife, Fatima, are at home happily together. Everything is not as happy as it would appear, however, as they are seriously in debt! Abu says to Fatima, "I have no money." Fatima says to Abu, "I have no money." Both together they say, "*We* have no money." Then they shrug their shoulders, pour themselves out a bowl of tea, sit down, stir it, smile at each other, drink the tea, and enjoy it. They move precisely together, as if they were of one mind in all they do or think. (This precision is essential to the light-hearted style of the play.) Suddenly, the big doors up stage centre open, and in comes Kayah, their trusted servant, shutting the doors quickly behind him. He agitatedly tells them that three creditors are on their way down the street coming to demand that their debts should be paid. Kayah looks several times through the grill announcing each

M

time that they are nearer than before. Abu says, "I will not see them." Fatima says, "I will not see them." Both say, "*You* must see them." There is a knock on the door, Abu and Fatima together say, "*We* are *out*." Fatima runs into her room, Abu hides behind the divan. Kayah opens the door, and there are the three creditors, one very tall, one of medium height, and one very small! They are all very solemn, and all move identically together. "We want our money," they cry. The servant protests that he cannot help, his master and mistress are out. "Nonsense," say the creditors and push their way in. Solemnly following one another (the tallest first, and the smallest last) they walk in a line about the room, peering into everything they can find in search of any money there may be. Abu is nearly caught several times, but avoids them by following round behind the last one, until they go out again the way they came in, angrier than before. Fatima has been listening and returns, and the three together discuss what is to be done.

Suddenly Abu has an idea. He and Fatima will each in turn pretend that the other is dead, then the Caliph will have to provide money for Fatima's funeral and the Caliph's wife will have to provide money for Abu's funeral. In this way, they will be able to pay their debts, and start life in another place. Fatima and the servant are in full agreement with the plan, and all is bustle and excitement. The servant is sent out to take a message to the Caliph that Fatima is dead, and Abu after instructing his wife to be prepared to appear to be dead, kisses her good-bye and follows after the servant to collect the money.

Fatima sets about preparing the room for the arrival of guests, when there is a knock at the door; she peeps through the grill, and to her surprise sees that it is Omar, the Banker. Rather reluctantly (for he is a renowned rogue) she lets him in, wondering why he has come. To her horror and astonishment he begs her to leave her husband and come away with him; Fatima refuses, but Omar promises that if she will come with him, he will settle all Abu's debts. Fatima begins to be frightened of his passion, so, pretending to agree, she persuades him to hide in the next room on the pretext that Abu will be returning. Duped by this, Omar willingly goes into her bedroom, and before he has time to turn round she has skilfully contrived to lock him in. At this moment Kayah returns saying that Ambassadors from the Caliph are close behind him on their way to establish that Fatima is dead. A moment later Abu returns; he is just in time to act the kneeling mourner over Fatima who is lying with folded hands on the floor, as the servant opens the door to the Ambassadors from the Caliph. Very pompously and with stylized extravagant movements they come to the centre moving precisely together; they observe the wailing mourner, the corpse and the miserable-looking servant. The first Ambassador lifts one arm of the corpse, the second lifts a leg; both remain stiffly and ridiculously in the air! The Ambassadors look at one another, tap the leg and arm, which fall suddenly to the ground; the Ambassadors look completely satisfied, hand two bags of money to Abu, and walk out in the same pompous way that they came in. Immediately they have gone, Fatima jumps up, and they all rejoice at the size of the money bags. Quickly the servant, Kayah, is sent out again, this time to the Caliph's wife to tell her that Abu has died, and to collect money for his burial. In the meantime, Abu prepares to put on an appearance of looking dead and teaches Fatima to act as mourner, and back comes the servant bringing two Ambassadors from the Caliph's wife to establish his death.

These two, belonging to a different household have a different set of movements but they are quite as stylized and peculiar as the other Ambassadors. To them, this is an everyday job and they have no interest greater than their own appearance, so they go through the same performance as the other two, give the money to Fatima, and depart. Now, of course, Abu is full of life again, overjoyed by the success of his plan and ready to be off, conveniently forgetting about his debts. But there is an ominous knock at the door. Kayah peeps out and reports that the creditors are again on the doorstep. Fatima remembers Omar, she cannot run to her room, together they crouch behind the divan with their bags of money, determined not to give it up now they have got it. Once again the creditors force entry, suspecting that money has come into the house, and once again, after trying to nose it out (and as before, only just missing Abu *and* Fatima by seconds) they depart disappointed.

Now all seems to be settled, and Abu and Fatima prepare to fly, when again there is a knock at the door. The servant now reports an unexpected turn of events; the Caliph and his wife are at the door together! Their suspicions have obviously been aroused by the two deaths, and they realize that they have been duped! What can be done now? Instantly, Abu has another idea, they can *both* be dead and the servant must turn mourner. Quickly Abu and Fatima lie with the soles of their feet touching and their hands clasped on their breasts. Kayah opens the door, and then runs weeping to his apparently dead master and mistress.

The Caliph and his wife are, of course accompanied by their retinue and their entrance is most impressive, still in the same stylized manner of the Ambassadors, but with even more ceremony. (They may be followed by a crowd from the street.)

Having expected to find they had been tricked, the Caliph and his wife are astonished to find that in fact both Abu and Fatima are dead; and the servant's grief is so real that no other investigation is necessary.

"Now," says the Caliph, "which of these two died first? One of them was due to receive money but not both. If Abu died first, you pay, if Fatima died first, I pay." There is consternation among the crowd, everyone substantiates a different theory, the servant is too grief-stricken to take any part; a quarrel develops between the Caliph and his wife, and the crowd stare bewildered as they argue. "She died first." "No, he died first." "No, *she* died." "*He* died." "SHE." "HE.", etc., rising to a crescendo of excitement as they speak (in mime, of course) more and more quickly, and then both together!

For a moment there is quiet, no one knows what to do next, then the Caliph makes the following announcement:

"I will pay 1,000 gold pieces to anyone who can give us a true and certain answer to this problem, and can tell us which of these two died first."

There is a buzz of excitement among the crowd; all of them would like to solve the riddle and earn the money, but now Abu again uses his wits, and much to everyone's astonishment, he jumps up, followed by Fatima, and apologizes to the Caliph and his wife, and claims the 1,000 gold pieces by confessing everything and so solving the problem. Fortunately for Abu, the Caliph enjoys the cleverness of the trickery and treats it as a joke, and after a solemn moral warning the Caliph gives Abu his 1,000 gold pieces. At this moment, there is a tremendous noise from the inner room, and Fatima explains her difficulties with Omar. Omar is disliked by everyone in the town, and her story is easily accepted; she now opens the door and he comes storming out in a great rage; he did not, however, expect to find the Caliph and his train, and is even more angry when the Caliph orders two of his attendants to remove Omar and punish him. The people of the town are fond of Abu and Fatima, so there is general rejoicing and amusement as the Caliph and his wife make their ceremonious exit in gayer mood than when they came in.

When the crowd has dispersed, Abu and Fatima sink contentedly on to the divan, and the servant pours them out a bowl of tea. They stir it, smile at one another, drink and enjoy the tea, just as they did at first—but their movement and mood of enjoyment is suddenly arrested when they hear from the servant (and *we* hear by the repeated theme in the music) that the creditors are once more approaching the house.

As the curtain falls we see Abu and Fatima gather up the bags of money they had received for the burials, and we know by their disconsolate faces that this time the creditors will be paid! But Abu gives us a knowing wink and hides away his 1,000 gold pieces just before we lose sight of him.

Notes. Whatever music is selected, the characters must be very obviously marked by change of theme and recurring theme, and the movement must be precise and clear on each beat. Traditional gestures would be quite suitable in this play, though not essential. With Seniors and Adults the miming of the mood with the music is half the fun. With Juniors it might be better to let them improvise with speech and use no music, unless they are especially skilled in mime.

THE WICKED PIPER

A mime play for Juniors with music composed by Barbara Lander. (Students might enjoy performing this also.)

Characters

A young peasant man
His wife
A wicked old piper
At least five elves (preferably ten or eleven)
At least four monsters (preferably seven or eight)

Set and Lighting

The scene is a clearing in the forest, a few trees and an old tree stump towards the left of the stage which serves as a seat. Up right of the stage is a grassy bank leading out and away into the distance. It is late afternoon, but the light fades from rather brilliant sun to twilight—so that there is a dim and misty effect when the old piper enters; by the time he goes out, the moon has risen, so that the ending is again in a flood of light, though of a different quality.

Costume

The peasants can be of any national costume provided it is in keeping with the set, or they can be dressed in simple English style. The elves in gay colours and the monsters predominantly green and brown, resembling evil spirits from the roots of the trees.

Theme of the Play

In a wood in early spring two little elves are playing; they run in and out of the trees playing hide-and-seek. Presently they tire of the game and sit together at the foot of a tree left, playing at cat's cradle with a length of gossamer thread. Two others come running down the grassy bank from up stage right, leap-frogging as they come; quickly they busy themselves scattering seeds and watching to see how quickly they will grow. Another elf comes from up stage left and looks round to see what mischief he can do; he is the naughtiest, and starts off by disturbing the two at cat's cradle—then he makes a nuisance of himself by teasing the other two each in turn in different ways.

The two playing cat's cradle tire of their game and set about making magic and willing the flowers to grow; all of them are busy and only disturbed by the mischievous elf, when suddenly they hear a sound. It is a weird piping, something they haven't heard before; they become frightened and huddle together, and as it comes nearer they run away to the right and hide in a thicket close by,—from time to time we see them peeping out, so we know that they are aware of all that is happening. The piping comes nearer, and from the left, coming from behind the trees, grotesque monsters appear, large and terrifying. They dance round in a circle and then turn and herald the entrance of an old piper; he is ugly and scowling, and the music that comes from his pipe is not beautiful but strange. The monsters dance again to his pipe, preparing evil magic, and the elves in their cover become more and more frightened.

Suddenly there is a stir among them, they have heard something which disturbs them, the piper makes a sign and quickly the monsters change themselves into trees, and the piper hides behind one of them—staring at the grassy bank up stage right. From the top of the bank we now see a happy young couple—a peasant and his wife—they have lost their way and are glad to find this clearing and a tree stump to sit on: the woman sits to rest, and the man gathers some flowers for her and comes and sits by her on the ground. Rested, they decide it is time to move on, especially as it is clear that darkness is coming fast; at this moment they are arrested by the sound of piping, and the old piper emerges from behind the tree coming closer and closer to them, as if bewitching them with his music. The peasant woman is fascinated, gets up and begins to follow the old piper, as if she hardly knew why; her husband realizes what is happening and entreats her not to follow, but she is spellbound and begins to dance in and out of the trees following the piper as he threads his way with malicious delight at the power he has over her. Her husband tries to follow, but the monsters that were trees come out and bar his way. He is fighting to get to his wife, struggling and nearly at his wits' end, when the elves boldly rush out of their cover and surround the piper; they battle with him and wrench the pipe from his lips. Immediately the piper is forced to stop playing. Having lost his pipe, his power is lost also and he is afraid; at the same moment that the pipe is wrenched from him, the monsters recoil, as if they too were powerless; the mischievous elf now finds a use for his quick wits, and runs with the pipe to the young peasant, pressing him to play it, for as yet his wife still seems bewitched and in a dream. Immediately the young man begins to play the most beautiful music issues from the pipe; the old piper struggles to get near enough to the peasant to regain his pipe and his power, but the music of the pipe is now too strong for him, and gains power all the time. The young man moves towards his wife, and the monsters and the wicked piper, struggling to free themselves from this new magic, run away on all sides looking uglier than ever, and writhing in contortions as if they were in pain. At the same time, the young wife is freed from her enchantment and returns with joy and relief to her husband; as he joins her he throws the pipe to the elves; they are highly excited, and playing happy music on the magic pipe they lead the couple safely away to show them their road home.

TEN LITTLE NIGGER BOYS

A mime based on the nursery rhyme, with musical variations composed by Barbara Lander on the traditional tune.

This mime could be attempted by any age. Juniors will enjoy playing it quite freely without troubling about the accompaniment, probably adding their own noises. Seniors and Adults will find it more effective if they realize that unlike some of the other mimes which are rather free in expression, this one needs to be *drilled*. The fun is gained from the precision of the nigger boys' movement interpreting each note of the music, and their movements when in unison being exactly together. Expert timing and finish is necessary.

Characters

Coal-black Mammy
Ten Nigger Boys (they can be all one size, or ranging from very small to large—grouped in height—smallest first)
A Mermaid
A Bee
A Beehive (three or more people)
A Fish (two people)
A Big Bear
A Baby Bear
Two Penguins (some other animals if desired)
A Parson
A Bride
One little girl

Set and Lighting

No special scenery or lighting, but as much space as possible.

Costume

The Coal-black Mammy will wear the typical coloured blouse and skirt and a handkerchief tied on her head, but all the other characters can wear a uniform basic garment (black or navy) and suggest the costume by slight additional accessories:

The Nigger Boys could have uniform white blazers with red stripes, and red neck-bows, also boater straw hats with red ribbon round them and elastic under the chin, so that they can at times be pushed back and hang at the back of the neck.

A Mermaid should have long hair which she can comb, a beautiful tail attached from the waist which she can spread out as she sits.

A Bee—antennae on the head, and possibly wings would be quite sufficient.

A Beehive—the three or four people concerned will together with uplifted hands support the straw top to a hive, so that they appear to be the walls—their uniform will be sufficient.

A Fish could have a mask attached to the right side of one person's face and the left side of the other person's face. Both will be facing forward with one arm extended forward palm to palm and bodies close together. The shape of the fish face can be indicated in the mask, the eye in the side. A tail will be draped from the mask on each side and trail after them as they walk. The front arms will represent the jaw which will engulf and swallow the boy, who will then come between them.

The Two Bears—Fur gloves (with claws attached) and fur bonnets.

Two Penguins—Penguin half masks, possibly flappers.

A Parson—A curate's hat, coat, and collar.

A Bride—Orange blossom, veil and bouquet.

A Little Girl—A sunbonnet.

With the exception of the little girl, who should have a

straight make-up, all the others should have negro 'suggestion' only—(not complete)—to fit in with the 'suggestion' of costume, i.e. black make-up ending at the sides of faces with a deliberate line, just as a mask would end; red lips (though actually wrong) will be effective with this.

Theme of the Play

This is of course apparent from the words of the nursery rhyme, but there are a variety of versions of it. Below is the version used for this mime:

1. Ten little nigger boys
   Going out to dine
   One over-ate himself
   And then there were nine.

2. Nine little nigger boys
   Staying up late
   One over-slept himself
   And then there were eight.

3. Eight little nigger boys
   Going down to Devon
   One saw a mermaid
   And then there were seven.

4. Seven little nigger boys
   Chopping up sticks
   One chopped himself in half
   And then there were six.

5. Six little nigger boys
   Playing near a hive
   A big bee stung one
   And then there were five.

6. Five little nigger boys
   Studying the law
   One stayed in Chancery
   Then there were four.

7. Four little nigger boys
   Swimming in the sea
   A big fish swallowed one
   And then there were three.

8. Three little nigger boys
   Visiting the Zoo
   A big bear hugged one
   And then there were two.

9. Two little nigger boys
   Lying in the sun.
   One got frizzled up
   And then there was one.

10. One little nigger boy
    Left all alone
    He got married
    . . . . .

Note. The play opens with the entrance of a Coal black Mammy, who saunters across and stands down left or right of the stage. She speaks with a negro dialect and introduces each episode by speaking the lines. She speaks one verse, then the music takes it up, never the two together. The action of the mime takes place between the speaking of each verse, the actors remain 'frozen' until the music begins.

All the extra characters (e.g. the Mermaid, the Bee, the Hive, the Fish, the Zoo, the Parson) remain on the stage after their part is finished as part of the tableau; so do the Nigger Boys after they have 'died'.

VERSE I

The ten Nigger Boys run on in single file and round the stage from up left in a semicircle to down right, and from there the leader goes again in a semi-circle up stage and round to down left, followed by the others, until he is opposite number ten who has by then arrived down stage right (see diagram). They sit exactly together, in a semi-circle, cross-legged, and facing the audience.

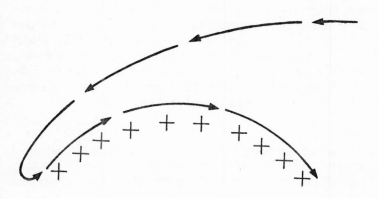

They all mime eating with alternate hands exactly on the musical beat, the greedy one (sitting up left centre) eats in double time; they mime drinking, putting glasses down, and they rise; the one who has over-eaten staggers across to down left holding his middle and falls, the others all point at him and hold the position in tableau.

VERSE 2

The Nigger Boys skip into position centre, five seated and four standing looking on in an uneven group. Those who are seated mime the dealing and playing of cards. They yawn and all of them go to sleep leaning on one another in various ways. At the sound of the alarm clock, all but one wake up and run and make a line across the front of the stage, leaving the one asleep down right. Exactly together they mime cleaning their teeth, then they put on their hats, turn to the left, and run off down left in single file.

VERSE 3

The Mermaid enters and sits down stage right miming combing her hair. The eight Nigger Boys skip from down left to up centre, forming themselves in a semicircle with the bulge towards the audience. With their backs to the audience, they mime digging sand and throwing sand over left shoulders, and one boy (just left-centre of the circle) catches sight of the Mermaid as he throws; slowly and shyly he walks across to her down right and sits at her feet; she chucks him under the chin. The others shade their eyes with their hands and stare shocked holding tableau.

VERSE 4

The remaining Nigger Boys spread themselves into a jagged group, and mime chopping wood; one (fairly centrally placed) does double-sized chopping in half-time. The others stop chopping and watch, and when he 'chops himself in half' the impetus is so great that he spins in several circles to the left, as if the top half of his body were disconnected, and so he falls. The others stare at him in various characteristic attitudes and hold tableau.

VERSE 5

The Beehive comes in and stands up stage right. The Bee is already in position in the middle of the hive. The Nigger Boys dance round in a circle holding hands as if playing 'ring a ring o' roses'. One of them tries to join in the circle, but they won't let him, so he goes curiously to the Hive. The Bee buzzes out and chases him all round the circle of other boys (who are by now on the ground 'we all fall down'); the Bee stings the curious boy who falls right, and the Bee returns to the Hive. All the other Niggers' heads turn towards the one who has been stung, holding tableau.

VERSE 6

Four of the five remaining Nigger Boys move into position and then walk very slowly from up centre diagonally to left, standing solemnly in a line. They mime carrying enormous books, which they put down and open; they put on their spectacles, pick up the books and begin to read, standing in a line. One Nigger Boy walks down the line studying the covers and looking over the top of each book. When he gets to the fourth one, the reader closes the book, lifts it, knocks him on the head with it, and the boy falls—his legs flop to the ground on the last beat of the music; the others stare, holding tableau.

VERSE 7

The four Nigger Boys mime swimming in various ways and in various directions. One is doing a back crawl to the right.

From the right appears a large Fish; its jaws engulf the boy and they sweep him to up left. The others stare after him in tableau.

VERSE 8

At the opening of this music a Large Bear and a Baby Bear come in from up stage left and stand left centre; then two Penguins waddle in from up right, and stand right-centre. The three Nigger Boys come happily down-stage centre eating ice-cream, one of the boys offers some ice-cream to the Baby Bear, who comes down centre playing with him; the Mother Bear comes up behind, hugs the boy and carries him to left, both sitting on the floor.

VERSE 9

The two remaining Nigger Boys lie in imaginary sun, centre stage; one mimes being frizzled up by the sun, the other stares in horror.

VERSE 10

The Nigger Boy who is left, rises. The Coal-black Mammy stops the verse after the line: 'He got married'— then a little Bride enters from down right and joins the boy. As the music changes to the 'Wedding March', they walk slowly up stage centre with their backs to the audience. By this time the Parson has come from up stage left and is waiting for them centre back. They kneel, give the ring, rise:— Then the Mammy speaks the lines:

> "He got married
> *and then there were———*"

At this all the nine Nigger Boys (excluding the tenth who stands centre with his bride) rise from their positions and run and sit in a row across the front of the stage, facing front: at the right end of the row we see there is a little white girl in a sun-bonnet (who has come from down right). The Bride and Bridegroom (now suddenly the mother and father of a large family) count them from left to right, registering great surprise when they see that the tenth is a little girl, and a white one! As each Nigger Boy is counted he turns his head to look at the little girl. The father looks disapproving, and the mother looks coy.

THE YOUNG KING

A mime based on a story by Oscar Wilde, with music composed by Barbara Lander.

This would be most suited to Seniors and Adults, but Juniors might well work freely on the story, without striving too hard with the technique required to interpret music and movement.

Characters

The Young King (a goat-herd)
His Companion (a boy lute-player)
The Archbishop
The Lord Chamberlain
The Usher
The Master of the Robes
The Master of Perfumes
Court Ladies (at least seven)   } more if available
Court Gentlemen (at least six)
A Herald-trumpeter-boy
A Page (who is also the crown bearer)

In the Dream

The Chief Weaver
Two other Weavers
A Child Weaver
A Diver
An Octopus
Two miners
The Spirit of Fever

Set and Lighting

The scene should give an impression of spaciousness, so that the main part of it represents a Throne Room. Up stage left there are some steps leading to the throne itself. Down

stage right and left are tables on which the Coronation robes
are laid out for inspection. Slightly recessed up stage right
are steps leading to an altar which is visible to the audience.
Up stage centre there is an opening leading to other parts of
the palace. A stool or two are placed easily down stage left
right of centre. The room should have as lavish an appearance as possible.

The lighting must give us a natural interior, with beams
of sun from windows right and left and from the entrance
hall up stage centre. There will be candles on the altar and
an extra light close to the throne which will be lit by the
usher when he enters, put out as he exits, and lit again on
his second entry.

After the entrance of the King and the trying on of the
robes, the afternoon sun from the windows begins to
diminish to evening, and the shadows lengthen, so that by
the time the usher turns out the light by the throne it is
nearly dark; there is still the reflection of a beam of moonlight from the window which makes the King and his
companions visible.

The three dreams will appear in the three unoccupied
corners of the stage; the weavers down stage left, the diver
up stage right, and the miners down stage right, each of
these corners will need to be separately lit, so that each
scene can fade in and out from a black-out; similarly
the throne must be lit separately, so that at the conclusion of each dream we are shown a glimpse of the
restless King, even though the light is only brought
half up.

At the end of the third dream the morning will be
approaching, and the whole scene will grow gradually
lighter as the sun comes up. By the time the Archbisop
arrives, there will be full morning light.

At the moment of the crowning, there is thunder and a

sudden black-out. During the black-out a mantle will be flung round the King and his staff changed for another; this can be quickly and easily done, and as light is restored and the transformation of the King is shown— there must be a spot on the King; the rest of the stage need not be fully lit until the last moment before the curtain falls.

Costume

The Goat-herd-boy-King should be bronzed and good-looking and carry a staff, and he should wear skins. At the end of the play, when he is transformed, a full mantle should envelope him, and though it should have great simplicity and no jewels, it might be made to sparkle with an ethereal quality. His original staff will be changed, and the new one will have a lily blossom at the top.

The Court Characters can be of any period; I would suggest mediaeval.

The Dream Characters should be simply presented—*the weavers* as peasants of the period. *The octopus* all black with hanging pieces from legs and arms. *The diver* in tights, with a large transparent cover over his head and down to his waist, as in the old tapestries. *The miners* in tights and bare from the waist up. *The Spirit of Fever* can be shown in any free imaginative way, or simply in red body tights and a quivering head-dress.

Theme of the Play

There is much excitement at the Court today. The old King has died, and it is now known that a boy goat-herd living in a forest nearby is the rightful heir to the throne. The boy has been found, and is today being brought to the Court for the first time. "What will he be like? How will he behave?" These questions are on everybody's lips. This is the eve of

the Coronation, and this evening the boy is coming to try
on his ceremonial Coronation robes which are lavishly displayed about the Throne Room. As the curtain rises we have
a glimpse of the room in quiet before any bustle and excitement begins. The rays of the afternoon sun heighten the
colours of the beautiful robes spread out in readiness; the
decorated throne, and small altar up the steps in a recess,
both seem to have a feeling of preparedness for something
great that is about to happen. Then, from another part of
the palace, a boy herald arrives in the great centre opening
to the room. He looks round for a moment, comes into the
room, faces smartly up to the opening, lifts his trumpet to
his lips and so summons the Court. He is followed closely
by the Usher—a pompous and fussy gentleman—who, after
lighting the lamp above the throne, surveys his preparations
with some pride. He moves around to make sure that all is
completely satisfactory, and, well pleased, he waits for the
arrival of the rest of the Court. And now they come, beautiful ladies and gentlemen greet one another at the central
opening, and swirl about the Throne Room adding still
more to the air of anticipation; there is much gaiety among
them, for whatever comes of it, this day is to be a great
occasion!

Soon we see the Master of the Robes arriving; he is a
busybody of a man, and seems to cause amusement to
all as he bustles about absorbed in the finishing touches
that must be put here and there, anxious that the crown and
sceptre are in their proper place, and finally mingling with
the crowd and making last plans with the Usher.

Now there is a little flutter among the ladies as the Master
of Perfumes appears in the opening. Eagerly they push
themselves forward into his path, and he sprays his perfume
and talks to them charmingly as he passes. He is such a
dandy that the gentlemen of the Court take little notice, but

he attracts the ladies, and they enjoy his little 'asides' to them.

A very small page arrives and whispers to the boy herald that it is time to proclaim the arrival of the Lord Chamberlain; so the trumpet again blares forth, and the Lord Chamberlain with great dignity enters the Throne Room and acknowledges the greetings of all who are present. Now there is even more excitement, for the arrival of the Lord Chamberlain indicates that the King must be close behind. Final preparations are now made under the vigilant eye of the Lord Chamberlain, and when the general excitement is at its height, the herald trumpets the approach of the King.

The whole Court makes obeisance as the goat-herd King stands in the great centre opening. He feels lost for a moment, and turns to his young companion—the lute-player—who is close at his side. Never before has he seen such grandeur, and he is overwhelmed and over-awed by the loftiness of the room, the grand dresses, and the fact that everyone is bowing to him—a goat-herd. His young companion smiles encouragement and they pass down among the crowd to the Lord Chamberlain.

The Chamberlain now explains to the boy that he must try on his robes as a rehearsal for the great ceremony, and while he does so we have an opportunity to study the different reactions and characteristics of the Court ladies and gentlemen; some are sympathetic with the boy's youth, others are inclined to laugh at his ignorance, some think him uncouth, but many feel that he has a natural dignity and that there can be no doubt that he really is the King. Among the younger ladies there are some who are so interested in their own idle gossip and their little intrigues with the various Court gentlemen that they think of little else, and there are also older ladies and gentlemen who have learnt tolerance and give balance to the Court; all are present in

the Throne Room for this occasion, and to everyone the
occasion has significance.

The Master of the Robes takes charge of the dressing and
fitting,—he is in a bustle of excitement, for him this is a
moment of personal triumph, and the Master of Perfumes
lends some assistance in his own particular languid way—
while the Usher keeps an eye on the herald and the page who
are almost ready to forget they are on duty, so exciting is it to
them both that the new King should be so near to their own
age. Some of the ladies and gentlemen offer assistance or
comment, and the Lord Chamberlain stands by and directs
when necessary. The boy King begins to enjoy his magnificent clothes, they are quite a novelty, and his companion is
amused to see his mood changing; the page, bearing the
crown on a velvet cushion comes and kneels at the feet of
the King, but at this moment the Chamberlain directs that
the gowns shall be removed and placed ready for the next
day's ceremony. This done, he leads the young King to his
throne and dismisses the Court.

Again the young King feels bewildered, he can hardly
believe that he is sitting on this grand throne as all these
beautiful ladies and elegant gentlemen curtsy and bow to
him and pass out of the great hall; finally the Lord Chamberlain too bows his way out, and the boy is left with his companion. The King sinks back on his throne, hardly knowing
what his feelings mean and his companion begins to play
the lute. As a goat-herd boy he too had played out on the
hillside alone with his flock; he now takes the lute himself
and plays another dreamy tune. The evening grows darker,
the feeling of peace and quiet spreads its influence and he
falls asleep; gently the lute-player releases the instrument
from him, puts down the lute and falls asleep himself on the
steps of the throne.

The day has been exciting and the King sleeps restlessly;

he turns in his sleep and it is clear that his dreams are not making him happy. The room is quite dark now, and suddenly out of the dimness the sequence of his dreams is shown to us: Here is a horrifying dream. Some weavers are at work, obviously half-starved and driven; there is a child among them who keeps dropping asleep from hunger and exhaustion. They are weaving the material to make the robe for the King's Coronation. As they work, the chief weaver passes to and fro goading them on, he wakes the child, and a woman entreats him to be merciful. The chief weaver turns and strikes the woman, and she falls senseless; the child is worse off than before, the other weavers continue to work as if the incident was a normal one;—the dream fades —and we see the King again turning uncomfortably on his throne.

Then out of the shadows we see another dream tormenting him. A diver is in great danger at the bottom of the sea— feeling his way against the heavy weight of the water; he is experiencing difficulty, and cannot stay there much longer, but he must find a pearl for the King's crown. He opens an oyster and finds a pearl inside, and just as he is struggling to reach the surface an octopus appears out of the weeds behind him. For a moment he is off his guard, and the octopus has caught his leg in one of its long tentacles. The diver takes out his knife and battles for his life, but other tentacles close round him, all his struggles are in vain, he is engulfed and sinks on to the bed of the sea with the octopus.

The dream fades, and again we see the King discomforted and longing but unable to wake. His young companion is relaxed in sleep on the steps of the throne, blissfully unaware that he should have gone with the King to his bedchamber, for he too was exhausted and sleep came too easily.

Out of the shadows a third episode in this dream sequence

appears; this time there are two miners working in the humid heat of a river-bed; their job is to find rubies to deck the gown that the King is to wear at his Coronation. They are weary, and their searching brings no success.

Suddenly we are aware of a wraith or spirit that hovers quiveringly behind each man in turn; they stumble and breathe with difficulty and we realize that this is the spirit of fever—and as they continue to sweat and struggle, fever rises triumphant and both men die in the river-bed.

It is nearly morning when this dream fades, and the light of the dawn is already in the room. The King rouses himself from his nightmares; he starts up realizing he has been there all night; he sees the robes lying ready to wear, he darts across the room to look at them again. Yes, there is the exquisitely woven mantle, the pearls on the crown, the rubies decking the magnificent gown. How could he have worn them, even for a moment, with pleasure, the previous night! After his dreams he could not possibly do so again, it is too horrible. He will destroy them. The lute-player, now awakened by the King's violent movements, realizes that it is dawn and that he has slept there too long. He runs across, intending to help the King to dress. He is astonished to find him crumpling and tearing the precious garments. Anxiously the lute-player runs to the entrance and calls for help. The page and herald are soon on the scene; they were already nearly dressed, and run in pulling on their tunics as they come. Other members of the Court follow closely, for already they were expecting the arrival of the Archbishop for the ceremony.

The Master of Perfumes drifts leisurely in to see why the crowd is gathering; but when the Master of the Robes arrives he is distracted by the sight! All his exquisite workmanship to be treated like this! What hooligans! The Usher is equally worried and goes back to report to the Lord

Chamberlain, and there is general consternation. By the time
the Chamberlain arrives the boy is beginning to explain his
actions and tell his dreams. He is so moved by the thought
that as he tells he half re-enacts all that he dreamt. At first
the crowded court are mildly interested, some are amused,
some are annoyed, but when the boy King ends his tale
with a declaration that he will not wear any of the royal
attire, then they are horrified. Some of the older people,
thinking it is just a childish whim, try to pacify him kindly
and tell him the effect of his dreams will soon pass; but he
will not listen; the situation becomes more serious, and the
Chamberlain exerts his authority and insists angrily that the
usual procedure must be observed, and the boy must now
dress quickly. To his astonishment the boy remains adamant,
and says he will not be crowned at all unless it is in his own
simple attire. At this juncture the herald trumpets the
approach of the Archbishop, and the time for the Coronation has arrived. From the great central opening we see the
Archbishop approach, followed by the crown-bearer, who
takes the crown from the table, and carefully placing it on its
cushion, stands in readiness for the Ceremony. The Court
make a great obeisance as the Archbishop comes among
them.

The Lord Chamberlain is in a dilemma; with a mixture of
awkwardness and anger he tries to give the Archbishop a
true idea of what has happened.

The Archbishop turns to the boy, it is clear that he appre-
ciates his feelings, but he tries to persuade him kindly to
follow the usual custom. Finding no response,—to the
horror of many of the Court officials—and particularly the
Master of the Robes—the Archbishop agrees that the crowning shall take place as the boy wishes and the fine robes are
removed. Then the Archbishop leads the goat-herd boy to
the foot of the altar steps, and the boy walks slowly up and

kneels at the altar, followed by the Archbishop. As the boy
rises, the Archbishop takes the crown and mounts the steps
to the altar, and looking kindly at the boy he places the
crown on his head. At this moment there is a clap of thunder,
which causes panic among the crowd—what disaster can
this be? What have they done to cause it? There is a sudden
darkness and thunder; then gradually the altar is transfused
with light that grows to a great brilliance and as the Archbishop moves away down the steps we see the boy King
standing at the altar suddenly transformed, no longer a
simple goat-herd, but dressed in a mantle more beautiful
than any courtly robes, and in his hand, his goat-herd's staff
is blossoming like a lily.

That this is a miracle everyone is sure, and in amazement
and wonder all kneel in recognition, and in acknowledge-
ment of their King. The Archbisop walks away from the
altar to the back of the crowd, and he too kneels among
them, showing that he recognizes the sign and the hand of
God in the vision of this boy.

CHANGE OF HEART

A mime, only suitable I think, for Seniors or Adults.

The mime is in five episodes with an introduction and a finale, and is symbolic of War and its attendant evils.

Music for this play has been composed by Josephine Rhodes.[1]

Characters

A Man (symbolizing Man's Indifference)

A Woman (symbolizing The Spiritual Light of His Conscience)

Two small children

Three bigger boys

A poor girl

A poor man

A wealthy woman

A wealthy man

Another wealthy man

A nun

Two street orators

One Figure—symbolishing the War Machine. (This can be played equally well by one person or by several people)

Two blind people

Five refugees

Three cripples

Other war victims

Children. Passers-by

Makers of armaments

Other members of the crowd

[1] The music is the composer's copyright, but may be obtained on hire. Anyone wishing to do so should apply to Miss Josephine Rhodes, 40 Nevilles Court, Dollis Hill Lane, N.W.2, or to The Rose Bruford Training College, Lamorbey Park, Sidcup, Kent.

Set and Lighting

As one episode must run without pause or curtain into the next, there can be very little help from the set; all that is necessary is a curtain set with cyclorama or sky-cloth behind, so that it is possible to have either an open stage, or closed curtains at the back, which may partially open for a particular episode or effect. An easily portable bench and a street lamp can be placed in the black-out for some of the episodes. In front of the proscenium arch and as far away from the main acting area as possible is a small table and chair. This remains throughout the play. Hand properties such as cards, bottles, marbles, can be real, but armaments, etc., should be mimed.

The lighting is of great importance. There are certain special areas of light:

(*a*) The large acting area, with a pool of light round the lamp-post when it is used.

(*b*) The area between curtains and cyclorama when there is an effect like the War Machine up stage centre, also for the finale.

(*c*) The table and chair outside the proscenium arch.

There will be a black-out between each episode and the slight change of set can then be made. Simultaneously with the black-out on the acting area the light on the table and chair will be brought up so that we see Man and his conscience between every episode; this fades again as each episode is played, except in the Introduction, in Episode V and in the Finale.

LIGHTING AND SETTINGS FOR SEPARATE EPISODES

Introduction: Man and his Conscience lit, the rest of stage in darkness.

Episode 1. Open stage and cyclorama—normal light of day.

Episode 2. Open stage and cyclorama—street lamp placed right centre of stage towards back—bench placed up stage towards left centre.

Episode 3. Open stage and cyclorama. Bench placed left centre of stage. Orators bring on their own tub and place it right centre of stage. Lighting as for an open-air scene on a sunny day.

Episode 4. The curtains are closed across the back, and the lighting as for an interior in the afternoon, without regard for sources of light, windows, etc., as the scene is abstract.

At a given cue the curtains at the back part, disclosing the War Machine high on a rostrum, and in silhouette, with a red glow on the cyclorama and some red on the stage, too. Towards the end of the scene almost all in silhouette.

Episode 5. The curtains are closed across the back. There is not much light at the beginning of the scene but enough to differentiate clearly between the characters. In this scene the light on Man at the table is full up throughout.

Finale and Resolution. At a given cue the curtains at the back part, disclosing the light of Man's Conscience dominating the scene from the rostrum in the opening (used earlier by the War Machine); there is a strong light on this figure and gradually the light increases on the whole scene until the final curtain.

Theme of the Play

INTRODUCTION

A man sits at a table at the side of the stage, if possible outside the proscenium arch; he is separated from the scenes that follow. The man is good-looking and as we see him now we feel he could inspire confidence, and be a leader of men. He is playing cards, but as he plays it becomes evident that he is bored with his life; the game is not going as he wishes, so he stops playing and throws a dice; he looks at it despondently, takes a drink from the bottle on his table, smiles, continues his card game, and we realize that he typifies Indifference. Standing close behind his chair is a beautiful woman; she observes him closely, but whereas at first he seemed aware of her presence as he drinks he loses that awareness and she can no longer influence him; she turns away; she is the Spiritual Life of his Conscience. The light fades from them and comes up on:

EPISODE 1.   INDIVIDUALISM

Two children are happily playing marbles; they are not very old and are obviously happy about the new marbles they have acquired and are enjoying their game. While they play, three bigger boys come along and see what is happening; they have no marbles of their own, so decide they will bully the little ones, and make them give them up. They set on the children from behind, take their marbles and tease them, finally running away and leaving the players disconsolate, one angry and the other very near to tears. As the light fades on this scene, we are again aware of Man and his Conscience for a few moments. Man is obviously affected by what he has seen; he is sorry to see the bullies win, but the episode is over, he shrugs his shoulders, takes another drink and continues to play.

EPISODE 2.   CLASS RIVALRY AND HATRED

We now see a poor girl standing under a lamp at a street corner, obviously anxiously waiting for someone. In a few moments she is joined by a young man; she meets and greets him eagerly, but he shows her he has had no luck, the work he wanted and tried for he did not get and he has no money left. He catches sight of a cigarette end lying in the gutter and eagerly picks it up and smokes it. At this moment a man and woman in evening dress pick their way across the street obviously looking for a taxi. The unemployed young man stands quietly and his girl goes towards the woman pleading for money; the wealthy man is annoyed that his lady should be troubled in this way and brushes the girl aside. She is so weak that she falls to the ground as the couple pass off. Her young man is incensed and goes to help her up; they sit on the bench. From lower down the street another wealthy and unpleasant-looking man appears, the girl again goes forward to plead for help, but hesitates when she sees the man alone. He stops, puts his monocle to his eye and looks her up and down; he comes closer to her, offering her money if she will go with him. She is horrified and instinctively steps back and appeals to her young man friend; then, realizing how great their need is she moves as if to accept the money and the conditions. At this, the young man can bear it no more and knocks the man down. He falls and they realize he is dead.

As this scene fades, we are again aware of the effect on Man and his Conscience. For a moment his card game is arrested and we hope he is moved, but again he shelves his responsibility, drinks to the future, and plays again, as the lights fade and we see:

EPISODE 3. PROPAGANDA

The scene has changed, and we are in a park; on the bench left is a nun surrounded by a group of children; they are absorbed in a story she is reading to them. The peace of this scene is rudely interrupted by the entry of two street orators carrying a tub; one of them mounts this and begins to address passers-by, while the other helps to collect the crowd. Gradually more and more people collect, and the children become more interested in the speaker than in the nun's story. The theme of the speech is 'Build up wealth for yourselves by making armaments'. One by one the children are prevailed upon to join the crowd right, and as the speech reaches its climax and the scene fades we realize that only one child was left listening to the nun.

Again we see Man struggling with his Conscience, but he plays and drinks with abandon and becomes the epitome of Indifference as we continue into:

EPISODE 4.   WAR

The scene opens on a large group of people whose movements make us aware that this is an armament factory; all are now busily employed. When the activity is at its height —the light changes and brings to life the next part of this scene. The curtains have parted at the back, and a magnificent and dreadful figure high above the workers dominates everything. This is the War Machine driving everyone to final destruction. A red glow suffuses the scene and before it completely fades there is a silhouette showing that the workers have become a mass of humanity struggling and fighting furiously; the movement gathers speed and impetus and ends with general destruction and despair.

The light dies and Man is seen again, but this time he is alone, his Conscience has left him. He is half drunk, he has stopped playing and is in a state of terror; he madly throws his dice, but nothing can help him now and he remains visible and part of the scene as we move into:

EPISODE 5.   AFTERMATH

Gradually, one or two at a time, we see a procession of suffering humanity filling the stage. Here come the cripples, the wounded, the blind, the refugees; it seems that all the world's sorrow is here. As the group grows it is noticeable that all their eyes are turned in one direction, they are staring or pointing at the Indifferent Man who has played and drunk his life away, ignoring all that led to this moment. As he feels all their eyes upon him, he can bear it no more. He leaves his table and rushes to the centre of the crowd, but feeling himself surrounded, he struggles to free himself and rushes to each corner in turn only to meet reproachful eyes which he cannot pass, until at last he falls in a heap in despair and remorse.

At last his better feelings have been aroused, at a great cost, and now:

FINALE AND RESOLUTION

The curtains up stage centre part and in place of the War Machine we see the Spiritual Life of Man's Conscience high above the scene, radiantly pointing out to the light and the way to Peace. The Man slowly raises his head, feeling that there is a difference; he slowly turns, recognizes his Conscience, and the truth is clear to him at last. He moves up to her, and as the curtain falls we see that he is moving up towards the light.

VILLAGE CONCERT

A comedy mime for Seniors and Adults, with music composed by Barbara Lander.

Characters

Farmer Briggs
His Son
The Lady of the Manor
Joe (the boxer)
Little Willie
Miss Hoodwink (the pianist)
Mr Hardy (the schoolteacher)
The Squire
The Vicar
His Wife
Little Millicent
Her Mother
Her Father
Jack (the sailor)
Maisie ⎱
Primrose ⎰ His girl-friends

Other members of the orchestra (as many as desired)
Members of the Audience (at least sixteen and more if possible)

Set and Lighting

The set should consist of a raised platform diagonally across the corner up stage left, for orchestra and performers, with an entrance from one side or at the back of this platform. A few chairs should be placed ready for the orchestra at the beginning. Chairs for the audience should be placed in rows facing the platform, half backing the audience, from down stage right to centre, on diagonal lines.

An entrance for the audience from up stage right.

The lighting is uncomplicated, a fairly sunny interior, with a shaft of light as if from a window giving the platform a little more illumination than the rest.

Costume

Modern dress, a little old-fashioned perhaps, and noticeably suggesting the characters as described.

Theme of the Play

At the opening we see an ordinary bare village-hall, with a low platform at one end; the scene is quickly brought to life by the characters who use it:

The first to arrive is Farmer Briggs, so deaf that he didn't hear what time the concert was to begin. But he always makes a point of being early and he is eager to start, for he plays leading fiddle in the village orchestra. While he is getting out his instrument and settling down, his son, George, arrives—a robust, solemn young man, who follows in his father's footsteps, for he plays second fiddle.

Now comes the Lady of the Manor. She is very popular with everyone, but they are all conscious of the honour she bestows in deigning to join the orchestra. She is a horse-woman who seems to ride the 'cello much as she would ride to hounds. When she plays, she thrashes it with vigour, keeping the pace if not always the time.

Presently they are joined by Joe, the boxer, who 'doubles' the triangle and the mouth-organ—and a very sensitive player he is too. With him comes Little Willie, the publican's son: though somewhat awed by the galaxy of local 'stars', he is none the less proud of his accomplishments as drummer, and he is the envy of all the other village-boys.

While they and other members of the orchestra are preparing for the 'fray', and only just in time, arrives Miss Hoodwink, pianist of local renown. For many years the

'May Queen', she has now passed her prime, but retains every bit of her self-confidence. Importantly she strikes the 'A' and the orchestra are busy tuning up as the audience arrives full of expectancy and excitement. All the village is there, and there is a bustle of anticipation as they murmur good wishes to the relatives and friends of performers, admire the programme girls and fight for the best seats.

Then the Squire enters, accompanied by the Vicar and the Vicar's wife. They sail into their reserved seats in the front row, and all is ready to begin.

Finally, Mr Hardy, the schoolteacher, walks impressively on to the platform and takes his place as conductor. Miss Hoodwink glares at him forbiddingly for she has a fixed idea that it is her job to keep the orchestra together and she has little respect for conductors. There is always battle between these two and the allegiance of the members of the orchestra is divided, though they work with a will following the one or the other. The orchestra opens with an impassioned rendering of a familiar 'number' in which their energy and effort are displayed to advantage. They receive an ovation from the thrilled audience and, flushed with success, they move back to make room on the platform for other performers.

On comes tiny red-haired Millicent, beautifully beribboned for the occasion, to recite her poem. Alas, she forgets and hesitates, but after making a fresh start, she attains sufficient impetus to carry her through to a triumphant end and the audience happily applaud the young prodigy. Her mother and father now take the stage (accepting applause with modest awareness that they are really a brilliant family). They sing their duet, given 'by request' in accordance with tradition.

Now we reach the high-spot of the evening—Jack, the sailor, hero of the village, is home on leave. Mounting the platform, he delights the girls with a brilliant execution of the 'hornpipe'. The applause is vociferous and he obliges with an encore and finally dances his way off the platform to further deafening applause.

The Vicar now rises and raises his hand for silence. Beaming benevolently, he makes an earnest appeal for the advertised charity, cracking his customary joke in conclusion. A collection is taken, and Mr Hardy returns to his position to conduct the orchestra in their final selection. After more applause, the audience begins to disperse. But who are these young ladies lingering behind, some supported by hopeful parents? They are waiting for Jack, vying with each other for the honour of his escort, much to the chagrin of the other lads of the village, who stand self-consciously by, doing their best to register indifference. Suddenly he appears from the back, but—what dismay!—he is not alone. With him are Maisie and Primrose who are strangers to the village. He bounces cheerfully out of the hall with a girl on each arm, the astonished group staring after him. Disconsolately they wander out, and the last member of the orchestra leaves the hall.

Note. The fun of this mime is in the clear characterization and the miming of the instruments—no props *at all* should be used—only chairs.

THE PLAGUE

An abstract mime suitable for performance by Seniors and Adults.

This would be effective if accompanied by sounds—e.g. drum, pipe and some human sounds such as singing or humming, laughter, hissing, or murmurs, also sudden moments of complete silence.

Characters

The Burgomaster
A Pedlar
A Friar
A Quack doctor
A Nun
A Boy who plays a pipe
Three abstract figures (representing Plague)
A crowd of mediaeval ladies and gentlemen
Some children

Set and Lighting

The scene is a mediaeval market-place with an entrance between the houses up stage right; there are also entrances from right and left. If possible some of the upper windows of the houses should be practical, so that at some moments villagers can watch the happenings in the market-place from above. There is an old well down left.

The lighting should convey the mood rather than the reality of the play, starting off with the bright sunlight of the morning, growing strange and dark for the entrance of Plague, but still light enough for us to see all the characters clearly; at the end the sunlight will return.

Costume

Plague may be represented as shrouded black figures, or in

black body-tights and masks, according to the conception of the producer.

The other characters in mediaeval costume.

Theme of the Play

It is early morning in this mediaeval market-place; house-doors are opening and people pass by happily greeting one another as they pass. A woman is singing as she cleans her courtyard; a boy, also singing, goes to the well to fetch water and returns to his house. Some children are playing in a little group on the right. Presently there is the sound of a small drum-beat, and a young pedlar comes into view, beating a drum to attract attention to himself and the wares he has to sell. The children stop their game and crowd round him laughing gaily. The pedlar is generous and gives them some trinkets to play with. One of the boys has been given a pipe which he begins to play and some of the children find themselves dancing and gradually men and women come from their houses to watch and join in.

Buying and selling is at its height when the Burgomaster passes by. He is much respected by all the citizens and they give him a great welcome.

The scene is at its gayest when an old friar joins the crowd; as he comes among them the mood changes, for he brings news that in a neighbouring village there is plague and many people are dying. The children do not understand why their mothers and fathers suddenly look so serious and quiet, but the dancing comes to a standstill and the tune on the pipe has changed to a minor key; the day is clouding over and a shiver passes through the crowd. It seems as if there is a faint hissing sound in the air although the crowd seem to hear nothing. Now we see three weird figures creeping among the people like shadows. No one can see them, but we see that they hover as a hawk hovers before seizing its prey. One by one they find their victim and stand close by like a shadow and immediately the victims are stricken with plague and fall to the ground, contaminated; no one dares touch them, and terror runs through the crowd. The boy with the pipe is taken with plague and his father runs for the quack doctor, who quickly comes and performs various rites; but in the middle of the cure, one of the shadows crosses his path; the quack doctor too has the plague and terror grows to panic. Many of the crowd creep back to their homes. A few of the people stay with a nun who has remained quiet and tranquil throughout; her faith revives their fearful spirits. Plague is defeated, the three figures lose their power and pass on to the next village.

Slowly life returns to its normal round. It is as though a cloud has passed by; and the singing is resumed as before, but it is a different voice, for she who sang before was a victim of the plague; but life continues.

*   *   *

Now follow four mimes which have been worked out by my students, by whose kind permission I am using them in this book.

THE FRENCH HAT SHOP

This depends very largely on precision of music and movement, and the student who worked it out has quoted music she thought suitable, but naturally permission would have to be granted by the music publishers before using it, so the ideas should only be used as an indication of the kind of music required.

This little play could be effective in smart French costume, but it can be even more amusing if performed in a simple basic costume. The only furniture needed is two chairs and a table. Doors, hats, handbags, etc., are mimed.

This could be performed by Juniors, Seniors or Adults, but again Juniors would approach it more realistically and without the same stylized precision as older and more sophisticated actors.

Characters

Madame
Her two assistants
A plump, frivolous lady
A slender, sophisticated lady

The scene is set in an exclusive millinery shop in Paris. It is essentially modern; with swing doors of plate glass down stage centre, and thick carpets on the floor. Two gilt chairs face the audience, one on either side of the entrance. Between them is a small, elegant table.

1. As the curtain rises Madame is standing down centre (facing the imaginary swing doors) filing her beautifully kept nails. Up left and up right her two assistants are unpacking hats. As they do so they cannot resist trying on one

or two of the latest creations, but unfortunately Madame turns round and sees them. Scandalized she hurries over, tears the hats off their heads and shakes her arms in despair.

2. Just then a customer is seen. Immediately Madame adopts her poise and charm again. The plump, frivolous lady enters, walking in very high heels with short, tapping steps. She wears a tight skirt, carries a dainty, if useless, handbag and wears an enormous hat. Pushing open the swing doors she is ushered into the shop by Madame and shown to the chair left centre. Taking off her large hat and placing it on the centre table she sits down, gracefully crossing her ankles.

Madame says, "What can I show you?"

The plump, frivolous lady replies, "I want a small hat with a frilly veil."

Madame turns to No. 1 of her assistants and repeats, "She wants a small hat with a frilly veil."

As if to impress it firmly in her mind the assistant says, "Yes, a small hat with a frilly veil"—and she finds one. She brings it to the customer and places it on her head.

But the plump, frivolous lady isn't sure that she likes it (Madame and the staff secretly think it hideous), but when she turns for confirmation of her doubts—"Voilà —it is exquisite!" She tries hard to believe this statement but regretfully says, "Non. What else can I be shown?"

3. But now enters another customer—a slender, sophisticated lady. She is superbly dressed. She walks slowly and languishingly. Madame shows her to the chair right centre. Taking off her small, dainty hat she places it on the centre table and sits down.

Madame says, "What can I show you?"

The slender, sophisticated lady replies, "I want a large hat with flowers on it."

As if to impress it firmly on her mind assistant No. 2. says, "Yes, a large hat with flowers on"—and she finds one. She brings it to the customer and places it on her head.

But, no, it is not satisfactory.

4. Then both ladies turn together and see each other's hats on the centre table.

Ah! At last!

Simultaneously they pick them up and try them on. Exquisite! They beckon the assistants (Madame stays up centre, horrified), pick up their handbags, open their cheque books and write and sign. They stand and prepare to leave, but as they are well satisfied customers in a friendly mood they go out arm in arm through the swing doors. Madame stands centre holding their cheques.

5. Outside the two ladies pause to admire each other's hats—then they recognize them as their own! Angry, the plump, frivolous lady snatches her hat away; the slender, sophisticated lady does the same, and then they realize they have been cheated. With one accord they march back into the shop where Madame is still standing holding the cheques. Together they snatch them away, place the hats back into her hands, tear up the cheques, and confident that wrong has been righted they stalk out of the milliner's—(hatless!)— and go their separate ways.

6. Madame, flabbergasted, throws the hats into the air with a final, "Ah, well!"

Notes on Music

Music suggested:
Piano selection from *Bless the Bride* by Vivian Ellis, published by Chappell, and *Carousel* by Richard Rodgers, published by Williamson Music Ltd.

1. *Carousel:* 'What's the use of Wond'rin' (Madame and her
   two assistants)

   Introduction   9th and 10th Bars
   Begin at 1st bar
   Madame files her nails. Assistants unpack hats   4 Bars
   They try them on   6 Bars
   Repeat last 10 bars angrily
   Madame sees them   2 Bars
   Runs to them   2 Bars
   Snatches hat off assistant No. 1   1 Bar
   Snatches hat off assistant No. 2   1 Bar
   Looks at both reprovingly. Shakes arms in despair 4 Bars

2. *Bless the Bride:* 'Ma Belle Marguerite' (Plump, frivolous lady)
   Cut first 6 bars and begin on 7th
   Plump, frivolous lady enters   2 Bars
   Opens swing doors   2 Bars
   Ushered to seat by Madame   2 Bars
   Takes off hat   1 Bar
   And sits   1 Bar
   Madame says, "What can I show you?"   2 Bars
   Plump, frivolous lady says, "I want a small hat
      with a frilly veil."   Play trill in place of next 2 Bars
   Madame to assistants, "She wants a small hat with
      a frilly veil."   Repeat trill octave higher
   Assistant 1. "Yes, a small hat with a frilly veil."
                                     Same, octave higher
   Assistant 1. Brings hat and places it on plump,
      frivolous lady's head   4 Bars
   Plump, frivolous lady looks doubtful. So do
      Madame and the assistants   1 Bar
   Plump, frivolous lady turns to them, but, "Ah, it
      is exquisite!"   1 Bar
   Plump, frivolous lady returns to mirror and
      shakes head   2 Bars

Cut last 4 bars of piece

3. *Bless the Bride:* 'Table for Two'. (Slender, sophisticated lady)

Slender, sophisticated lady enters	3 Bars
Open swing doors	1 Bar
Shown to chair by Madame	3 Bars
Takes off hat	1 Bar
Madame says, "What can I show you?"	3 Bars

Slender, sophisticated lady says, "I want a large
hat with flowers."   Insert trill

Madame says, "She wants a large hat with flowers."

Trill octave higher

Assistant 2. "Yes, a large hat with flowers on."

Trill octave higher still

Assistant 2. Brings hat and the slender, sophisticated lady tries it on
She studies it carefully, but regretfully, "Non"
} Cut 4 bars and play the following 8

4. *Bless the Bride:* 'Oh, what will mother say?'

Plump, frivolous lady and slender, sophisticated lady see each other's hats on centre table

Cut first 4 bars and begin on 5th

Together: "Oh! How wonderful!"	2 Bars
Try the hats on	2 Bars
"Yes, it suits me."	2 Bars
"Exquisite!" Beckon assistants	2 Bars
Open bags, take out cheque books	4 Bars
Receive pens	2 Bars
Sign	4 Bars
Tear out cheques and fasten bags	2 Bars

Repeat last 12 bars

See each other's hats	1 Bar
"It is mine"	1 Bar
Plump, frivolous lady walks left and takes her hat	2 Bars

Slender, sophisticated lady walks right and takes
    hers   2 Bars
Point at shop, push swing doors open and enter 6 Bars
Repeat last 8 *bars*
Together take cheques from Madame and return
    hats   2 Bars
Tear cheques   2 Bars
Open swing doors
Throw pieces away and exit, each a separate way 2 Bars
5. *Carousel:* 'What's the use of Wond'rin'. Play 1st, 2nd
and 8th bars and the first chord of the 9th bar. Madame
throws hats up. "Ah, well!"

THE CIRCUS

This play could be attempted by Juniors or Seniors. Some
adult classes might enjoy doing it if accustomed to a good
deal of movement.

Characters

The Ringmaster	3 Clowns
6 Horses	Girl equestrienne
Tamer of seals	Weight-lifter
3 Seals	Tight-rope walker
Fish-man	Children (audience)

Music

I would again suggest well-known songs, a change of
theme for each new character or group of characters.

Setting, Lighting, and Costume

While it is obvious that elaborate setting, lighting, and
costumes could be used, the scene could I think be more
effective with an empty stage and basic practice costume,

allowing the miming only to rouse the imagination of the audience. Suggestions of costume might help the effect as in 'The Ten Little Nigger Boys', e.g. a cloak for the ringmaster, funny hats for the clowns, sunshade for the tightrope walker.

The scene opens with a group of excited children sitting on the floor in a circle, with a space up stage centre. Their excitement increases as the characters of the circus enter.

First comes the Ringmaster. He wears a cloak and comes with a great flourish, bowing to everyone on all sides and introducing his troupe. Then he calls on his beautiful prancing horses, six of them, high steppers with beautiful heads tossing as they come; he commands them and round and round the ring they go, then off again.

Next come the performing seals, three of them, wriggling their way into the centre, using their flippers to propel themselves along, following the directions of their tamer. He throws a big ball to them and they bounce it on their noses from one to the other. At the end of their performance he sends for some fish, which is brought in by the fish-man, and he throws them their reward before they go out, accompanied by great applause, and applauding themselves by flapping their fins.

Then come three clowns, riding on each other's shoulders, laughing at their knockabout jokes, climbing through hoops, making the children laugh to the end.

Then the girl equestrienne is seen coming; she is standing on her horse, riding bare-back, just like a dancer, as exciting as any trapeze artist.

When she has gone there is the weight-lifter with his immense muscles making all marvel at his strength.

Then comes the little lady with her sunshade who walks on a tight-rope, miraculous and breath-taking; but she ends safely and bows her way out.

Back come the prancing horses and all the performers, taking their final bow as they circle and go off, the high-stepping horses making a final circle.

MACHINES

A mime suitable for juniors, seniors or adults.

Again basic practice costume could be used, and a bare stage, which would be helped by a silhouette effect in the lighting.

No music—the appropriate sounds to be made by the actors themselves.

Action

We now see characters grouped in twos, threes or fours, each representing a machine. Some are wheels, others pneumatic drills, or pumps or automatic slot machines. As they begin to move, each group separately, they make their own sound, so that no music is needed. The sounds are appropriate and varied, and the rhythms of the machines are fitted round a basic slow steady beat,—though they may be in time, or double, triple or even syncopated time.

The machine making the smallest noise starts first, and is gradually joined by the others according to size and noise. When all the groups are in action the rhythm is intensified and quickened, and suddenly, at the height of the excitement, a whistle is blown, and the machines die away in softer noise and slower movement, and remain static as they were at the beginning.

THE PLAGUES OF EGYPT

An abstract mime which could be attempted by Juniors, Seniors or Adults, provided they know the Bible story of the Plagues of Egypt. Again a bare stage and basic practice costume is all that is needed. No music—appropriate sounds to be made by the actors themselves and the effect of thunder and lightning off stage.

Characters

Egyptian Father
Egyptian Mother
Egyptian First-born Son
Frogs, Flies and Lice and Locusts
The River Nile
Thunder and Lightning

Some of the characters represent the River Nile, lying on their backs and gently undulating their arms.

An Egyptian family enter, man, wife, and son, and walk slowly to the river to fill their water-jars, but as they stoop to do so they draw back in horror, finding their jars are being filled with blood. They throw them away in disgust. Then the frogs appear; four or five of them croaking and leaping around. The Egyptians mime that they are treading on others and surrounded by them, and the frogs group themselves on one side. Next comes the plague of flies and lice, buzzing and hissing and jumping with darting movements—the Egyptian family desperately trying to avoid them, until the insects settle in another group. The next plague is of boils, a horrible sequence in which the Egyptians feel great pain as the boils appear on their arms, necks and bodies. After this some terrifying figures enter, darting and flashing in every direction—these are thunder and lightning. Then the locusts appear, hovering with outstretched wings, finally settling in another group. The next group is slow and mysterious in movement—and a darkness comes ominously from the back of the stage. It seems that the Egyptians cannot suffer any more, but the most terrible punishment is still to come in the smiting down of the first-born. Slowly the son collapses and lies dead, leaving the parents grief-stricken in each other's arms.

Now follow two examples of solo mimes.

SOLO MIMES

SEVEN YEARS BAD LUCK

or

UPS AND DOWNS IN THE KITCHEN

Costume—A maidservant of the 1930s.

Set—A kitchen. Natural interior light.

As almost all the properties are mimed, a curtain set is quite adequate, as long as there is a chair and a small table with a cloth on it to the left of centre and a magazine lying on the table; also a standing-mirror somewhere handy which can be brought to the table, and an effect off stage for a knock at the door and also for breaking glass at the moment when the mirror falls.

Tray, crockery, cigarette, matches, comb, meat, cat, etc., should be mimed, and of course the butcher-boy is shown only by the girl's reaction. Choose a gay tune for the main action; change to three sentimental up-to-date songs for the three film stars, and on the entrance of the butcher-boy something as obviously appropriate as 'Oh, Johnny, Oh, Johnny, how you can love . . .'—then back to your original gay tune after his exit and for the end.

Action

The scene opens on an empty kitchen. Then from up stage left we see Lily, the maidservant, kick the door open and come in, carrying a tray of crockery. As she crosses the room with her head held high, she trips over the cat, and down she goes, crockery and all. That cat has always been a trouble, and this time he is literally her downfall! Lily shakes her fist at him as he slinks away, and then she ruefully looks at the pieces. She collects the upturned china and gathers it together again on the tray, painfully aware of her bruises as she does so; then she picks up the broken tea-pot. She tries the pieces together, but it is too splintered and would never stick. And now, oh dear! She hears footsteps and recognizes her mistress's step. Quickly she jumps up, puts the tray on a side-table, hides the broken pieces in a drawer and stands waiting; but it was a false alarm, no one comes. With a shrug of relief Lily takes off her cap, sits down at the table near the fire, picks up the magazine that lies there and begins to read. What bliss! Dare she smoke? That would make this moment perfect; she would feel dreadfully abandoned! She would enjoy that too! She delves in the pocket of her apron and out comes half a cigarette which she has picked up, and a box of matches. She lights the cigarette and smokes, sighs with delight, crosses her legs, picks up the magazine and acts the grand ladies she has seen upstairs; but after a few minutes she finds the cigarette is not quite as good as she expected, so she takes it out, throws it in the fire, and contents herself with her magazine, which we see clearly from the cover is concerned with films.

As Lily turns the pages we see by her absorbed interest, her obvious admiration and her envious sighs, that she has aspirations and would like at least to look like a film star. Suddenly she runs for the mirror, stands it on the table in front of her and stares first at herself and then at a picture in the book. From her apron pocket she produces a comb and arranges her hair, her eye-brows and her mouth, to look like a serious beauty, finally standing and adopting a slinky mannequin-like line of body to match. But, alas! she catches sight of her effort in the mirror and sinks down dejectedly. It's no use, she can never be that type.

She turns to another page; here is obviously a gay young thing, full of life and a tap-dancer, perhaps this would be more suitable. Rapidly another hair-style is tried, the mouth and eye-brows go up instead of down. She gets up, leaves the table and with the picture for a model in one hand she starts to dance, imagining her audience before her and world success. But this too comes to a sad end, for at her great moment she trips over her own feet and disconsolately sits again, deciding that dancing is not perhaps, after all, her strongest point.

Another page is turned and it is clear that this time she has seen a 'fluffy' blonde with a beautiful smile, one silk-stockinged leg crossed over the other, reclining in a deck-chair with pussy on her shoulder. "This is my chance", thinks Lily, and once again hair and face are arranged, and her dear friend the cat can at last come into his own. He is persuaded to play his part, and Lily is just developing the right feeling, when there is a rat-tat at the door. Now who is going to disturb her fun? The cat leaps away, Lily takes another look in the mirror and very conscious of the charm she is exuding crosses grandly to the door down stage right and opens it with a flourish. How opportune! Here is the butcher-boy, what could be better! Lily takes the meat, smells it suspiciously, crosses to the table, transfers the meat on to a plate, smiling encouragingly to the boy as she does so. Then she languidly returns to the door with the basket, which she hands back with 'invitation' in her eyes. Leaving the door open, she crosses to the front of the table and sits on the edge, beckoning the butcher-boy to come and join her. He needs no encouragement, and soon they are both perched on the edge and it is clear that they are enjoying a little flirtation. At the moment when enjoyment is at its height, Lily suddenly feels something behind her on the table; she turns and leaps away quickly. Horror! The cat is eating the meat! Lily claps her hands to distract him, but he is too deeply engaged, so she picks him up and throws him to the ground. Once more she hears her mistress's footsteps and she hurries to push the butcher-boy out of the door, reluctantly waving him away as he goes down the street. Then she runs for the meat, throws out offending pieces, hurriedly looks for somewhere to hide it, and without hesitation runs to the oven down stage left, pops the meat inside and slams the door. Still running, she gets to the table, picks up her cap and puts it on her head, hides the magazine under the tablecloth, BUT, in doing so, sends the mirror flying to the ground and sees it lying there smashed to atoms. As the curtain falls, Lily sinks into her chair, showing that she realizes that this time it means 'Seven Years' Bad Luck'.

THE JUGGLER

A mime based on the story of 'Our Lady of Notre Dame', suitable for seniors and adults.

Music for this mime has been arranged by Josephine Rhodes.[1]

The Set may be simple or elaborate and should represent the precincts of the Cathedral of Notre Dame, close to the porch, above which is a statue of the Virgin; the statue is off stage down right.

The Lighting should convey late afternoon and the setting sun should illuminate the juggler's face at the end of the play.

The Costume is that of a mediaeval juggler.

Properties should all be mimed, and the monks shown only by the reaction of the juggler.

(If so desired, this could become a group mime by introducing a group of monks, and the statue of the Virgin which will come to life.)

[1] Anyone wishing to hire copies of this music should apply to Miss Josephine Rhodes, 40 Nevilles Court, Dollis Hill Lane, N.W.2, or to The Rose Bruford Training College, Lamorbey Park, Sidcup, Kent.

Theme of the Play

As the scene opens an old juggler enters from up stage left; he carries a bundle which contains his equipment for his juggling, and he looks so weary that we wonder if he can travel any further. He looks round at the Cathedral Close and settles down with some relief to rest, centre stage. It is obvious that he is getting old and tired of life, and this quiet spot seems to him to be a sanctuary. Just as he is settling down to sleep, he hears voices approaching from off left; he realizes it is the monks coming to the Cathedral for their evening prayers. Quickly he gathers himself together, opens his bag, gets out his balls and prepares himself to juggle for them, so that he can earn a few coins to save him from starvation.

Now the monks come into view and stop to watch the juggler's antics, but suddenly he is overcome with fatigue and hunger and falls to the ground, fainting. Two of the monks run to his assistance, one produces a flask of water, another a crust of bread, and gradually the juggler is restored and able to rise to his feet and thank his kind friends. At this moment the Cathedral bell rings out inviting them to service, and one by one the monks make their way into the Cathedral, down stage right. The last to leave turns and asks the juggler to join them; he hesitates, but refuses; to him it would not be natural, he would feel out of place and awkward; to go to church is not his custom.

The monks have gone, the juggler is left alone; he seems to be feeling a little sad and wishes he had taken the chance to go with the monks. He peers into the Cathedral but does not dare to enter; he looks up at the statue of the Virgin above the porch, crosses himself and wonders what he can do for her; he seems to have so little to offer. Suddenly he thinks of his juggling; of course, that is all he has to offer, and that he will give her. Excitedly he gathers up his balls

and his pole to balance on his nose, all his best tricks shall
be shown to her. This shall be the finest performance he has
ever given! He sets to work, he juggles, balances, dances,
does every trick he knows, using all his energy in his effort
to worship the Virgin in the best way he can; but now the
monks come from the Cathedral and they are astonished to
find the juggler, looking up at the Virgin, and, as they
think, dancing irreverently in the Cathedral Close. Is this his
gratitude? Did they tend and succour him only to have their
religion flouted in this way? Angrily two of them take off
their girdles and begin to scourge him; he must be punished.

Weary with his efforts and not able to comprehend what
wrong he has done, the juggler once more sinks down
exhausted, and it seems that he will be whipped to death.
But the Virgin has accepted his prayer and by the reaction of
the monks he realizes that something strange has happened.
The juggler realizing the scourging has ceased and becoming
aware of the silence around him, slowly rises. He sees the
monks are kneeling and all are looking at the church door,
and there above the porch is the Virgin, smiling at him; she
has accepted his offering. Full of joy and praise, the juggler
staggers to the centre and kneels to her. This is all he is
able to do and he falls to the ground and dies in ecstasy.

INDEX